To DWD

THE CUNNING HOUSE

Richard Marggraf Turley

SANDSTONEPRESS
HIGHLAND | SCOTLAND

First published in Great Britain
and the United States of America by
Sandstone Press Ltd
Dochcarty Road
Dingwall
Ross-shire
IV15 9UG
Scotland.

www.sandstonepress.com

Commissioning Editor: Robert Davidson

The moral right of Richard Marggraf Turley to be recognised as
the author of this work has been asserted in accordance with the
Copyright, Design and Patent Act, 1988.

The publisher acknowledges support from
Creative Scotland towards publication of this volume.

ISBN: 978-1-910124-10-9
ISBNe: 978-1-910124-11-6

Jacket design by Mark Ecob, London
Typeset by Iolaire Typesetting, Newtonmore.
Printed and bound by Totem, Poland

Richard Marggraf Turley is a British author and literary critic. He is Professor of Engagement with the Public Imagination at Aberystwyth University, and works in the University's Department of English and Creative Writing. In 2007, he won the Keats-Shelley Prize for poetry.

"Is any one here who knows how to play the cups and balls?"

Encyclopedia Britannica (1810)

1.

MONSTERS

1. Self-destroyer

At least he could be sure of the corpse's name. James Tranter, footman to his Royal Highness the Duke of York. He had two slick chickens to thank for that. Both jack-a-dandies, Neale and . . . he opened his notebook for the foreign-looking one with the odd name . . . Sellis, were valets to York's younger brother, the Duke of Cumberland.

By their account, Tranter had acted up the previous evening, charging about with a hatful of bullets. Lots of loud talk about putting a slug through his brains. Seemed he'd been good for his word.

He watched as the Royal Surgeon, a short man with bad skin called Jackson, gave the corpse the once over. Every appearance, the St James's surgeon pronounced, glancing up, of the pistol having been discharged from within the mouth, rather than at the temples, which was the more usual position. The bullet had blown out the palate. The missing area of the orbital bones – he indicated with a finger, as if there could be any doubt – marked an exit.

There was, Jackson added, getting to his feet and rolling his shirt sleeves down, no single location of a gunshot wound that on its own conclusively disambiguated suicidal from homicidal injury. (He obviously enjoyed the words.) But as far as he was concerned, the hole satisfied in every respect. Biathanate in nature. Tranter was a self-destroyer.

The beginning of March, and unseasonably warm. Hadn't lit a fire in his office for a fortnight. Somewhere nearby, a bird was singing. He couldn't find it.

"Care for a closer view, Mr Read?"

He'd have to see this travesty through. He was the Chief Magistrate at Bow Street, after all. He turned back to the surgeon and smiled grimly, adjusting the buttons on his waistcoat. One was coming loose. He gave the thread a little tug.

Tranter's body lay on its back at the cobbled entrance to the palace stables, a discharged pistol held loosely in its manicured fingers. The Chief Magistrate glanced up. A high brick wall rose behind these outbuildings, and just behind that – a world away – lay Pall Mall, one of the city's busiest pavements.

He turned his gaze down. The footman's corpse looked lank and worn. There was an intimate whiff about it. Kneeling, Read noted the upper teeth protruding into nothingness, the broken crust of the skull. Lifting his eyes skywards, he allowed himself to imagine for a moment the slug's flight onwards, beyond the constraints of the footman's skull, its acute plane over the dovecots, the inevitable parabola, pictured the projectile coming to rest, chinking curiously, next to a flowerpot, where the contrast between its brutal grey and the plant's living colour briefly detained any servant whose eyes happened to be drawn in that direction by a strange insect, busy at the sticky parts.

A lot easier if that were true.

What the Chief Magistrate also noted, and knew better than to mention, was the lack of sufficient frothy matter on the cobbles and stable walls to account for the contents of the footman's inner thoughts.

2. Ones & Zeros

"What of space, Mrs Cooke?"

Sarah stopped wiping down tables. She looked

quizzically at old Mr Shadworth, the only patron who remained below, half-hidden in a cloud of blue tobacco smoke.

"Has its immensity no end? Are the suns and planets without number? How deep is the void?" He lifted his sparse eyebrows.

She gave him a smile, and a non-committal shrug.

"What is infinity?" he persisted.

The old dog claimed to be a mathematician at the Academy. She sent her cloth back over the tables, the air keen with citrus.

"Indubitably," Mr Shadworth continued with a touch of piqué, placing his tumbler on the counter, "it is endless repetition, all there is, all there can ever be, divided endlessly."

"Then you already know." An odd fish, but a big tipper. His silver guineas had her handsome jacks lining up. Only the Country Gentleman dropped more coin.

Roars from the attics sieved down through the ceiling boards.

"Stargazers," Mr Shadworth said, crossing to the brass spy glass that perched on a tripod in the corner of the taproom, "speak of the infinity of space as a never-ending progression, a voyage through ideas of emptiness."

Mr Shadworth had the telescope brought in – at his own expense – and personally supervised its placement at the window. But the only vista it opened was a view along the whole length of Clare Market.

He squinted into the eyepiece, then returned to the ale counter. "They say, since the universe is infinite, other worlds like our own, incalculably remote yet equally adapted for rational life, must roll afar. Perhaps the moral world extends even to such distant realms." He knocked back his tumbler, licking a dark residue from his lips.

Sarah stretched for the back of a table, wincing where James's fingers had dug in below her shoulder blade that morning.

Good fer nothing since yer come back. Should never have let yer go, family or not.

"Speaking for myself," Mr Shadworth said, pulling at his jacket, watching her massage the tender spot, "I can't think the chances are high."

"Why's that, Mr Shadworth?"

"Oh," he said airily, "the answer is best described mathematically. 'One', or '1' – " he drew the numeral in the air " – representing our world, is the middle – " he raised an eyebrow " – let us call it 'attribute', between 'zero' and all other values. Between all barren worlds and those that may be supposed to nourish life."

"I don't – "

"Remember, Mrs Cooke, 'one' is no closer to 'zero' than it is further from infinity." He smiled, the perilously thin skin at the corners of his eyes becoming a mass of spiculated folds. "Infinity is all other possible numbers. It might be two, it could just as easily be two-trillion-and-two. It would certainly be a fallacy to take the sign of infinity for infinity itself."

"I – "

"Indeed, Mrs Cooke." His face fell a little. "Of course, perhaps there's no inside or out, space limited only by space." He leaned forward. "His Holiness has appointed a circle of astronomers to advise him on the latest scientific ideas."

The cloth stopped. "Surely that's bla–" She checked herself, afraid of the word.

"Blasphemous?" Mr Shadworth shook his head. "Far from it, my dear. The Pope's perfectly willing to entertain the possibility of the existence of other planets. He's even instructed his agents to prepare for missionary work among the stars."

She looked at him dubiously. "Would the Pope really baptize monsters?"

"I'm quite certain he would."

The ancient being pushed himself up from the counter with an easy motion that, not for the first time, caught Sarah by surprise.

"Errands to run, Mrs Cooke. Well, bene darkey. Your arm to the door?"

She led him across the taproom, certain he didn't need any help. His frame was oddly solid, she'd almost say muscular, if that weren't impossible. All the old men's bodies she knew were soft and stringy. She thought of old men's cocks, hairless, buried in fat, tricky to coax out.

Sarah glanced up. The noises from the attics were getting louder.

"Stay away from the Charlies," she cautioned, picturing coats and rattles.

With a little wave, Mr Shadworth disappeared into the murk of Clare Market.

When the last of her mollies had gone, Sarah slipped into bed beside James, who was snoring drunkenly. Her thoughts turned to those three . . . what had Mr Shadworth called them? *Attributes.*

One of James's girls from his other tavern, a regular knocking shop, possessed the private organs of both man and woman. Sarah had discovered it while treating her for blotches. The creature laid back on her bed, lifted her skirts above the waist, and presented two red lips like the wattles beneath a cockerel's throat. Nestling above these incomplete female parts were the beginnings of a man's organ, about the thickness of a little finger. That part shared by both sexes was unusually large: a halfpenny might have been dropped into it.

She mulled over her patrons. Ones, nothings, all possible numbers.

3. Tools of the Trade

The rat crept along the wall of the burying ground in Portugal Street, where stinks and other odours of the dead were given off, before doubling back the length of Clare Market. Past the disreputable tavern with its ramshackle bays.

The July air was even more unsustaining than usual, and he was no longer at his best ... He gazed down at the silky patches showing through his coat. Still nimble enough, though. Filling his shallow lungs, he darted across the street for no other reason than to prove he still could, aware he'd needlessly drawn the eyes of a huddle of men cutting for guineas on the pavement, then slipped into the alleys and dark passages fanning out between Vere Street and Stanhope Street, the shortest way down to the river.

Someone not far away was making a poor imitation of a blackbird's call.

On the Strand, Rat-man judged it safe to rear on two feet. He stepped into a shadowy doorwell to catch his wind. Above him, Venus and Mars were bright specks; he imagined the chill between planets, that unbearable space. But a body in motion was a body not yet cold – and there was work to do. The latest intelligence from France spoke of a munition so potent, wherever a man stood when it ignited was the centre; of grenades packed with chemicals that rendered soldiers irresistible to each other.

It had always been the Frenchies. He remembered

handing General Wolfe his gloves at Quebec after a day of clinging to rocks. Long ago now. France, a nation of barley and buckwheat eaters, moustachioed fawns and stinky women.

He set off again, ducking at the corner of Somerset House into an ill-lit passage strewn with ashes and oyster shells. Above him, chandeliers flamed in a high gallery. Then he was on the river bank, pattering over loose pyramids of burnt clay tiles.

The unfinished bridge towered ahead, its cunning inter-frictions of iron and granite reaching out from either side of the river towards a deafeningly dark hole. Rat-man's sharp eyes found the tiny entrance to the service tunnel. He flipped open his watch. He was early.

He walked to the second shuttered pier, scaling the scaffolding with spry, connected movements. The bridge was unmetalled, and without sides, a set of makeshift railings all that prevented workmen plunging into the oily water. He peered over the edge, feeling the cold air rise. A great hoy shouldered up the watercourse. There had been talk of turning the river into one vast wet dock with sliding vanes and wickets, capable of accommodating the new copper-hulled behemoths. But the plans raised spectres of French ships-of-the-line sailing up the Thames, pontoons of enemy dinghies, landing boats tethered at the foot of Parliament stairs.

Movement below. A shadow was creeping along the bank. Alone, as instructed.

A clatter of debris . . . a muffled curse. Rat-man smiled. This would be easy.

His foot connected with something that glinted blackly against the freshly ashlared stones. Blunt and metallic, short-handled. Just the job. He picked up the hammer, swung it in a scything arc as if intending to dislodge an offending nodule of granite from some otherwise perfectly rectangular block, then slipped it into one of his deep coat pockets.

He scurried down the scaffolding, jumped off at the footings, and trailed the shadow into the service tunnel. A familiar sour smell of urine coiled into his nostrils. A few hops, and the darkness was complete.

Someone coughed up ahead. Whispered his name. One of his names.

Rat-man felt his way along the masonry, which came smooth and humid beneath his palms.

4. Dandy-Charger

Back in the village, helping the mowers in the churchyard. As always, the scythe's handles were set too far apart for his young arms. The blade's cradle kept catching on his boot. Every second blow produced a squint stroke.

"Thou ain't taking it clean," one of the men said, licking spit from his lips.

"Strike into the grass," another suggested in broad forest accents. "Thou be standing too far afield, an' all bumble-footed."

A third man took the blade from him. The other boys stood off, watching with blunt eyes.

"A good scythe, well 'ung, saves 'arf the labour," said the mower, deftly cutting a tight swathe. With a smirk, he held up the tool, measuring. "Him be be'err off wi' a rake."

"Orra trowel."

With burning cheeks, he snatched back the handle. This time he compensated for the length with a rounder stroke, and had almost managed to clear a second grave when a slow-worm spasmed from his cuttings, sheering in panic over the dead stones, caught in the open. The other men huddled round, children again as they stared down at the creature's notched tongue, its human lids.

All of them, beneath those thin slices of sky, caught in the open.

A commotion at the trying bar jolted Junior Prosecutor Christopher Wyre back to the present. The younger of the two sodomites, a handsome jack called Leager, had fainted. An officer was propping him up to hear his punishment recited in full. In the light from the glass mirror that hung in the centre of the chamber, both felons had a washed-out appearance, as if they were already fading from the world.

"I have done wrong, I have done wickedly," the other public criminal, a thickset coalman named Oakden, was mumbling.

The Judge finished unfolding his black towel, and laid it solemnly on his head. According to custom, flowers had been strewn about his desk. Jacobea lilies.

To cries of *Monsters!* the mollies were led away. Wyre remained seated till the courtroom had emptied, then pushed himself up from the bench. Leighton would be waiting in the entrance hall. It had been a fortnight since he'd last seen his friend; Leighton had been laid up in a Guy's Hospital bed, wounded in the thigh, a guard at the door. He'd survived his encounter with the notorious French spy Vallon, unlike his Bow Street partner . . . How had the newsrags put it? *The Tyrant's agent fired into his belly, blowing a hole above the navel.* Fancy phrases to sell copies, but Wyre thought of a wife deprived of a bedfellow, two children of their papa.

Public opinion was divided over Bow Street, Wyre mused as he walked. Some officers policed with excessive bravura, while others practised what *The Gentleman's Magazine*, in that fancy way it had, termed suborning, and *The Post* called bribery. As far as Wyre was concerned, anyone willing to take on one of Boney's best men deserved the city's gratitude.

A barracking mob pushed and heaved in the Courthouse's marble foyer – molly trials could still be relied on to draw a crowd. Hearing his name called, he turned, breaking into a smile as he saw Leighton's athletic form. Noticeably leaner. *Thin as the shank of a spoon*, his grandmother would say.

"With me, Kit! A success should be celebrated." The Runner extended an arm.

Wyre followed his friend out onto the wide civic steps, where he was blinded by the blenching sun.

"A double conviction," Leighton called over his shoulder, jostling through the sensation seekers, making a good job of hiding his limp. "You must be feeling cock-a-hoop."

"It was high time things went my way. Three duff cases in a row. Those walkers cost me, Leighton. They still do. Reputation's everything in the courtroom."

"Think of them as acquitted felons – " The Runner stopped abruptly and pointed. "Down there . . ."

Wyre followed the police officer's finger through the pasteboard hats. A little way up from the Courthouse, three well-dressed cits were stepping into a flash phaeton, all vaudy lancewood and whalebone.

Wyre shrugged. "Ruffled shirts, come to wave off some old friends."

"They ought to be called to account, same as any common bum-bailiff."

Wyre didn't say anything to that. The chances of successfully prosecuting a grandling were vanishingly small. Men of Leager's and Oakden's station were easier.

"I suppose it explains how those two backgammoners could afford such a slick defence. As a matter of fact," Leighton went on, as the phaeton began to move, "I thought their hired windbag was about to get the better of you. *Mr Wyre here would have you believe . . .*" He was a skilful mimic. "Just as well you kept the handkerchief in reserve. Got the fish-fags, heel to point." He turned as he moved, eyes narrowing. "*Entre nous*, they were guilty?"

Wyre frowned. "Two witnesses swore to seed. They saw the swines wipe their yards."

"Of course they did. And that *was* Leager's handkerchief you showed the jury." He winked. "No denying the egg-fry, but neither defendant seemed to recognize the lace. Nor did their wives."

"If you think those two were married."

Leighton grinned. "That cross-examination of yours was enough to make any ordinary man fall into a thousand contradictions. I might have confessed to buggery myself."

"Sodomy, Leighton. Let's get it right."

The Runner was making a beeline for some sort of mechanical contraption fastened by a leather strap and padlock to the Courthouse palings. Two wheels, connected by a bright yellow wooden perch. It resembled nothing so much as an oversized hobby horse.

"Well?" Leighton said. "What do you think? The only running machine in London. Found it in the Bow Street stores. Someone was supposed to be testing it. Thought it would help me get around, till my leg's healed properly. The lads have christened it the dandy-charger."

Wyre eyed the mechanical gelding with suspicion. "How does it work?"

"It's a bit like skating," Leighton said, pulling the machine towards him. Wincing, he raised his right leg over the perch, sat forward, and extended his elbows.

Using both hands to grip what Wyre took to be an iron rudder of sorts, with a sudden kick and a puff of exhaled air he moved off. Covering twenty yards with surprising rapidity, he swung the hobby horse around in a tight arc. "Better than seven-league boots," he called up the road. "Best of all, it doesn't need feeding or billeting. And it doesn't shit."

Wyre had a sudden vision of lines of redcoats all astride wooden chargers, bearing down with jutting hips and outstretched rifles on the bewildered ranks of the grande armée on the plains of Talavera.

"It suits you." What else could he say? Besides, in an odd way, it did.

Wyre watched as the Bow Street officer attached his contraption to a rickety drainpipe outside The Sun, an alehouse on the Bromwich Road where they'd become accustomed to meeting for lunch.

"That won't put anyone off round here."

"We'll see," came the answer. A touch of pride.

The Sun's victuals were on the unexceptional side of nothing special, but Leighton seemed to prefer the tavern to the other ordinaries and chop-houses in the area. "No fiddly French sauces," was his explanation.

The taproom presented the usual gallery of thieves, half-thieves and ragged coats.

Wyre ordered broth and took custody of two mugs of fusty beer. They found places at the far corner of a long table. Stubby candles ebbed and flared, casting shadows over the pock-faced patrons eating off knife-scored wooden platters.

The Runner lifted his mug, closing his lips over the scum, his Adam's apple shockingly mobile.

Wyre sipped his own beer. The innkeeper seemed to

believe he'd discovered some nostrum that made his brew stand out, but to Wyre's palate it was yeast-bitten.

A stocky waiter moved between tables with steaming bowls. He winked at the lawyer.

"Last night in bed, Kit," Leighton began, "I imagined I was puking up tiny crouching things – claimed their names were Gimiken and Juicy Boy."

"Not fevering, are you?" Wyre glanced nervously at the saucers of quassia dotted about on the windowsills, all swimming with dead flies. Even the Duke of York's daughter, Princess Amelia, was sick. What would his friend William say? *The angels of Albion come armed with the diseases of the earth.* That would be his comment, or something very much in that vein.

"Were you anywhere near Saffron Hill? The hospitals there are turning people away."

Leighton shook his head.

"Well, stay on the safe side. Take a few grains of blue."

"Mercury? It was just a nightmare." He leaned back in his chair.

Wyre regarded Leighton. He remained a little bemused by their friendship; nevertheless, over the past year, despite the gulf in temperament, they appeared to have developed something approaching affection. Yes, it was that, he was sure. At any rate, he knew the Runner well enough to be certain Vallon was the incubus disturbing his sleep. He also knew that while it might be the fashion nowadays for men to show themselves capable of being moved, Leighton wouldn't welcome inquiries into the cast of his imagination.

"Look at them . . ." Leighton stared morosely around the dining room, "stuffing themselves with pigeon pie, without the least notion of what we hold at bay." He picked up a well-thumbed pamphlet someone had left on the table. One of Joanna Southcott's disciples, if the title – *The Woman Clothed by the Sun* – was anything to go by.

"*You* hold at bay. While you're out swinging night-stick and knuckles, taking on scum like Vallon, I spend my days scouring provincial judgments for some obscure precedent or other, deciding between bad behaviour and prosecutable. Blue-bag and beeswax candles are about as exciting as it gets for me."

"You do your part." The Runner drained his mug, immediately hooking the attention of a barmaid with a motion of the hand that was perfectly languorous yet absolutely direct. Whenever Wyre tried it, it looked like writing in air. "I take 'em – " Leighton winked at the black-eyed woman – "but you make sure they dangle." He knocked his empty mug against Wyre's almost full one.

At the ale counter, a thickset swad sporting a new regimental jacket had seized a bombazined tapgirl by the hand, and was now leading her in a drunken jig.

"When we held frisks in my youth," Leighton said, nodding towards the couple, "we sprinkled ripened rose seeds on the floor before the ladies entered. The seeds would get kicked up and lodge in their nether regions." He gave Wyre a broad grin. "The burred coats caused a fearsome itch. Did half our work for us." A fresh mug arrived; his fingers closed eagerly.

"You're right about the new defence counsels," said Wyre, changing the subject. "It's getting harder to convict. Men like Mitchell make juries squeamish about committing to the rope."

Leighton shrugged, flicking through the dog-eared pamphlet. "William the Conqueror favoured castration over the noose."

"*The Post*'s petitioning for the return of the gelding knife. We might not have seen the last of old Will's methods."

"Must sting, but it's limited as a deterrent. There's not much to see from a distance."

"The rope's the bigger spectacle," agreed Wyre. Today's two gallows-birds, Leager and Oakden, would be dropped within the week. *The Post* would send someone along to concoct a suitably sensational report – not that much embellishment would be necessary. Fifteen minutes to die, spasmodic evacuation of the bowels. A voiding of the offence, some said. On top of that, many creamed themselves. It was just, if unsubtle.

Leighton lifted his mug. "More mollies in London than ever before. The godly point to scripture."

Wyre had heard the talk. End days, cities of the plain. The language was everywhere. Southcott's lot were the worst.

"Scripture, or do you mean the rants of radicals? And don't tell me you go along with that Southcottian bibble-babble."

"Shouldn't discount it, Kit. She foretold the harvest of '99, fulfilled just as she predicted. Surely you, of all people, would agree backgammoning is a sin in the sight of God. Men violating the divine image. *Vox dei*, and all that." He laughed.

"Sodomy in the towns, bestiality in the villages."

"Right. Whosoever lieth with a beast."

"It's been a while since I prosecuted one of those." Wyre allowed himself a smile.

The Runner quaffed his beer noisily. "I once took a sodomite in Marlborough Gardens. He pleaded with me, claiming if whores' quaints were reduced to the width of a boy's arse, he'd happily return to women."

"You didn't release him?"

Leighton answered with a smirk. "When were you last squeamish? First hanging?"

Wyre winced inwardly, picturing the Sussex catamite. Wintour had been a notorious malefactor, even among his kind. For his part, Wyre had been newly articled to a small practice in Felpham. St Mary's, where he lived with his new bride, became an island twice a day with the tides. His wife, Rose, practised piano in the drawing room – those left hand exercises, like time ticking off. The cottage overlooked a beach littered with shells. Rose collected everything from common limpets and dog whelks to the more exotic sting winkles and glistening borealis, which she strung to make necklaces for her besotted nieces. Wintour had been a handsome devil. He'd been able to pass. No one believed such things possible of him. By the end, his blackened tongue had protruded two inches from his mouth.

He nodded, sipping his beer.

"How did he croak?"

"It was what they called dying hard – " Wyre squeezed his lips together. What on earth had possessed him to take Rose to the press yard? Things had changed that very morning; in all probability, she'd made her decision to leave then. At least his performance had impressed someone: a fortnight after Wintour's turning off, a letter arrived from London, offering him a position in the Courthouse. Signed Mr Best. "When I arrived here, I thought I'd be leading treason trials within the year." He smiled sadly. "Rose begged me to turn Best down. She was right, as usual. He had me pegged for molly briefs. Said I had a particular talent for it. Ten-shilling cases, Leighton."

"Some would say that's good enough recompense." Leighton slapped his empty mug on the table.

"It's not just the coin." Wyre stared gloomily into his own cup. "Rose used to say . . ." No, it was too excruciating to talk about his wife, even to Leighton. Especially to Leighton.

"Be kinder to yourself, Kit. Lawyering's an honourable profession."

"I spend my days sifting through accounts of unnatural acts, blow by obscene blow. I doubt there's a man in London who knows more about crimes of the arse. That's hardly a topic a man can discuss with his wife over dinner."

"Look at it this way, you'll never run out of pretty ganymedes to haul before the dock. They say one man in a hundred carries the sickness."

"That's just scaremongering." Wyre glanced over at the ale counter, where a burly man was casting looks in his direction. There was something familiar about the phiz.

"Well, I read it somewhere."

"Probably in *The Post*," Wyre answered. "These days, you're more likely to find their news rats sniffing around a trouser leg than a crinoline dress. Besides, if the city seems overrun with sodomites, Bow Street's methods are partly to blame. I know how it's done, Leighton – agents loitering in bog-houses, waving their yards around, arresting any poor sap who clutches. You're putting ideas in their heads."

"Not me. We have special officers for that."

The stocky waiter arrived with two steaming bowls of broth. A wrong turn taken somewhere in the middle of his nose gave him the look of a backstreet pugilist.

Leighton looked at Wyre for a moment. "If you'd really like a taste of my world, you could give me some advice. As a matter of fact, it touches directly on what you call our methods."

Wyre regarded him cautiously.

"My constables found a body under New Bridge last week, down by the workings. Someone got their head knocked in."

"That place is a known molly rendezvous. And I'd have thought getting brained was an occupational hazard."

"What if I said this particular nodgecock was more than just a turdman out for a ride?"

"A fly?"

"In Paris, he'd be called a *mouche*."

Wyre considered for a moment. "Sounds like a pinch that got out of hand."

"It's possible. Flies operate on their own. Supposed to be safer that way." Leighton hesitated. "But let's say I happen to know he was working on a case with reach."

A flicker of movement at the bar. The bear-garden bruiser was lumbering towards them. In seconds, he loomed over the lawyer.

"Mr Wyre, ain't it? Promised bro I'd pass on his respects, if I ever got th' chance."

Now Wyre was able to put a crime to the face. Silverthief: older, and larger, of the Michaels brothers. A year had passed since he'd put his twin in gaol for an assault in Marlborough Gardens. Junior had vociferously denied unnatural motives, but who didn't?

Wyre looked at Leighton, who was toying with his spoon, his face the very model of what the Italians called *sprezzatura*. When he turned back, it was in time to see Michaels' broad knuckles begin their scything swing.

Wyre was only dimly aware of Leighton rising from his seat, the soup spoon flying up in the air, Michaels' ham-like fist being plucked from its arc in space. With a sudden transfer of weight, the Runner pressed the bigger man to the table, pinning his arm. The soup spoon clattered across the table and dropped to the floor. Leighton bent over the silverthief, bringing his lips close to the man's ear.

"Right, piss-flap, I'll let you up, and you'll leave without a word, understood?" A sharp, upwards jerk produced a strangled grunt. "Let's try that."

Leighton leaned back, and Michaels rose, scowling.

Tugging at his rumpled jacket, the bruiser took a heavy step towards the bar. When his right hand re-appeared, it was as if from outside the frame of a picture. Wyre watched dumbly as the enormous fist slewed towards the Runner's jaw.

With stoat-like agility, Leighton slipped the punch, letting it pass harmlessly in front of his face. He played two hands to Michaels' ribs, robbing the man of air. A short right followed, exploding above the silverthief's cheekbone, the sound brutally hollow. It was a flush, knock-down blow. Michaels sat dazed on the floor, one eye a tumid ring. Wyre had known plenty of felons crippled by blows to the head, doomed to drag their feet or slur their curses for the rest of their lives. Perhaps Michaels would be one of them.

The springs of Leighton's action returned to their source somewhere deep inside. He shrugged off Wyre's gratitude, merely raising his hand again in that manner that brought a barmaid scuttling.

When Leighton finished his ale, they made their way through the tavern's subfusc, Leighton with his customary confidence, Wyre more warily.

Outside, the yellow dandy-charger was still there, as Leighton predicted. In bleaching light, the officer unfastened it from the rickety downpipe, and swung his leg over the wooden perch.

They parted on the corner of Tenby Street. Wyre watched his friend's coat billow out behind him. Half-runner, half-rider.

5. Marrow Bones

By sticking to side streets they'd managed to avoid the worst of the mobs. Just Blackfriars Bridge to clear now . . .

Through the glass-sliders, Parson's keen eyes, sharpened by years of caution, spotted trouble crouching at the entrance. He banged on the folding roof, signalling to the jarvis, who'd been hand-picked for just such an eventuality. The hearse, lighter now by Oakden's and Leager's bodies, picked up speed. Trailing from foot-long staves, little adventures of silk fluttered outside in the still air.

The bridge faction, Southcott's people, he was sure, were busily chalking slogans on the flagstones. Before they noticed the hearse's approach, it was practically on them. The sect jumped to its feet, hoisting placards and grabbing cudgels, swiping ineffectually as Parson and the principal mourners flew past.

This last obstacle negotiated, the remainder of the journey was conducted at a more sedate pace. They entered Southwark, rolled along Gravel Lane, past Mr Hill's alms houses, and juddered to a halt outside The Hat and Feathers, where Parson was led away by supporters into the tavern's dark.

Seated, he accepted a mug of hot gin and ale. Huckle n' buff, the locals called it. The room buzzed.

Yes, the turning off was bearable.

Yes, Oakden went as quickly as could be hoped.

No, forty-five years old wasn't bad for a sodomite in these times.

Harmless as a fly.

Who ain't?

Smile on his lips as he climbed the ladder.

Poor bugger only showed it when they dropped the rope over his head.

Very dignified, Parson.

The pomp of the gay world, and all its pursuits.

Indeed.

Oakden's passing had in truth been easy. To slip from

the world with barely a struggle . . . Parson was half in love with the idea. Leager's end, though . . . Dear God! Fitter, he'd fought the knot. Parson screwed his eyes shut, but couldn't put the morning to flight, picturing on the back of his lids how, to a rousing cheer, his sweetheart began to tread furiously with his feet as if trying to climb a particularly steep flight of stairs, his beautiful hands clenching and unclenching . . . the eventual diminishing of the furious motion to a slow, swinging ellipsis of the rope . . . the blackened face, tongue protruding idiotically.

"Through bloodshed we'll be reborn, eh? Eh?"

He lifted his head to find a drunken scaramouche standing at his table. "Aye, reborn in the Word." He managed a pale smile.

Leaning over, the scaramouche passed him a scribbled note. Parson glanced down at it. With a frown, he excused himself.

Other than for the two men seated at a revolving card table, the side room was empty. Parson approached like a ship dragging its anchor.

The taller, muscular-looking man was clad in something blue that resembled a regimental jacket. He leaned on a silver-headed cane, a skull-and-marrow-bones ring glinting unpleasantly from his little finger. An aura of brutal air hung about him. The other made a more subdued impression in a faded black coat and patched canvas trousers. Handsome and heavy.

Blue Jacket introduced himself as Mr Yardley. His hand was grimy. "The 'earse wuz a nice touch, Rev'rend. No difference these days twixt a duke an' a dancing-master when it comes to ceremony."

"If my friends had been dukes," Parson replied crisply,

"they wouldn't have found themselves in the dock to begin with."

"True 'nuff." Blue Jacket nodded sagely. "Well, look at it this way, they may 'av trudged about on their trotters all their days, but they wuz carried by 'orses after their deaths. Belated congratulations to yerself, by th' way. We wuz taking wagers on a six stretch, or worse. Who d'yer bribe?"

Who had he bribed? Parson stared, the memory of his trial a year ago suddenly raw again. *Who had he bribed?* Hadn't he been dragged from his own pulpit in the Obelisk Tabernacle, hauled past a burning effigy on the steps, *FILTHY SODDY-MITE* scrawled on the door?

The heavyset man offered a hand at smooth odds with his rough exterior. "Mr Cooke, at yer. Who paid fer th' service?"

Parson brought the tips of his fingers together piously. "The Obelisk's faithful." No need to mention the dead men's benefactor, the Country Gentleman (who'd also paid both men's legal fees). No need *ever* to mention him. "The warden's a worse felon than Leager or Oakden ever were," he said, changing the subject. "Takes five shillings for a man carried at shoulder height, seven pence for a child under the arm."

"Does that include the digging?"

Parson nodded. "The digging, but not the filling." His eyes slid to the side. "We'll need to take another collection for the stones."

Yardley shrugged. "Should have persuaded 'em to flog their carcasses to the surgeon. They could've chipped in with the expense of seeing themselves under th' earth."

Parson's lips smiled.

"We've got a proposition for you," Cooke began quietly. "You have a congregation, we have a new house. Might be some mutual interest."

"A house?" Parson was on his guard now. Bow Street had special officers trained in the art of tempting men into misdemeanours. "What kind of house?"

"The kind your friends would've been at home in."

"A house of private meetings," Yardley added, twisting his ring around his knuckle. "Lots of 'em about town, fer them as know where to look. Oh, it's a vast geography ..." He rubbed his palms together. "Don't fret, they're tolerated."

Parson tried to ignore the dull katoum of pulse in his ears. "The name of this establishment?"

"The White Swan," Yardley replied evenly. "Jus' a simple matter of marrying our patrons a couple of ev'nings a week. In an upstairs room. Well away from prying eyes."

"Think of yer chapel funds." Cooke winked.

"Think of them stones you mentioned," Yardley said. "An' if yer pick up some handsome converts, all t' the good, I say."

Parson felt a stirring in his lap.

"An upstairs room? Away from prying eyes."

6. Briefs

"What are you, would you say? Thirty-five?"

"Not quite so old, sir." Wyre wondered in turn about Mr Best. The old barrister's sharp, classical features were at marked variance with his lined complexion.

Pursing his lips, London's legal *éminence grise* signed a heavily embossed letter with tiny dancing movements of his crow-quill. "And where are you from, Wyre?"

"Felpham, sir."

"Before that." Best glanced up.

The question appeared to exist in a simple enough

dimension, but nothing the Chief Barrister uttered ever did.

"I grew up in the Forest of Dean."

With a precise action of his wrist, Best dropped a bleb of wax onto the envelope's flap. He pushed his seal into it, leaving an impression of a beetle, or possibly the more exotic scarab. "Your name, is it common in those parts?"

"I believe it's originally Welsh, sir. I'm told it would have been pronounced with two syllables. *Wier-rey*." He repeated his name, suddenly no longer his, with a Welsh catch in the throat.

"Glad to have left it, are you? The forest?"

Wyre hesitated. For most of his adult life he'd struggled to see Dean. Not wanted to see it. He thought of the thickets of twisting trees, the clints and grikes that pocked the land, left over from centuries of digging. Of the Buckstone, a cottage-sized boulder perched at the top of Buckstone Hill. Three or four men working away at either side could rock it quite easily. He'd taken his turn beneath it with the other boys, felt its unholy weight nudging over the fulcrum.

It had all started there. If 'it' could ever be said to start anywhere, really.

Despite himself, the old names resurfaced. Sinkaway, Bogo, Pauncefoot, Kyllicote Wood.

"It's an odd place, sir."

The old barrister kept his eyes on Wyre as if completing a puzzle only to find it had no picture. "I suppose," he said at last, rising, "we all have to come from somewhere." He extended an arm.

Was that it? No word of advancement, not a single syllable alluding to more dignified, more lucrative, briefs? Wyre tried not to show his disappointment. He'd dared to hope Rose was wrong about Best, dared to imagine the Chief Barrister had simply been testing him with seemingly endless molly work before offering a portfolio more commensurate with his talents.

No, Rose had been right in Felpham, and she was right in London.

Best followed him out of the office. Their footsteps made echoing halls of the Courthouse's narrow upper corridors. At a row of wide arched windows, the barrister stopped, and turned to the city, the enormous dome of St Paul's rising above the roofs and chimney pots.

"When I was a boy," he said, "I used to spend hours sketching plans for great gardens. Vistas with grand arcades, balconies, double deceptions. I still have them somewhere."

7. Signs

Sarah Cooke bustled along Carey Street, cutting through Clare Market with its lean-to stalls and out-of-plumb façades, its butchers and higglers. Past the area they set aside for Jews to slaughter lawful meat, and stamp with leaden seals. Past the hocks hung from hooks. Vere Street was the second turning on the right. Such places always were.

She started as an enormous booming sound rang out around the city, like some heavy object falling in the attics, instinctively hunching her shoulders as if something was indeed about to come down around her ears. The noise echoed around the rooftops, gradually fading. She didn't think it was thunder, though rain would be welcome after a fortnight of baking weather. The dust got everywhere. In all the nooks and crannies.

Sarah reached the ancient tavern, which nestled six doors down from the old theatre where Mr Ogilby first drew his lottery of books, squashed between two taller buildings across from the blackened ruins of the Bear Yard. Number 11. Hers to govern. She still couldn't quite believe she'd persuaded James she was capable of turning a profit. She glanced around at the little lanes, cross-alleys and courts leading off, all with their funny names, or without names altogether, and not to be found on any map.

The instant she'd set eyes on the alehouse's uneven bays, the roof that rose to three points, St Clement's Church with its good ring of bells close by, she'd known it was meant to be. The leaseholder claimed the building went back to the time of Queen Bess. Sarah could credit it. She thought of those queer spellings carved above the twisted lintel – *O Lord in the is al my traist* – and above them, the words that still made her swell with pride: *Sarah Cooke, licensed to sell Spirituous Liquors*.

When James acquired the premises the signboard was a roughly drawn cat, its front paw resting on a cartwheel. Old Mr Shadworth, who seemed to come with the lease, explained that 'Cat and Wheel' was a corruption of Catherine's Wheel, the instrument on which the virgin-saint was broken. The legend of the four cutting wheels had upset Sarah, who asked James to paint it over. He did so with a smirk.

The swan had been the child of James's imagination. Mr Shadworth was able to shed light on that design, too. The bird was the device of Edward of Lancaster, Prince of Wales, slain at Tewkesbury along with Sir William Bottler and John Daunty of Wooty-Under-Edge.

"Thus," Mr Shadworth lectured, brushing crumbs from one of her coveted Parliament cakes off his waistcoat, "time is preserved in the signs attached to our inns and taverns."

The old buffer also approved of the address itself. In

Babylonian religions, he'd explained, '1' stood for the male member. "How doubly propitious, then, Mrs Cooke, must be two such numerals, standing proudly side by side. How apt for what you have in mind."

Her first act as landlady was to wash the hallway dark blue. It kept the flies down, she explained to James. The creatures were fooled into thinking day was night, and flew straight out again.

8. Charity

Freshly ejected seed turns paper stained with mallow blossom green. Exposed to air, it forms crystals in the shape of wheel spokes, which gradually become four-sided pyramids. Beautiful under the microscope, acrid almond to the taste.

Miss Crawford sat at her writing desk, a foxed copy of Bache's and Thomson's *System of Chemistry* in front of her. She hesitated a moment before lifting it to her nose. It still smelled of Spanish Town. With a rush of sensations, she remembered the childhood thrill of smuggling the volume from her father's library, of slipping it into her travel chest before they left for England.

Her mother had raised a cordon round her father's groaning shelves, afraid of the bald truths lying in wait among the musty treatises on such topics as anatomy and wounds . . . Eyes filling, she smoothed her dress, chasing a few ugly wrinkles from her lap to her knees.

That first, expansive afternoon with Bache and Thomson had taken place a decade ago, in a different world. She suddenly saw again the face of the mulatto she'd questioned about the taste. It depended on what the man had been eating, the reply came, on whether he was a drinker, smoker or in ill-health. But – the mulatto brushed Miss Crawford's cheek with her fingertips – it depended most on the woman's mood whether the flavour was stronger or less strong.

Watch my eyes while I'm spoiling the Captain, and you'll know.

Miss Crawford pictured the pretty mulatto at work in the barn. Tears were a relief for women and a torture for men. It was the other way round with seed.

An odd-shaped insect hung above the door. It seemed to be peering into her study. The scorching weather had dragged all kinds of strange creatures up from the equator, causing her father's English maids much consternation. But Miss Crawford didn't recoil – her Jamaican girlhood had accustomed her to all the tribes of crawling things. She thought back to the cockroaches that used to devour leather saddles as easily as ladies' gloves and shoes, or the bindings of her childhood picture books. She recalled the carapaced monsters scuttling over the fruit bowl, dropping their egg-cases. Back then, she used to race them with her friends as they'd seen the black boys do.

Her mother swore by castor oil, and used to rub it over father's boots. But mother was dead, succumbing to ship-fever during the crossing. Father's boots were her responsibility now.

Miss Crawford's mind drifted back to the Sugar Islands. She remembered being told to watch for spiders, the deadliest no larger than a pea with a single bright scarlet spot on its head; officers straddling alligators and riding them down the high street; long-tailed pigs wandering past bone-white European façades into the slums; rats destroying sugar cane; gabbling-crows with human voices. She remembered wading for groopers, snappers, snook. Land-crabs running on the beach from black devils with

30

torches. The fishy flesh of turtles. Moths huge as plates. Big brown snakes, said to be fatal but which caused no more than a slight fever and swelling (an inflammation she'd suffered at eleven was removed with sweet oil and warm lime-juice). Yellow snakes, which slaves stood on, believing the ritual cured bone-ache. And black snakes that darted at the eyes when attacked. Their pet dog had been blinded.

Once, deep in the woods, she'd found a snake's skeleton wound round that of a cat. Her mother said the pair must have fought and perished together. Osonoko told her she'd found a mumbo jumbo charm.

Her fiancé made her promise to take him to the islands. He wished, he said, eyes gleaming, to present an account to his improving society. Even as she'd agreed, she'd known the idea was absurd. Robert Aspinall, junior mental physician at the Wood's Close asylum, would never grasp her family's past. Was incapable of grasping it. For him, Jamaica was, always would be, a den of exploitation, the backdrop for Three-Fingered Jack and his glorious maroon uprising. She knew it as a land of prickly pear and Turk's-head cacti; of heavy rains and fireflies.

From her study, Miss Crawford heard the maid drawing back the bolts. That would be Robert, late as usual, rushing back from his morning's meeting for the manumission of slaves, or the relief of unfortunate lunatics, or indigent, or both. The endless adjectives of Charity.

Rogues and vagabonds, her father would say.

She prayed Robert wouldn't allow second-hand principles to get in the way of a business opportunity. She pictured the iron-haired engineer and her father waiting in the drawing-room. It was a rare opportunity to get on, if Robert could be persuaded to take a practical view of things. Half the members of his improving societies had interests of one sort or another in the Sugar Islands, so why not Robert? Indenture touched them all. Could he name a manufacturing town on England's coasts whose pavements, theatres and libraries hadn't been built on the wealth of the triangle voyage? Worthless beads to Africa, human cargos to the Caribbean, rum, sugar and cotton back to the seat of empire.

Her poor gullible, principled fool.

Through her study window, a sound like a great gun being fired made her jump, as if Three-Fingered Jack had risen again, and was touring the fine houses, slighting them with captured munitions.

Pushing Bache's and Thomson's filthy treatise from her, she rose to meet Robert in the hall. His neck-tie was askew, his pale cheeks flushed from hurrying. Without a word, she ushered him to the threshold of the drawing-room, then stepped behind the door to observe through the safety of the crack.

9. The Bridge

He ought to be at his desk going over affidavits, rescuing a flagging case against a drayman. (The swine was charged with assaulting a banker's son.) But the offer that sweltering morning of some angelic shop-talk with Leighton at the scene of an actual misdeed had proved too precious to pass up.

Today, the Runner was *sans* velocipede, his limp seemingly much improved. Not that the dandy-charger would have been much help here, Wyre thought, as they picked their way across the vast, brick-strewn waste that led down to the workings.

"You'll like this," the Runner said with a grin. "In

the early hours, one of our lads made a pinch at Pye Corner. The gentleman was decked out like a milliner's dummy, and the pego was a solider he'd propositioned at a pissing-post. First thing our gem'man did, standing before the magistrate, was to accuse the swad. Claimed he'd threatened to blacken his name unless he handed over his silver buckles."

"Standard defence," replied Wyre. "We hear it all the time."

"Queer rogue: all lisps and mincing steps, done up in a tye-wig. The ladies in his cell were ready to puke at him. He sat there canting to be let out."

"Let me guess, some fancy lawyer swanned in?"

Leighton nodded.

"You won't see him again. He'll be halfway to France by now."

A huge crack reverberated over the city. Wyre cringed, drawing his arms about his head. Had the Tyrant arrived? Were his ships sailing up the Thames? He imagined vast arrays of sea-mortars. Priming irons thrust into touch-holes. He thought of the door Rose slammed, the day she left.

Leighton scoffed. "Artillery practice, Kit. Don't say you haven't heard it before?"

The building site was deserted save for half a dozen builders who stood around a steaming kettle leaning on spades, bare-chested, muscle-bound. The largest took a step towards them, a questioning look on his face.

"Bow Street," said Leighton.

Continuing onward, they plotted a course around scattered planks, loose piles of burned clay tiles and thick coils of ropes, the half-completed bridge looming over them, dark and skeletal, a decayed abbey or cathedral. Ladders and pulleys added to the picture. Fat Henry's thugs must have erected similar scaffolds when they stripped the lead from the roofs. It would make a fine painting, if a touch gothic. A huge sea of mist rose up obligingly from the water around the granite pillars, lending the whole scene a spectral sublimity.

Leighton made for a low service tunnel of some sort, its diameter barely that of a span. Wyre turned at crude laughter drifting across the site; surely the workmen didn't think . . . ?

When he turned back, Leighton was already a vanishing shadow. Wyre stepped gingerly into the passage. Why hadn't Leighton brought a lantern? If this was something to do with his 'method', he should have given advance warning. The darkness was that of the Sibyl's cave. Soft underfoot, a smell of damp plaster and piss, worse than a bog-house. Hardly the place he'd choose for a romantic assignation, yet mollies flocked to the bridge for a clinch. He supposed a great deal of police work was conducted in such dire undercrofts.

How far did they need to go? The muffled thuds of Leighton's shoes ahead gave no indication the officer was slowing. Wyre raised an arm, brushing his fingertips along the rough granite ceiling, imagining the weight of stones above their heads, the new road above that, carriage wheels turning incessantly, hoofs beating down, fine gentlemen and their prinked-up sloys seated vis-à-vis, making cow eyes at each other. He shuddered.

Leighton was here to 'absorb' the place. A strange modus, standing about waiting for inspiration to strike, like a poet palely loitering. Wyre's eyes strained uselessly. A simple bull-lamp, Leighton!

He sensed more than saw the Runner's wraith-like figure moving ahead of him. Behind, the entrance's circle of light was a fast-receding stamp on the brain.

Wyre started as a hand was placed against his chest.

34

"This is where we found him." Leighton's voice was compressed, strangely unechoing. The outline of an arm moved as if laying a bed sheet. "The fly knelt forward here, where he received a single blow to the back of the skull. Pushed the bone two inches into his brain. Must have hurt like fuck ever so briefly, whatever the surgeons say. According to the attending officers there were no signs of altercation. No scuffed ground. No cuts or scratches about the body, either. And incidentally no signs of intimacy. This was no dick-and-arse."

"Could your constables have missed something?"

"Our lads are well trained."

"I'm surprised a gany-boy had the strength to inflict that kind of damage." Wyre hesitated. "Did you know the fly?"

A pause. "By sight. Not top calibre; came to us from a regiment of foot. But he was handy enough. Should have smelled trouble, even if he couldn't see it." Leighton was on his knees now, patting the brick floor. "They found a mason's hammer beside the body. Killer must have picked it up on site, cocky sod."

"One of the bridge builders?" Wyre suggested, the laughter outside still burning in his ears. "Working late, saw the fly creep into the arch, made the not unreasonable assumption the victim was a backgammon man, followed him in. Then . . ." He mimed the blow.

Leighton's shadow shrugged. "This is still a book of beginnings. There's a lot more we need to – " He held up a finger, then bellowed up the tunnel. "Stand where you are! Do NOT fucking move!"

Leighton darted forward, vanishing completely, leaving just the sound of heels sliding on slimy brick, before that sound, too, was lost in air that seemed bent on recomposing itself as if nothing were happening.

Then, alone.

10. Stare Case

Brockton looked up at the high, barred window that opened at street level, the only source of light in the subterranean office he shared with Wyre. Dainty ankles flickered in front of it. Bare, dirty feet too.

No sign of any let-up in the heat. Under his legal robes, he was sweating horribly, and his shirt stuck to his chest. It had been another bread-and-butter morning. Tedious hours spent on boundary disputes, petty thefts, drunken assaults and a so-called rape. Nothing that presented the least opportunity for a man who wished to get on.

An enormous explosion somewhere or other outside had been the only mildly interesting event that morning. He'd thought 'earthquake', at first. The religious zealots spoke of little else; God's punishment for the city's depravities. But it was more probable the army had let off a mortar. A large one.

No, it had been an earthquake, he decided. It wasn't all that uncommon for them to strike in northern cities.

He glared over at the empty desk. Wyre's felt presence made his teeth hurt.

The clerk appeared in the doorway, an insolent fellow with a stump where one arm had hung before some salvo or other in the Peninsula game came his way.

"Mr Best's asking. Yer'd better run, lad."

Brockton's face clouded over at the clerk's too-familiar cant. He'd better run. Lad.

"Did Mr Best mention why he wished to see me?" Brockton heaved his bulk to its feet, squeezing through the gap between desks. He glanced down at the files spread haphazardly on Wyre's table. Molly briefs . . . Brockton wrinkled his nose. There were worse things than boundary disputes.

The clerk watched him with an amused expression. "Not so much as a syllable."

"Nothing at all?" Forewarned was forearmed.

The clerk winked.

Brockton made his way along the corridor to the staircase. Stare case, more like. Fleeing girls, ingeniously carved in the decorated marble panels, seemed to pant up the acclivity with him, tunics flapping. He hauled himself up, leaving brief, intimate palm prints on the chilly handrail.

The swirling walnut veneer of the Chief Magistrate's door gave him his reflection; in his court garb he looked like an absurd blue mushroom. Brockton tugged at his powdered wig, which sat badly today, and knocked in what he hoped was a stylish manner. How curiously hollow his knuckles sounded on such a heavy door.

Best's lacquered den continued the classical theme. Statues of Venus lifting her pudic veil, a boy riding a goat. The old barrister himself was peering down at a book of law, a heavy-bottomed glass at his elbow. Fine Cognac brandy, judging by the tawny dregs.

Brockton instantly recognized the book as a volume of a much longer work. Coke's *Institutes*.

"Buggery, Brockton," Best said in a silky baritone, "from the Italian *buggeroni*." He looked up and nodded. "You'll find that it is. Tell me, what do you know about molly houses?"

Brockton strained to anticipate the cast of his master's thoughts. "Nauseating places, sir, where men gather in pursuit of abominable fruits."

"Euphoniously put. Worthy of old Coke himself."

"The mark of the moral life," Brockton added, pleased with himself, "is to choose to conceal the private parts, to have sexual interunion privately. Buggery is the vortex that engulfs the moral life."

The old barrister winced as if something had frayed in his lower back. "Let me share something with you. I was once present at the anatomization of a young woman. The surgeon was a handy fellow." Best's eyes were oily, unreadable puddles. "Now, there's a cracked engraver in South Molton Street who claims a lady's nakedness is God's glory. Can't say I saw any of that, just transparent walls. She was a conjuror's trick, Brockton, an inside-out-woman."

Best gave him a look of such intensity, Brockton wondered if his superior were trying to peer all the way into his own internal cavities; then, with a sniff, the barrister passed across the mottled book on his desk. The spine had cracked at Chapter 10. Most black, most white.

"Edward Coke," Best said. "I seem to have lived with his ideas, or in them, for half my existence. You'd think I'd be tired of them."

Brockton cradled the tome. "Sir, the *Institutes* are the cornerstone of modern law. The history of morality itself."

Best nodded. "A history filled with terrible things, each one intended to protect the present of today from any futures that may injure it."

Brockton stared, uncertain.

"To put it another way, the law is behovely. Have you ever been in love?" A pause. "I take it you have not," Best said with a hint of the cross-examining style. "Love – " he smoothed his blue robe at the shoulders " – may be compared to a ship sailing a perilous tract between two shores, Ruin and Destruction."

"A striking conceit, sir." Had the flat chains of that great legal brain jumped their cogs?

"The law is founded on conceits, of which the conceit of custom is uppermost." Best brought his hands together as if about to recite a prayer, or catch a fly. "But tell me, why

38

does the law seek to intervene in our choice of mate? Why does it balk at citizens acting according to their unbiased wills? If two men consent to love each other, why must the state empty a vial of wrath on their union?"

Brockton was quick to perceive a test. "I believe you are alluding to sodomy, sir, which is counted as one of the *clamantia peccata*, the crying sins, not to be named among Christians." (Was he expected to go on? It seemed he was.) "As a crime, sodomy outranks rape and kidnapping. It is *contra natura* because the anus lies on the other side than the vulva."

"A crime without benefit of clergy. Meaning?"

"That sodomites can be hanged, sir."

"Thank you, Brockton." Best looked pleased. "The business of the Courthouse is to drag into clear light the worst human actions that can be imagined. The *very* worst. Thankfully, extraordinary vices, like extraordinary virtues, are very rare, but where they exist, the public demands they be punished to the limits." He closed one eye as though taking aim. "To prosecute sodomites to the very end of the law, how many witnesses are required?"

Wasn't this Wyre's sordid domain?

"Two, sir?"

Best nodded. "Two. Both of whom must be prepared to swear to seed. Naturally, in capital cases where the state seeks to take a life, the highest standards of jurisprudence must be upheld." The old bar-gown's smile did not reach his lips.

A molly brief? Surely not ... And yet, it didn't feel as though he were being demoted. Quite the opposite. Brockton's eyes narrowed. Coke was growing heavy in his arms.

"Some two or three prosecutions a year, taken to the limit." Best tilted his head at an angle that implied the gallows. He held out his hands for the volume, clapping it together before replacing it carefully on his desk. "Between you and me, in a short while we'll be seeing a good deal more molly men than that, several of them citizens of means." His eyes locked with the younger man's. "What you decide to do with the others is entirely your business."

The junior prosecutor looked at him.

"The law is hungry for sodomites, Brockton. Shall we feed it some?"

11. Descent

The blame was as much hers as theirs. Her father had only consented to the meeting in the first place because he'd mistaken Robert's sudden interest in engineering for signs of commercial ambition, a fairy tale she'd been happy to promote. In her defence, her father regarded mental surgeons as worse quacks than bone setters, and she'd merely jumped at what appeared to be an opportunity to win acceptance for her fiancé, and thus speed the date of what Robert liked, jokingly, to call their nuptials.

For the tenth time, she replayed the fiasco in her imagination, the tears still hot on her cheeks. When she'd delivered her fiancé to the drawing room earlier that morning, Mr Bolton had been crescendoing over a set of plans for an improved steam engine. The industrialist's forefinger moved up and down as if it were itself powered by steam.

"And here, figure *c*," he'd boomed, "the descent in the cylinder, and figure *e*, the improved reservoir. Double cooling of the condensate, Crawford, yields ten more horses." (Her father had nodded appreciatively.) "The smoke," Bolton descanted in his rich northern brogue, "is also in great measure ameliorated by being mixed with unburnt air." Bolton had paused then, noticing Robert's silhouette in the doorway.

"I see your valves move by gears very similar to Smeaton's . . ." (Her father). "If you were able to guarantee delivery before the year is out, I'd be pleased to be counted among your investors. Any later . . ." Her father sniffed. "Agitators, Mr Bolton. I'm thinking of stock, you understand." Her father frowned, also registering Robert's presence. "Aspinall," he said stiffly. "Well, sit down, man." He pointed at Bolton's plans. "Ten per cent more efficiency. What do you think?"

Miss Crawford had known only too well what Robert thought. Only of his Society's fulminations against plantations. That, and his infernal case notes.

"Perhaps," her father continued, "Mr Bolton can persuade you to invest in sugar. A sweet tooth will always be the mark of a true lady, eh?"

Her fiancé hesitated. A fraction too long.

"What's the matter?" Mr Crawford frowned. "Sugar beneath you?"

"Not at all, sir!"

"Then perhaps you'd care to express yourself clearly."

Her poor fool, always digging a hole for himself.

"It's just that sugar cane agriculture has been proven responsible for – " Through the crack in the door, she'd seen her fiancé's hand move to his jacket pocket, coming to rest on that hateful black volume. Sometimes she thought it was the only thing he truly cared about, the only thing he'd save from the flames.

"Mr Bolton and I are perfectly familiar with that system of husbandry." She recognized the dangerous edge to her father's voice. All too well.

Robert's eyes shone. "And the system's a bad one, sir, since it depends on the enslavement of – "

"What the devil – " her father slapped both palms on the table " – do you mean by using that word here?"

Robert appealed to the engineer. "Mr Bolton, as an abolitionist yourself, you must – "

"You presume, sir," thundered her father. "By God, you presume!"

It was Bolton's turn to colour. "Aye, an abolitionist, like my brethren in the Lunar Society." He tugged at the buttons of his sleeve. "But I trust you'll allow a difference of opinion as to how that noble end may best be brought about."

"If stringent legislation were – "

"Legislation?" her father exploded. "The mortal enemy of free trade and profit!"

Sell at the dearest market, buy at the cheapest. Her father would wish all little children to repeat that credo at every rising of the sun. He'd introduced her to Ricardo's economic theories the same summer he taught her how to load and discharge a pistol at speed. They kept a weapon in every room of the house. That was the year of the Maroon Rebellion. She'd been eight.

"Sir, no one could wish the plantations' steam engines unbuilt, but – "

"But?" Bolton had leaned back in his chair, his eyes two blazing furnaces. A man of sun and planet gearing, wax and resinous bodies. "But? But?" He shook his head slowly. "Well, Crawford, I was sure at least one country was still grateful to its benefactors." Turning back to her fiancé, he'd said, "My business, sir, is to calculate the economy of heat. These drawings offer steam in lieu of horses, the work of a month, done in a day." (Her father murmured approval like a Welsh deacon feeding on the

Word.) "A negro who does his duty – " the light cast by the copper table lamp made dark folds of Bolton's face – "who obeys his master's orders to his satisfaction, need fear no mistreatment."

"I didn't meant to suggest – "

"The present system of governance in the Caribbean will continue, or it will cease, whether I lend it my patents or not."

"But I – "

"All I've done is make the work in those dark places as efficient as possible, requiring the least number of bodies."

Her father laid one hand solemnly on top of the other. "I must apologize, sir. The iron has plainly entered Mr Aspinall's soul."

Robert began to protest again. Bolton spoke over him. "It is poverty that cuts the sinews of moral energy. If a state of squalor is allowed to persist, it doesn't matter whose reforming philosophies are introduced into the islands. You will simply find the chains no longer on a man's limbs, but wrapped within. The moral darkness will be unbroken." The industrialist's face seemed to gather itself into one tight point. "By improving the lot of the planters, you improve conditions for all. Even those of your sable-skinned brethren."

"If regulation were fully endorsed by parliament – " Robert said weakly.

"Would you strike off their fetters?" Bolton gave him an incredulous look. "What then? Wait for the ploughshare to pass over the dust of Jerusalem? The brutes would settle old scores, beginning with the slaughter of their masters. Their mistresses, too – " His eye came to rest meaningfully on Robert. "Would you see maroons living in the governor's house, boko sorcerers burning entrails in churches, white babies impaled? Is that an acceptable price

43

for enlightened thinking, a whole hemisphere of naked, wandering savages? Not to mention the spread of other violent passions. Men familiarized with each other in the heat." He sat back, wet with passion. "I've done God's work. Can't you see that?"

Miss Crawford knew precisely what Robert Aspinall could see: whatever had appeared in that month's muddled articles in the liberal journals. Engravings of bodies chained like beasts, or hanging to scaffolds by the ribs; accounts of women pressing shrivelled infants to their breasts; fathers swallowing poison.

Robert had jumped to his feet, eyes gleaming, and dashed from the room. Pushed past her in the doorway.

12. Uppish

Wyre entered that state of soul in which all motion seemed suspended. The sensation was that of standing on a stone barely wide enough for his feet in the middle of a vast pool of water. A sudden sound, like a single ripple propagating across the pool; light breath over his nape. He swallowed, and swallowed again, waiting for the blow that would send him tumbling from his stone into the frigid depths.

Have a care, Mr Wyre.

The voice seemed to come from everywhere. His eyes darted uselessly, the shadows shifting so he was always peering into the darkest place. What did a blade slid between the ribs feel like? Perhaps it had already happened. His conjectures gave way to icy panic, but an attempt to run for it produced only unconnected twitches in his legs.

"Leighton!"

The Bow Street officer's shadow skidded to a halt along

the damp crumbling bricks. "Did you see his face? What did the smutball say?"

Wyre's chest had set like stone. His shoulders heaved, but no air came.

"What did he say?" A whip of anger in his friend's voice.

"Nothing – " Wyre managed to gasp, hands on his knees. "He told me to have a care. He must have followed us in!"

Leighton shook his head. "He was already inside."

Wyre stared blankly. "Why risk it?"

"Some murderers like to haunt the scene of their crime. Either that, or he was tipped off."

"He called me by my name. *Have a care, Mr Wyre.* Those were his precise words. If Michaels thinks he can intimidate me . . ."

"It wasn't Michaels." Leighton stepped past him, heading for the tunnel entrance.

Wyre hurried after him. "Who, then?"

"Someone who isn't afraid of the dark. Come on."

The flat light was as welcome to the lawyer as air must be to a man just pulled from under the sea. They plotted a slant return up the slimy banks – Wyre trying to control the tiny tremors travelling up and down his limbs – and onto the Strand, where the midday sun had made a fiery sea of the cobbles. He was a sorry mess: shoes soiled by river mud, his good jacket slimy at the shoulders and sleeves. He couldn't return to the Courthouse in that state. And there would be awkward questions from Brockton to field.

Leighton offered to accompany him home. Wyre nodded gratefully, then frowned. Did the Runner fear other covert agents would be waiting?

"Don't worry, Kit," said Leighton, looking amused. "If our slinker had wanted you cold . . ." He left it at that.

They headed west in silence, cutting through St James's

Park, the Palace's lofty windows just visible above the high brick wall. The war with France was going through one of its hot periods; perhaps at this very moment the King's generals were advocating tremendous outflanking geometries to the two soldiering dukes, York and Cumberland.

Leighton was the first to speak. "Did you tell anyone where you were going, Kit?"

"Not a soul. And anyway, no one at the Courthouse would . . ."

"Wouldn't be the first time one of you lot proved partial to a handy-dandy. Remember the gay Parson?"

You lot? As for Parson Church, though, Leighton had a point there. It had happened just after Wyre joined Best's team of lawyers. His novice status had been all that saved him at the subsequent inquiry.

"Seems some of you got their defence and prosecution mixed up. Bribes have a way of confusing the issue. When I think of the trouble we went to. Made the pinch in the Parson's own tabernacle, tipped off the news-rats, even brought along the boy who made the accusation – that little stinker, White."

"It wasn't our finest hour," Wyre conceded. Some good, at least, had emerged from the shambles: the court case had been his introduction to Leighton. Wyre pictured the officer stepping up to the trying bar, explaining in his sardonic way how his men had broken through the Parson's supporters, how the culprit had turned to his flock and said – Leighton had perfectly mimicked the man's sanctimonious pulpit tones – *The boy has told a simple plain story, and you would do right to believe him. I have been imprudent, but I am not conscious of having done the actual crime. If any thing of that nature has been done, it must have been without my knowledge, when I was asleep, dreaming I was in my own bed with my wife.*

Leighton was the one who'd initiated their acquaintance, coming up in the Courthouse foyer afterwards. "In bed with his own wife?" he'd said, without the formality of an introduction. "As if anyone could confuse arse and quim."

The pair turned into Oxford Street, footstepping north to Cumberland Place, and from there entering the smaller avenues fanning up into Crawford Street and the many different flavours of Devonshire. Wyre's ankles were swelling against his shoe leather in the heat. He began to wish Leighton had brought his hobby horse.

"Got to hand it to him, though . . ." the Runner showed the pink behind his teeth. "That Parson was a showman. When we took him, he threw back his head and roared, *Rejoice not against me. Though I fall, I'll rise!* How in hell did he slip Best's hook?"

Wyre shrugged. "No one could have foreseen Hamer." That was true enough. By first recess, it was clear certain phrases deployed to stinging effect by the defence counsel could only have come from the Courthouse's own files. Since prisoners were forbidden from seeing evidence ahead of their trial, it meant only one thing – someone from the prosecution's own ranks had been peddling information. There was no hard evidence implicating Hamer, but Best dismissed him all the same. The man lost his pension. He was still protesting his innocence when two stout clerks threw him from the Courthouse steps, breaking his collarbone. "Once Mitchell had seen our cards, the game was up. Then it was the usual tricks. Resorting to the law's delay, putting things off till the next assizes. Costs went up, witnesses moved away, the case fell apart."

"I expect you would have done the same in the Parson's position."

"That's a position I hope never to find myself in."

"No danger of that." Leighton grinned. "These molly men like 'em smooth."

"To cap it all, Parson Church found an upright widow to marry and vouch for his tastes. Keeps a seminary for young ladies in Hammersmith."

"You'd think a jury would see through that one."

"They lapped it up. As for the letter of confession, Church claimed he only signed it under duress."

"The one who made the original complaint – " Leighton looked thoughtful " – that caddling drummer-boy, White. Hard to imagine a more cock-spoiled specimen."

Wyre nodded. "In the end it came down to his word against the Parson's. The jury decided the lad was on the make, and that was that."

"Ever hear any more of the drummer-boy?" Leighton looked straight ahead.

"Kept his nose clean as far as I'm aware. Why do you ask?"

Leighton didn't answer. They'd reached the new pavement outside Mrs Mason's apartments. The Runner whistled through his teeth. "Uppish new lodgings . . . What's your secret? Stocks or bonds?"

"No secret, I wish there was." That was the truth. Short of a miracle – or, what amounted to the same thing, a promotion – he'd be relinquishing his tenancy at the end of the month. He'd only taken these rooms to entice Rose back, gambling on Best giving him more lucrative briefs. That seemed fanciful now.

"Forget her, Kit," Leighton said with a bluntness that caught Wyre by surprise.

With a trademark mock-salute, the Runner left him in the shadow of Mrs Mason's grand entrance.

13. Lights

In the evening's odd light, everything in the city seemed fabricated. Even the trees lining the alleys appeared to have been cast from great foundry moulds, their branches swaying on unseen pivots connected by invisible rods.

The city hovered between possibilities. Robert Aspinall could easily trace his steps on a map but no longer knew convincingly where he was. London was a fierce shrill note wedged between the world and nothing, a city of dukes and dustmen, of paced-out plots, where harlots wailed and children plucked at sleeves.

On Dunstan Avenue, the overhanging branches cast a lattice of shadows. Suddenly, Aspinall was no longer a mad-doctor at Wood's Close asylum, but a vanquished gladiator netted by a retiarius, awaiting the emperor's thumb. That, at any rate, was precisely how it had felt in Mr Crawford's drawing room that morning.

How many miles had he covered since then?

So utterly disarmed; so utterly shamed. What choice did he have, other than to dash out? He couldn't draw a proper breath in that ghastly room.

There and then, he'd made the decision to seek the tavern out, to witness for himself the source of his patient's – *former* patient's – mental torments, the prompts to lunacy. If Mr Crawford placed no value on his profession, perhaps he'd recognize the worth of celebrity. Because once the public heard of Mr Parlez-Vous, was inducted into the phenomenon of 'double character', he'd be the doyen of lecture halls up and down the country. Six shillings a ticket. Let Miss Crawford's father sneer then!

Mr Parlez-Vous ... At first, Aspinall thought the moniker charming. That was before, over the space of four shocking weeks, he'd begun to touch the sides of a most appalling case. That a human being was capable of entertaining such fantasies, let alone acting on them!

But there were certain risks that accompanied a visit to the tavern. Not moral ones; he was immune to *that*. No, the risks were more practical, and presented themselves to his liberty. Parlez-Vous had left nothing conducted in that place of unlicensed sale to the imagination. Anyone found within its walls would be tarred with the same brush of sinful trade. No excuses.

He kept walking.

Up ahead, half a dozen hellcats were waiting in front of a grille-work gate, caterwauling to passers-by, a shocking motley of petticoat and fringe. The tiny muscles beneath his eyelids began to jump. One of the wagtails, dark hair tied in plaits, stepped forward, blocking his way. She hoiked up her skirt, revealing a dark mess that belonged on the anatomy slab.

"Chew on that, Mistah!"

"Nice n' meaty, is our Elsie's," one of the women called in encouragement.

"Nah, can't you tell? He'd rather eat a Scotch hedgehog."

"Quean!"

"Percy Bumington!"

Someone opened the iron gate and slammed it shut again. The noise made him jump. At first he thought another cannon had been fired, like the crack that had sent him half out of his skin that morning as he'd rushed to Miss Crawford's from his Society meeting. The wagtails laughed.

Aspinall's fingers crept to his jacket pocket, closing around his black medical notebook. What a Sisyphean task faced those publicly minded souls who worked to improve the condition of such females. Even if his own time weren't already occupied twice over with the city's psychically oppressed, he'd balk at the challenge.

Besides, the mental vitiations that led women to such behaviour were dreary and predictable, compared to the spectacular phantoms of mind afflicting Parlez-Vous. This evening, if he held his nerve, should see him complete the picture, furnish him with a finished portrait of mind.

Or . . . should he return to Miss Crawford? Better still, send a cab? There was still time to visit the theatre. Last week, he'd taken her to see Kean act. The play had been a war of lungs; King John pronounced 'ache' as if the word possessed two syllables. After the performance, they'd attended a demonstration in the Rotunda, where a chaffinch was suffocated in a glass jar. They'd watched helplessly as the bird broke its wings against the sides. Aspinall remembered trying to live himself into that absence of air.

If memory served, this evening's lecture, by a Dr Prydderch of Cardiff, addressed the meaning of bread in Wales. Miss Crawford had always shown an interest in the quaint customs of the Principality. He fished out his timepiece from his yellow waistcoat. Yes, still time to send a cab.

Five or six fleshless veterans in threadbare military red were loitering at the turn into Little Moorfields. They regarded him with placid eyes. His father used to say: if the whole world were given to a beggar, he'd still beg. Aspinall dug for a coin, dropping it into a skinny palm.

The crumbling walls of Bethlem Hospital rose before him. Once dubbed the Palace for Lunatics, the institution had long since decayed into that place of cruelty known to the city and the world as Bedlam. It was no longer an asylum in any meaningful sense, rather a house of lurid entertainments.

At the far end of the street lay a coaching inn with freshly whitewashed walls. Aspinall paused at the arch leading into the stabling yard, where a low-sized boy with shiny auburn hair was crouched over, playing jacks. One of the flints flew out towards Aspinall's foot.

"Is your father around?" Wyre said.

"Father's dead," the lad answered in a broad city accent. "Mr Rawlings done 'im in."

The physician stared. What a singular child.

A large black dog with sad eyes came pattering up. The boy threw his arm around the animal's neck, and buried his face.

"Well. I am sorry to hear that." Aspinall threw fivepence among the jacks, and set off again.

At the entrance to Princes Street, a coalman stamped up from the void, clutching an empty sack in each hand. He hawked phlegm, and spat it out at the physician's feet.

Aspinall's fists clenched.

One by one, lights were being lit.

14. Electric Air

Plunge one hand into a vessel of water as hot as can be borne . . . Let the other be immersed in a vessel containing an equal amount, but nearly freezing. Pour the two fluids together into a third, then thrust both hands in the mixture. Always the same result: hot to the cold hand, cold to the hot. The medical man shook his head wryly. A pretty parlour trick, he conceded, drawing himself up to his full height. But only he who had deceived his own heart – he patted his hands dry on a linen towel – could infer from such basic deceptions the absence of fixed principles. Cold and heat were distinct properties, with actual existences, not fantasies. It was folly to entertain any other hypothesis.

A faint boom . . . something drifting up from the city. Military manoeuvres. The worst of the present martial epoch was the fact the Continent was closed off. Getting the latest medical books from France and Germany was difficult, impeding progress. But the case he'd stumbled on here, in this modest house of mental relief on the outskirts of the city, would cause reverberations across Europe.

Stumbled on ... stolen. Such distinctions were meaningless in the history of science.

The medical man moved to his wheeled trolley, and slid his instrument case towards him, popping the clasp hinges with two satisfying clunks. From the case, he selected a pair of hollow cork plugs, and pressed them into the nostrils of the monster he'd bound to the gurney earlier that morning. The prisoner, limbs arranged neatly, struggled against the flat, unbreakable leather straps, begging to be released. Quite impossible, he explained patiently, tightening the man's gag. Anyway, they'd been over it all before. Ignoring the muffled cries, he deftly inserted a bifurcated tube for inflating the lungs. Then he summoned the patient he'd grown used to calling Mr Parlez-Vous from the back room. It was time to begin, and he'd promised not to start without his new assistant.

Parlez-Vous entered, hair slicked back, face cast into turbulent yellows by the lamplight. The medical man explained in detail how the apparatus worked, in what order its components must be actuated. The first nozzle released gas (he mimed a twisting motion), the second introduced a potent admixture of elements into the electric tube, whose sole function was to assist the gas in uniting with the blood. Next, the gullet was relaxed by means of a laudanum preparation, after which a stiff stilet of whalebone could easily be pushed down into the belly. When, and only when, these operations had been completed to his satisfaction, could the third nozzle be opened.

The strapped man was also listening attentively. At the mention of the whalebone stilet, the bulbs of his eyes strained, and a fresh round of piteous entreaties began.

With precise movements, Parlez-Vous began the sequence, slender digits taking the first ivory stopple through an exact quarter revolution. As the azotic air whistled through the tube, the man on the gurney stiffened, his fingers setting like cement around the wooden sides.

So far, all in order. But, the fact was, the medical man no longer entertained high hopes for electrical air. It seemed all too likely that Dr Hales's *Vegetable Statics*, which once promised so much, had been a red herring all along. Months wasted investigating a dead avenue. The idea that particles of air might attract sulphur, that molecules thus compounded could store repulsive force ... a wild surmise, another scientific chimera.

He followed the strapped man's eyes to the large, pot-bellied glass jar that sat on top of his mahogany cabinet. Sheathed metal cables coiled up from the cap, held out of harm's way by insulator spikes. To a casual observer (not that such a thing could exist down here), the elaborate device must resemble some fantastical loom, a web of humming braids rising above the tumblers. A bluish skyre clung to the apparatus – beautiful in its own, terrifying way. The man on the gurney began to plead again.

The medical man's eyes followed the leather-sheathed wire that led away from the electrical jar, terminating in a metal globe a precise foot in circumference. From this instrument a thicker tube ran to a second nozzle. He gestured for Parlez-Vous to open it, handing over the whalebone stilet. His student proved remarkably adept, unperturbed by the strapped man's spluttering and choking as the stilet was fed into his belly. He'd seen professional doctors put off by a patient's mewling.

A spiders' mesh formed on his face. He stepped briskly onto a glass-footed insulating stool, instructing Parlez-Vous to stand well clear. A jar of these proportions was easily capable of scorching a man. From his new vantage, he looked down on the patient. What was the human body itself, if not a sort of Leyden jar? Movement – Galvani had proved it with the severed limbs of frogs – and perhaps volition itself depended on an excess of electricity in one part of the animal frame, and a deficiency in another.

Having insured himself against accidental discharge, he made certain the stilet was still firmly in place and could not be regurgitated. The third nozzle he opened himself, and watched as the strapped man's stomach swelled until it resembled a mother's in the sixth month of utero-gestation. He began to count, his deep voice joined by Mr Parlez-Vous' higher, softer tones. When their duet reached twenty, he took a lancet from his wooden tray and made a deft nick in a raised vein in the man's left arm, collecting the blood in a glass bulb. This he held up to the light. Bright red. Perhaps the brightest yet, if a little sizy.

Electric air . . . A handsome phrase, a modish term; but it had delivered little. Today's proving would be the last. If the newest monster to have been delivered to his basement, at no small personal risk, showed few signs of relief from his moral sickness, he would indulge Parlez-Vous' desire to return to older, surer methods. It couldn't be disputed that the desire to sin vanished with the removal of those parts responsible for its commission.

The sight of the creature gasping on the gurney, livid lips separating convulsively, caused a momentary twinge. But he reminded himself his work was in service of futurity, carrying light to the otherwise incomprehensible regions, the abyss, of sexual darkness.

Fortified by this thought, he took a long-barrelled syringe

from the top drawer of his desk, and lightly depressed the plunger, producing an opaque bleb at the needle's end. Refrigerating syrup, he explained to Parlez-Vous, who leaned in, a model of attentiveness.

15. Water Service

Could the air really teem with tiny pearly creatures that fell with the rain? Living things so small they resisted microscopes, just as the stars did telescopes? Sarah Cooke's brow gathered into a tight knot. Mr Shadworth once told her he'd observed an ... *animalcule* (she relished the word) in a drop of river water. To the naked eye it resembled a small piece of see-through, but in the lens it went about with a fringe around its mouth that shook. When rubbed by other beasts it drew up its tail.

As she pictured it, one of her Chinese girls, Liu, poured another pitcher of piping water at her feet.

Sarah lay back, doing her best to ignore the stabbing pain in her belly. Perhaps she should just vanish from the city, leave James as a bad memory. Another one ... But why should she give up her alehouse, just as it was beginning to show a profit? She rested her head on the tub's wooden rim. Mr Shadworth told her how Egyptian women bathed together in hammams, and rubbed each other all over with hands coarsened with pomegranate skins. The mothers used these occasions to choose brides for their sons. Afterwards the bathers cracked each other's joints in a ceremony called ... Sarah tried to remember ... *tuck-tuck-ah* ... and painted their toes crimson.

The heat spread beneath her skin.

"Fragrant bath," Liu whispered in her ear, "attract lovers, good spirits."

Sarah's eyes traced the tiny woman's plump lips and dark nipples. Even a woman would be better than James. Or an old man; perhaps Mr Shadworth himself. She smiled at the thought.

Shimmering in the perfumed steam, Liu sprinkled aromatic flakes into the pent-up water, then slipped her hands beneath the suds, stirring. Sarah pissed lazily through her fingers. Men paid good coin for such sights in The Horse.

She winced at another stabbing pain deep inside.

Hog's grease, James called it. Sarah made it by melting a pint of animal fat on the squat dog-iron in the kitchen, adding civet and olive oil with crushed, sweet-smelling petals. She left the concoction to congeal overnight in a wooden bowl, scraping it out into little round tins for the mollies.

When she'd arrived in The Swan that morning, her husband had been waiting. He called her to him, waving one of the tins, still drunk from the night before. Then he'd scooped out a big dollop with two fingers. Sarah had shrunk from his graceless touch.

"Everyone should contribute their mite," he'd said, seizing her, bundling her like livestock in a back room. James flung her face-down over some rough sacks, gripping both wrists in one large hand, raising the lever of her arms as though drawing water, forcing her head down. Then, with an oath, he pushed into her.

The room filled with burning seraphs.

Afterwards, he cursed her for the filthy confusion of seed and dung. "There," he said, smearing her lips with it. "You give a child a spoonful of honey when she's good."

She'd hardly heard him over the sound of her mother's voice scolding her for plunging a bright hot pan into cold water. Didn't she know the sudden change in temperature made metal brittle? Stupid girl.

Her head grew heavy. Sarah breathed out, let her eyelids close.

If she wasn't dreaming, she wasn't wholly awake either.

St Margaret of Antioch's was much as she remembered it. From the lectern, the priest was praying for flattened wheat to rise. He denounced government inspectors. Playing to the gallery, as usual.

Sarah hung back at the church door, scanning the pews.

Shake the poppies from your brows. Heed these visions of futurity. Come to your heart's delight. The times we have fallen on are evil.

The priest was right in one respect. The village congregation *was* formed of clay, compounded of dust. The clod of the valley.

Shit of the valley.

There, in a side aisle, hunched in prayer! The old weaver. Elderly now. With an icy spasm, she dipped her fingers in the stone stoup, stole down the aisle, and slipped into the pew behind him. Seeming to sense a presence that disturbed, he turned. So old, his rosy skin appeared young again, only thin as sewing paper. His face tightened.

What? Hadn't he expected ever to see his little dyer girl again?

Clutching his cap, the old weaver lifted the pew-door latch and hurried down the nave. Sarah followed . . . past the cross-legged effigies in chain mail, past the pudding-breasted woman held down by a stone shroud that had so terrified her as a girl. All the way to his little cottage at the foot of the hill.

She pushed at the warped board door.

The wheel sat where it always had, cylinders of carded wool strewn around its feet.

One thread in every dent.

She resisted the urge to tidy away the dark.

His loom squatted to the side, a cobweb of braids rising above it. Two pieces of shirting a week, each piece twenty-four yards in length. Sarah's eyes ran along the rough shelves. Bottles of alum, cream of tartar, sulphate of iron, potash, tin crystals: everything you needed to persuade wool to accept the dye. The weaver swore no one else could tease such yellows as hers from onion skins. She used to collect the ingredients herself. Ladies' bedstraw, dandelion, tomato, cow parsley. Elderberries made a dull violet colour, walnut hulls thick fawn. Nettle and dock produced deep suns, and dandelion gave out magenta. She used cutch for the reddish-brown of fishing-boat sails at sunset. It wasn't always the shades you expected.

One thread in alternate dents, one thread in every dent.

"Count yourseln lucky," he piped up from his chair next to the fire.

The burr was a shock of memory. She'd cast off her own bumpkin accent the day she arrived in London.

"Tha's roight. Could've 'ad the lads waiting."

Her eyes moved to a tool for beating down weft leaned up against the hearth. He'd been using it as a poker.

"What, to tie my hands with hitch-knots?"

"Nobbut sport," he wheedled. "You used t' laugh."

Two threads in each dent, three threads in each dent.

She drew out the blade she'd brought with her and showed it him.

"Don't be witless," he blustered. "They all saw you in church."

She stepped up to him, holding it low, easily batting away his skinny arms.

"Still th' little whore," he snarled as she held the edge of the fish-knife to the scrag of his throat.

She stepped behind him, cradling his head. The weaver

clutched uselessly, a spider held by a wasp. One good pull would see it done.

He began to wail, begging her to stop, the noise seeming to come from everywhere at once. He was telling her something, if only she'd listen. The room began to burl; dark stains appeared on her slip. Then a clatter as the knife fell to the uneven flagstones, its blade a jig of yellow flames.

"I'll send fer the magistrate," the weaver said, struggling to his feet, some of his old boldness returning. He moved to block her way to the door.

Sarah seized the weft-iron from the hearth and hurled it with all her strength. The tool struck the side of his head with a thud. He sank to his knees, groaning, his eyes filling with cochineal. Lifted his fingers to the gash.

She crossed the room, and retrieved the weft-iron. Raised it high.

Four threads in every dent.

St Clement's bell struck six. Liu had gone, but left a length of coarse linen within reach. Sarah pushed herself up, stepping stiffly from the tub.

The first mollies of the evening would be arriving.

16. V.S.C.

The sign proclaimed *Vere Street*. His erstwhile patient – *the* patient – spoke of little else. Aspinall's hand slipped into his pocket, cradling the black notebook. That soft leather binding, at such odds with the contents.

A book of skin; a book of pain.

He had to remind himself what he was pushing himself to such limits for – that, once his reports began to appear in London's medical journals, they would usher in nothing short of a new era in the curation of mental distress.

And appear they would. They couldn't stop him. He didn't think they could.

The jutting shop signboards stretched away like recursive images to a man caught in the chasm between two mirrors. Tallow-chandlers, grocers, cheesemongers, booksellers . . . all the filthy names of commerce. Torches flared at the theatre entrances. A brougham whistled past, sending up choking dust. It was seven o'clock in the evening, and respectable couples were making their way to the playhouses.

Like a hanging wave about to crash onto shore, he stepped onto Vere Street's cracked flagstones.

The unthinkable house itself was a hodgepodge of crumbling bricks stacked haphazardly between twisting timbers, which at some point appeared to have survived a fire. Above an antiquated door hung a makeshift sign displaying the silhouette of a white swan. Aspinall recalled one especially trying consultation, during which Mr Parlez-Vous had sketched this symbol over and over, filling pages of foolscap.

The tavern door opened inward, making him start. A woman's face appeared, her hair tricked up in wagtail ringlets. Beneath a thin calico dress her nipples protruded like damson stones.

"Saw yer through the window," she said (though the windows, he noticed, were heavily draped). "I'm Mrs Cooke, the proprietress." She waved him in.

The mad-doctor hesitated, as he knew he would. But if this was the price of understanding Parlez-Vous' sickness, of wresting the once-in-a-lifetime case back from his superiors at Wood's Close, he'd step into the storm itself.

Making sure his jacket pocket was buttoned, he stepped in.

In the hallway, the tavern madam pressed an oblong card into his hand. He glanced down to find a crude profile of a swan, facing dexter, above three amateurishly curlicued letters. Mentally, he filled the gaps. *Vere Street Club*. A heavy oak side-door opened into the taproom. Aspinall's yellow waistcoat suddenly felt as tight as the strait jackets they sometimes used at Wood's Close.

He took in what the dim light cast by low table-lamps revealed: rough labourers and finely dressed gentlemen mingling freely, flies evidently deemed as good as peacocks in this garden. Tiny vases of bluebells jarred like oranges in winter.

The proprietress touched his sleeve. "I'll introduce you to some nice gem'men. Don't worry, they won't bite," she said, laughing. "Not these, anyway. Can't say the same for all my patrons." Gently, she pulled him towards a small circle of drinkers seated at a table beside a jasper-lined fireplace. A mounted lithograph of Caravaggio's lizard boy hung from the chimney breast.

Snatches of lewd talk arrived from all directions.

—— *To me, my precious little rogue!*

Impossible to block them out.

In his attic tabernacle, Parson Church rubbed the rib of flesh on the back of his hand where they'd branded him with a hot wire for being an orphan. Abandoned as a three-week-old baby on the steps of St Andrew's Church. That's where he'd got his name, where he'd got his calling. Truly, a child of providence.

The orphanage governors chastised him for his bad writing, and for leading the other illiterates into the devil's sad snare. He'd spent his life running from accusations. Mr C. said this; Mr C. said that.

He cast his eyes around the cramped loft. Hardly genuine

bon-ton, as he'd been led to expect. The odd handsome footman or farmer, otherwise a ministry of waifs and strays. (And some had strayed further than others.) But hadn't Jesus preached to similar congregations?

Club members were still squeezing in, eager to witness the evening's first wedding consummated on the truckle bed. Parson's eyes returned to the youth in the third row. The boy's cobalt brows were matched to a set of paste jewels. Was that a new ring glinting on his finger? A present from the Country Gentleman . . . Who else?

He pronounced the insoluble ties of matrimony, praised the sweet fruits of genuine, disinterested friendship.

"Friendship that rules every power of your minds, bodies and souls. Forgive each other your faults."

Friendship that would save them all.

O what unhappy men we are! Addicted to abominable propensities. Led into error. O, Christ! O, God!

Yes, dry, thirsty creatures, harassed by devils whom it pleased to perplex those they couldn't destroy. His eyes drifted back to his marvellous boy. His White. Why had the lad found his way here, of all places? Renting out his favours in plain view.

Shut up meditation with prayer.

Dear God! O Lord!

Familiar phantoms of the brain rose before him, playing out his arrest a year ago. Dragged like a felon to the watch-house, accused publicly of crimes too horrible to relate.

Lord, how they are increased, that trouble me.

Lovely White. Cash-corrupted White!

It took every ounce of will to control his breath. "Know the plague of the heart and the value of Jesus. Dear friends, you have been forewarned."

Each night, a dream of scorpions.

His trial had been a farce, concluding with the bodily

ejection from the Courthouse of one of the prosecution's own lawyers. The case against him dismissed, Parson returned to his Obelisk Chapel, where he preached defiance to a teeming audience.

Truth told, he'd been resigned to dangle; was almost relieved at the prospect.

Why shouldn't I administer the sacrament to those intoxicated with gin?

"My Temple is open. Do not be led astray by unprincipled men. Avoid gossip and tattling about ministers. These are dark days."

Why not throw in my lot with the Queen of Bohemia and Kitty Cambric? Why not bless the coming union?

From the third row, White finally met his gaze, before slinking off. Back to the Country Gentleman and his stinking guineas. Parson pictured his true love in that devil's clutching arms.

Remembering the bride and bridegroom, he composed himself, and led the happy couple from the dressing-up chest that served as an altar to the truckle bed.

As he joined their hands, the pair swapped shy glances.

"Show us yer ring!" someone roared.

"Sincere friendship . . ." Church trailed off. Tried again. "Dear friends, do not be surprised that a trial by fire is occurring among you."

For God's sake, do not.

"What God has brought together, let no man – "

Etc.

"Sarah, haul your fat arse over here!" The heavyset barman glared at Mrs Cooke. "Ain't bin the same," he explained to the drinkers at the ale counter, "since she cum back from visiting her ol' man up north."

Aspinall observed Sarah Cooke through the guttering

candlelight. Pretty, with bright eyes. His Society would certainly consider her worth saving. His eyes returned to the men at the fireside table. Very well . . . If he was to fathom this place, he must engage the patrons in conversation. He'd think of it as an interview no different from those he conducted with the residents at Wood's Close. With that consoling thought, he left the bar, drifting over into earshot.

"Stricken with remorse?" (the lean one was saying in a bat-thin voice, arm draped over the shoulders of his neighbour). "Devil on a stick, our Thomas is one of the monstrous Donnestre of th' Red Sea. They possess the heads of birds wi' human bodies, an' lure unwary boys with poetry, only t' devour them – " he touched the tip of his finger to his nose " – apart from the head, which they weep over noisily."

"Then set about ensnaring the next gullible young colt," a plump man added. His flabby eyelids opened and closed spasmodically as if he suffered from some ocular disorder, though it was several years since Aspinall had studied maladies of the eye.

"Where'd yer learn such abrac?" the one named Thomas said, his accent thick and glottic.

"In Africa, where the sea is full of moons," the other replied, holding up a ruby-coloured handkerchief. His flaggy cheeks recalled a butcher's shambles.

"Take care when you leave tonight," the lean one said. "There's a new guild against us. They've christened themselves the Society for th' Suppression of Sodomites. Their leader's a jack o'lantern – calls himself The Bee."

"Eh? Does he intend t' sting me to death?"

"They say he sports regimental colours. Yellow and black."

"Not a queen bee, then?" Thomas looked up, his eyes meeting Aspinall's.

It was too much. The asylum physician changed course, squeezing between tables, the air thick with bitters and spices. He came to rest at the taproom counter. Sarah Cooke came over and presented him with a mug of hot beer.

"Mind you enjoy yourself," she said, beaming.

A fiddler launched into 'At Her Wheel, the Village Maiden', a tune Aspinall knew from boyhood. He sipped at his hot ale – pleasantly sweet – and listened to the flurry of grace notes, slurs and furious détaché passages.

As the fiddler called the switch, Aspinall felt the slightest of tugging sensations at the hem of his jacket. His hand shot to his coat pocket . . . the precious medical volume nestled safely beneath the tight weave of his jacket . . . his heart found its next beat. Frowning, the physician glanced round.

An athletic-looking man with cropped hair stepped from the bar, and was soon lost in the crush.

—— *Sing wack, dilly-dooly! Wack, dilly-dooly!*

Aspinall took another sip of beer, and moved off himself. Talking was out of the question, he decided. Instead, he'd satisfy himself with investigating the tavern's interior – furnish his imagination with the details he needed to make a proper description of the house that haunted Mr Parlez-Vous.

—— *a wonderful association between the bigness of the buttocks and stones*

—— *keep poking till he blows!*

Behind the bar was an alcove reached by a low wooden arch. Aspinall ducked under it.

—— *tastes like jugged hare*

A couple were embracing there on a high-backed bench, one middle-aged, the other a youth. The older figure was dressed in satin breeches, his silver-buttoned long coat cut nattily away at the skirts, the upper part of his face entirely hidden beneath a dark-blue visor. (Aspinall thought of a Venetian masque.) He cradled the younger man in his lap. Aspinall blinked, at first unable to make sense of what his eyes reported . . . Something thick and heavily veined was moving languidly in and out of the youth's deepest depths.

—— *Sing wack! dilly-dooly!*

The whole tavern seemed to tilt towards the couple. Aspinall felt himself tumbling, caught by the obscene gravity . . . He cried out as someone seized his wrist, pulled him backwards through the arch, then spun him like a wax doll. The taproom became a whirling panorama.

When everything came to a standstill, the physician looked up to find an enormous, bullet-headed man bending over him. The tallest man he'd ever seen.

—— *Sing wack, diddly-oh!*

17. Pretty Chickens

"I assure you, Mrs Cooke, the deepest truths are all female."

Sarah gave Mr Shadworth a faint smile, having no wish to encourage him. The tavern was busy this evening.

"How we arrive at them – " the elderly man continued blithely, "that's the male part."

Sarah's eyes swept the room. Where was the new cit in the bright yellow waistcoat? Surely he hadn't left after a single mug?

"Women live a life of hunches. We men, on the other hand, concern ourselves with thoughts. With reason."

"I'm perfectly capable of reasoning," she murmured.

"You are, Mrs Cooke. After all, what is thinking but

basic calculation?" His brow creased into a skein of fine folds. "If I were to assert, all horses are brown, I could communicate the very same, substituting a mathematical symbol for each word. Why, I could conduct a whole conversation in such a manner. I could – " He broke off.

A yellow bruise like sticky pollen dust gleamed beneath one watery eye.

"An individual thought," he said with a melancholy smile, "is like a single move in chess. On its own it has little significance, but add a hundred of them together, and you have a master, and perhaps a mate."

He pushed a stray corner of fraying cambric shirt back into his breeches.

"Whoever you've been playing with doesn't seem to know the rules."

Sudden noise from behind the bar. She peered through the hanging beer mugs into the alcove, where a disturbance of some kind was taking place. It was that awful long-shanks who followed the Country Gentleman about like a puppy. The monster was molesting someone . . . the nice man with the yellow waistcoat!

Sarah dashed out from the bar, hardly hearing Mr Shadworth say, "Oh, he understood the rules. He understood them perfectly."

Aspinall stared up numbly. Much of the height, his physician's eyes told him, lay in the legs, as if the man were standing on stilts. But there was no doubting the tensed power in that upper torso.

The brute lowered his forehead till it made contact with Aspinall's own. "Kitson . . . Inspector of Hides."

The voice was odd and high; Aspinall suspected something had gone amiss in childhood. He tried to free his wrist. "You're hurting me, sir."

The Inspector ignored him. "How d'you tell if a hide's well dressed?" He left no gap for an answer. "Observe if the cut be shining. The inside should be th' colour of thorny nutmeg. To spot a hide that's badly dressed, let a drop of water fall from yer finger onto the grain. If the drop don't remain perfectly round, but spreads, the hide is badly tanned."

At last the monstrous thumb and forefinger released. The mad-doctor backed away hurriedly.

"Don't cut too deep, or too early," Kitson called after him. "The ooze hardens the surface. No one will buy."

That was it. He'd risked enough. If Mr Bolton or, worse, Miss Crawford's father, should ever learn he'd set foot in this filthy place . . . It was unthinkable! Mrs Cooke arrived, her face a mask of concern; he pushed past her, just as he had Miss Crawford earlier that day, and weaved his way to the door. His fingers were closing around the knob when a heavy hand landed on his shoulder. He had what seemed an age to assess its size and pressure. Had the giant Kitson come after him? Or had some clandestine Bow Street officer stepped out of the shadows? He turned, struggling to breathe.

"Lost a shilling on the Porpoise," a square-shouldered man slurred, revealing a row of pebble-like teeth. "Useless bugger got himself floored in the twelfth." He covered an eye with one finger. "What d'yer say to me standing you a glass of grog. You can console me."

Aspinall shrank from him. "I was, I was about to – Good day, sir."

The man's grin vanished. Reaching past Aspinall's head, he laid his palm against the door. "Oh dear, oh dear. What's this? Too glorified for The Swan, are we?" He leaned in, placing his other hand on the physician's lapel. The stench of sour gin made the physician want to retch.

"Hoi!" An arm went up at the fireside table. "Tha's right! Come over an' warm tha' cold brass balls."

Aspinall slipped under his accoster's arms, and moved gratefully towards the hearth.

The hallooer rose to greet him. "Mr Thomas, your most humble – " He trailed off with a swan-like arc of the arm. Bottles, glasses and newspapers were pushed aside on the table. A platter of jellied meats appeared from nowhere, then a chair.

————— *the rest of the chink is named the perineum*

"Pretty waistcoat!" said the plump one, eyes lost in rolls of flesh. He rubbed the yellow braid between thumb and forefinger. "*Tres bon!*"

"Ignore t' bacon-faced sirrah," the one who'd called himself Thomas said, jerking his thumb. "Oracle of the pot-house, our Mr Donne."

————— *by the holy prepuce*

Donne harumphed, brushing imaginary dust off his sleeve.

"What shall we call thee?" Thomas took a swig of brandy, his eyes fixed on the physician.

————— *Mr Pinker's about to blow!*

A crumpled sheet of paper lay next to Thomas's elbow – a diagram of some kind. Something was scribbled in one corner. *Lines of Torres Vedras*. It meant nothing to Aspinall.

"Tha' name, sir?"

Aspinall felt like a river about to lose itself in the sea. He plucked a name out of thin air, aware how absurd it must sound. *Xenophon.*

————— *Look at th' pretty chick'n!*

Thomas winked. "Xenophon it is, then. Pleased to make your acquaintance. Quite right, an' all," he said, looking round as if the room were filled with covert agents. "Dun't

70

hurt these days t' be careful. At this table, tho',
" he added, "we all go by our Christian names. I'm Thomas – " he clapped a hand to his breast " – this scoundrel is Francis – " he pointed to the thin man " – and this round villain is Donne."

The plump man, who was busy renovating the physician's glass with the inside of a flapping shirt sleeve, looked up and grinned.

"I suppose you've heard about the recent turnings-off? We had front row seats. Proper wriggle, it was. Poor ol' Leager, poor Oakden. You'll find *The Dispatch*'s account upstairs in the privy, where it serves as bum fodder."

―――― *no surgeon would attempt anything with a knife in there*

"A pox on the editor," declared Donne. "That rag's a drain for other newspapers to carry off their worst trash."

The fiddler called a switch.

"Pinch of tha' sentry-box?" Thomas said, helping himself to Donne's snuff. An image of Napoleon was embossed on the silver case.

"Francis fetch'd it back from th' campaigns," Thomas said, seeing Aspinall's alarmed face.

Donne tugged at his collar. "This heat! Bingo and water, anyone?"

―――― *mumming with the fetishes*

Francis held up a creased copy of *The Times*. "Woman in India, placed between two boards, sawn in 'arf." He turned to Aspinall. "Third Regiment o' Foot. Pleas'd to make yer acquaintance."

―――― *milk-maiding with the vishnoos*

"What wor her crime?" Thomas goosed Aspinall's thigh.

Another stool arrived from above. To Aspinall's horror, it was his pebble-toothed accoster.

Thomas nodded. " 'Ow do, Jameson?"

The broad-shouldered man leered around the table. "Caught at a game of flats wi' her mistress, would be my guess."

"Occult rituals?" Donne offered.

—— *I don't like the smell*

"There yer go again," Thomas said. "Told yer before, the occult ain't jus' the reserve of savage nations. The forward-looking city's also a place of superstition. Take them disciples of Southcott, now . . ."

"I pity anyone gullible enough to purchase seals from that impostor," said Donne primly.

"Southcott's lot hate us," said Thomas. "They'd queue for a week t' see a molly man choke."

Donne pulled a face. "And do they *ever* tire of the 'coming apocalypse'? Sword, famine and plague marching through the land. I wouldn't spend a single afternoon, let alone eternity, with those glum Johns."

—— *Look for the golden ball hanging over his back door*

"I remember conjuring parsons as a boy." (Donne refilled his glass.) "Met Mary Bateman once, an' all . . ." His voice dropped to a whisper. "Aye, thass right, the Witch of Leeds. Kept a hen that laid eggs inscribed wi' the words, *Christ is coming.*"

Jameson gave a loud sigh. "I thought they stretch'd that embezzler's neck in York last year."

—— *Mercury is king!*

Thomas sniffed. "Crowd rushed fer strips of her flesh, cured 'em in jars t' sell as souvenirs." He leaned towards Aspinall. "A friend of ours, the Bricklayer, wor found down at the bridge last week. Someone had taken a hammer t' him. Comely lad, loved t' chat." He looked round the company. "Some might say tha' wor his problem."

72

—— *If your water's clear, you've nothing to fear from the doctor*

Silence.

"Don't let Thomas put you off," Jameson scoffed. "He's just a Covent Garden waiter who thinks he's a scholar. The man would bow to a Quaker hat. Even his accent's sham."

"Born 'n bred in't north," said Thomas with a grin. "But I've bid farewell to my loiner brogue. Sound as queer in Leeds today as if they'd exiled me t' Peking." He pulled a handful of coins from his pocket, and proceeded to stand them up on their edges.

"Farts in French, tho'," Jameson added.

Thomas looked away. "Tha' must be confusing me wi't Bricklayer."

—— *like butter in a hot skillet*

Aspinall suddenly became aware of an elderly man standing at his elbow. His skin reminded him of old legal parchment. How long had he been there?

"*Navia aut caput*, Mr Thomas?" the gentleman said, peering down at the coins. "Ship or head? Neither, I suppose, in your case." He rested a liver-spotted hand on Aspinall's forearm. "Remember, in The Swan all bets are suspended. Shouldn't you be getting home?"

"Daft old bugger," Thomas said, as the man turned and disappeared in the alehouse's twilight. "Don't mind 'im, Xenophon."

Donne turned to the physician. "Are you married?"

—— *easily the bigger of the two*

"Yes. Betrothed . . ." Aspinall faltered.

"Don't fret," Francis said, misprisioning his discomfort. "We wun't think any less o' you. We're all married men here." He hoisted his glass. "Besides, a wife can always serve as an improvised man, if you ask her nicely enough."

——— Oil your rods in the summer. Take care the parts lie flat

"My wife swears it makes no difference if she's deep enough in gin." Donne smirked, showing the wattles of his neck.

"Worse than ol' Bum Cutter," Jameson said, wrinkling his nose.

Thomas set his glass down loudly. "In Turkey tha can get fer a few shillings what we're forced daily t' risk our necks fer." With a deft movement he swiped the coins into his cupped hand.

——— taken with a certain cow

From the bar, an unkempt man was making a stumbling beeline for their table. Donne nudged Thomas.

——— a square building seen at a distance appears round

"Miserable fornicators – " the newcomer slurred, peering down with rheumy eyes " – wae'd stiffen tae aye well-groomed horse."

"This grum friend," Donne said in a stage aside to Aspinall, "is known to her friends as Miss Pasiphäe. If it couldn't hang with propriety between the hind legs of a bull, she isn't interested."

——— a young Colossus to be seen at the sign of the French horn

Francis giggled. Aspinall, despite himself, joined in the mirth. Miss Pasiphäe rounded on him.

"Whae's this, eh?"

"Now, now, don't pester," Thomas chided, placing a protective arm around Aspinall's shoulders. "This one's the pea under t' tumbler."

"Or the lady in the pack," Francis added.

"Wouldnae last a minute i' the Crochallan Fencibles," Miss Pasiphäe pronounced, pinching Aspinall's cheek. "Noo but a tom-turd man."

—— avoiding the gibberish of physics

Thomas cleared his throat, and extended an arm in the declamatory style. "When at the Despot's dread command bridg'd Hellespont his myriads bore – "

Donne gave a snort of derision. "Who's responsible for that crambo?"

—— Eh! you dear little toad. Come buss!

"Why, only Mr Pye himself, his celebrated meditation on th' finitude of existence." Thomas winked at Aspinall.

"It's a snapping-turtle of a poem," Donne replied. "Cowper, now *there's* a poet."

"Verse shood turn th' emotions loose," Miss Pasiphäe said, and belched loudly.

"It ought to be an escape from the emotions," Donne suggested.

"A good florencing serves that purpose," Francis said.

—— Tight-built, an' out in all weathers

"Modern poetry – " Donne pulled a face " – always slippery without being sweet."

—— all handsome wi' his baubles dangling

"Hear about the captain who lost the sea?" Thomas said.

—— Paris could be anywhere

Donne gulped at his brandy. "Horse-piss," he said, wiping his lips.

"You'd know," said Francis.

"A true friend should be like a privy ..." Thomas looked at Aspinall. "Open in a necessity."

"You'll pay dearly for licking honey from thorns," Donne muttered.

—— hot-shot in a mustard pot

Thomas raised his glass. "Tie up your stockings, my dears. She ain't a good 'ousewife as won't wind up her bottom!"

—— *his mouse-trap smells of cheese*

Jameson hoisted the brandy bottle. "May the yard-arms be long – "

" – an' the sterns be steady!" said Miss Pasiphäe, finishing the toast.

—— *Oh, go at it, my jumbo!*

The bar-door flew open on its hinges and three brawny men burst in.

18. Campaigns

The six-fisted maelstrom rushed into the tap-room, cuffing drinkers indiscriminately. Mrs Cooke shot out from behind the ale counter, and was dashed unceremoniously to the sawdust. She lay there, dazed.

"Turd-suckers!" roared the stockiest intruder. One side of his face was a hatch-work of jagged, blue-edged scars. "Laldy t' ye all!"

Aspinall began to rise, but Thomas put out a restraining arm.

"The fistic universe's nowt fer thee, lad."

"But Mrs Cooke . . ." Aspinall protested weakly.

"Used t' far worse from her husband."

The tars cut a deep swath into the bar, a circle of panicked drinkers forming a receding tide before them. Victims were hauled out at random, the mollies falling beneath flurries of looping blows. It dawned on Aspinall that the bruisers' slogging course was set to arrive at the chimney. Even Thomas seemed to shift nervously.

An enormous form stepped from the demi-light. The stocky tar weighed anchor, sizing up the Inspector of Hides. He turned to his mates. "Big bastard here, Jez."

"Bigger they come, Sutton," the other answered

philosophically. "Lemme n' Sam have a go at the scaly rip. We'll stow 'im on top o' the others, bilge to the cunt-line."

Sutton shook his head, stretching his arms out like a bird about to take flight. Without warning, he delivered a right hook to the Inspector's chest that would have stunned a whale.

Aspinall gasped in horror, but the only sign the colossus had even registered the clout was a slight shifting of his muscles, a redistribution of weight between the feet.

Sutton's next blow was fired straight off the shoulder. A concussive third concluded the salvo.

"Whop 'im!" Jez roared with approval. "Draw his fookin' cork!"

Kitson shrugged one shoulder, then the other, methodically. Started to advance . . . Forced to work laterally, Sutton strung together a vicious sequence of hooks and rabbit punches, but Kitson seemed content to soak up the punishment, pressing ever forward. The tar – with a look of immense concentration on his face, as if sitting an exam – resorted to pecking and feinting, conceding ground until, with an audible thud, his heels made contact with the skirting board.

The giant threw his first punch. Easily read, it struck only a glancing blow to the tar's cheekbone, but its slant weight was such that the whole upper part of Sutton's face seemed to slip to the side, leaving the right eye bulging from its socket. The sailor steadied himself, then slumped. Seeing his man lose bottom, Kitson dropped a vast left hand over his shoulder, and pulled him in, driving a slow right fist repeatedly up into the tar's soft parts. Sutton's slack face was a totem of expunged colour.

Aspinall stared – was he witnessing a murder? He tried to get to his feet, but again Thomas prevented him.

Sutton's mates launched a desperate rescue party. Sam

broke off the leg of a stool, and swung it wildly at the giant's shoulder blades, while Jez kicked at the vast shins. Terriers baiting a bear. Kitson felled Sam with a hammering fist to the top of the head. Then, as Jez stared stupidly, the colossus leaned over, clamped two plate-sized hands over his ears and, with a high-pitched squeal, raised the sailor clear from the sawdust.

Aspinall instantly realized what the brute had in mind: a sideways jerk that would dislocate the sailor's head at its articulation with the neck.

To his astonishment, Jameson stepped out of the shadows. "Not here, John . . ." he cried, pulling down on one of the long, knotty arms. Kitson's pale, yellow eyes swivelled. Aspinall braced for the inevitable, which did not come. Instead, the monster let the kicking tar fall, and allowed himself to be led away behind the bar.

The tavern drew breath.

It took four mollies to lug Sutton's bulk into the street, one to each limb. The fiddler launched into another whirling rendition. Someone called for black strap.

Aspinall jumped – Francis was pouring brandy through his fingers.

Thomas frowned at the physician. "What's a banging boy like you doing in The Swan, Xenophon? Shouldn't tha' be out making feet fer children's stockings?"

Aspinall took a gulp of brandy, hasping as it went down.

"I put one sullen miss in the family way not once, but twice," Donne interrupted. "As soon as a girl has a baby," he added darkly, "she becomes an enemy."

"Y-e-s . . ." Francis said dubiously.

"Ye mean tae say," Miss Pasiphäe said, incredulously, "there micht be two wee Donnes scamperin' aroond?"

"Each more depraved than me," Donne said. He wafted the air. "Od's heart, this heat."

"Teel us a tale, brither!" Miss Pasiphäe thumped his fist into his palm, looking at Thomas.

They all turned expectantly.

"Since you ask so prettily. Some years back, I found myself in Brussels. They wor cutting men down to size in th' main square. To judge from the quantity of claret on the boards, the executioner had been at it all day. Three rogues wor up next, two o' them likely lads, one a simple boy wi' straw hair, son of a pretty widow. The mother knelt at the young Capitaine's feet, all cherry lips and jutting bubbies – " he mimed with both hands " – pleading with him. Promised him a new phase of heaven. Hell, if he wished it." Thomas sniffed. "At that time, it worn't uncommon fer three generations of one family to be dispatched at a single sitting, each set of progenitors strapped onto a bascule slick wi' the blood of their darlings. Needless to say, our Capitaine wor deaf to the widow's petition."

There was a pause.

"They chopped the lad?" Donne said.

"Aye, they did. The simpleton turned his head to his dam jus' as the blade fell. His very last word wor – 'mama!'."

"Tha's 'ard," Francis said quietly.

"Issa gud story," Miss Pasiphäe slurred approvingly.

"Because it's true," Thomas replied.

Mrs Cooke arrived with more brandy. Her lip was split and swollen. She gave the physician a rueful smile. "It's not always like this."

"What? Of course, it is. Public houses – " Francis said extravagantly, "the sin of all great cities." He gazed around. "I'll tell you a tale, boys, one to rival old Harlequin Billy's." He took a swig of gin. "It concerns a French trooper, wot I slew in the dunes."

Thomas groaned, pulling his chair closer.

"They promised us black-eyed houris," Francis began.

(Aspinall leaned in with the others.) "Didn't see a single one o' those. Jus' marched round in circles till our foreskins wuz red-raw with sand. Hotter than a punk's notch, the air jingling wi' grape. One morning alone, we had t' put twenty lads to bed with a spade. Few miles out from Damanhur, we surprised a ragged-arse column of Frenchies wot'd bin battling clouds of Arabs all week. Bested 'em smartly enough. Soon after, word cum down we wuz to pay 'em back for Omedinar – "

"Omedinar?" asked Donne, rapt.

"Little place, right up in the cow's belly. Two dozen of our rocketeers 'ad surrendered there the week before. One of their squibs had gone off at the French commanding officer's feet – left him a branchless trunk. In revenge, the Frenchies had our lads hoisted on the ends of pikes. Two in the back – " he made quick thrusting motions with his fists " – two in the front, just under the ribs. Then . . . *allez-hup!*" From his seat, Francis made a gesture like a man forking a stook of hay up onto a wain. He let out a heavy sigh. "We wuz told to bay'net anyone still drawing stream. All them wounded men, worse butchery than Vinegar Hill."

"Oh, you poor darling," Donne crooned.

"When it wuz done, the order came t' march on Coron. But before I could form up wi' the others, it came on sudden – shittin' like a mink. Nerves, it must have been. I crouched up 'gainst a wall t' let nature take her course. Told the boys I'd catch 'em up."

A long pause.

"Was tha' th' teel?" Miss Pasiphäe said.

Francis glared at him. "Must have passed out. When I regain'd me senses, I spied 'im – young swad in a soldat's uniform, creeping over the piles of Frenchie dead. Dunno how he'd given our marauding van the slip. He wuz handsome, mind, wiv his pistols swinging." Francis looked around balefully. "Should've seen his expression as he took in our 'andywork. All them guts out." He rubbed his eyes as if there was desert sand in them. "He spotted me then, breeches round me ankles, legs covered wi' filth, an' come on with a blood-curdlin' cry – sabre pointing straight at me thigh-'ole.

"What on earth did you do?" said Donne.

"Scrabbled to me feet, best I could – " Francis grimaced " – then keeled over. Jus' lying there like an up-ended turtle waiting fer the soup pot. Fortunately, I had the presence of mind t' draw me fire-piece. Quick, like, I spat a ball – last one – in the barrel . . . waited . . . ." he closed one eye, taking aim with outstretched finger and cocked thumb, "waited . . . wai—ted . . . till I saw the pink of his cheeks. Then . . . ." the thumb went down. "Smoke everywhere! Cuntin' hell, I thought the pistol 'ad burst on me. But when the puff cleared, the bastard lay a few yards away, belly split open like a ripe mango. Weren't dead, tho'." He shivered. "He started fumbling for his own pistol – an' there's me, shot all spent . . ."

Donne's breath whistled through his teeth.

"Nothing for it, wuz there, but to draw me knife – the one Da' give me before I sailed. I crawled over, farting an' belching, an' stuck the quaint right in the neck. Oh, he tried to fend me off, but there wuz no heft to 'im. Christ, you should've heard him mewing as the blade went in."

"It was kill or be killed," Donne said simply.

"Tha's right!" Francis's head moved up and down. "When he'd finished twitching, I went through his pockets." Catching Aspinall's look, he said tetchily, "It's a soldier's right t' root fer spoil. Anyway, I could feel something 'ard beneath his tunic – "

"Which reminds me . . ." Thomas said.

Francis ignored him. "I began tuggin' at his buttons . . ." He stopped.

"And?" Donne brought his fist down on the table. "And? And? Don't leave us hanging?"

"Bandages – " Francis gave the men a puzzled expression. "Yards an' yards of 'em. Funny, cuz he 'adn't moved like he wuz wounded. Oh-ho, I thought to myself, there's something precious squirrelled away there. Meybe loot from Pharaoh's tombs, enough to buy myself out of the army. I pulled away."

"We all know that feeling." (Thomas again.)

"What had the cull stashed?" Donne said.

"Wot I found," Francis said with an isolated look, "wuz a fine pair of dairies."

Blankness.

More blankness.

It sunk in.

Thomas smirked. "You mean, you pinked a woman?"

"I could see her then. The soft skin, high voice. The panic." He sucked at his bottom lip. "She couldn't 'av been more than sixteen."

"Whit the fuck was a bitch daein' oan campaign?" said Miss Pasiphäe.

"The law allows soldiers to kill anyone, man or woman, so long as they're wearing uniform," Donne said tartly. "You did no wrong."

Francis's eyes glistened.

"Hang an arse," Thomas said slowly. "The Nile was when? '97, '98? How old were you?"

"I wuz there."

Donne passed the brandy round, clucking his tongue.

"I wuz there," Francis repeated, more quietly now.

Miss Pasiphäe reached for a glass. "London – a whore whae'll welcome anyone, and anything, intae her."

Aspinall began to lift his own tumbler when Jameson laid a firm hand on his wrist.

"Wait on, Xenophon. The White Swan's an opportunity, but it's also a risk. We're sworn to murder any mollying bitch who betrays us."

Aspinall's heart contracted to a tight fist. "Betray you?"

"Ye cud be a spy," said Miss Pasiphäe.

"Or one of Southcott's servants," suggested Donne. "Hadn't you better tell us your name?"

"I already told you," the physician protested weakly.

"Yer real name," growled Jameson.

The tavern seeming to be unbuilding itself around him. Aspinall plucked a name from the air, the first to occur. That of a childhood tormentor.

Jameson glanced across at Miss Pasiphäe. "Mr Amos, you're a customs inspector. What do you do when you hear an untruth?"

"You try tae get behind tha' statement," the other replied.

"Last chance," Jameson said, "before we call Kitson. He has a particular talent for getting behind things."

When he finally said his name out, it was a relief.

"Not so hard, was it," said Thomas. "And how does Mr Aspinall make ends meet?"

The physician blanched. There must be dozens of Aspinalls in London, but only one Aspinall the mad-doctor. Word was certain to get back. His fiancée might understand his motives for his nocturnal visit, but her father wouldn't.

"Why so coy?" Jameson said. "I'm a fusilier, Thomas and Donne are waiters, Francis is a sentinel in the foot guards, or so he claims. When I first met him he was growing something in Mr Sabine's garden." The others passed sniggers around the table. "We like to know a bit about each other. Just the bare facts."

Aspinall stared at them. Tell them a story. Any story. The one about his second cousin, come back from the Sugar Islands, about her dead mother's silk dresses, puce-coloured and full of pins. Tell them about Wood's Close, about the Windsor chair suspended from the ceiling in the basement, how their kind are strapped in and spun till they vomit, or void their bowels. That this is considered progress. Tell them about Professor Ashcroft, who thinks sodomite dogs deserve torture, not treatment; who refuses to pander to sin as if it were a mental derangement. Or Dr Ellesmere, who calls their vice *crimen contra naturam,* and says their contagion will seep through the city and raise a new Sodom. That the consequence of their awful fruit must be heavenly vengeance, for isn't the Bible clear? That molly men give birth to themselves, clutching at each other's yards – that there's no heart in them left to look on the Sacrament. That their desires are like apples that fall unto dust when touched.

He looked round at the faces, and wondered if he'd said any of it aloud.

From the corner of his eye, he saw the bartender was lumbering towards them, apron dangling from one hand.

"My father's a baker," he blurted.

"Not that fud baker in Keynsham market, whae sells hot bread full of darnel? Couldnae stop jiggin' for twa days."

The bartender was unholy in the half-light. "Any sisters wishing to navigate the windward passage should present their passports." He looked at Aspinall as if enjoying a view.

The others fished out their membership cards. With fumbling fingers, Aspinall found his.

V.S.C. He was in it now. Up to his neck.

19. Country Gentleman

The attic corridor was feebly lit by recessed lanterns. Aspinall walked with uncertain steps to the first of the doorless lofts and oratories. The fusty room was packed with men playing chambermaids to men on low truckle beds. He fought the instinct to retreat. But he'd come to take the temperature of Parlez-Vous' sickness – to understand the heat itself. He told himself that.

Where the devil had Donne and the others got to?

On the nearest couch – dear Lord – a bearded club member lay beside a toga-clad youth; an ivory totem caught the lamplight in a way that seemed at odds with its unyielding geometries. Each pull saw it extracted to its full length.

———— *get it from rubbing*

Further inside, Aspinall spotted the visored dandy from earlier in the saloon. The youth was completely naked now, his yard describing an extended arc.

———— *I've heard it comes from sharing spoons*

A moustachioed nurse, perched on the edge of a bed at Aspinall's knees, looked up. "White's a lucky lass," he whispered. "The Country Gentleman a generous pussmaster. He pays in gold sovereigns."

———— *Mr Howard's pencil's broken*

A friar burst into the loft, cassock hoiked up, his appendage comically hangdog.

"Show us yer bumfiddle!" roared the nurse.

———— *Cum 'ere, m' sly boy*

Aspinall stared blankly. There was nothing to be learned here. Just men rutting like beasts. With a shudder, he backed out into the corridor, meaning to make for the stairs, when a tide of flesh hit him, carrying him further into the hanging shadows.

—— *remember to use me honourably*

When the rush stopped, he found himself at the entrance to a smaller attic filled with men huddled over an enormous clothes chest, shuffling identities in a rack-jack of activity. In the phantasmagoric half-light, chequered ribbons and furbelow scarves floated in the sticky air. A gasman rose a milkmaid, a rouged drayman in laced shoes fought a female grenadier for a green hat edged with bright blue quilling.

—— *A dirty thing wet becomes more dirty*

Aspinall spied Francis and Amos clinching on a sofa. He turned away, just as a golden-haired youth seemed to step out of the brick wall into the little well of light cast by one of the set-back lamps.

"Come ride a rump," the boy whispered. "Come do the story." He undid his breeches, showing Aspinall a callous, heavy-skinned thing.

—— *buried in dung like a limbeck!*

"*There* you are!" Donne came hurrying up, looking warily at the youth. "How do, Miss Selima?"

—— *Take it out, see how sticky I am*

The plump man seized Aspinall's hand with a sense of purpose. "This way . . . Thomas is looking for you."

They'd gone a few paces when their way was barred by a tall figure in clergyman's robes, his black, oiled hair drawn up into an imposing cowlick. Aspinall felt Donne's body tense through his hand.

"Parson – " Donne began.

—— *honest as a banknote*

"Where's White?" the other demanded, running a hand through his hair. "I know you've seen him, don't pretend otherwise." His eyes were red and peery.

—— *Taffy was a Welshman, ar hyd y nos*

Donne hesitated, then pointed to a narrow passage that led away sharply.

"God be with you in all things," said Parson with a grunt.

"Don't fret," Donne whispered, when the clergyman had strode off. "He won't find White there."

—— *next to the pastry-cook's at Charing Cross*

Aspinall looked at him. "Who on earth is this White fellow?"

"For Parson," Donne answered, "Ensign White is his personal paramour." His pudgy cheeks twitched. "I don't think the Country Gentleman sees it quite that way."

"The Country Gentleman?"

"The cit in a visor," Donne said. "Rich as Croesus. No one knows his real name. Wouldn't *want* to know it. Wouldn't be healthy."

—— *Coo-ee, it's the gobbler!*

Francis appeared at Aspinall's side. "Did you say Country Gentleman?" The guardsman rubbed his hands together. "Everyone's guessing. Assizes judge or King's Counsel is my guess."

—— *hungry dogs will eat dirty puddings*

"Meybe ah know exactly who he is," Thomas said, approaching with a yellow false gown draped over one arm. "Let's just say he's a lusty fellow, and leave it at that." He leaned over and – shockingly – nuzzled at Aspinall's neck.

The physician recoiled in horror, but found Donne had him in a firm grip.

"Come on, you," the plump man said, pinning his arms to his side, ignoring his protests, steering him towards the back lofts.

—— *fat as a pork chop!*

20. Molly Rites

According to Fielding's Treatise of Midwifery, *dedicated to assuaging the sufferings of parturition, the calamities that may beset a physician attending at child-bed number no fewer than one hundred and seventy-two. Strangulation of the infant by umbilical cord, haemorrhaging of the placenta and sloughing of the passages from an impacted head moving like a plough through soft tissues are only three of the more alarming scenarios now being entertained by Doctor Sweet-Lips and his assistant, Mistress Fox.*

It is an unconventional birth.

On a side table is a bowl of uneaten panado, along with a cup of water, in which half a drachm of powdered nitre has been mixed. The child's mother exhibits all the signs of scarcely imaginable anguish, but between deep, heaving groans she remembers to ask after her child. Is it blue? Can it be saved? Someone laughs. Mistress Fox, wearing the high-crowned black hat of her profession, makes practiced soothing noises, waving back the twenty or more bystanders who have taken a step closer to the bed. Give the doctor room, she commands. The doctor or Doctor Sweet-Lips looks up from Fielding's Treatise *and frowns at the friends, relatives and hangers-on.*

It is by no means extraordinary in this modern age for a man to deliver a child. Thousands of doctors up and down the country usher infants safely over the threshold every week, although many – perhaps most – husbands, deep down, foster a prejudice against male presences at such intimate quarters. It's not so long ago that apothecary-surgeons conducted deliveries from behind screens, or called instructions from adjoining rooms, relying on the female kin for descriptions of how the child lay in the uterus, the strain on the perineum, the extent of dilation.

That more of these births did not end in disaster is a miracle, thinks Doctor Sweet-Lips, removing sweat from his forehead with a lint cloth. These days, thank God, men are permitted to get their hands wet. Midwifery, the science, or art, of tending to women in every aspect affecting the sexual system, has been taught as an optional component of Edinburgh University's medical degree for decades. However, the present tableau is not staged within the safe walls of that institution, nor does Doctor Sweet-Lips count it as his alma mater.

In fact, he has never read an obstetric report, and a professional looking in would surely tut, then shudder. But at the present moment, Doctor Sweet-Lips may be this labouring mother's only hope.

He knows it is whispered that his last delivery ended with an incomplete child, its face resembling an old man, with wide mouth and ears like membranes. The parts of the skull, it is said – though this may be mere spite – were moveable, and the lips of the mouth resembled bloody pieces of flesh. He has also been accused of giving life to monsters, both perfect (in the shape of a dog or ape), and imperfect (with defects in the head or genitals), that should have been allowed to die. But even a perfect monster must be considered a human being. So Sweet-Lips believes.

Perhaps that's it: this child is malformed in some way that impedes its progress through the canal.

The mother screams. It begins as a long, low, animal sound, rising to a theatrical shriek that gives the lie to those who claim we have risen above our nature. Something here is not as it should be. The doctor scans Fielding's Treatise *once again. There has been no movement for some time, not since the head first emerged from under the arch of the pubes. He studies the child's head. It is almost entirely freed; the cord is, to be sure, partially wrapped around the infant's neck, but there is no strangulation and the doctor can easily hook his finger beneath the thread connecting mother and child. There is – astonishingly – no blood. Neither the lively and florid blood of the small arteries, nor the darker, viscous, pooling blood of the veins. No slow haemorrhaging. That, in any case, is encouraging.*

Reflection is the basis of all rational philosophy, and Doctor Sweet-Lips steps back to think. It may not be too late to resort to more conventional treatments. Perhaps the arm should be bled, and half a pound removed, as recommended by all the authorities. It might, indeed, relieve pressure. Should he fall back on orthodoxy?

The woman gasps, the head falling limply to one side. She is cheered on by the audience. The long, dark curls that have escaped from her sarsenet hood are plastered across her hot cheek. Sweet-Lips takes her pulse, which he announces is weak and intermittent. It is clear to any observer she is sinking. With a flourish, he turns his attention to the infant, which protrudes obscenely, comically, from the mother. Its face is ruddy, almost as if painted, with no signs of the blackness or swelling associated with being too long delayed in the passage. Perhaps the child, at least, can be saved. He gazes on the creamy belly and wonders about the Caesarean operation. It is rarely performed on a living mother, but is permitted if the signs of life in the child are strong, and those of its dam dwindling. He considers the second, equally unpalatable, option that still remains to him: to divide the cartilage that binds together the bones surrounding the womb, and in that way enlarge the opening. He has heard of this being done with success.

On a table, out of sight of the mother, is arranged an array of forceps and other metal instruments of various kinds, including sharp knives and hooks.

Mistress Fox leaves the Treatise *propped open and moves to the head of the bed to ease the mother, whose pains are reaching a new climax. She adjusts the woman's hood, placing a cool hand on her forehead. Then she pulls the night-gown higher to give Doctor Sweet-Lips the clearest view of all. She bends to rub the woman with a little soft pomatum, and applies a cloth wrung out of warm water over the belly, still high and cushioned. In an effort to dilate the parts, she inserts her fingers below the child's head and pushes in. She seems surprised to feel nothing but a soft, fleshy substance where she might have expected things hard and loaded. She communicates this to the doctor, then, while he consults Fielding, prepares a clyster of warm milk and water. Finally, she places the woman's feet firmly against the bed-post, evidently hoping it will assist in expelling the child – however, the mother is too weak even to help Mistress Fox move her legs.*

Time is running out. Sweet-Lips resolves to try one last procedure to save the woman. If he has misjudged the tautness and remaining length of the cord, the child will suffocate within minutes. He selects a metal instrument from the table, one with a suitably thin, short blade, and inserts it between the base of the child's head and the mother's anus. He gives every impression of making a sudden incision, and with a dramatic scream from the mother, the child's whole body comes loose at once.

The doctor seizes the motionless infant while Mistress Fox severs the skein of fine umbilical thread. Then he places the marvellous progeny flat at the foot of the bed. He removes any mucus that may be in its mouth, wiping as far as he can reach down the upper part of the trachea with his little finger and a piece of rag. There is still no movement. He crouches over the tiny figure and applies

91

his mouth to its lips, holds the nostrils, breathes hard. He waits, repeats the procedure. Again. Again.

From somewhere there is a sound like that of an infant bawling. He picks up the tiny body, his face creasing into a broad smile, and hands it over to Mistress Fox, who displays it in triumph to the bystanders. The men, tricked out in women's clothes, close in, clapping and whooping.

It is a perfect jointed baby; a perfect wooden child.

21. Charlies

"Let go of me, sir!" Aspinall was only dimly aware of entering the stifling chamber at the far end of the corridor, of being pushed onto a couch. A circle was forming. The attic's solitary lamp cast only shadows. *"Wait. Please – "* His voice seemed to be coming from a different room.

—— *Careful of that one, teeth in his arse.*

Thomas leaned over him, undoing his shirt. "We're all sinners here, if tha' believe there's any crime in a man mekin' what use he pleases of his own body."

Not like this . . .

Thomas's lips pressed down over his. Aspinall tasted metal.

"Dost tha' wish t' live fer ever in the valley of dry bones?"

Aspinall made to get up, but was shoved down again.

"No harm – " Thomas crooned, laying a firm hand on Aspinall's neck. "Nowt here but love." With his other hand he released his member from his breeches. It was long and heavy, hooded like an assassin.

—— *To be found guilty, the emission of seed –*

Frantically, Aspinall struggled to escape, but the muscular man forced his head down. Aspinall bucked and choked, till he felt the man's melting period.

———— *I'm finding this 'ard t' tug to*

Thomas gasped, spent, and fell back on the couch, leaving Aspinall to stagger to his feet and spit, drawing shrill laughter.

Something dripped from Thomas's yard, the colour of cataracts.

———— *"Ergo, salvabitur!" quoth he, and said no more Latin*

Brushing away scalding tears, the physician pushed through the onlookers, and rushed from the loft. In the corridor, he dropped to his knees and retched on the floorboards. Then, clambering to his feet, he moved unsteadily towards the landing, passing a packed chamber where someone in a black peaked hat was playing matron to a man on a couch, a seaweed-green tunic crimped up around his waist. Aspinall watched numbly as a doll was snatched from between the man's – Jameson's – legs. The oily-haired clergyman stepped forward, and sprinkled brandy over its head.

What on earth was he to tell Miss Crawford? Aspinall turned towards the landing, to safety, as a musket tip rose from the stairwell, followed by a dun leather helmet. For a suspended moment, soldier and physician gazed at each other impassively. Then dozens of heavily armed men thundered up the stairs, night sticks crooked.

Alerted by the noise, *V.S.C.* members emerged blinking from the attics, scrabbling to fasten breeches, caught in the glare of the Watch's bull-lamps. Some of the men rushed for the stairs, becoming a wave that crashed back into itself.

———— *Holloa, hold a light!*

———— *Here's a pretty nest of you!*

———— *Don't kill me, and I'll tell you everything!*

Any remaining mollies were dragged out and beaten with cudgels. Men were being bashed and flattened, and battered where they stood. Aspinall's heart leapt as he saw Amos crawl clear from the writhing mass. The Captain waved over four troopers, who pulled the customs man back in by his hair.

"Lit me gang, ye open arses!" Amos cried out.

The soldiers struck at his joints.

"Don't hang back, boys," the Captain urged. "Give the crab cull a basting."

V.S.C. men were falling like wheat before flails. With a yell of "Boney!", Francis mounted a lone charge, and was felled by a rifle butt that split his nose. A crimson arc slopped against the wall.

At the other end of the corridor came cries of *Stand! Stand!* A sucking darkness resolved itself into the Inspector of Hides. The giant began to advance at a steady trot, shucking off officers like stricken toreros. Aspinall gazed in disbelief: *two* sets of lips grinned at him along the passageway, as if the Inspector were now some two-headed ogre from a child's storybook. It took a dislocating moment till he realized someone was hanging from the Inspector's back. Silk Visor from the saloon ... The Country Gentleman!

As Kitson's thundering strides brought the pair level with Aspinall, the dandy's mask rode up. Their eyes locked: it was like peering at all the world's fires in one place. To add to the horror, Aspinall realized he knew the face – and not just from engravings in a print-seller's window. He'd actually met the man. It had been in Wood's Close.

With the noise of pitched battle around him, he pictured the Country Gentleman in the asylum drawing room, standing imperiously at the tall windows (Aspinall couldn't bring himself to speak the man's real name, even in his thoughts). He hadn't arrived alone, but brought a disturbed young charge with him in his clandestine barouche. Professor Ashcroft had summoned Ellesmere and Aspinall, and together the two physicians had examined the mental sufferer whom they were told to address as Mr Parlez-Vous.

Ellesmere, the senior man, broke the news that it would be advisable – *strongly* advisable – to detain the patient, but it had been Aspinall who ventured the diagnosis: *congenital misdevelopment of the brain*. It had not gone down well. As the haughty gentleman left the drawing-room to discuss terms of treatment with Professor Ashcroft, a stout, grey-haired man in a blue hat had entered. In a perfectly even voice he'd instructed the physicians never to speak, publicly or privately, of the visit. There was no need for an "or".

Parlez-Vous' therapeutic regime had fallen to Aspinall. Within a few days, his new patient had become *the* patient.

A loud crash brought Aspinall back to the present ... With a bat of a vast arm, the Inspector had sent two Charlies skittling. Then the gargantuan charged for the stairs. He stumbled once, recovered, surged forward again, was at the threshold, when an olive-skinned soldier, an assortment of daggers, throwing-blades and short-barrelled fire-pieces hanging from his white cross-belt, stepped out behind him and took deliberate aim with a stubby pistol.

The Captain of the Watch lunged, pushing the barrel down. There was a thunderous crack as the weapon discharged into the floorboards, sending splinters of wood in all directions, then a great choking belch of smoke.

A molly standing nearby shrieked and clutched at his calf, scarlet blood welling under his cream satin stockings.

Through the pall, Aspinall watched the Inspector leap down to the half-landing, the flapping jack dangling from his back, visor back in place. Then gentleman and his giant were gone.

A stunned space of unfaith, then mayhem resumed on the upper landing. The revolt was short-lived; within minutes, all offenders still able to stand were under armed guard. The others were pulled into a groaning heap.

Aspinall stood with his back against the crumbling brick wall. Personal searches were being conducted further along the corridor. He thought of his medical notebook – everything was in it: observations, conversations, speculations on the precise nature of Parlez-Vous' mental lesions. Everything. He thought, too, of the Country Gentleman's grey-haired retainer. He'd have to act fast. Wiping sweat from his eyes, he looked around, alighting on the recessed wall lanterns. The nearest one had been smashed in the mêlée, its flame extinguished, shards clinging to the lead work. In a hot fit, heart catching on his ribs, he fished out his notebook, slid it up the wall, and dropped it in.

Barricaded in the attic bog-house, the agent known in The White Swan as Thomas cursed savagely. The Charlies were securing lofts one by one, obviously intent on making an example of the whole fucking den. Just as long as they got the queen eel . . .

As for himself, he should have been long gone. He hoped he wouldn't have cause to regret that gob-stopper with Aspinall. As if he weren't already running enough risks! A molly to mollies, Runner to Runners, and beneath it all – *Merde!* Why the fuck had the Watch arrived so early?

He'd wager the blame lay with those fanatical culs down at St Clements Watchhouse. 'Southcott's army', the fools styled themselves. *Death to all mollies!* It was a simple motto, no room for ambiguities. Well, if this was the opening salvo in their holy war, the fuck-wits couldn't have picked a worse time.

His thoughts returned to his own predicament. It was

sticky. In all senses of the word. No shortage of witnesses, either. The best course was to lay low for a stretch. Wait to see who came up trumps. He'd work with what was left, as he always did.

The sound of heavy boots at the door . . . Untangling his heel from his skirts, he clambered onto the privy seat and pushed himself up into the window recess. Levering open the stiff casement, he manoeuvred himself over the ledge, and down onto the thatch. He managed a few steps before his heel caught again in the eyelets of his hems, pitching him forward. He tumbled over the stooks, arriving at the precipice head first, was halfway over, when his fingers found a tarred under-rope.

It creaked as he swayed, but held his weight.

Above him, a splintering thud. That would be the privy door going. *Allez vite!* He dropped the remaining ten feet to the dust. *F-u-c-k*, his ankle! No time for that. The Charlies would be at the window, looking for the shot.

He gathered his hems in both fists. Using the over-hanging roofs for cover, the triple agent hobbled off into the undarkening night.

2.

CRYING SINS

22. Etchings

The corpulent printer stood, leaning back, arms flung wide, on his porch in South Molton Street. Thicker round the middle, a little greyer, but still extravagantly, still inimitably, William. Which was was precisely why Wyre had called. In truth, he doubted his warning would make an atom of difference.

Wyre followed his erstwhile client through to the cramped first-floor parlour dominated by a large round table piled with sketches and proofs. Pencil drawings fought for space with copper blocks, curious twists of cloth, broken nibs and dirty quills. The printer pulled out a mismatched chair with a scuffed leather back.

As Wyre waited for William to fetch wine, he glanced at the drawings. Slender women in suggestive poses. The usual, then.

"They deceive, men – " William's airy voice floated over from the drinks cabinet " – who claim the spiritual principle is like a bird flying above the air in the ether, where the eyes can't reach. They'd have God exist in the midst of a cloud." He returned with a bottle of dark claret and two small fine china cups. Tongue pinched between teeth, he poured the liquid, crouching so as to dispense it right up to the cups' thin lips. "I say the spiritual principle is perfectly visible to those with enough courage to break free of the church's manacles." He pushed one bushy eyebrow up with his finger, making his eye big. "There's a world of difference between not knowing how to see things and any actual deficiency in the organ of vision itself." He shot the lawyer a conspiratorial look. "I saw a tree full of angels at Peckham Rye – "

" – and the devil in South Molton Street. I know." Wyre smiled despite himself. "But there are those who regard your credos as dark fanaticism. These are watchful times."

"Fanaticism?" The printer made a clucking sound. "I desire only a celestial Jerusalem, the purifying fire." He sipped at his claret. "The tongue, Wyre!" He hoisted his cup. "Effortlessly capable of distinguishing the *moelleux* from the *rancio*. Would that the brain were so dextrous in its own distinctions."

"Some men fear conflagrations of any kind," Wyre said in a low voice. "The millennium's been and gone, William."

"Not really," came the response. "It's available to us here, now, in this room, if you could only put by your philosophy of the five senses. Not everything can be measured, Wyre, with a pair of compasses."

"You see, that's exactly what I mean. People won't understand. What's all this I hear about you advocating concubines?"

"Rather that than the hearse of marriage, eh?"

Wyre reached for his own cup. If the allusion was to Rose, he refused to be drawn. "That's the cant of Hindoos."

"Sexual love *can* be holy," the rotund man insisted, hinging his weight forward on his elbows. "Isn't the carnal body both spirit and flesh? By breaching sexual custom we trample the stony law to dust." He lifted his gaze as the door opened and his wife arrived with a side of ham.

"Why such scepticism towards the law?" Wyre asked. He tasted the wine. It always seemed to be thicker and stronger at William's. "The country would collapse without it. The Tyrant's henchmen would pour in like rats."

"Would that be so bad?"

"You sail close to the wind. Don't forget what I am."

"What you've become, Wyre. You weren't always a prosecutor. Moses gave us the law for our hard hearts." He rolled his eyes at the lawyer, the affection evident. "You know perfectly well that sexual pleasure has been perverted into commandments. We err only when we yield to reason. Vere Street, now . . . Such a fuss about buggery – and all because the iron-age scriptures happen to say it's wrong."

"Sodomy," Wyre corrected him. "All forms of unnatural copulation between men come under the blazon of sodomy. Buggery is the act of intercourse with beasts. And as for scripture, all civilized societies require a bedrock of morality."

But that was the difference between William's personal system of religion and that of other sects: he didn't consider *any* form of sexual ecstasy unholy. On first making his acquaintance, Wyre had assumed his new client was an unthinking follower of Joanna Southcott, parroting her 'end days', rascal-multitude rhetoric. But he'd come to realize William's credos were far stranger than that.

The portly man waved his hand as if the distinction were specious. "Sodomy, buggery . . . Don't forget there's an inside and an outside to truth." He pursed his lips as if about to whistle. "Besides, don't pretend you hold with that biblical hogwash. You'll find more sense in those newspapers you enjoy reading so much. Opinions change, my boy, often within the space of a week. Two millennia ago the earth turned, then it stopped, and recently it has begun to turn again. What men consent to do by their own firesides . . ."

"No one can consent to be assaulted."

"What they do in private – "

" – influences the well-being of the public," Wyre interrupted.

The printer shook his head. "Desire is no fault in the young. Though it's certainly true," he said, pursing his lips again, "that all that wanton energy could be put to better use. By withholding the seminal fluid those young men would nourish their brains. Abstinence, though, is a priestly invention. Desire is imprinted in human nature, it can't be criminal."

Wyre studied his face for signs of levity, but found none. "You're either the devil, or inspired."

"And perhaps you're not all unbeliever."

"I've come with a warning."

The printer tilted his head. "How am I to take that?"

"They're preparing a prosecution against you – for indecency, this time." Brockton hadn't used that term, but his snigger made the likely charge clear. "Can you blame them?" He sighed. "If you will insist on printing such images – " Wyre gestured at the lewd sketches fanned out on the table.

"I like my women glowing," William protested.

" – however prettily done, people will think you no safer than those lunatics who fall into ecstasies thinking they're sucking at Christ's wounds." He drained his china cup; William promptly refilled it. "What's this, for heaven's sake?" He lifted a pencil sketch of a bare female form standing between two angels, or devils, their male parts coiling up like serpents.

"I won't deny the sexual being."

"You think only of your balls."

William looked arch. "If the structure of the testicle is properly examined it will be evident it is so wonderfully constructed that anything more perfect cannot be. I see the universe in it. The testicle, you might say – " he winked broadly " – is a gonad of the infinite mind."

104

"This sexual religion of yours is considered dangerous." It was as hopeless as he feared. "We were lucky back then in Felpham. The trooper who accused you had a rough character." He thought back to the tiny cottage built from ship timbers; its low ceilings used to creak as if the beams believed themselves still at sea. "Don't mistake the present climate. If your case were examined today . . ." He left it at that.

"We all have to find our own ways of bearing witness against the beast," came the gnomic reply.

Yes, it was pointless, but at least he'd satisfied himself he'd done all he could. In the corner of the room a butterfly dangled from a single thread of cobweb, twisting in its fruitless efforts to extricate itself.

Wyre finished a second bumper. No matter how much he drank, the china cup at his elbow was always full. Before long, the sinuously coiled forms in William's pictures were dancing for him on the table, and the parlour's burnished shadows themselves took on the appearance of scaly cross-hatching. He heard himself giving a lurid account of the New Bridge murder, ignoring a quieter voice telling him that details of ongoing investigations were off-limits to casual chit-chat. Leighton wouldn't thank him for it. The investigation clearly intrigued the printer, who sat, leaning forward on his elbows, demanding Wyre recount the smallest detail of the uncanny encounter.

"There are no leads," Wyre said, "at least, none of any value. My acquaintance at Bow Street believes there may be no solution to the case."

"Beneath the cup always lies the half-cup."

Wyre frowned at his glib philosophy; so much of William's discourse tended to sound like this.

"Our problem as a species," the printer continued, "is our quickness to see things not as they are, but as we are."

105

Wyre closed one eye. "I see you clearly enough. That is, I think I do."

"A police mission, and perhaps a Courthouse case, are not so unlike a copper plate when the artist first takes it in his hand." William smiled mysteriously. "Both begin black as night. The work is to introduce the lights."

"Each of your metaphors is more opaque than the last."

"Move through the literal, Wyre, and something is sure to come."

"I'll be certain to pass that on to my friend," he said, waving his hand imprecisely, "but only if you promise to take seriously what I said about your pictures. They mean to make an example of you." (Brockton had boasted about his role in the planned action.) "Don't give them the excuse they require." Wyre pushed his cup to one side. It was late.

William merely fetched another murky bottle from the depths of his seemingly bottomless drinks cabinet. Something else, Wyre knew, nestled deep within. Something of his – assuming William hadn't pawned it for engraver's acid. He pictured the fire-piece, which he'd purchased in Sussex from a gunsmith named Egg. Rose had made him hand it over soon after they'd arrived in London, not being able to abide its presence in their tiny Southwark apartment. When would a lawyer need such a thing, she'd demanded to know. It was a fine weapon. Wyre had half a mind to ask to see it.

They talked into the early hours, roaming from faith and philosophy to the drying periods of oil. Eventually, Wyre heaved himself to his feet, steadying himself on the back of his chair.

"Next time, my boy, bring that portrait you're trying to complete."

Had he really mentioned the painting? When? He didn't

remember. Wyre pulled a face. "Whenever I start up again, I spoil it further."

"Keep at it." William's expression was suddenly serious. "Forget convention – all you need's contained here – " he touched his forefingers to his eyelids " – and here." He tapped his head. "Everything else is sham."

They parted on the porch. At the bottom step, Wyre turned. He *had* to say something.

"For goodness sake, William, put some clothes on. I never know where to look."

23. Drill

The botanist begins the evening's lecture by dividing the quadrupeds into five orders: anthromorpha, *or those resembling the human form;* ferae, *wild beasts;* glires, *wild rats;* jumenta, *beasts of burden;* pecora, *cattle. Within the third order he is scrupulous to include the porcupine, hare, squirrel, beaver and common rat.*

"Some English natural philosophers," he says, not troubling to conceal his scorn, "would make rats and beavers parts of separate trees. They deny that the analogy between the number of teats and teeth in these animals amounts to kinship." He steps out from behind the lectern. "Would it not," he mimics, switching to English, which imparts a feyness to his speech, "be more true to say an ass is an ass, a rat a rat, rather than making a rat a squirrel, or a beaver – or, by extension, a man?" The grey locks of his periwig shake as he moves his jaws from side to side, in something resembling a human laugh.

At the rear of the auditorium an elderly gentleman rises, and moves down the central aisle with an ease that belies his age. The botanist watches him steadily from the front, the air in the theatre acquiring the charge of a great event.

"Your taxonomy, sir," the ancient gentleman says with a clipped accent (plainly a lodger in the French language), "is a laughable delusion. A rat is not daunted by size like the squirrel or hare. It will attack even one of the lords of creation. It will, if hard-pressed and sufficiently famished, devour its own kind. Will a beaver do that?"

Someone in the audience laughs. Others join in. Soon the noise is deafening.

The sleeper opened his eyes with a start to find a figure crouched on its haunches in a corner of the room.

"What th' fook are *tha'* doing 'ere?" The safe house in Crispin Street was supposed to be just that. Tossing aside his thin blanket, he jumped out of bed, wincing at a shooting pain in his right ankle. He pulled out the leather-knife he kept under his pillow.

The intruder regarded the instrument with apparent interest, though not fear.

Definitely not fear.

The penny dropped. How had he missed *that*?

Fuck!

Silence. More silence. His eyes moved to his writing desk. Ransacked . . . All his painstakingly transcribed copies of command dispatches, diagrams of defence lines, escarpments, redoubts . . . *Fuck! Fuck!* Had the wily old fucker found his letter to the Palace? He cursed himself for not posting it earlier. His half-turned man at St James's was his last chance of bringing his mission in this shit stain of a country to a successful conclusion. He experienced a sudden, all-consuming wave of regret. The strain of maintaining a triple identity, of lying with pox-ridden filth . . . *Tout ça pour rien!* All for nothing. His target – the bantam-cock, mad George's own stinking scion – had flown the weather-coop. There'd been no sensational arrest, no morale-sapping scandal. Everything now depended on the unpromising seeds he'd planted at St James's Palace (in that respect, at least, Vere Street had been good for something). But it was a long shot. He pictured the weak-willed, pathetic boot-licker on whom his hopes rested. A devilish long shot.

Still – he slashed the air with his blade – if they imagined he'd be easy, a man with fifteen years active service, one of Fouché's black agents!

The ancient assassin had moved from the far wall, and without seeming to occupy any intervening space, now stood an arm's distance away.

He didn't feel anything being taken, but his leather-knife now lay in his opponent's open palm. Credit where it was due. Desperately now – for he recognized a master's talent – he attempted a parrying feint, a manoeuvre designed to keep his adversary's blade arm out of play. He did it instinctively, the drill deeply instilled. For a moment he seemed to hear his first instructor, long ago now, praising his boyish agility – *C'est bien, Vallon!* – explaining how the balance must always be spread evenly between the balls of the feet . . . and knew it all to be futile.

He watched with almost detached curiosity as the knife was thrust into his live matter, given a quarter twist right, a half turn left, before being withdrawn with a prolonged sucking noise. Staggering, he grabbed at the back of the precious desk chair, upsetting it, before collapsing against the wall, slowly slumping to a sitting position.

Dark blood welled up around him. Surprising how quickly his nightshirt became sodden.

There was no pain. Absolutely no pain.

24. Intelligencer

These days, *The Post* was a shadow of its former self, just the odd item of news padded out with electioneering tirades and society drivel. Wyre stepped from the news-vendor's into the steady stream of foot traffic moving down Welbeck Street, his head aching violently from the previous evening at William's.

He opened his copy at a petition for the gelding of sodomites; it had been reprinted daily since the raid on the Vere Street Club, and had caught the eye of Parliament. Opposite it, a column proclaimed the Princess Amelia's health had taken a turn for the worse.

Wyre plotted an unsteady route through the match-sellers, china-hawkers and plump servant girls whose faces made him think of fripperies filched at odd hours from their mistresses, the air ripe with unwashed bodies. The miasma was doing nothing to help his urge to retch.

The red cobbles of the Cavendish Square coach stand lay ahead. Wyre could ill-afford the expense, but tardiness carried its own penalties at the Courthouse, Mr Best never failing to dock pay when one of his lawyers was unpunctual. A slovenly waterman waved him over towards a superannuated four-wheeler; its original baronial insignia survived only as a collection of ghostly outlines on the rusty-hinged doors. With a strangled gee-ing sound the equally antediluvian jarvey cajoled his beasts into the nose-to-tail traffic, where they moved at scarcely walking pace. Half a crown lighter to little purpose ... Watt had recently proposed a steam coach. Who wouldn't prefer such a machine? Wyre imagined the city filled with them, emitting nothing more than little wreaths of silvery smoke, the streets newly paved for their silent wheels.

He mopped his brow. The handkerchief was cool, and soft – part of a silk set Rose had given him the week before she left. Tears pricking the corners of his eyes, he flicked through his paper, hoping for distraction. *Another Monster Captured* . . . The city was running mad for tales of Vere Street, he tutted. That, and the comings and goings of royal second cousins visiting the stricken princess. It seemed she'd made a ring for her father, the Duke of York, with a lock of her own hair wrapped inside. That was on the mawkish side of sentimental.

His eyes were pulled to a short piece on the facing page – a familiar name was picked out in tight Grub Street capitals:

Yesterday afternoon, Rivett, the Bow Street officer, arrived in town from the Isle of Wight, with an Ensign, Hepburn, belonging to a West Indian Regiment, charged, on the evidence of a Palace servant at St James's, with a most diabolical offence with a drum-boy, White, at the Vere Street club house.

Surely it wasn't the same juvenile who'd made the complaint against Parson Church? He assumed the misrule, after coming so close to having his neck stretched, had left the city far behind. As for the other military bum-boy, he didn't think the name Hepburn had ever crossed his desk. At any rate, he supposed he'd be dealing with both soon enough. Or maybe not.

Wyre frowned at the column.

The prisoner underwent an examination before Mr Best, and acknowledged being at the house, and also part of the circumstances stated against him. He was committed

111

for further examination. The boys are presently in safe custody at the Tower.

Both miscreants had already been examined ... and by Mr Best himself. Wyre stared blankly. Wasn't prosecuting mollies supposed to be *his* job?

He went back over the details. 'Rivett, the Bow Street officer' – Wyre had seen him giving evidence once. Barely twenty-five, the man was already running to seed. It wasn't difficult to picture him in a Cheapside dive among the hired informers and bawds, accepting his fourth drink from some salivating news-hack on a retainer. As for this 'Palace servant', that was probably a reference to some cock-corrupted footman trying to wheedle his way out of a prosecution of his own. So far, so familiar. (God's teeth, an ensign and a drummer boy: it was hard to think of a worse cliché!)

But the report felt off. Best's role, for starters. But it was more than that. Hadn't *The Post* just casually placed Vere Street next to St James's Palace? Even if it was only in a news-rag's column, the proximity was suggestive. He couldn't imagine the Palace being ecstatic about that. And why had Best felt it necessary to summon the ensign out of his regimental camp all the way down on the Isle of Wight, when he could have simply left him to the army's own cruelties?

Perhaps it was nothing more than the desire for a public dangle. To be sure, the whole city would turn out to watch the base pair exchange a sickening last glance – or, more likely, spit and hiss at each other with a big bone in their breeches. He shuddered at the idea of those final, aching expulsions. Rose had never come to terms with the pageantry that accompanied a municipal hanging, never appreciated the two-fold necessity of deterrence coupled with civic humiliation. "But the law isn't infallible," she would remind him. "Imagine yourself, standing alone at the edge of eternity, deserted by all of humanity and the world, a white cap drawn over your face, the rope placed around your neck. As for humiliation," she'd continued, waving aside his attempt to speak, "the inability to find gainful employment and provide honest bread for one's wife and children must be a far worse source of shame for a man than anything a baying crowd might present."

A few days before she'd vanished, she'd begged him to return to defence lawyering. Hadn't he once saved that odd printer from a charge of treason? And hadn't they since become firm friends? Wyre had demanded to know who'd put such nonsense in her head. Prosecuting was a cast of mind, he told her. Rose replied he didn't know what a couple was supposed to be, that by pouring things out to him she thought life would come back to her, only to find herself empty.

Six months, now, since she left the cramped apartment they'd shared in Southwark. No forwarding address.

At the foot of the page was a diagram the size of a cartwheel tuppence, labelled *A Human Tear Under the Microscope*. The crosshatch engraving was a series of stark fishbones. He looked from it to the coach's glass sliders, and beyond, and saw its repeating pattern projected onto the city.

The rest of *The Post* amounted to a digest of stocks, sensational accidents and electioneering harangues. If the rag were an accurate representation of the world, London was a pit of freaks. He refused to believe it, closing the pages, folding the city into itself.

He watched as a fly, drunk from the heat, crawled along the leather armrest. Rolling up the paper he leaned forward. Resisted. Settled back again. After all those royal arses, the padded seat was still comfortable. Someone had been picking at the buttons.

25. Chemistry

The Chief Barrister's smile was a code without a key.

"During your unsanctioned absence yesterday – " (Wyre cringed inwardly) " – I instructed Mr Brockton to begin collating the Vere Street evidence." He gave Wyre an appraising look. "But *you*, Wyre – " the barrister's hooded eyes narrowed " – *you* will be prosecuting."

Wyre bowed his head in cautious acknowledgement. It was still a molly brief, but at least one the whole city was talking about.

"It will be a case with reach," Best said, his eyes two tight points. "The Secretary of State himself has addressed the House. An ambitious man would make much of that."

Wyre bowed again. "I hope I know my job, sir."

"We all hope that, Wyre." Best's gaze drifted to the window. "The city is awash with moral dissidents. We are all that keeps it from utter degeneracy."

Wyre returned to his office to find the most basic of notes waiting for him on his desk, just a scrawled address above a single spidery letter: *L.* All he needed. Twenty minutes later, the lawyer was clattering through districts the Society for the Suppression of Vice would gladly see cleared by cannon.

He disembarked at the entrance to Crispin Street, a tight, nondescript avenue near the corner of Howden Place. No. 23b, it transpired, could only be reached via a rusty grille-gate to the side of a milliner's shop. It was a fireman's nightmare. He spotted Leighton's hobby-horse padlocked to a down pipe, surrounded by curious wagtails, who no doubt made a habitual lazaretto of the street.

A constable was waiting. "Ain't a pretty sight, sir," he warned, leading Wyre up to the third floor. "Someone's had a right go."

Wyre paused on the landing. It wasn't quite a stench yet, but was well on the way. Sleeve to his nose, he followed the constable into a tiny den at the end of the corridor. The smell there was overwhelming, sending his stomach into spasms.

No sign of Leighton.

In the far corner, a waxy figure sat slumped in a dark, viscous pool, head lolling a little sideways. His open eyes seemed to be staring at an upturned chair in the middle of the room as if he wished to right it. The chair belonged to a writing desk, the lid of which had been prised.

Wyre took a step forwards, and felt something crunch underfoot. Looking down, he saw he'd stepped on a little pile of spent brimstone matches.

"Watch the empiricals, there's a good man." Leighton's voice from the doorway.

Wyre turned, relieved. "Empiricals?"

"Our quarry's soiled the turf."

How do you know they're his?" Wyre cast a glance back at the body.

"I'll tell you." Leighton crossed to the dead man. "But first, what do you make of this?" He bent over, fishing out from the gore a blade with a round handle. Four inches or so in length.

"I'd say it was a leather-knife," Wyre answered.

Leighton nodded, handing the blade to his constable. "Something a tanner might use. Why's it still here, though?

115

Suggests the blade didn't belong to the assassin, doesn't it. Oh, and this might also interest you." He produced a small card from his pocket.

Wyre took it, whistling under his breath at the design. A crudely embossed white swan.

"Thought you'd like it," Leighton said. "Authentic Vere Street Club . . . proper *objet de vertu*. Worth a bit now, I'd have thought."

"Did you come by it here?"

Leighton gestured towards the escritoire. "Whoever forced the lock evidently didn't think it worth keeping, or destroying for that matter."

"So the victim was a White Swan man. And worked in the tanning trade."

"Seems safe enough to assume."

"Who found him?"

"One of the wagtails. Complained about the smell, poor dear. Said it was putting off her customers."

"Any idea who he was?"

"I was rather hoping you'd be able to help me with that. Have a good look, Kit. Ever seen him before?"

Wyre forced himself to look. "It's no one who's ever appeared on my books."

Leighton nodded. "Well, it was worth a shot." Kneeling, he took a thin pencil from behind his ear, and pushed it into an inch-wide slit in the man's nightshirt. His ersatz physician's probe disappeared to his fingertips. "Smack in the liver. Someone knew his job."

The Runner seemed different, somehow. His eyes were restless, almost convulsive in their movements. Had he slept at all in the three nights since their encounter under the bridge?

Leighton hoiked the man's bloody nightshirt up over his shoulders, revealing a well-defined torso; then, to Wyre's disgust, he reached down for the dead man's yard, which he retracted, exposing a large, pale bulbous head. After staring at it for a moment, he heaved the body onto its side.

"No sign of cordial," he announced, as he inspected the corpse's seat. "Our man didn't shoot his bolt that night, and as far as I can tell he wasn't used that way by anyone else. This wasn't some spat over a half-shilling ride."

"A burglary, then?"

"No sign of forced entry . . ." Smiling grimly, he pushed himself to his feet and moved to the casement, craning his head over the ledge. "It's a good thirty feet down to the alleyway." He looked left and right. "No drainpipe or trellis. Nothing that could take a man's weight." He peered back over the ledge as if calculating where precisely on the scale of impossibility scaling a vertical wall with no handholds lay. "At least we know one thing for certain: our assassin came for something specific." He nodded at the escritoire's prised lid. "The only question is, did he get it? Come and see."

Wyre followed Leighton over to the desk. Inside were rows of corked glass bottles. Squinting over the Runner's shoulder, Wyre saw that each phial had been labelled in a spidery hand: *Galls, Sulphate of Iron, Cobalt, Potash, Nitric Acid, Sulphur, Vinegar.* Two larger compartments contained a Florence flask, and a quarter-pound bag of something chalky that puffed up in Leighton's face when he touched it. "Our victim was quite the little chemist. Everything here you'd need to manufacture sympathetic ink."

Wyre looked at him quizzically.

"Don't tell me you never tried it as a boy? First draw a tree trunk and branches in ordinary ink, next add the leaves using a solution of cobalt. The page stays winter,

117

but only till you play a brimstone under it, then spring and summer arrive at once. It's not much of a code, though, if someone's expecting it, which our assassin plainly was." He pointed at the little pile of twisted spunks Wyre had crushed underfoot.

The Bow Street officer crossed to the hearth, and put his fingers into the ash, rubbing a little between his fingers. He held the residue up. "The killer was after encrypted letters, Kit. From our spymaster here . . ." He nodded at the corpse. "Came armed with a phosphorous bottle. After he activated the ink – " he pointed to the hearth " – he incinerated the evidence." Leighton chopped his hands together, sending fine ash floating into the room.

"He did all that calmly after killing a man? Why not hot-foot it, read the letters somewhere safer."

"Oh, I don't think our man is given to panic. The real question is, who were the letters addressed to? But I don't suppose we'll know *that* till the intended recipients turn up, looking like our friend here."

"You think there'll be others?" He stared at the wax figure.

"I'm quite certain of it." Leighton rose stiffly from the hearth. "Come on, we've done all we can here."

As Wyre moved from the desk, he banged his shin against the upturned desk chair. Leaning over angrily, he grabbed a leg, intending to set the chair upright.

"Touch nothing," Leighton said quickly. "That's a credo at Bow Street."

Chastened, Wyre lowered the chair again. Then froze . . . The impact had caused a corner of the seat to become dislodged from its frame. "Wait a minute . . ." Using his fingers, he worked at the crack until first the corner, then the entire panel, lifted out, revealing a shallow cavity in which a neatly pressed envelope nestled. Wyre snatched it up, snapping the maroon bleb of sealing wax between his fingers.

Triumph turned to despair. The letter was blank.

Leighton smiled at him. "Remember what I said. Spring and summer come at once in this game." He held his hand out to his constable, who produced a small German fire bottle and a box of spunks. The Runner played one around the lip of the fire bottle until, with a wet hiss, its tip spluttered into life.

Wyre felt like a man collared for a conjuring trick. He watched as the match burned down to Leighton's thumbnail without emblazoning any furtive inscriptions. Two more attempts produced nothing. "Cockstand!" The Runner shook the last spunk out, handing the letter to Wyre with a pained expression.

The lawyer tilted it as Leighton had done, and similarly saw nothing. At a flatter angle, however . . . a silvery prismatic wash. Frowning deeply, he carried the sheet to the casement. In seconds, green letters, then whole words and sentences formed, as though his own thoughts were being thrown onto the page.

"Leighton, you really ought to see this . . ."

The Bow Street officer strode over. "The trigger's not heat, it's *light*. I was right to bring you along. Well, what does it say?"

The letter trembling in his fingers, Wyre read aloud.

My dear Sellis,
Yrs arrived unopened. Give thanks that England's cabinet noir is less efficient than my master's. You mustn't despair. The Palace is not a prison, whatever they wish you to believe. Yr cause has been taken up by men of action & I shall have the pleasure of writing before too many days with encouraging news. Hold fast, and take comfort in the knowledge that your friends have not forgotten you.

COULD NOT *forget you. What does it matter if you are made to ride backwards? Suffer the indignity in the knowledge it must be short.*
  Yr friend,
  Thomas

Wyre turned to the slumped body. "Pleased to meet you, Thomas. Or is it Sellis?"

"That bit's easy. A member of the royal household wouldn't doss in a dunghole like this. Which makes our corpse Thomas." He let out a long breath. "Next question, what do we know about this Sellis character?"

"That he doesn't like riding backwards?"

"Who does?" Leighton looked thoughtful for a moment. "But he needs to be warned."

Wyre looked at the Runner.

"Even supposing the assassin remains in the dark about Mr Sellis's existence, I very much doubt it'll stay that way for long. Back-blows from Vere Street, Kit, that's what this is. And it's not over yet." He rubbed his temples. "Anyone associated with Thomas and the Vere Street Club should consider themselves in the firing line."

"Shouldn't we go directly to the Palace?"

"Getting access to St James's won't be as easy as you imagine. The Palace has its own jurisdiction; they call it the Court of the Royal fucking Verge." His face tightened. "I'll need permission from the old bird just to approach the Verge." (Wyre assumed the allusion was to Bow Street's Chief Magistrate, Mr Read.) "Believe me, he won't like it." His face wrinkled. "Has to be done, though. It's clear the reason Mr *V.S.*-frigging-*C.* got pinked lies somewhere at St James's Palace." He looked away. "Things are about to get complicated. Let's keep the letter to ourselves for now, agreed?"

Wyre gave him a cautious nod. Leighton would know his business.

They made their way downstairs, followed at a respectful distance by the constable.

"Has this got anything to do with the New Bridge murder?" Wyre said, as they stepped out into the glare of Crispin Street. "I rather hoped you'd keep me abreast. Might be my ticket out of molly briefs."

Leighton was unlocking his mechanical gelding. He grunted non-committally.

"You never even told me what your fly was investigating."

"Vere Street," the Runner said, suddenly grinning. "What else?"

26. The Lower Levels

Brockton heaved his bulk to its feet, and headed for the steps down to the coups. He held a handkerchief to his mouth. As the fever had spread street-by-street above, so it was putting out its tendrils below. It didn't pay to take chances. He was a practical man.

Joanna's disciples were talking of a tremendous judgement to come. Fiery lakes, monstrous apparitions, halos and mock-suns, companies of marching toads not seen since 1660. Much of the talk concerned the Tyrant, said to be assembling invasion barges across the channel. But Brockton had no time for such ranting, even though he had himself once seen a great light emanating from the peak of a mountain. He'd been twelve. Some would have made much of it, but he'd had other fish to fry. He still had. And, since that unexpected interview with Best, his fish were sodomites.

It was said that in France crimes such as blasphemy,

heresy, sacrilege and witchcraft weren't prosecuted. Even the detestable sins of incest and sodomy regularly went unpunished. The fiddle-faddling man of feeble organs prospered in that nation of heaped ordure. The French would make heroes of the Vere Street gang. But sodomy would remain a felony in England. Perfect sodomy, in which the sodomite ejaculated in the anus, as well as its imperfect varieties. It would remain a felony because it was a true crime.

Puffing, Brockton reached the bottom of the tightly winding steps. Earlier that morning, he'd interrogated Cooke, keeper of The White Swan. The interview had borne fruit, if not quite as much as he'd hoped. The reptile clung to most of the sordid mental freight he called his 'names'. He had, though, given up a few identities as tokens of good will. Men who'd camped at The White Swan for nights on end, respectable men who'd pay handsomely rather than risk being dragged into public view. Brockton had written these names down, and thanked the monster.

The next prisoner – he squinted through the cell-door grate – was pressed from different clay. Where Cooke's was a rough, solid presence, this Dr Aspinall seemed truer to type: massless and unphysical. He motioned to Mr Suter the head gaoler, who adjusted the long-handled pistol in his belt, and reached for his key.

Brockton waited until the heavy door had closed behind him, and Suter's footsteps had receded to faint thuds, before setting his ledger down on the cell's low wooden bench. Then he lowered himself down next to the captive, so their elbows were almost touching. With a priest's respect for silence, he said nothing. He was in no hurry. For men in Aspinall's position, time was something that was done to them.

"In sermons throughout the city," he began at length,

"they're calling the earthquake the inevitable corn of an unbending harvest of vice. You and your Vere Street friends are the link between sin and catastrophe . . . but the law will uncouple you." He watched the prisoner's eyes grow round. "You've finally committed a crime worthy of your monstrosity. We should thank you for giving us something to purge." Brockton looked levelly at the prisoner. "They say a dog that laps the piss of a hanged man dies within the week. I would advise you to draw up a will, but sodomites cannot make a testament."

If the physician seemed about to speak, the impulse deserted him.

Brockton tapped his ledger book. "They mean to hang you, Aspinall." He watched the prisoner's face drain. "However, it might – " Brockton tilted his head " – *might* be possible to bring you through. Naturally, for a consideration."

Some men were said to be able to tell coins from the handling, a few from the mere smelling alone. Talents of gold, talents of silver. Brockton named his sum. Steep, yes. But the others had managed it. The prisoner buried his face in his hands, and through sobs insisted he couldn't raise a quarter of it. Brockton struggled to his feet, using Aspinall's shoulder for support. He said no more. Such claims belonged to the process of compromise, and here there was no middle ground. Besides, Mr Best had been quite clear. Not all the beasts could be allowed to slip away. Some two or three would have to bear the brunt. The question now – for Aspinall, the only question – was whether the physician would be among them.

"Are you married, monster?"

Aspinall lifted his eyes.

"Engaged, perhaps?"

A wary nod.

"Then there may still be a way. I'll call on your betrothed, have a word with her father. See if we can't come to some arrangement."

A faithful lawyer was like gold thrice tried in the fire.

The physician groaned. Mr Crawford wouldn't –

Brockton took the physician's hand in his own. Its warmth amazed him.

27. Case Notes

With deep repose of the conscious organs, the pictures revived by the mind should be considered less remembrances of a vast reservoir of events than attempts to overcome them . . .

His own words, meant for his psychical treatise, composed on the very desk that now stood in a damp cell in the city's Courthouse. The sun sieving through the high grate that opened onto the press yard threw a Coptic cross over the stained flagstones.

"Answer me!" barked the Judge, a knotted towel hanging from his head. "Are you a French quaint or not?"

The sworn jury of two, one swarthy with slow, sunken features, the other pale and sharp, had pinned Aspinall to the ground. They cocked their heads attentively.

"Nothing t' improve his case, m'lud," the leathery one said.

The jurors hauled the physician to his feet to hear the verdict.

For coughing maliciously, for being a Frenchie and for attempting to sodomize his cellmates while they slept, the punishment was death.

"Pull th' dung beetle down," instructed the Judge.

Aspinall was battered savagely to the floor again.

124

Groaning, he watched as the legs of his desk chair were lowered over his head and shoulders. The jurors bound his elbows to the chair legs using shreds of his own shirt. Aspinall flailed, but was firmly pinioned. The faces of his tormentors floated above the woven cane seat. He gasped as a boot landed in his belly. Someone laughed: quick, wheezing spasms.

The mad-doctor's cries turned to frantic yelps as the bulb of the Judge's yard appeared above the seat, and scalding urine sluiced through the weave. It dripped onto Aspinall's face and neck. He flapped again, earning a shod foot to the groin.

"Downcast sinner," the Judge said. "Just our luck, chummed wi' a back-door man."

"Respectful of Brockton to let us know, tho'," the pale juror remarked.

"Brought some swag furniture wi' him, lads." The Judge nodded at the red-and-gold writing desk. "We could sell it."

Aspinall moaned. Miss Crawford had paid half a guinea to have it brought in; he'd tried to write, sought to piece together his case notes, but work in this dire hole was impossible.

"Right. But first, we'd have t' . . ." The pale juror looked meaningfully in Aspinall's direction.

The Judge nodded, and knelt beside the physician. Sliding his hands under the chair, he unfurled his fingers like birds' wings, closing them again around Aspinall's neck. The tattoo inked on the felon's lower forearm showed a large map of London over which prison bars had been superimposed.

"Shall I?" He looked up.

"They can't hang you twice, Ned."

"I want to do it."

125

Aspinall's eyes widened as the coarse fingers tightened. His cries for help became chokes as the edges of his vision began to close in. Then everything was black. His chest felt like it was exploding inward. He slapped his palms frantically on the floor.

A distant clattering sound, like a truncheon rattled between bars. Aspinall felt the fingers release.

"Fainted in the heat," the Judge said, glancing up at Suter. Collapsed at his desk."

"He was trying to un-man us."

"Can't leave us breathing his steam!"

The jurors untied Aspinall, and helped him to his feet. They brushed off the shreds of his shirt.

"Don't you be committing no more crimes now," the Judge said as Suter returned to the shadows, "our court's always in session."

Miss Crawford's pulse kicked an irregular tattoo in the hollow of her throat. She took in the sight, her fiancé's chair upturned, his expensive writing paper strewn across the flagstones. Robert sat huddled in the far corner, knees pulled up tightly under his chin.

"She yours?" A voice came from the shadows.

"We'll help you keep her happy . . ." A tall man stepped from the gloom, his mouth twisted into a grotesque leer. "Won't we, my hearts?"

"Keep it down, you rogues!" The gaoler called through the grating, hoisting his bull's eye lantern, casting bluish shadows on the unshorn men.

Robert rose unsteadily, face bruised, framed by matted hair, and came to her.

The tall cellmate thrust his hand into his breeches and let his eyes roll back, howling like a dog. Miss Crawford stamped her foot at him.

"My notebook . . ." Robert whispered, leaning into her, "have you recovered it?"

She gave a little shake of her head. "They've posted a soldier at the door."

His shoulders sagged.

"I'll get it," she said quickly. "I promise."

Robert turned then to Brockton's offer. What had her father said? Would he consider a loan?

Miss Crawford pressed her lips together. How could she tell him her father had sworn to stand beneath the gallows rejoicing as Robert was launched into the ever after?

28. Handy-Dandy

Wyre glanced up from his files at the clerk's silhouette in the door. The fellow hadn't bothered to knock. Standing next to the sly ex-fusilier was a handsome young woman, slim, below average height, with a dark complexion. The skin had a peculiar soft lustre. Her eyes and lips were also dark, and her treacly hair hung in fetching, natural curls. What was most distracting, though, were her large eyes. So large they put him in mind of a primitive votive statue; though where he'd seen one of those, he couldn't remember. What was it that lay in them?

"Pardon th' intrusion, Mr Wyre," the clerk said insincerely, lifting the stump of his missing arm. "Missy 'ere wuz awful keen t' see Mr Best. Most insistent for 'im. Would have sent her packing, 'cept it concerns Arse Street. Claims she's engaged to one of the mollies. Aspinall. Says she's in possession of information purs'ant to his case." He winked.

It was an old scam, and the clerk was right to be sceptical

of it. The first thing a clever molly did on being taken was to send word to his confederates, who arranged for some pox-ridden drab to pose as his wife. 'Vouching for taste', it was called. If the magistrate was inexperienced, the ruse had a chance of success.

This woman's dress was cut fashionably, even if its tints were brasher than the customary London duns. Like most of the furbelowed Pollies and Susannahs who drifted around the Courthouse, she'd been crying, but there was none of their brassy attitude.

No, it was an old scam, and it wouldn't wash. Aspinall would stand trial. He *had* to ... Of the twenty-seven culprits taken in Vere Street, there was, according to Brockton, sufficient evidence to arraign only five of them. In the plainest terms, Wyre couldn't afford to lose another molly, and especially not Aspinall. How many of the public would turn up to see a few bedraggled waiters dangle? A professional man, however, and a physician, no less ... That was a different matter.

But he'd have to hear her out.

The clerk touched his finger insolently to his temple, and vanished.

The dark woman stood beneath Wyre's bookshelves, pressing her fingers together.

"The clerk said you had new information?"

"My name is Miss Crawford. I am engaged to Dr Aspinall. That is the truth."

A hint of sugar in her dense, intricate accent.

"So the clerk says." Wyre looked away.

"My fiancé's a respected physician at the Wood's Close asylum – "

"Who was arrested with the other culprits at The White Swan, a notorious molly house."

Her hands began to tremble. "He was taken into custody

during the raid, but he was ignorant of the nature of the premises. He – "

"Miss – " Wyre interrupted again, letting her remind him of her name " – Crawford, Robert Aspinall was arrested in the attics along with men caught in the middle of despicable acts. There can be no mistake."

He leaned back, waiting for the inevitable. Her fiancé had been tricked, threatened, made an uncharacteristic error of judgement. If she was hoping for an indulgence, he could do nothing for her.

"I assure you, Robert isn't that way."

"It comes as a shock when someone we think we know deceives us."

Miss Crawford shook her head: small, contained movements. The air was full of constraint. "Not Robert. A woman knows."

Wyre cleared his throat. "You say you have information."

She answered with a wavering voice. "I visited Robert in his cell yesterday. He was afraid for his life."

"Cells aren't nice places. The company is bad."

"It wasn't that, Mr Wyre . . ."

The space around them was quickly developing the character of frozen time.

"You must understand, there's nothing I can do. The law will take its course."

"Robert told me," she said quickly, "that Mr Brockton swore that an example should be made of him unless he paid a substantial sum of money. But my fiancé doesn't have the means."

Wyre looked at her sharply. It was just as well Brockton was out. He wouldn't take a libel easily. "That's a serious accusation."

"This morning, your colleague called at my father's house, and demanded one hundred pounds for Robert's release. My father threatened to send for a magistrate. Mr Brockton told my father he'd just damned Robert to the drop, and we were welcome to whatever was left of him. Why don't you ask Mr Brockton?"

Wyre said nothing. Brockton wouldn't be the first Courthouse lawyer partial to a handy-dandy . . . But it was this woman's word against his colleague's, and Best seemed to have taken the man under his wing.

"Legitimate expenses are incurred during an arraignment, Miss Crawford. Someone has to cover the costs of additional work."

"One hundred pounds?" The silence hung. "Won't you at least look into it?"

He pursed his lips. There was no new information.

"For men like Mr Brockton," she said, her voice full of scorn, "the law is an opportunity. Robert's nothing in this, and you know it."

She strode to the door, her hand obscenely small as it closed around the handle.

"Miss Crawford . . ." He called after her. "Wait. Please." Aspinall deserved the halter, of that he was certain; but the thought of this fine-looking woman not only suffering the humiliation of being known for a molly's dupe, but also preyed on by the likes of Brockton . . . It was too much. It was enough. "I promise nothing, and if two witnesses can be found to swear to – to what they saw, then your fiancé will find himself far beyond my help.

The clocks were striking four o'clock as he stood for the second time that day before Best's walnut desk. The Chief Barrister's hand formed a fingerpost tilting down at the note Wyre had written after his interview with Miss Crawford.

"You allude to grave concerns."

Wyre shifted uncomfortably. Perhaps his rhetoric had been a little excessive.

Sir, allegations have been made. They involve significant sums of money."

"And?" The single syllable rang.

"Well, at first I was sceptical, but I've been through the Vere Street files, sir, and in the last few days, more than a dozen White Swan culprits have been released." He cleared his throat. "Directly after being interviewed by Mr Brockton."

"A case of witches being weighed against parish bibles, you mean? Say it out, Wyre. Bribes."

"There may be a perfectly satisfactory explanation, sir, though I have to say, it stretches credulity that a properly conducted examination would exonerate practically all the men taken in the raid."

Best rose stiffly, and crossed to the sideboard, where he poured two glasses of brandy. "The work of a lawyer – " he said, replacing the mushroom stopper " – makes him inward with perverted longings." He returned, handing Wyre one of the glasses. "Men may swim against the stream of their inclinations, but in the end their actions are always ruled by their nature." He lowered himself into his chair, wincing. "The sodomite, Wyre, is wedded to the bowels, and thus to the bowels of the earth where men rot and decay. He can no sooner change his disposition than a fish can one day decide to breathe air instead of water. Where men act according to their natures, and offend, we must chastise."

Wyre left a respectful gap. "Twenty-seven culprits were arrested that night. Five remain in custody, and none from the higher ranks."

"Do you hold your brother in such low esteem?"

Hot prickles rose on Wyre's nape. "Sir, at the rate

Brockton's going, there'll be no one left to prosecute. No one better than a customs officer and the landlord of a disorderly house."

"You forget the mad-doctor." Best's logic had the momentum of a miller's spur wheel.

"As a matter of fact, sir," Wyre began awkwardly, "in that particular case, the question of guilt may indeed be ... moot." His throat felt thick. "As I mention in my note, it was Dr Aspinall's fiancé who alerted me to possible irregularities in Mr Brockton's investigation."

"Aspinall was caught red-handed. He was taken in the act of conspiring to commit sodomy, which lest we forget is the term reserved for intercourse with the dung passage. In plain English, he is a buggerer. The same is true of the other four who remain in detention for the public good. They are agents of their own distress." He signed a vellum document with a sharp flick of the wrist. "Mr Brockton has sifted the men," he said, without looking up. "These are the ones."

"And the others, sir?"

"Not the ones." The Chief Barrister dipped his quill. "Don't let a pair of pretty eyes cloud your judgement."

29. Contractions

Wyre peered into the chiaroscuro of The Sun's dining room. Was one of the silverthief's accomplices sitting among the motley assortment of ploughtails, joskins and drysalters? All the patrons had an oddly stitched-in appearance.

Leighton smiled, apparently able to read Wyre's thoughts. "Meant to tell you," he began, "Michaels was taken a few days ago. Sap-head battered a shopkeeper who caught him palming. Victim forgot to wake up. It's the noose for that scad now. What do you say to a spot of German duck? What Sally can do with nutmeg is a revelation."

Leighton raised a finger, hooking a serving-maid most men would probably call buxom. Her blonde hair was stacked up in piles in imitation of the fine style. She smiled down at Leighton, her puffy white top showing something of the ingenious hammock pushing up her ample breasts. Leighton frowned at the two mountains of flesh as if about to admonish a wayward daughter.

"Three mugs of beer, Sally, two knuckle stews and a long, juicy kiss. Not in that order."

Wyre looked at Leighton, who was now tapping combinations of fingers on the table top as if practising chords on a pianoforte. It was difficult to imagine two men at greater variance in temperament, and yet the masculine bonds were strong.

"I still haven't seen anything in the papers about the New Bridge murder," Wyre began.

The Runner lifted his shoulders. "Takes more these days than a hammer to the noggin to shock the reading public."

Sally returned with two mugs of hot beer.

That was true enough. All the rags this week were leading on the arraignment of the Vere Street gang – column after column speculating on the nature of the charges, the range of punishments available to the judge, the predicted size of the crowd.

These very topics were being rehearsed around them. A pinkish sort seated opposite was recommending to his neighbours that the felons' testicles be cut away like gangrenous flesh. *Let their French masters see what we do to filthy bastards.*

Wyre glanced at Leighton. Had such jack o'lantern talk resulted in Thomas's murder in Crispin Street?

133

Leighton gave him a noncommittal look. "It's possible, but then everything is." He drank a deep draught. "It was commendable, you finding Thomas's letter, Kit. But don't get your hopes up. Slayings of that kind are rarely brought to a resolution."

Wyre frowned. He'd never heard defeatist talk from Leighton before. "You knew the fly. Surely you'll keep going till you've got your felon?"

The Runner shrugged. "He wouldn't have expected it."

The waiter with the bent nose arrived with their bowls of meat and potatoes, setting them down roughly.

"What about the Palace man?" Wyre lowered his voice. "Sellis. Did you get anywhere with them?"

Leighton looked up, his face all acute angles. It was easy to see why women liked him. With a pang, Wyre recalled his initial reluctance to introduce the Bow Street officer to Rose. He needn't have worried. Leighton had been subdued as they'd all sat together in those cramped Southwark lodgings. Wyre and Rose, fresh from Felpham. He pictured his wife pouring tea from her mother's china teapot.

Leighton moved his spoon listlessly through his stew. "'Fraid not, Kit." He looked up. "I'm under surveillance. Better you're not seen with me till I sort things out."

Wyre stared blankly. "The Palace? You said they wouldn't appreciate you sniffing around."

The Runner's expression was suddenly savage. "Not the Palace. Try Bow Street . . . my own fucking office."

Wyre pressed for details, but Leighton's mood had turned inward. For the rest of their meal, he did no more than play with his broth, leaving Wyre to eat in silence.

Outside, the sun had filled the street with furtive shadows. Leighton winced as he lifted his leg over the dandy-charger's perch. Wyre watched him move deftly along the pavements in the direction of the Public Office. It hadn't taken him long to become a skilled operator.

The pain began as spasms in the legs, creeping up to his belly. At first, Wyre tried to hide his discomfort from Brockton, who was observing him with evident interest. When a stabbing sensation sent Wyre's hands to his midriff, he admitted defeat. Through clenched teeth, he announced he was going home for the afternoon.

By the time the growler prowling for illegal fares outside the Courthouse dropped Wyre off at Mrs Mason's apartments, it felt as if the integuments of his belly were unknitting beneath his fingers. He struggled through to the foyer, and collapsed against Mrs Mason's desk. With alarm in her eyes, his landlady called for a porter to help him to his room while she went for a doctor.

Wyre waited in bed, coverlet pulled around him, shivering and sweating at the same time. *Schüttelfrost*, the Prussians called it. Was this the fever? God knows, he'd been to some bad districts this last week.

The porter had lent him his copy of *The Gazette*. More electric strokes from Vere Street:

Mr Mellish, the Member for Middlesex, has expressed his determination to bring in early in the next Session a Bill for making the attempt to commit a certain horrid crime punishable by transportation for life. This, however, will not be sufficient. The monsters must be exterminated, or a curse will fall on the land, contaminating even our colonies.

As he read, pearly drops pattered onto the pages, and were absorbed into the coarse weave. Slowly, the sentences flew apart before his eyes.

Monsters. Curses. Stones.

30. Interlude

Looking down, he finds himself dressed in full lawyer's robes, as if about to step to the bar . . . He ducks to avoid densely overhanging waxy green leaves, each with a spike that could put his eye out. Absurdly coloured flowers dangle above the foliage in a suspended explosion of scarlets, mauves, carmines and pepper reds. His captor's face is half-hidden beneath a broad-rimmed umbrella hat.

"A brief is an accumulation of facts." The man's tone is matter-of-fact; he introduces himself as Dr Clutterbuck.

Walking alongside the doctor with a swaying gait is a large bird, grotesquely lashed with a leather collar. It cranes its long neck, peering up at the captive. The doctor swipes back and forth with a machete to clear a path. Long-legged carapaced creatures jump from shiny leaves at their approach.

Through occasional breaks in the flora the captive spies a hot-air balloon decorated like the tricolour on La Fête Nationale. A brass telescope has been mounted on a pivot fixed to the wicker basket, and is trained down on them.

They arrive at a stagnant pool simmering with mosquito larvae. The captive peers into the water as a face floats to the surface. Half the flesh has fallen away. His father's features can still be discerned . . . He turns away in disgust.

A woman with her hair tied up in the severe Roman matron style steps from the undergrowth carrying a tureen of soup.

"That heated air will sink is easily proved," says Dr Clutterbuck, dipping a spoon in the soup.

The bird squints at Wyre. "Costive bowels, a promising symptom."

They proceed along an avenue of coconut trees bordered by prickly pears and aloe blades. Dark figures are loading something onto a wagon. A horse trots past, followed by a running footman in rags, his black hand twisted in the horse's tail.

They are standing now at the edge of a great cliff. Far below in the bay a Guinea ship is arriving. Uncountable faces crowd at the portholes, staring up.

"*In this heat,*" *says Clutterbuck,* "*sheep's wool is gradually converted into hair.*"

"*A black horse will become perfectly brown,*" *says the bird, bobbing.*

The island appears to be an archipelago of small, oblong bodies of land, surrounded by an immense depth of water. Salt oozes from the ground, crystallizing into solid cakes. Gangs of ebony-skinned men are gathering the salt into bushels using long rakes.

"*Winchester bushels or customary measures?*" *Clutterbuck frowns.* "*Who claims the rights to the surplus?*"

They plunge back into the undergrowth, stepping over ripe, tawny fruits. The flowers here are hairy reddish tufts hung with juicy green capsules.

"*The plant in its natural proportion,*" *says Dr Clutterbuck.*

"*Each part in its proper situation,*" *echoes the bird.*

They arrive at a peach-house. Warmed by two fires, the building is filled with all manner of forced forms and grafted specimens. Clutterbuck heads straight to an enormous clay pot that has been placed in the middle of the perfumed house. The pot contains a gigantic puce flower straining from a shroud of flesh.

"*The male plant produces male flowers only,*" *says the doctor. He stands on tiptoe, peering over the rim of the pot.*

"*Water it,*" *commands the bird.*

Appalled by the sight, the lawyer pushes the creature's neck from him and dashes from the peach-house. The bird follows, swollen to ostrich size, holding its elongated beak low to the ground.

The captive arrives breathless at the perpendicular edge. Another Guinea ship lies far below. Sailors gaze up from the deck, millions of black eyes at the portholes. How do they fit them all in?

He turns at the sound of the ostrich's beak snapping.

Leans forward, endlessly.

31. No-Show

Wyre woke with aching stones. The air smelled of sour milk. Roses's chair was at the foot of the bed, but Mrs Mason sat in it.

"They say when we die, Mr Wyre, we're never really alone, but hear our loved ones going about their business as if they were in the next room. At first, it's said to be a comfort, but gradually their concerns become of less and less interest. Could you hear anyone, Mr Wyre?"

He said nothing for a moment; then, "Did Rose come?"

Mrs Mason got up, and squeezed his hand.

When he was strong enough to sit up in bed, his landlady brought him a copy of *The Chronicle*. It was just as she'd said ... 24th July. Seeing the date in solid roman type suddenly made the passage of time seem real. The Vere Street trial was long over. For all he knew, Miss Crawford's fiancé was already surgeon fodder. Exhausted, he let his head fall back.

When he next opened his eyes, a familiar lean face stared across at him from the lady's chair.

"You had us worried, Kit. Your landlady sent for a doctor – and a priest. We were even considering Mr Birch's Electrical Magic."

I had a funny dream," Wyre said, eyes filling.

"Had your funeral speech all prepared . . ."

A tear brimmed over; Wyre couldn't help it. "You may still get to use it."

"Nonsense!" Leighton smiled. "Remember, illness arrives on horseback but leaves by foot. Anyway, you're one of the lucky ones." The Runner pushed himself to his feet. He'd changed. Those dark rings under his eyes, for a start . . . (Wyre didn't want to think about how different *he* must look.) And was that a livery of some kind? A foot-man's perhaps?

Looking around the room, Leighton gave a low whistle. "Uppish lodgings. Sure you're good for them?"

Wyre made a face. "I'd rather talk about Vere Street."

His friend looked levelly at him. "You won't like what I have to say."

Wyre listened in disbelief as the public officer ran through recent events. *Best* had led the prosecution? Since when had the Chief Barrister sullied himself with molly briefs? Still more difficult to credit was the fact all five gang members had escaped the noose. An hour's stand in the pillory would be unpleasant, but it hardly fit the crime. There was some comfort, at least, for Miss Crawford: her fiancé had more chance of surviving a stand in the stocks than the rather more terminal drop from a ladder.

The question was, how had it happened in the first place? Mitchell was sharp, but there was no way he could have trumped Best in the pit.

Leighton had a final shock to deliver, the key to the others. Before a sodomite could be condemned to a capital tariff, two eye-witnesses had to swear to seed. It seemed

139

one of the prosecution's star witnesses had failed to show up. Some puggard named Wardle.

"Never heard of him," Wyre muttered.

"No one had, crawled out from under a stone at the last minute. Claimed to have seen everything."

So Best's faith in Brockton had been misplaced.

"Where's this so-called eye-witness now?"

Leighton shrugged. "Your guess is as good as mine. Read has officers out looking for him. What they call scouring the land."

"And the other witness?"

"Fellow called Taunton. Captain in the Watch."

"Was he prepared to swear to seed?"

Leighton grinned. "Gallons of it, bubbling from every orifice. He almost made up for Wardle's absence. But Wardle fucked things up royally."

Wyre's eyes felt heavy. "Has a date been set for the pillorying?"

"Tomorrow, as it happens. Bow Street's been taking on men all week. With a bit of luck, we'll get the culprits to the stocks in one piece. Getting them back again might be trickier."

It seemed Aspinall wasn't out of the fire yet. But there was more at issue here than a molly's fate. The whole thing reeked of handy-dandy. He'd know more once he'd seen the trial proceedings. The transcripts should have been placed in the Middlesex Records Office by now. He'd make an appointment.

He asked about the New Bridge murder, but there was nothing to report. Mr Have-A-Care had vanished into the ethereal. It was the same story with Thomas and Sellis. As for the Palace's co-operation . . . Leighton lifted his shoulders.

"It's just as I said, Kit. They don't want to know. No

support from Bow Street, either. The old bird was plain: the Palace is off-limits for the likes of me."

Wyre looked incredulous. "Encrypted letters that linked the Vere Street Club to St James's, molly assassinations . . . Isn't that too much to ignore?"

"Read's writ runs," Leighton answered. "Of course, I went anyway. But before you get excited, it's a closed shop. I was passed from gentlemen of the privy chamber to equerries, to the King's fucking cock-crower. They won't confirm, or deny, whether anyone with the name Sellis even works or has ever worked there, citing jurisdiction of the Court of the Royal-frigging-Verge. National security's become the full stop to every sentence."

Wyre pictured Miss Crawford's handsome features. He'd let her down. He'd failed to protect her from Brockton. He'd allowed Best to fob him off.

"There's something else you should know, Kit," his friend said hesitantly. (Wyre had never seen him so uncomfortable.) "The doctor told Mrs Mason he hadn't come across your symptoms in any of the fever patients he'd attended."

"I remember a falling sensation . . ."

"You were puking up blood. There were blisters on your tongue. Your piss was black. Shall I go on?"

Wyre felt faint again. "Poison?"

"What did you eat that day?"

"Only the broth we ordered in The Sun." He looked oddly at Leighton. "You didn't eat yours, remember?"

The Runner didn't flinch from his gaze. "I wasn't hungry."

"Who'd want me out of the way?" Wyre said after a pause.

Leighton dragged his nails over an unshaven cheek. "Probably wasn't you they were after." He rubbed his eyes with the pads of his thumbs, then patted the lawyer's shoulder. "This isn't over yet. I'm resurrecting some old contacts, people I can trust. We'll talk in a few days. I'll know more then."

Wyre was too weak to protest.

32. Tussy-Mussies

A sharp lurch to the left, an echoing pitch to the right. The cavalcade set off for Charing Cross. Like the other gang members, Aspinall hung by a shackled wrist to the high central rail running the length of the open-sided cart. The same caravan, he'd been told, used to take the transports to Portsmouth.

The fruit and dung began to land. He hunched over, using his free hand to protect his head as best he could. Miss Pasiphäe remained stubbornly erect, laughing like a maniac. Aspinall yelled at him, but the customs man continued to laugh, eyes bulging.

—— *Reap the whirlwind!*

Citizens were creeping along the house-tops carrying bedpans and buckets. Their loping shapes put Aspinall in mind of troops manning the battlements of some night-marish fortress. Francis had also seen them; he gave a little whoop of terror. Donne's eyes were shut tightly. The landlord, Cooke, stood apart, sneering.

—— *Robert!*

Aspinall peered into the spectators, falling back with a gasp as a clod struck him on the temple.

—— *Prick-eared bastards!*

The crowd tightened about the cart, a blizzard of filth arriving from all sides now. Stinking flounders, fermented fruit, the contents of bedpans. Volleys of slaughterhouse gore rained down on marshals and mollies alike, slowly melting all to one identity.

—— *Dung-lickers!*
—— *Bumheads!*
—— *Taste the fruit!*

Amos grinned madly, bruised and bloodied, somehow still upright. Aspinall saw the brickbat coming that thudded into the custom man's skull. The defiant old sodomite tipped forward, dangling from the rail.

Thirteen years old, and fresh in the city. James Cooke had flown to her like a crow to carrion, offering her a room in The Horse on Carey Street in exchange for odd jobs. An old brood mare had shown her round. Sarah's task was to carry buckets of water up to the attics, and return with the slops. Soon she was guiding soused men through the tavern's passages, paid to fend off their clumsy attempts; and then not to.

One of James's harlots, whippet-thin and handsome, liked to dance for her, catching up her skirts, sparing nothing. Sarah removed the fug in the girl's airless chamber with tussy-mussies of thimble-flowers, which she picked herself in the fields above Finsbury. London-pride and columbines, candy-tufts and catchfly.

"Set them in water," the thin prostitute begged.

"They live longer parched," Sarah replied.

She thought of those flowers now as she waited with the crowds for the cavalcade to approach.

The firm of Starkey & Jennings had seized James's license; soldiers had been posted outside The White Swan. The cart with her husband in it appeared, and slowly drew level.

Time hung above the men like bad air. Like summer-fever.

An ounce of nutmeg, an ounce of cloves, an ounce of

143

*mace. Sixpence for plague water. Take care your still does
not burn.*

Crouching, she picked up an apple from the cobbles,
drew her arm back with the others.

To a serenade of hisses, the procession arrived at the
entrance to Panton Street. Aspinall remembered celebrating
Nelson's victory at Trafalgar here. The crowd was bigger
today.

The pillory's crossed wings were capable of accommodating four heads at once. Francis, Donne and Aspinall
were chosen to stand first. The guardsman began to tremble
violently, clinging to the side of the cart. Two officers held
him up horizontally, while another prised open his fingers,
wrenching him free.

Aspinall laid his head through the iron carcan as
instructed, heart contracting as the upper portion of the
stocks was lowered.

The crowd roared, tame tigers allowed to taste blood.

Twenty women were called forward, and arranged
into a semicircle beneath the platform. Aspinall watched
helplessly as butcher boys passed egg-sized white stones
around the wild sorority.

A musket discharged skywards was the signal to begin
driving the machine around its iron-collared shaft. He
leaned forward for the city's discipline.

The first stones arrived among the fruit and dung. Some
clattered from the wings, but those that struck stung like
hornets. The pinioned men groaned and cried out. Soon,
they were shuffling through a smeary circle of crimson
blood.

A pebble to the forehead dazed him. For a while, he
seemed to stand above the spectacle, perfectly lucid while
his physical body was slack. He gazed down sadly at his

defenceless head. He'd been put here to learn to suffer, to undergo the punishment of a rogue, like a butcher exposed for selling measly pork, or a baker bad bread. If they'd offered him poison, he'd have accepted it gratefully. He watched his feet trudge, his face raised to the pitching and pelting; welts rising; blood dripping.

Fresh salvos landed like punches. Behind him, Donne's bellowing was frightful to hear.

With a shriek, one of the women rushed forward. Drawing a blade she'd concealed in her skirts, she clambered onto the platform, pointing the weapon at Francis's fore parts. Aspinall watched in horror as – to cries of "Slice it off!", "Cut it close!" – the guardsman began kicking out madly. Before she could inflict any injury there, an officer arrived to haul her back by her hair.

The rest of the stand passed as a timeless nightmare of yells, muddy salvos and the creaking of the unoiled shaft. There must have been a second shot fired in the air, but the physician didn't hear it. He stopped pushing only when he felt the flat of an officer's hand on his back.

Aspinall was first to be released, and led numbly from the platform. The carcan was raised next from Donne's neck. The man's eyes were bulging, his face a cartographer's fantasy of welt-roads and bruise-conurbations. Francis looked like he'd been dragged from the Pit. Aspinall had seen such fixed stares and empty faces many times at Wood's Close.

The three were returned to the cart and re-shackled. Then it was Cooke's and Amos's turn to mount the platform, to absorb the city's scorn. The customs man gazed out at the sea of faces, a dark, spreading stain appearing at his crotch.

The crowd grinned back with a single pair of lips.

145

33. Transcript

The hackman who drove Wyre to the Middlesex Sessions House behaved as if he had custody of a stately barouche, rather than a clapped-out dust-cart. A Carey's *New Guide* man, he gave the lawyer chapter-and-verse in miles, furlongs and poles. As they rattled past the Panton Street crossroads, Wyre used scenes from *The Gazette*'s account to populate the public square, picturing the air as it must have been a week ago, thick with missiles. It beggared belief no one had perished. So far, at any rate. The landlord was back in the Courthouse's cells – for his own protection, according to *The Gazette* – where he was receiving medical treatment for his hurts.

Wyre disembarked at the Sessions House, where the city's trial transcripts were kept. The exertion made his head swim. Perhaps Mrs Mason was right, he should still be in bed. Leaning for support against a length of iron railings, his eyes fell on a brass plaque that supposedly marked the exact spot where an oar landed in 1784, dropped by Lunardi as he flew above the city on inflammable air. He could do with some absurd levitation himself.

He waited in the Reading Room for the trial transcripts to be carried up from the stacks. The archivist, a thin, laconic man, placed a stiff pasteboard box of tightly tied docket rolls in front of him. It seemed the Vere Street vellums had been misfiled; he'd found them swaddled with a set of filthy accounts dating from the sodomy trials of 1744. Whoever boxed them didn't know the first thing.

With a sudden image of the whole city as an archive of misplaced items, Wyre began picking at the knots. Unravelling the transcript, he flattened it out with his palms. At least there appeared to be a full account. These days, it wasn't unusual for court scribes simply to note 'crimes too horrid to relate', before recording a bald verdict. The document before him seemed candid enough, though, even if the customary *fucks* and *fig-holes* of a sodomy trial had been civilized into *f–ks* and *fundaments*.

Taking a deep breath, he began to read.

437. JAMES AMOS (alias Miss Pasiphäe), EDWARD DONNE (alias Sweet-Lips), ROBERT ASPINALL, RICHARD FRANCIS (alias Jemima Kiss), and JAMES COOKE were indicted at the Middlesex Sessions, Clerkenwell, for not having the fear of God before their eyes but being moved and seduced by the instigation of the devil, wickedly and feloniously did make a filthy nasty lewd beastly assault; and for diabolically and against the order of nature, having venereal affairs in the fundaments of each other in a certain room in The White Swan tavern, which they entered for the sole purpose of perpetuating that abominable and detestable crime called sodomy, on the 9th day of July in the fiftieth year of the Reign of this Sovereign Lord George the Third by the Grace of God.

(The CLERK identified the PRISONERS. MR. BEST opened the PROSECUTION.)

The case you are called on as Jurymen to decide appears to me one of the highest importance that can come for consideration in the shape of a felony. The men before you are prosecuted under laws of old standing. Their behaviour exceeds that of the worst creatures of the field. Once before in history, sodomites caused the destruction of two cities by defying the code of the Lord. To allow these men to live is to court disaster.

SAMUEL TAUNTON Sworn. – Examined by Mr Best.

Q. What are you?

A. I am the officer who had the execution of the warrant.

Q. When did you apprehend the men?

A. On the 9th of July, at about eleven o'clock. I went with other officers to The Swan and took up the before-named persons, except the landlord, in the attics.

Q. What did you see in the attics?

A. The upper part of the house was given over to appetite. Men of rank and respectable situations were found wallowing on beds with wretches of the lowest description.

Q. Did you see any of the prisoners engaging in sodomitical practices?

A. I did.

Q. How many men were there?

A. There were about thirty of them in all, gentlemen and gentlemen's servants together.

Q. What do you know of the prisoner Amos?

A. I saw him guilty of a very dirty action. They were all in liquor. Their conversation was full of lewd conceits.

Q. Can you positively undertake to swear that this man was in The Swan?

A. Yes, I am positive of it.

Q. What action did he engage in?

A. I saw Amos unbutton Donne's breeches and put up his shirt.

Q. Did an assault take place?

A. Amos turned him on his belly and kept him down. He told him to lie quiet. I saw him take his yard and put it to Donne's fundament.

Q. Did it enter his body?

A. It went a little way in, not far.

Q. Was there any seed?

A. Amos wiped it on his shirt.

Q. What else did you see?

A. I saw Donne use Francis as if he were a girl. He put his hands in his bosom and made signs of amorous intention.

He took hold of the nut of his yard. Francis offered to sit bare in Donne's lap.

Q. Where did this take place?

A. In the attics of The Swan.

Q. Did Francis make good on his offer?

A. He did. Donne drew out his p – k. He used spit to make it glib.

Q. Was there any seed?

A. I saw something run from Francis's body, and saw him wipe some wet off.

Q. Do you recognize the prisoner Aspinall?

A. Yes.

Q. Did you see him commit a bestial act?

A. I saw another man place his instrument in his mouth.

Q. Which man was that?

A. I do not know his name. He is not among the prisoners.

Q. Are you positive Aspinall is the man you saw commit this bestial act?

A. I saw the other man follow him upstairs, and say what sort of a c – k have you got? Let me feel it, which he did. He said it was not so big as his. Then he took him to a couch and set him down on it, unbuttoned his breeches, then worked it. Then he sat down, put his hand behind him and put it into his b – e, and worked up and down. Then Aspinall took his yard and sucked it.

Q. Was there any seed? A man's life is at forfeit.

A. I believe there was.

Q. Take care when you answer since another man's life may be at forfeit.

A. They lay in a darkish place and other men were crowded round them. I believe there must have been some because Aspinall wiped his mouth.

Q. Are you willing to swear to an emission?

A. I am.

Q. Did the prisoner submit quietly to this abuse?

A. He seemed to reconcile himself to his treatment.

Q. Did anyone attempt to use you unnaturally?

A. A gentleman offered me three guineas if I would lie with him in one of the upstairs rooms, and afterwards he offered to make it up to ten.

Q. Did you indulge this unnatural desire?

A. The thought of that transaction made me sick.

(JOHN WARDLE was called for examination by Mr. Best, but did not appear.)

(MR. Brockton was employed for the DEFENCE)

MR. Brockton – Mr. Taunton has given a full account of the behaviour of the Vere Street club, and I believe it was Mr. Wardle's intention to do the same. In the light of this evidence, I decline to trespass on the time of the Jury by offering a defence. It cannot be consistent with my own character. Instead, I call on each of the prisoners to tell their own story and will leave the Jury to form their own conclusions.

FRANCIS Sworn. – Examined by Mr. Brockton.

Q. What are you?

A. Guardsman, 3d regiment. 23 Tottenhall Road.

Q. Do you deny the charges?

A. Every word. I drank beer, nothing else. I was not in the action. Every word he says is as false as God is true. I do not deny that bad opprobrious language passed between us, and Mr. Taunton may have drawn false conclusions from it. Our talk was the jest of men in liquor. I had not such a thought as the things suggested here, which are obnoxious to me.

DONNE Sworn. – Examined by Mr. Brockton.

Q. What are you?

A. Waiter. 10 Drury Lane.

Q. Do you deny the charges?

A. I deny them.

Q. Do you deny the testimony of Mr. Taunton?

A. I do. He was worse than any of the men there, and perjures himself to strike back at those who refused his unnatural longings. He has a piqué against us. I saw him emit in his hand in sight of everyone.

(The prisoner was reminded that he, not MR. TAUNTON, stood under examination)

AMOS Sworn. – Examined by Mr. Brockton.

Q. What are you?

A. Customs man. 7 Foster Lane.

Q. Do you deny the charges and testimonies against you?

A. I deny them all. I am a loving husband and a tender father, an honest man in all my dealings.

Q. Did you take your private member out of your breeches in the presence of the prisoner Francis?

A. I asked Francis whether he was ever clapped, and he said, no, nor poxed neither. I said I feared I had shankers, and asked him to look. Nothing further took place.

ASPINALL Sworn. – Examined by Mr. Brockton.

Q. What are you?

A. Physician. 15 Store Street.

Q. Do you deny the charges and testimonies?

A. I do.

COOKE Sworn. – Examined by Mr. Brockton.

Q. What are you?

A. Landlord of The White Swan, Vere Street, Clare Market.

Q. Did you allow lewd behaviour in your house?

A. I did, and I am sorry for it. I saw the prisoners f – k each other many times. They assembled in my house for the purpose of lewd behaviour. I admit that I participated in all the guilt, except the final completion of it, which is abhorrent to my nature. But I consider myself more criminal since I had no unnatural inclinations to gratify. I was prompted by avarice only.

Q. Did you never indulge in the lewdness?

A. I did not.

(CHARACTERS)

ELIZABETH MASEY. I have known Mr. Francis about three years. He lived with Mr. Headley. He always behaved to me as one that had affection to women, so far as I was able to judge.

JANE PINKNEY. I have known Mr. Amos between two and three years. He behaved as a man that had a high regard for women. I never suspected him guilty of any indecencies with his own sex, and do not think him capable of it.

ELISHA WARD. I have known Mr. Donne about two years. I never saw, or knew anything by him, tending to this kind he is now charged with. His general character was good, as far as ever I heard.

In order to convict a person upon an indictment for sodomy, the act of PARLIAMENT requires that emission of seed should be proved, as well as penetration, sworn to by two eyewitnesses. The JURY, not feeling there was, in any case heard, sufficient evidence of spermatick injection to convict with a CAPITAL sentence, but rather of the attempt at a crime, produced the following VERDICT:

AMOS – GUILTY. Aged 52
FRANCIS – GUILTY. Aged 26
DONNE – GUILTY. Aged 40
COOKE – GUILTY. Aged 35
ASPINALL – GUILTY. Aged 27

Sentenced to Stand One Hour in the Pillory,
Tried by the second Middlesex Jury,
before LORD EYRE.

Wyre stared at the vellum, feeling his throat tighten. Brockton had *defended* the Vere Street gang? It made no sense. What the devil had gone on that afternoon? Had everyone forgotten their roles? Brockton didn't know his to begin with. The man's incompetence came through strongly in the transcript. He'd as good as thrown his charges to the dogs. If Wardle had actually turned up, they'd all be stinking on a surgeon's anatomy slab now. But why had it been necessary to give Brockton the defence brief in the first place? Surely Mitchell wouldn't have passed up his big chance to impress.

It didn't add up. None of it did.

34. Modus Operandi

At a news hut near the Sessions House, Wyre exchanged tuppence for a copy of *The Gazette. Mollies Discovered in St James's Park!* All the newsrags were at it, rootling Vere Street titbits into soul-shaking headlines. Wyre made his way to the hackney rank, and was directed to a bright blue rig. He clambered in, and settled back to absorb the latest commotion.

A miscreant of the name Carter was taken into custody on Saturday night, charged by a young man of the name of Purdy, servant to a cheesemonger in the Strand, with a criminal assault in St James's Park.

The avenues leading to the Watchhouse of St James were choked with at least 5,000 people early in the morning, waiting for the escort of the prisoner to this office. He was handcuffed with a man charged with felony. Before they had got out of the street, the features of both celebrants of indiscipline were dark with blood. The monster was committed for trial.

The magistrate's office was surrounded by thousands of persons during the examination, the greatest part of whom waited to assail the prisoner on his way to prison.

A cheesemonger . . . What next, a Royal Shiner of Shoes? He dozed the remaining three miles to his apartment.

Wyre climbed the stairs in a daze, stopping short at his entrance. Framed in his doorway was a slender woman in a dark mulberry dress and blue shawl. Had Rose come back to him? It was Miss Crawford who turned. He felt a hot flush. If the clerk had given up a lawyer's private address, there'd be a reckoning.

"Mr Wyre," she began, blushing. "I told your landlady you'd agreed to look over some legal documents. I apologize for the deceit. I had to speak to you."

He regarded her for a moment in silence, then opened the door, motioning for her to enter. He owed her an explanation.

Miss Crawford stepped inside. She looked around his flash apartment.

"I was taken ill before your fiancé's trial," he said, leading her to Rose's lady's chair. "Things might have been a good deal worse." As he said it, he felt absurd.

"*Worse*, Mr Wyre?" Her head made an odd jerking movement, like some expensive clockwork toy. She sat down, clasping her hands in her lap. "But it isn't the trial I've come about."

"Then I'm afraid I don't understand."

"When the verdict was made public, the Director

154

of Wood's Close wrote to my fiancé terminating his employment."

"I'm sorry to hear that." Wyre didn't say he wasn't surprised.

"Three days ago," she continued, "Robert took a coach to the asylum to collect his belongings, and to bid his patients farewell." Her face was suddenly desolate. "He didn't return, Mr Wyre. I'm afraid something's happened."

Wyre looked levelly at her. "I take it you were expecting him back?"

She blinked. "Yes, Mr Wyre, I expected him back. We planned to leave London as soon as his injuries healed. I wrote to Professor Ashcroft, the Director, the following morning, demanding to know where Robert went after leaving Wood's Close. I have yet to receive a reply."

Miss Crawford's thin shawl slipped to one side. That smooth, bare shoulder, dark where Rose's skin was almost translucent. Wyre had an unbidden vision of his wife, the pretty clergyman's daughter, the flower of a provincial forcing-house next to this natural beauty.

"Your fiancé went alone?"

She nodded.

"Did he take anything with him?"

She gave him a quizzical look.

"Such as a change of clothes." He pictured Aspinall making for the coast in a fast mail coach, his hands all over some wiry terrier of a man.

Miss Crawford blinked. "You think Robert returned to those men."

He shrugged. There was no point denying it.

"He vowed he wouldn't."

"Does your fiancé have any enemies?"

Her lips twitched at the corners. "Robert is a scapegoat for the city's ills."

"I'm not sure what you expect me to do," he said truthfully.

"Help me find him, Mr Wyre."

What, help a gallows-cheating molly? She was asking too much.

"I can offer a retainer of ten pounds," she said, her voice suddenly intense, "with full expenses. An additional ten pounds if you manage to locate Robert. I'd also ask that you accompany me to Wood's Close, to ask the Director in person where Robert went after collecting his belongings."

He paused for a moment. He said it as tactfully as he could. "Have you stopped to consider your fiancé might not wish to be found?"

Brilliant flecks lit her eyes. "Ten pounds, Mr Wyre, payable on acceptance of the commission." She reached in her skirts and withdrew a banknote.

Wyre stared at it, a month's rent practically dropping from the sky. But he wasn't a Brockton. He wasn't for sale. His job was to see rump-riders hanged in the public square, not to find them when they went prodigal.

"I hardly think Courthouse prosecutors are at liberty to take on private cases."

"Please, Mr Wyre."

"You're asking the wrong man. There's nothing I can do."

She pursed her lips, then rose to her feet. "I can be found at 23 Great Windmill Street, if you change your mind."

"I'm afraid that's unlikely."

She let herself out. He watched her go, the sheer back of her dress hinting now at nothing.

35. Afterclaps

His first day back at the Courthouse, and he'd slept badly. Feeling faintish, he left the apartment, his thoughts turning, as they had throughout the night, to Miss Crawford. Why in God's name did a woman of her calibre cling to Aspinall? A man who, in terms that brought it home, fucked other men.

People disappeared all the time; according to Leighton, most had no desire to be found. Besides, Robert Aspinall had good reason to lie low. In his shoes, Wyre would do the same. He'd take the first mail coach out of the city, and not stop till he was on the Holyhead road to Ireland. Christ, it was hot as Hades. His head swimming, Wyre stopped at the next hackney stand and climbed into a dilapidated barouche. The devil with the expense.

Had he been too salty towards Miss Crawford? She was hardly responsible for her fiancé's actions. He felt guilty at having brushed off her complaint about Brockton, when there had likely been substance to it. Would he really let her confront this asylum director alone? In all likelihood, the fellow had merely neglected to reply to her letter to spare her the torpedo touch of truth. Namely, that Aspinall had flown the coop. That he was back with his kind. But it wouldn't hurt to have a word with him, professional to professional. Find out what really happened. Put Miss Crawford's mind at rest, one way or the other.

And then there was the ten pounds to consider.

Wyre slipped in through a side door, not feeling up to fielding insincere inquiries about his health. Brockton wasn't in their shared cubbyhole, which was something. In fact, his colleague's desk had been cleared. So he'd been given his marching orders after the Vere Street trial debacle. Good.

By mid-morning, Wyre was back in his old routine, although the backlog of molly briefs would take weeks to clear. He flicked through charge cards, witness statements, character references. One or two briefs looked reasonably promising. Odds on chance of securing convictions.

His thoughts kept returning to Miss Crawford; that slender figure, and large eyes; to that peculiar mix of forthrightness and vulnerability. Finally, he reached for a crisp sheet of paper and began to write. If she were at liberty to meet him at the Panton Street coach stand at five o'clock, he'd accompany her to Wood's Close.

Miss Crawford's reply arrived with the clerk's midafternoon rounds.

36. Bone and Soda

The four-wheeler was a dirty, converted relic, its yellow paint picked out with waspish black. They jiggled north through tree-lined streets, districts of pots and windowboxes, past chalybeate drinking fountains, up and down paltry suburban dips and summits, London's last houses arriving with their backs to fields, out to the city's wheat work. A single pheasant stood stupidly among the season's out-of-reach crop. As always, somebody was making a killing.

Miss Crawford had a red-covered octavo volume on her lap, *John Donne* spelled out in gilt lettering along the spine. One of those plush ten-shilling editions. Did she read any moderns? He was unprepared for the fierceness of her reply.

"Only that of one man, as yet little known. A young lord whose hand I would kiss and I'd burst into tears."

Wyre looked blankly. He had no time for the age's vogue for heaving couplets, preferring sprightly lyrics; he was quite content with "finny tribe" where fish were intended, with "fleecy fold" for sheep, and with "tenants of the air" for birds. It was a mystery to him why people had to contort their imaginations to think up pointless little allegories for the world's things.

He gazed out through the glass sliders at leaves parched by the drought into early duns and coppers.

The way wound between two fields, Hampstead Heath visible away to the east, before funnelling into a compact curve. Soon, the turreted silhouette of a large house appeared above the hedgerows. Wyre and Miss Crawford pushed against the sides of the bone-shaker as the driver turned a tight circle in front of the asylum's enormous wrought-iron gates. The horses strained at their leathers, centre pole creaking loudly. A judder of whip springs. Wood's Close.

The neat gravel drive to the house was flanked on one side by topiary clipped into intricate bestial shapes. Wyre offered Miss Crawford his arm. They moved easily together; with Rose, he always had to perform a little hop and skip to compensate for the difference in stride. As they passed an elegant chaise-and-pair parked at the top of the drive, a tall figure in a long black coat appeared in the porch. High collar, white satin tie – the epitome of a professional man. Miss Crawford's fingers tightened around the Wyre's sleeve.

"Welcome to the Retreat," the dark-suited man said, with a hint of Yankee twang. "A pleasure, Miss Crawford, even under the circumstances." He bowed stiffly at Wyre. "Professor Ashcroft, Director of this institution." His moustache reminded Wyre of an alluvial fan at a river mouth.

Miss Crawford lifted her chin. "Mr Wyre is acting as my legal representative."

"Indeed ..." Ashcroft's smile dimmed. "This way, if you please." The professor extended an arm into the hallway. "Dr Ellesmere is waiting in the drawing room. He was Dr Aspinall's mentor," Ashcroft said to Wyre as he conducted the couple into a severe rectangle of a room. Beneath a double-height sash window, a clean-shaven man sat in refined congruities of dark cloth, face almost obliterated by sunlight. One leg was crossed to reveal a long black shoe, buffed to a high sheen. He looked up as they entered, and laid aside the book he was reading. Something on fruits by someone called Hooker.

"Believe me," Ashcroft spoke as the other man rose, "the decision to relieve your fiancé of the burden of his duties was not taken lightly. He was an outstanding theorist of psychic disorder, whose oneirograph on dreams showed marks of true genius. But you must appreciate, Miss Crawford, allowing him to remain in this house, dispensing moral guidance ..." The sentence became a meaningful dip of the head. "Quite out of the question."

"You misunderstand me, Professor Ashcroft." Miss Crawford's voice acquired a steelier inflection. "I'm not here to discuss my fiancé's position."

A horizontal fold appeared at the bridge of the asylum director's nose, perplexing an otherwise smooth, egg-like countenance. "Then I'm guilty of a presumption." He made a slight bow.

She regarded him evenly. "I wish to know the cast of Robert's mind when he left Wood's Close. I wrote two days ago to that effect."

Ashcroft exchanged a glance with his colleague. "Forgive me, I assure you no such letter arrived in my hands. I assumed Dr Aspinall had returned to town."

"He did not."

Ellesmere coughed tactfully. "Miss Crawford, when your betrothed arrived to collect his belongings, he was visibly moved by the sight of these familiar prospects." The stylish physician brought his hands together. "I believe he was acutely sensible of what he'd thrown away. After that, he said very little, retrieving a few items from his office, which he packed into a leather trunk, before leaving. He couldn't have been here above half an hour. I accompanied him to the gates, and we parted with a handshake. He left in the same hackney coach he arrived in."

"Could you describe that coach?" Wyre said.

"Alas, I'd have to say it looked much like any other. As for his destination, he took the London road south. Of that I'm certain." He paused. "Perhaps I flatter myself, but it was my distinct impression your fiancé held no grudge against Wood's Close. He appeared resigned to the fact his position had become untenable. I'd say that was his cast of mind."

Wyre frowned. "You'd have us believe Robert Aspinall left the institution he loved with no more than a friendly handshake."

"As I believe I just said, Mr Wyre, he seemed reconciled to the circumstances. Beneath the surface, who can say? Who can ever claim to understand the inchoate forces that lead to our actions?" He turned to Miss Crawford. "There are enough reasons to suspect that which the self thinks it knows about itself, without venturing to account for the motives of others." He opened his palms in the manner of a reverend at his pulpit.

"I don't see – "

"My point, Mr Wyre? We have patients in our care with whom you might play cards for hours and not notice

161

anything. Yet touch their favourite string and the relapse would be sudden, accompanied by shocking displays." He brought his hands back together in a conciliatory gesture. "Miss Crawford, would you care to accompany me through our grounds? I have some candid thoughts to share about how best to help your fiancé when he returns, as I have no doubt he will."

Ellesmere's voice seemed to be that of reason itself. Between them, Wyre realized, these two mental physicians had cut through his interrogating style as if they were King's Counsels and he a mere legal tyro.

The professor excused himself, leaving Ellesmere's dark-sleeved arm to gather them into the long hallway, which led through to a large, iron-studded door. This opened onto a garden vista that sent Miss Crawford's hand to her mouth. Tiered rockeries, a rose garden, allées of hornbeam, velvet lawns, clever shrubberies . . . all lay spread out before and below, a mass of gorgeous colouring easily the match of Vauxhall.

"We encourage our guests to take regular air-baths," said Ellesmere, as they followed him out. "There isn't the slightest danger to the public." The physician halted at a well-tended bed; pointing out a plant that appeared to have turned a somersault, he said, "This specimen lives entirely on atmospheric moisture." He smiled, running his fingers through the plant's wispy roots, which stuck up preposter-ously in the air. "The little fellow arrived last summer by crate from China. We also keep carnivorous vegetables." He pointed at something hard and waxy rearing from the peaty soil. "They bait their prickles with sticky. Insects can never resist. Flies and bees know there's richest juice in poisonous flowers, little suspecting they might end up themselves as . . . juice." He turned to Miss Crawford and smiled. "Our other plants are fed on nothing more sinister than soda and bone-dust. Take this beauty, now – " He stooped to stroke the pulpy petals of a starkly coloured plant with bulbous protrusions. "Fruit good-sized, a little oblong, perhaps. Flesh very white, though nice and red next to the stone."

Setting off again, they entered a trellised walkway, to emerge onto lawns edged by balls of waxy flowers and thrusting broach spire. A ha-ha broke the boundary of the visible and formal.

"Where does madness come from?" Miss Crawford asked in a quiet voice.

"Oh," Ellesmere replied airily, "there are many causes. Anything from ulcers in the legs to worms. The majority of cases can be marked down to disappointment, but the most distressing occurrences can't be followed to any cause."

"Can the sickness be passed down from sire to son? From father to daughter?" She looked away.

"Certain hereditary insanities, yes," he answered. "Those are particularly difficult to mend."

"What kind of lunacies do you treat at Wood's Close?" Wyre asked.

"All of the thousand mortal shocks flesh is heir to . . . disappointment, jealousy, inherited disorders, madnesses arising from injury." He broke off, clearing his throat. "But let us not apply the chains of definition too tightly."

Beyond the ha-ha, a family of geese took fright at something unseen, one after the other scrabbling into the air, broad wings clapping furiously.

"What about Robert's . . ." She trailed off.

"His sexual insanity? I assure you, Miss Crawford, our methods are forward-looking."

They entered a grove of fine espaliers with whitewashed trunks. At the foot of each tree was a chafing-dish of burning sulphur for strangling caterpillars.

Ellesmere held a branch out of Miss Crawford's way. "Your fiancé's illness is entirely a way of thinking. Most men in the early stages of his sickness can be taught restraint. Those, however, for whom sodomitical pleasures become habitual ... Well, let us say it is for their own good we call them what they are. Madmen. Only then can they be given the treatment they deserve."

At the other end of the orchard, ravers sitting in a horseshoe were spooning coloured powders from metal buckets into cylindrical cases. Sky-rockets, it dawned on Wyre. One of the women, long hair hanging wildly down, skirts bustled up around her waist, was tearing out great fists of grass, which she appeared to be stuffing into herself.

He touched Miss Crawford's arm. "We should go. The coachman won't wait much longer."

"Before you leave," Ellesmere said quickly, "let me repeat, there's much we can do for your fiancé."

"*Do* for him?" Wyre said incredulously. "Ladling powdered serpents into rocket heads for the rest of his days?"

The physician gave him a pitying look. "I should have thought you, Mr Wyre, of all people, would welcome our efforts. We've cured the most shameful criminals. Men whom repeated sojourns in your cells have only hardened."

"The law exists to punish," Wyre answered. "As for madness, perhaps God is of sound mind, but I've never met a man who was."

Miss Crawford straightened. "I've heard a good deal of cold theory. What I wish to know is whether Robert will ever come back to himself."

The physician wet his lips. "Some of my colleagues teach that the foundations of wrong desires are laid down in childhood. Only poets and philosophers would deny the

164

complex legacies of our early days . . . yet I'm not one of those who say our destinies may not be changed. I once heard of a goat that lost its front legs: within a year it had learned to hop about on its hind legs. After it died, an anatomist discovered it had developed an S-shaped spine like a human, as well as other correlates of bipedal locomotion."

The dark woman looked at him. "How long might such an accommodation be expected to take in a case like Robert's?"

The doctor spread his arms, letting a professional smile answer for him.

"I see you don't like direct questions," Wyre said.

"There's no such thing as a direct question. By the time it completes its passage from brain to tongue, it has ricocheted along so many obtuse angles its journey resembles that of an ivory ball around a billiard table." Ellesmere turned to Miss Crawford again. "The Persians have a saying: with time and patience the leaf of the mulberry tree becomes satin. This house will be kind to your betrothed. You have my word."

She bowed her head. "I'll consider your offer."

The physician regarded her for a moment. "It's often said the fault of the soft sex is to shy from uncomfortable decisions. But be under no illusion. The alternative to treatment is to grant your fiancé the freedom to make a mockery of himself in theatres and fun cafés, a continual embarrassment to yourself, like a monkey that masturbates in public."

Wyre stared in disbelief. Leighton's response would have been a straight punch to the nose. The moment passed.

They journeyed back to town in virtual silence. Miss Crawford's hand lay on the quarto of Donne the entire way. The jarvis let them out on the still bustling Strand, where they parted with a stiff handshake.

37. Lines of Inquiry

Wyre rose late. No time to eat the steaming eggs Mrs Mason had left for him on a tray at the foot of his bed. Washing quickly, he threw on his legal-blue jacket and scurried out.

A queue had formed at the St Thomas's Row news booth. The vendor's hands shuttled back and forth like a weaving machine. Wyre took a wild stab – spiralling bread prices in Taunton? Fresh insurrections in Norwich? Perhaps Princess Amelia had finally succumbed to her mystery illness. He craned over the shoulders of the man in front of him, half-expecting to see black borders.

To the side of the queue, a man in a rancid raincoat was raising his pulpit, shaking a copy of *The Dispatch*, raving about lakes of fire. A Southcottian – Wyre shook his head slowly – afraid of steam-engines, telegraphs and all the age's improvements. A prime candidate for Wood's Close.

Wyre paid tuppence for *The Chronicle*. His face changed as he absorbed the news.

A most extraordinary attempt was made late last night to assassinate the Duke of Cumberland. His Royal Highness dined on Wednesday at Greenwich, returned to Town in the evening, and went to an Opera Concert for the benefit of the Royal Society of Musicians. He returned home at about half past ten, and went to bed about eleven. Some time around twelve, lying in bed, he received two violent blows and cuts on his head. His first impression was that a bat had got into the room, and was beating about his head. He leapt up, when he received more blows. From the light glimmering, and the motion of the instrument of destruction reflected from a dull lamp in the fire-place, they were like flashes of lightning.

He tried to escape, but the assassin followed him, cutting him across his thighs. His Royal Highness, the Duke, not being able to find his alarm-bell, which there is no doubt was cut, called several times for Neale, his valet, who came to his assistance and sounded the alarm. The Duke told Neale not to leave him, fearing there were assassins in the room. Shortly afterwards, he proceeded to the porter's room, while Neale went to awaken Salis, another of the Duke's valets. The door of Salis's room was locked, and Neale called out, saying: "The Duke of Cumberland is murdered." No answer being given, the door was broke open, and Salis was found dead in his bed, his throat cut from ear to ear.

A razor was discovered in his room. It is supposed that Salis, conscious of his own guilt (for there appears no doubt he was the would-be assassin), imagined they were about to take him into custody. Fearing torture he cut his own throat. A pair of his silk slippers with his name in them, along with an extinguished dark lantern, were found in the closet adjoining the Duke's chamber, where Salis had concealed himself until his Royal Highness fell asleep. The sword – found discarded at the door of the Duke's bedroom – was a large military sabre, which the Duke lately had sharpened. The whole edge appeared hacked and blunted with the force of the blows.

Salis had five different rooms to pass through from the Duke's bedroom to his own. Traces of blood deposited on the left sides of two of the doors were found. When Salis's coat was examined, the left sleeve was discovered to be thick with blood.

We understand his Royal Highness received six distinct wounds. Mr Jackson, the surgeon, who was immediately sent for, arrived at one and pronounced none of them mortal. The Duke of York, who also resides in the Palace, visited his Royal brother first thing in the morning. A Coroner's Inquest will be held on the body of Salis, led by Mr Read, Chief Magistrate at Bow Street. The inquest jury's report is expected by the end of the week.

The motives that drove Salis to make this atrocious attempt on his master's life are almost impossible to develop. The Duke is recovering slowly.

An attack on a royal, in the Palace itself – unthinkable! And the perpetrator, *Salis* ... The occult name from Crispin Street had been *Sellis*, but he wouldn't quibble. 'Hold fast', that phrase in Thomas's sympathetic ink, rang like a baroque fugue. The mollying bastard hadn't been *consoling* Sellis, he'd been egging on a co-conspirator who'd lost his nerve. A man who, if *The Chronicle*'s account could be trusted, appeared to have found it again, before ending himself with a razor. And what was this? Leighton's Bow Street superior, the 'old bird' himself, had been appointed to head the inquiry into Sellis's death. That was one in the eye for the Court of the Royal Verge. Wyre supposed unbiased scrutiny was paramount; the conspiracy mongers would have a field day, otherwise. All the same, it was quick work to have organized an inquiry already. Absurdly quick, some might say. As for allotting the jury a single week to reach a verdict on violent death ...

Wyre turned into the lime avenue leading to the Courthouse. The trees cast dense, intricate shadows. A Duke attacked in his nightgown – that was treason, which went a long way to explaining why Sellis had slashed his own throat. He pictured the valet in his chamber, razor pressed to his neck, weighing windlasses in the public square against the blade's sting. The choice, dreadful as it was, seemed clear enough. The executioner would start by cutting away Sellis's yard and stones, burning them in a brazier before his eyes. After that, he'd drag things out, keeping his man conscious long after work with the jointing knife began.

He'd take a razor to the jugular every time.

The clerk stopped him in the foyer.

"Quite an evening, Mr Wyre?"

Wyre nodded curtly. He had no intention of swapping theories about Sellis.

"Palace ain't the only place of excitement, tho'. What, you ain't heard?" He raised the stump of his arm. "Someone took a pot-shot at one of our backgammon men. Landlord o' the White Swan, ol' Cooky."

Wyre stared at him. James Cooke had been returned to the Courthouse cells, stupefied from a brickbat to the temple. Safe custody it was called, though evidently not safe enough. "Who shot at him? From the beginning, man!"

"After you wen' home last night, sir, Cooky started performing. Give Mr Kean 'imself a run fer his money. Suter sent two lads in t' calm 'im down, but he kept ravin' about a conspiracy. Insisted the King 'imself was in danger, that he'd speak to no-one but th' Secretary o' bleeding State. Didn't trust none o' the Courthouse fuckers. Beg pardon, sir, his words, not mine. Mr Brockton went down to talk to him, together with Mr Cavendish."

Brockton? Hadn't his desk been cleared? Cavendish was a different matter. He was old school, not easily alarmed.

"What did Cooke say to them?"

"Refused t' say a word. Wanted the Secretary."

"Surely Mr Cavendish didn't take him seriously?"

The clerk winked. "Had him whisked off, right there an' then, sir, under armed guard. That's where it 'appened, outside his lordship's mansion, right at the gates. Right at the gates, Mr Wyre."

"Was the assassin taken?"

"Nah. Guards said the shot seemed t' come from everywhere at once, but I reckon it must 'av been popped off from one of the roofs opposite. That's where'd I'd hunker down. Used t' be a Green Jacket in the 7th. Me an' me Baker rifle, pride of the regiment. Before the arm, that was." He flapped his stump. "Shooter got his slug away, saw blood on Cooky's forehead ..." The clerk flicked open the fingers of his clenched hand like a little detonation. "Must've thought his job was done, then legged it. We leave it to others t' take the glory, us sharpshooters. What he weren't to know was the bullet got lodged in that thick skull o' Cooky's."

"He knew the landlord was coming," Wyre said in a quiet voice, thinking of that cool voice in the service tunnel.

"Looks that way, sir, don't it? Tip-off, as yer might say. One of them fancy bum-funners of yours, I shouldn't wonder."

Wyre frowned. "What do you mean by that?"

"Cooky was blethering on 'bout his ledger. That's what he calls his list of names. He's in the extortion business, mark my words. Seems someone took exception."

"Where's the landlord now?"

"Back in his cell. Sat up blusterin' all night. Doctor took twelve ounces of blood. But he's quiet enough now. Sleeping it off. Smells like a ship's surgeon. Doctor says to leave 'im. Either he'll wake up, or he won't."

Wyre cursed under his breath. Another attempt on a Vere

Street man's life. The picture was acquiring a disturbing singleness. He needed to talk to Leighton.

There was something else to consider, too: things suddenly looked a lot worse for Aspinall. It stretched credulity to suppose the mad-doctor's disappearance was unconnected from the events of last night. Poor Miss Crawford, she didn't deserve any of this. He gave the clerk a firm look. "Tell Suter I wish to know the instant Cooke comes to his senses." He dug in his pocket for a half-crown he could ill afford to dispense. "Make sure I'm the first to know. Before Brockton, you understand?"

"Won't get no logic out of 'im, Mr Wyre," the clerk said, pocketing the coin. "Cooky's lost his pebbles."

"Come with me, while we're at it," Wyre said. "I've something for you to deliver to the Public Office." He led the clerk to his office, where he scribbled a quick note to Leighton, asking to meet the Runner at midday. The Wheatsheaf, this time. He'd be giving The Sun a wide berth from now on. As the one-armed man turned to go, Wyre asked, "Where's Brockton now? Didn't Best send him packing?"

"Oh, that he did, Mr Wyre," the clerk said over his shoulder, "up to th' second floor. Risen in th' world, is our Mr Brockton."

Wyre stared. It was time to have a word with the fat toad.

Brockton's office had its own brass nameplate. Wyre rapped sharply.

"Come."

The adenoidal tone was unmistakable. His colleague's room had a fair view over the chimney-tops.

Wyre launched right in. "You might as well know I've been through the Vere Street transcripts."

171

"A complex case." Brockton's face betrayed nothing. "It already feels historical."

"Was Wardle *your* informant? Why didn't you mention him to me?"

"He came forward at the last minute. After you were taken ill," Brockton added, smiling.

"And he failed to show up on his big day."

There was no answer to that.

"Twenty-seven culprits, all taken in the act – and the net result? Five pilloried men."

"I suppose there's a purpose to all this," Brockton said.

"Defending the Vere Street gang was Mitchell's domain. How did you end up in the advocate's role?"

"Mitchell was seconded to Crown business in the Principality. It wasn't possible to find another lawyer prepared to represent filth. I did my duty."

Wyre looked around the office. "Seems you've been rewarded for it."

He turned. There seemed no point in further comment.

Nothing from Leighton. There wasn't any good news about Cooke, either. Still comatose. The hulking gaoler corroborated the clerk's report – the doctor didn't expect the White Swan's landlord ever to be *compos* again. There was nothing to be gained by hanging around the Courthouse, so Wyre left for The Wheatsheaf, trusting Leighton would turn up.

He took *The Chronicle* with him, refamiliarizing himself as he walked with the details of the assault on the Duke of Cumberland, placing the details in space. Two shabby trees became Sellis the faithless valet and Thomas his conniving correspondent. The more he read, the less convinced he was that a jury could wrap up the inquest in a single week. Too many moving parts. The principal evidence against Sellis appeared to be entirely circumstantial, boiling down to little more than a pair of slippers. What kind of would-be murderer left his slippers at the scene of a crime, his name absurdly stitched in the lining?

He turned from the first scrubby tree to the other. Sellis – dupe or mastermind?

If there was an upside, it was that he had a chance to make good in Best's eyes. If Vere Street really had gestated a plot to kill a royal, the case would have to be reopened. This time it wouldn't hinge on punishing sodomites, but had all the makings of a full-blown sedition trial. Though *that* depended on finding some of the principal players still breathing. It looked like Cooke could be counted out. That left the other pilloried men: the guardsman, waiter and customs officer. Odd as it sounded, his best bet probably lay with Aspinall: there was a connection he could exploit through Miss Crawford.

He picked a third tree, a lime, its leaves caked with white dust, to stand in for the other man mentioned in the report, the manservant who'd discovered Sellis weltering in blood. Neale. That was another thing that made no sense. Why the devil hadn't the fellow . . .

The Wheatsheaf's four-bay façade hove into view. Wyre looked for Leighton's dandy-charger, half-expecting to find it strapped to a downpipe. It wasn't there.

The air in the tavern's back room was charged with the words 'assassination' and 'Frenchie bastards'. Wyre's poor imitation of Leighton's hooked finger eventually caught the attention of a barmaid, who leaned across the bar, hair hanging in loose ringlets. Wyre ordered two mugs of hot beer.

At half past one, there was still no sign of Leighton. Giving up, he took a mouthful of beer and pushed himself to his feet. It was a long shot, given Leighton's itinerancy, but he'd try the Runner at the Public Office.

No. 4 Bow Street, Leighton's circus. The non-descript high stone building with its single chimney had always struck the lawyer as at mundane odds with the extravagant behaviour that represented its stock-in-trade. He squeezed into an entrance corridor packed with short-weight bakers, disorderly apprentices, fortune-tellers, harlots, pork butchers and card-sharps. Wyre presented himself to the desk sergeant.

Mr Leighton 'adn't bin in that day. Weren't in yesterday, neither. What weren't unusual. "When he's got th' scent, Mr Wyre. When he's got th' scent!"

Surely, the lawyer reflected, Leighton would have seen Sellis's name in the papers by now. He'd be as eager to make contact as Wyre was, especially given the Crispin Street intelligence they shared. After all, they were in possession of information that linked the Palace manservant Sellis to the Vere Street mollies.

"I'll tell 'im you were 'ere, sir."

On an impulse, Wyre asked the desk sergeant about the officer named in *The Post*, the one who'd dragged those military turdmen, ensign Hepburn and the drummer-boy White, up from the Isle of Wight.

"Rivett, sir?" The sergeant called over a wispy-cheeked officer, and with a wink instructed him to show Wyre up.

Rivett's desk was under a tiny back-facing window.

"Mr Wyre from the Courthouse, sir," announced the young officer.

The Runner turned, presenting a portrait of unshaven

cheeks and sensual mouth, unpleasant gaps between the snaggle teeth. Nothing of the patriot-flame.

"Mist-a Wy-ah . . . from the Court'ouse," he parroted in broad city.

"Are you the one who brought in the drummer-boy?" (Rivett regarded him steadily.) "I'm interested in the man who informed on him."

"Oh, it's all up wi' Whitey boy," Rivett said. "No 'elp fer 'im nah." The man seemed constitutionally adverse to a straight answer.

"White will get a fair trial," Wyre said, resenting the implication.

"Yer fink?" Rivett sneered. "Shoulda seen th' bastard when I got the drop on 'im. Filled his breeches, an' who can blame 'im?"

Wyre ignored that. "The papers say a Palace servant put the finger on White. What was his name?"

Rivett's eyes slid away from the lawyer's as from the repulsing poles of a magnet. "Never met him. We wuz jus' told the identification had been made."

"At least give me the man's name."

"It wuz an alias. Told t' use it at all times."

"Is that usual?"

"Depends . . ." Rivett smirked. "Dunno much, do yer?" He exchanged a grin with the young officer.

"Well, then, tell me what his alias was." Wyre's tone became sharper.

Rivett looked the lawyer up and down. "Dunno as I'm under any obligation to answer yer interrogations. But the alias ain't no secret. Funny name, but then they usually are. Mr Parlez-Vous. That's what we wuz told t' call him."

"Who stands behind that cypher? Listen, there may be a great deal at stake."

"Nah, Mr Wyre," Rivett said with a slow shake of his

head. "Even if I knew." He lifted his upper lip. Those dark gaps again.

Wyre returned to the Courthouse via the Strand. The heat was beyond. He passed the new St Clement's church, which gleamed in the sun. Tiny lanes began there to fan out north, splitting off into further avenues, one of which eventually became Vere Street.

Mr Parlez-Vous. It was an unpromising starting point. Wyre traipsed up the Courthouse's grand steps; at the entrance, he was flagged down by the clerk. It seemed Cooke wasn't dead, after all.

Wyre never looked forward to his descents into Suter's stygian realm, but this one might be worth it. The head turnkey led him to the landlord's cell, and Wyre put his face to the barred upper portion of the door. It smelled as if something had gone off. The landlord was sprawled on a straw bed facing the wall. Seeming to sense Wyre's disturbing presence, he pushed himself up into a sitting position. Slowly, his head turned. One eye was caked shut with blood, the other darted wildly, coming at last to rest on the lawyer.

"Suter!" he roared. "Get him away! He's come to eat me."

"Calm yourself, you mad bastard. This is Mr Wyre, one of the lawyers here."

The gaoler unlocked the heavy door, and Wyre entered warily. The putrefying miasma was a physical thing that had to be pushed into, heart and lungs. The landlord's condition was patently precarious. His black hair was sodden and hung lankly, one cheek was buff leather, and his breathing came laboured as if each inhalation was raising a weight. But most shocking was the penny-sized hole above his right eye where a portion of skull was missing. Something Wyre didn't want to think about glistened there.

Cooke put his head at a grotesque angle. "Did Sarah send yer? Daft bitch is lost to me anyway. Brockton's had five pounds off her, and God knows what else."

"Tell me about last night."

"Job half-done . . . Yer talking to a dead man. Best don't mean for me to leave this place on my feet."

Wyre frowned deeply. "What's Mr Best in this?"

Cooke's look became sly. "Only the worst banger of foreign dung-holes. What in th' trade we call a regular."

"Don't be ridiculous." Wyre cast a glance back through the bars at Suter, who made a throat-cutting motion.

"Promised to bring me through, if I kept me clam shut." The landlord began to whine, his sensual lips widening. "Head o' the sect, Mr Wyre, the Mother of all Mollies."

Wyre ignored him. "Who shot at you? It's in your interest to tell me."

The landlord's swollen face seemed to collapse in on itself. "Ask Suter." He dragged the back of his hand across his mouth. "*There's* a man who tells less than he knows."

"Speak plainly. I can't help you otherwise."

"Fink I'm beyond your 'elp now, Mr Wyre." He squinted over the lawyer's shoulder. "When I wus carried back yesterday, Suter forgot 'imself. 'Cooky', says he, 'What the devil are you doin' here? It weren't meant for you to come back'. Go on, Mr Wyre, ask him."

Wyre sensed Suter's bulk shifting behind the bars of the door.

"There'll be time for allegations of that nature," the lawyer said. "First, I want your list of clients. Who were the habitual men? That's what you went to tell the Secretary, isn't it?"

Cooke touched a finger to the missing circle of bone on

177

his forehead. "Funny thing, Mr Wyre, it don't hurt." He fixed the lawyer with his single good eye. "I saw a six-foot grenadier take a little master 'arf his size, three or four couples in the same room riding each other like rams." A slop of something slid out of the hole, which he wiped away with the pad of his forefinger. "Word got round, see. Weren't long before the cits rolled up in their fancy coaches. Tipping an 'od-carrier a guinea meant nothing to 'em, jus' so long as they got to squeeze a nice fat, healthy yard."

"Their names, man."

Cooke's face grew cunning. "Everyone wants those. The White Swan was never just about arse, see, Mr Wyre. Those pegos thought they was customers, but they was jus' names to be sold on. Still are, if I understand Mr Brockton's game. Should've had Yardley's sense, melted away at the first signs of trouble like ice on a milliner girl's gash." He grinned. "Eh, Mr Wyre? Some of 'em were worthless, mind. Miss Sweet Lips was a waiter, Mistress Fox a sawyer. The better men, tho', yer Kitty Cambrics an' Lady Godivas, yer Black-eyed Leonoras. That's a different story. Bankers' sons, 'onrable Members. Even 'ad a sub-librarian at the London Institution. Higher than that, maybe." His look became sly again. "Oh, it was a club wi' reach."

Wyre straightened. "If crimes have been committed, it's my job to see them prosecuted. Rank won't protect anyone, you have my word."

Cooke's good eye suddenly flared. "Cut their sacks off, Mr Wyre, it's the only way, or yer'll never make decent citizens of 'em." A strange noise brewed in his throat, starting low and rising.

The door scraped open behind the lawyer.

With a firmness that took Wyre aback, Suter ushered

him out into the tight passage. "For your own protection," the gaoler said.

So there was nothing to be expected from Cooke. But the day had at least provided one new thread to pull – Rivett's allusion to his Palace source, to this 'Mr Parlez-Vous'.

He needed to know more about him. He needed to know more about everything.

It was time to try Leighton at his lodgings.

What it pleased Leighton to call his 'whereabouts' was situated in a haveless part of town, not far from Cheapside's own unambitious streets with their covered ways and yards. Wyre stepped into the dark building, passing the Runner's yellow hobby horse in the hall. Picking his way through the doe-eyed trulls who slouched or slept on the stairs, Wyre climbed up to a narrow first-floor landing, and followed the apartments along to No. 17. The door was ajar. Faint voices could be heard inside. Wyre knocked; when there was no reply, he entered, half-expecting to find the Runner in a clinch.

He wasn't prepared for the smell, worse than Cooke's cell, somewhere between sweetness and pungency, and it was getting stronger. Wyre squeezed past Leighton's tasselled sofa to reach the back cubbyhole that served his friend as a drawing-room-cum-study. Two men were conversing there. The shorter one had his back to the door, the other stood side-on; tall, with elegant wire-framed glasses held on by a coloured ribbon.

Two Bow Street officers in distinctive blue garb were busily pulling books off Leighton's shelves.

Leighton himself sat slumped at the writing desk, his face contorted, neck a spider's nest of scratch marks. It looked as if the phlegm was still boiling in his throat.

38. Symptoms of Death

The stocky one was the Middlesex Coroner, a pinched man under the burden of the name Solomon.

"When did you last see the deceased?" he asked bluntly.

"About a week ago," Wyre replied numbly, eyes fixed on Leighton's hunched form. "He hadn't been replying to my letters."

Solomon lifted a flat round tin from the Runner's desk as if in explanation. "White oxide of arsenic, soluble in water. The moral circumstances indicate brandy tincture of the poison was ingested seven or eight hours before the onset of death."

Solomon turned to the spectacled man, who nodded before introducing himself as Mr Cline, surgeon at Guy's Hospital. "Often called on to advise Bow Street on such matters." He took a corked ampoule from his inside pocket, and passed it to Wyre. "Heat isn't kind to corpses."

Wyre dabbed a few drops under his nose. Lavender oil. It was a relief, though the smell seemed somehow prosaically beside the point.

The arsenic, Cline continued, was discovered among an assortment of miniature chemical jars. The surgeon raised the lid of Leighton's desk to reveal a row of bottles. Wyre recognized the spidery script on the labels from Thomas's escritoire in Crispin Street. Why weren't the bottles in Bow Street's evidence room?

"Sympathetic ink," Wyre murmured. He looked up. "Leighton wasn't a self-destroyer."

Solomon opened his mouth to speak, but Cline got in first.

"Unpalatable though it may be, there's little doubt this gentleman took his own life." The surgeon pointed to signs of what he clearly enjoyed calling external lividity

180

and contraction of the fingers. "The stomach was bloated and deeply shadowed, both symptoms in keeping with arsenic poisoning."

Footsteps echoed in the hallway. Solomon ushered in two stretcher bearers. Unshaven and slovenly, they linked arms under the Runner's thighs and lifted him from the desk chair. They had to press on his knees to get the legs to lie flat.

"Did he have a wife?" Solomon asked.

Wyre shook his head, with a sense of spreading unreality.

On the count of three, the stretcher bearers hoisted the body, and carried it through the cramped apartment.

"My friend was investigating an armed cult of sodomites. It was all connected to Vere Street. He confided to me he was under surveillance. He wouldn't have . . ." He trailed off, seeing the men's faces.

Mr Cline nodded sympathetically. "This has come as a shock to you."

With less feeling, Solomon added: "Fantasies of persecution are a common indicator precursory to suicide."

"But those marks on his neck . . ."

"We saw them," Solomon said. "Your friend probably clutched at his own throat, thus – " He acted out the movements, making choking noises, stopping only when he saw Wyre's incredulity. "It's an instinctive response," he added, now in the far corner of the room. "I've seen such bruising before in cases of this kind."

The two blue jackets were still rifling through Leighton's books. Wyre glared at them. "If it's a simple case of suicide, why go through his belongings?"

The Coroner gave him a thin smile. "Just in case."

The Bow Street officers swept Leighton's chemicals into a large leather clasp bag, and made their way out. Bowing, Solomon and Cline followed them, the surgeon pausing briefly at the door to offer his sympathies again.

Then Wyre was left with what had suddenly become Leighton's personal effects. He gazed around at the detritus. It didn't seem right, everything left strewn on the floor. Not that Leighton had ever placed a premium on tidiness. The lawyer dropped to his knees and began sorting through. Among the papers and files were volumes on topics as diverse as atoms, birds' eggs and French architecture, as well as a triple-decker by Mrs Radcliffe. Rose used to devour such trashy novels, books that set up a mystery only to rationalize it with ridiculous artifice in the worst sort of literary *coitus interruptus*, where haughty little pusses always somehow married into fortunes, and moustachioed Italian aristocrats preyed on fatherless wards. What was the one she'd tried to get him to read? *The Orphan of Montefalco*. The title said it all.

Leighton's novel was *The Italian*. He recognized the closely printed type, the very same 8-shilling edition his wife had spent last winter reading, eking out the pages towards the end. Leighton had teased her once, dismissing novel readers as dupes of the imagination – but he'd been a secret enjoyer all along.

Wyre lifted the volume by its spine. As he reached up to replace it on the shelf, something fluttered from the fanning pages . . . a folded sheet of paper, quarto-sized, tear marks down one side. He inspected it, brow knitted. The sheet contained cramped notes in a sinuous hand, with many foreign marks and interlineations. Evidently, it had been written at speed. There was a date, the beginning of that year, 7 January 1810. In the top corner, something was inscribed in different handwriting, which Wyre recognized as Leighton's scrappy own. Despite the scrawl, there could be no doubt of the spelling: underlined twice, followed by a question mark, 'Mr Parlez-Vous'. He turned wonderingly to the notes themselves, disgust rapidly turning to alarm:

May do anything that pleases
Exists in a state of permanent mental orgasm
Relishes the nightmare, prays for it to descend.
*

Maintains evil is anchored in the body.
Manichean?
Excited by blood.
Exhibits self-hatred.
Relates in detail the effect of a bullet passing through a human head
*

Claims to have been an unwelcome child.

Rivett claimed Parlez-Vous was merely the grubby alias of a Palace servant snitch, but Leighton clearly thought the man was something more. *Permanent mental orgasm* . . . Could such a lunatic really be dressing a duke each morning? Leighton hadn't been sure – the question mark showed that. But he was dead for a reason. The lawyer's blood ran cold. He was in over his boots. Solomon and the other medical man, Surgeon Cline, had clearly been looking for something specific. Was he holding it in his hand? Might he expect to be relieved of the note downstairs, and of more? The case had done for Leighton, so what chance was there for him? Why the devil hadn't Leighton turned the note over to the authorities? Thomas's letter to Sellis, too, for that matter. Leighton had asked him to keep quiet about the correspondence, and he'd blindly agreed. Some might construe that as neglect, he thought uncomfortably, as an attempt to pervert the course of justice. When did silence become treason?

He opened a page of *The Italian* haphazardly, his eyes landing on something typically overblown: *Oh! when shall I dare to call you mine?* How could his wife bear such prose. How could Leighton?

No one was waiting for him in the stairwell. Feeling the weight of the torn-out page in his pocket, Wyre stepped out into bleaching sun.

Halted on the top step. Leighton's yellow hobby horse . . . It didn't seem right to leave it to the cockatrices and their pimps. Moments later, Wyre re-emerged, wheeling out the dandy-charger. Mounting it unsteadily, he rode the outlandish machine back to the Courthouse, grief for his friend blinding him to the startled looks of pedestrians.

39. Notes

Best pushed aside the torn-out page of notebook. He looked up. "Once again, Wyre. From the beginning."

Struggling to keep his breath steady, Wyre went over the salient details: the bludgeoned fly, the cool voice at his ear, Thomas's obscenely crooked leg, those slow sympathetic letters, Sellis's slippers, the slug fired at Cooke . . . bringing it all within the orbit of Leighton's death. His murder. The only element he left out was Aspinall's disappearance; the bendyman's name still lay on his tongue like dust. Then he felt better. He'd been an idiot for not confiding in his superior earlier.

The old barrister studied him. "I take it you think there's a bigger picture."

"Leighton thought a seditious conspiracy was being gestated in Vere Street. There's reason to suppose the plot is still ongoing."

184

"Reason to suppose. Is that conjecture merely, or do you have evidence? This is no trifling matter, Wyre."

"Key witnesses, and now a principal investigator, are dead, sir . . ." He'd expected Best's legal instincts to see the connections, but it seemed he was expected to spell them out. "The valet, Sellis, was corresponding with Thomas, a card-carrying Vere Street gang member, who was discovered murdered in Crispin Street. Sellis's suicide might be more than it seems. We should inform St James's Palace about Thomas."

Best raised a laconic eyebrow. "I'm looking for the intellectual thread."

"The crux is Vere Street, sir," Wyre said with an insistence of tone that surprised him. "Each of the victims frequented that living sewer, and each possessed information that threatened the conspiracy."

"Your conspiracy . . ." Best frowned. "You still haven't said what its purpose is."

He hadn't thought that far ahead, but heard himself say: "The target's the Duke of Cumberland."

"Read the newspapers, Wyre. The assassination attempt has already been thwarted. The Duke's man, Neale, was the hero of the hour."

"The plot's still active, sir. Leighton must have been getting close."

"Your Mr Leighton – " Best showed the tip of a surprisingly pink tongue " – how confident are you of his own loyalties?"

"I trust him." Was that even true? "As a matter of fact, Leighton was concerned about Bow Street's own allegiances. He claimed he was being surveilled."

A faint smile flickered across the Chief Barrister's lips. "Did he, now?"

"And then there's the attack on the landlord. The

185

shooter knew exactly where to wait, exactly when Cooke would be arriving." (Best pursed his lips.) "Before he died, sir, Leighton spoke of an armed cult of sodomites."

Best snorted. "You're beginning to sound like a street-corner fanatic."

"But what if The White Swan was more than just a convenient meeting place for mollies? What if the Vere Street Club was hiding a political conspiracy within a sexual one?" William's words sprung to mind. "A cup within a cup."

"That's a pretty phrase." Best's eyes were perfectly still.

Wyre knew the hackney was driverless and careering towards a hairpin, but it was too late to stop now. "Sellis was desperate to quit St James's Palace. That hardly fits the bill of an assassin-in-waiting. The newspapers are painting the valet as the plot itself, but what if he was its victim?"

Best sniffed, seemingly a signal to continue.

"Leighton was on the heels of a shadow man, Mr Parlez-Vous." Wyre pointed at the torn-out page of notebook. "As far as I can gather, he's still employed by the Palace. Parlez-Vous was the one who blew the gab on the drummer-boy."

Best's eyes were tiny points now. "A made-up name, a ridiculous moniker scribbled on a page of gibberish that's scarcely more than an innominated tip-off. The result of some Palace rivalry or other."

"Parlez-Vous exists, sir. Leighton thought so. This man may still be going after the Duke."

Best placed his head on one side as if guessing the lawyer's weight at a fairground stall.

"What do you suggest is to be done, Wyre? Replace the entire staff of St James's Palace? Think of the consequences for morale. The war is at a tipping point."

Wyre was silent for a moment. "Our best chance is the inquest, sir. Someone with cross-examining experience, capable of breaking through the penetralium, should be present."

Best's lips twitched at the corners. "Penetralium? You speak as if St James's contains the secret of a god." He shuffled a pile of loose legal vellums. "Besides, I think Bow Street's Mr Read can be relied on to smell out any misdeeds. He is overseeing the inquest, and personally collecting the witness statements."

"But, Leighton – "

"Asked for specifically," Best cut him off, before adding, "which I concede is never a good sign."

Wyre looked at him, trying to contain his surprise.

"The inquest began this morning," Best said, business-like. "In three days, the jury will deliver its verdict." He paused. "The inquest is a quasi-internal affair, conducted under the auspices of the Court of the Royal Verge. A cynical man might conclude Mr Read's presence is intended to head off objections about secret courts from the usual quarters. Now, it would be a great shame if the Chief Magistrate at Bow Street were to be caricatured by reformers as a mere sop to impartiality. I think even Mr Read would agree on that." He fixed Wyre with steely eyes. "The imprimatur of the Courthouse will go some way towards dampening popular theories. Perhaps it's time to offer to do our bit for King and country, eh? Mr Read will certainly take it amiss if a senior man were sent. But a man such as yourself, Wyre . . . I take it you have no objections?" The surprisingly yellow tips of the old barrister's teeth were showing. "Present yourself at the Palace gates, half past nine tomorrow morning," he said briskly. "I'll see you're expected. Oh, and Wyre," he added, "mind your Latin."

Wyre pulled the ribbons of Rose's twilled muslin dressing gown tighter. First Rose, now Leighton; both gone. He sipped at his claret – French, if honestly labelled – and raised the glass to his friend, picturing him perched on his preposterous running machine. The yellow dandy-charger, he thought with a pang, was currently leaned up in Mrs Mason's foyer. He'd meant to return it to Bow Street, but couldn't bear parting with this last vestige of his companion. Also – Leighton was right – it was a remarkably handy way of getting about.

He took another sip of wine, tears pricking. If Parlez-Vous *had* been involved in the Runner's death, he'd personally pay Jack Ketch to botch his drop. With an uncharacteristic flick of his wrist, he drained his wine. A success should be celebrated, he thought bitterly. After all, he *was* the Courthouse's man at the Palace. He'd stolen a march on Brockton. Perhaps it wasn't absurd to think a promotion lay in the offing. He'd be able to remain quartered at Mrs Mason's, pay the rent in a timely fashion.

The word tolled him back to himself. Sixty-five pounds in debt and counting . . . His one-off windfall of ten guineas from Miss Crawford for the Wood's Close debacle wouldn't keep a roof over his head beyond a fortnight. Should he have accepted her retainer? Money in these times wasn't to be trifled with. But the moral absurdity was glaring. If he hadn't fallen sick, he'd have hanged her molly fiancé. If only he could ask Rose. He pictured her here now, imagined showing her around Mrs Masons's apartment, leading her to the big bed, smothering her in fine linen, telling her what a brave girl she was.

He jumped at a knock on the door, and got to his feet.

Someone had slid a note under the bottom rail. Frowning, he stepped out into the corridor in time to see a pair of child's kicking heels vanish round the corner.

Wyre bent down for the note; it was succinct and unpunctuated:

Obelisk Tavern 8 o'clock Information awaits pertinent to a recent case of poisoning No polis

The reference to poison sent a chill through him. Was he or Leighton meant? The rest was clearly a bear-trap. The Obelisk. As if he'd venture to that south-of-the-water bagnio alone.

His thoughts were interrupted by another knock, quieter this time. "Who is it?" he called. Miss Crawford's muffled voice came through the door.

She wore a high-cut russet jacket and matching reticule Rose would think too . . . In her left hand she clutched a note, the sibling of his own.

"It was delivered an hour ago, Mr Wyre. It alludes to a missing person. I assume Robert is meant."

"I got something similarly cryptic," he said, leading her to a chair. He hesitated. "The Obelisk is little more than a lazaretto. I take it you've no intention of going?"

Her colour rose. "If there's the slightest chance of information, I have to know."

Such misplaced loyalty. Could he really let her go alone? It seemed the great wave had arrived. Either he swam, or was pressed to the bottom.

Sidmouth Street hackney-coach stand was a stone's throw away. Miss Crawford agreed to cover the expense. The evening's roads were a pell-mell of clattering vehicles, ranging from aristocratic drags and fancy gigs to sturdy dray carts, the former champagne to the latter's bottled stout. The journey in sultry air took them along the improved Lambeth avenues; soon they were traversing the old marshes on a hard mile of new boulevard. In what seemed almost no time, the first of the district's two obelisks loomed ahead, then the notorious tavern itself appeared.

The jarvis pulled up hard. Wyre tipped him to wait, and helped Miss Crawford down. Drops of moisture had collected in the notch of her throat, beginning their own little journeys down her breastbone.

Inside the public house, low table lamps did little to lift the shadows. Wherever he looked in the gloaming, punks and their customers were fondling and mussing. In one lightless nook, a jade in unhooked stays was using a conical nipple to tickle the nose of a thickset swad. The soldier's fingers were lost between her legs.

"Warm hand fer yer jock, fella?" the degraded female said as Wyre drew level. "Yer missus won't mind. Will'ya luv?"

With a shudder, he shepherded Miss Crawford past.

The dark woman brushed his sleeve. "How will we know the man we're here to meet?"

"I think we're supposed to wait till he declares himself," he answered, one eye on a burly trio who had just entered from the street, dressed in smart town clothes. The men seemed to be heading straight for them, but turned at the last moment, moving deeper into the taproom. The lawyer's attention turned to two men standing at the chimney.

He nudged Miss Crawford. "Let's try over there." Taking her arm, Wyre made a beeline for the fireplace. The taller of the two, a solid type in regimental trousers, whispered something to his neighbour, a man with thick black hair, oiled-back. Surely not! The man possessed nothing that conjured the apartness of sanctity, but there was no mistaking the Parson. What role was that piece of human refuse playing here?

"Parson Church," Wyre said bluntly.

It was the taller man who stepped forward. A death's head ring glinted from his little finger. "You're mistaken," he said, quietly but perfectly distinctly.

Ignoring him, Wyre fixed the Parson with a level gaze. "We got your little notes."

A flash of silver marrow bones, and Wyre was gazing up at a circle of jeering faces, the room swaying about him. Through a fog, he saw Miss Crawford fly at Death's Head, fists flailing. A flat hand sent her tumbling over a table like a loosely jointed doll. She came to rest on the floorboards, dark hair unpinned, one tawny leg exposed above the knee. Wyre struggled to rise and, with an angry cry, aimed a jab at their assailant. Death's Head picked the fist out of the air, responding with a blow to the temples that sent Wyre back to the sawdust.

For a second, he was vaguely aware of the three burly figures from earlier crashing through the circle of spectators, arms outstretched . . . Then the sensation of a great, dark wave descending.

When he opened his eyes, Miss Crawford was crouching above him, her hair loose on one side, shining in the sun.

A voice came from the bar. "Back wi' us, then?"

"Yer reflexes are all wrong," another wiseacre added. "Yer wife's less cunny-thumbed than you. Nice piece of clockwork, that 'un, mind."

"No gud actin' the gemmen in a scrap." The first voice again. "No 'arf taps. Yer gotta blacken yer 'art."

Wyre sat up, and spat blood into the sawdust.

191

"Ignore them, Mr Wyre," Miss Crawford put her arms out to help him to his feet, but he pushed her away roughly.

"There's no mystery here," he exclaimed angrily, "only your fiancé's sordid pleasures. Robert Aspinall took up with extortionists and buggerantoes, and this is the result. He can rot."

"Mr Wyre!" Her perfect mouth acquired the absurd pitch of a tragic mask.

Struggling up alone, pressing one hand to his thudding brow, the lawyer staggered towards the door, Miss Crawford's tiny heels clicking behind him.

The journey back was a dismal amalgam of pounding hoofs without, hypnotic silence within. The cabman's wheels, once Hermes-like, now seem weighed down by lead. Gradually, the pain in Wyre's jaw began to subside into a dull ache. By the time they arrived at Sidmouth Street the sun had gone, but an immensity of light still hung behind the sky. A painter like William would have a field day.

Coming over faintish again, Wyre accepted Miss Crawford's assistance up to his apartment. He joggled the key in the door, and pushed it open. Inside, someone was sitting in Rose's lady's chair. The ring glinted bluntly from his finger.

"Ev'ning, Mr Wyre. How do, Miss Crawford."

40. Protocols

Miss Crawford stepped forward, her slender fingers clenched into fists.

"Haven't you beaten him enough already? Leave this instant, or I'll fetch a constable."

Death's Head gave Wyre a broad grin over her shoulder. "Spirited lil imp. Ain't the type t' cry o'er a pug dog."

The Parson's face appeared, as if levitating, above the concertinaed room-divider.

"Come out of there at once," Wyre cried. "How the devil did you get in? If you've harmed a hair on Mrs Mason's head . . ."

Death's Head extended his hand. "No 'ard feelings, mate. The name's Yardley."

"The Courthouse doesn't tolerate bully-boy tactics," Wyre said, ignoring the hand, "as you'll find out."

"Now, now," Yardley replied, "don't leap to conclusions." He took back his hand. "Let's see if we can't get off on a better footing. Them three what entered the tavern after you, two of 'em were Bow Street plain clothes, th' other wuz Palace. Naturally, me and th' Parson concluded you'd brought 'em along for the ride."

"Well, we hadn't," Wyre answered hotly. "Why did you have us traipsing halfway across the city? Was there ever any information, or just a ploy?"

"Depends, dun' it?" Yardley said. "We hear Cooky's bin squealin', the salt-swollen quim – " he stopped, grinning at Miss Crawford " – beggin' yer pardon, miss. Who'd 'av thought, me ol' business partner squeezing me out?"

"Selling you out, more like," put in the Parson. "Both of us."

"What do you know about James Cooke?" Wyre demanded.

"Oh, he wuz in deep, Mr Wyre. Right up the 'ole of the arse. Beggin' yer pardon again . . ." Yardley bowed at Miss Crawford. "The cull's game wuz extortion. Yer can 'ardly blame the Palace fer smiting back."

Wyre gave him an incredulous look. "Are you suggesting

the Palace was involved in the attempt on James Cooke's life?"

Yardley leered. "Who'd yer fink's behind all them Swan men droppin' like flies? Yer friend among 'em . . ."

"Mr Leighton had nothing to do with that den of foxes."

"As yer like it, Mr Wyre. Fact o' the matter is, on account of Cooky bleeding the high-ups, anyone who so much as farted in Vere Street is a marked man now." He pointed at the Parson. "We're obliged t' skulk about the city. What ain't our style at all."

"Any innocent man has nothing to fear. That's how the law works."

"Guilty . . . innocent. Baby terms!" the Parson said contemptuously.

"You take good care tomorrow," Yardley continued slyly. "When a man gets invited to table at th' Palace, he'd better hope he's there as a guest, not part o' the menu."

"Especially if it's a French dish," added the Parson.

"Who told you my business?"

"Wouldn't you rather know who Cooky wuz squeezing?"

Wyre gave him a dry look. "I imagine Sellis was among them."

Yardley looked at the Parson. "Sellis, he says." He turned back. "An' if I told yer Vere Street wuzn't the secret at the heart of the Palace, but th' other way round?"

"I don't care for riddles," Wyre said primly. "If you have a story, tell it to the magistrate."

"Really? How long d'yer think we'd outlive that tale?" He shut one eye meaningfully. "There's a secret ministry of men at St James's, what acts as it fancies."

"Who told you about my secondment to the inquest? I suppose it was Brockton." The toad had gone too far this time.

"Nah, not 'im . . ." Yardley laughed wheezingly. "Their chain of command is wonderful subtle, Mr Wyre. Half of 'em dun't even realize they're in it." He sniffed noisily. "But we'll give yer one identity for nuffink – a slimikin, name of Neale. That's why we invited yer to The Obelisk. Now, yer wouldn't think to look at 'im, but trust us, he's up t' his waterproof beaver-hat's nostrils in it." Yardley ran a grubby sleeve across his nose. "Sellis is nafink in this business, forget what the papers are saying. Nah, if yer really mean all that guff about the law, talk to Neale. Start with that cunt, an' work yer way up." This time, there was no bow to Miss Crawford.

"Playhouse fantasies." Wyre said dismissively. "It was Neale who saved the Duke of Cumberland from his assassin. If you have any serious information, make a clean breast of it. None of the rest is real."

"Not real, he says? Then perhaps he'll tell us where Mr Aspinall may be found."

Miss Crawford froze. "What do you know about Robert?"

Yardley looked amused. "They say two cunning knaves require no broker, don't they, Parson?"

"Get to the point," Wyre said.

"Already told yer. The point's the Palace. Oh, it's a fing of infinite modalities." The powerful-looking man crossed to the latticed windows, and gazed out over the courtyard.

"Where's Aspinall?" Wyre demanded. He repeated it, his voice rising.

Yardley was perfectly calm. "Neale first. Soon as that quim's hanging in chains, missy gets her molly back. Fer all the good it'll do her."

"There's a coup against the Duke," Wyre said. "How do we know you're not part of it?"

"The Duke's a devil," the Parson spat.

Wyre rounded on him. "So you'd add sedition to your crimes?"

"Steady on," said Yardley. "No use blamin' Parson. Got locked in a coal 'ole as a boy, didn't he?" He smiled indulgently. "No, Parson 'ere just wants his White back."

"White?" Wyre frowned. "What's the drummer-boy in this? They're going to hang him, anyway," he added.

The words were pistol slugs to the Parson, who groaned and clutched at his chest.

"That was cruel, Mr Wyre," said Yardley. "Needless cruel."

The Parson rolled his eyes spitefully at Miss Crawford. "Poor Robert Aspinall," he said in sing-song fashion, "caught between the gallows and Bedlam."

Without saying more, the intruders left. The sound of marrow bones clicking on the polished door handle stayed with Wyre long after.

They sat in silence. Twice now, without any thought for her own safety, this delicate-looking woman had tried to protect him. Was he really going to discard her? She turned to him, exquisitely vulnerable, open to the city. Was this a taste of Leighton's world?

"I should go, Mr Wyre. I'm sorry for what happened."

"Wait," he said. A pause. "I don't trust those thugs. I'll get my coat, accompany you home."

She bowed her head in a manner he thought grateful. But he had less idea than ever what to make of her.

The air above the pavements was hot and sweet. They walked along marble crescents and shining terraces as street lamps were being lit. Miss Crawford's pelisse brushed his sleeve. What Rose would call walking snug.

It wasn't far, the dark woman assured him; but not far had to be reached via dubious districts where commodious new limestone residences ceded to older brick-and-timber buildings, to dark taverns and torch-lit theatres, and from there to zones of lickspit frippers, where punks and harridans yowled from alleyways, banshee lines of communication that always seemed to outpace them.

"Great Windmill Street," said the lawyer, stopping with a frown. "It's along there, isn't it?" He glanced into a tight side street.

Miss Crawford clutched his sleeve. "The night Robert was arrested, he was forced to leave something in that awful house. I promised I'd recover it. It won't take long."

What? Tamper with evidence?

"It won't take long," she repeated. She turned and, going up on tip-toe, brushed her lips against his cheek.

He stared back mutely. Is this what Best meant by pretty eyes?

Vere Street was a narrowish lane running above Clare Market. Wide enough to admit a coach, but the over-hanging galleries made it feel more constrained than it was. They stopped at a dark, three-storey façade. The first two levels were brick, the upper one half-timbered. Three different-sized bays protruded from the roof, rising to uneven peaks. The tavern's sign arm was empty, but Wyre didn't doubt they were standing outside London's most notorious address. The White Swan's lower windows were all broken, stopped with sheets of newspaper. Two slops of white paint above the lintel revoked the inn-keeper's license. Crude slogans had been daubed across the tavern's frontage – scrawled beneath a grotesquely distended yard that was half-buried in a coarse approximation of a rump was the name *Ass-pinall*. He winced. No woman should have to think of such things.

He looked at her. "Are you quite sure?"

"I promised I would."

Wyre rapped on the oak door. He was about to knock again when they heard shootbolts being coaxed back. A freckled face appeared in the gap.

"Both of you together?" The tavern madam opened the door wider, revealing unlit depths; a waft of gin fumes escaped. "Or has one of you come to watch?"

"We're not here for that," Miss Crawford answered with surprising gentleness. "One of your guests left something here."

"They all do, love." The beginnings of a ribald smile, which must have come easily once, ghosted her lips. She tugged at her shift, which was sheer enough to leave nothing to the imagination (Wyre tried to ignore the dark shadow below her waist). "The Charlies took everything that wasn't nailed down, but if it's still here, you're welcome to it."

They stepped into a clammy passage. Damp and smelly, like the service tunnel. The tap-room was a slovenly mess. On the unswept floor, between two overturned tables, lay a dirty grey mattress, slit open like a gullet.

"He can do me in the arse, if he likes," the landlady said plaintively, touching Miss Crawford's sleeve. "It wouldn't cost extra."

The dark woman didn't say anything, but proceeded through the tap-room, seemingly knowing where to go. Wyre followed her, dried bluebells crumbling to powder under his feet, to a back staircase. It rose, dog-legging, to a narrow corridor, along one side of which sepulchral recesses gaped, all – obscenely – without doors. More of the grey, stained mattresses within. Miss Crawford, however, was studying the glass lanterns set at intervals into the wall. She counted off three, then, looking across at Wyre, lifted her foot for what children would call a bunk-up. He laced his fingers obligingly. Stepping on, she pressed herself against the dusty bricks, and hooked her arm over an empty muntin, reaching into the cavity. (Wyre felt intimate shifts of weight through his palms.) With a little cry of triumph, she stepped down, clutching a black quarto notebook.

When she spoke, her voice was so quiet it seemed to come from one of the shameful lofts themselves. "The inmates at Wood's Close entertain strange fantasies. Some imagine themselves made of clockwork. These poor souls threaten no one but themselves." Her fingers tightened around the notebook's leather covers. "But there was one patient who was different in every respect." Her breath seemed to catch in her throat. "Robert told me there wasn't a man in England he'd consider safe in that lunatic's presence."

Wyre frowned. "Was this patient in your fiancé's care?"

"At first, yes. During that period, I hardly saw Robert. He was convinced he'd stumbled on an undiscovered ailment of the brain, and laboured every hour at its explication. He coined a term, 'double character', and said publication of his notes would cause an upheaval in the medical world. But the case took a terrible toll. It emptied him out." She pulled her top lip under her teeth in a desolate fashion. "When, after a month of treatment, a senior physician assumed all responsibility for the case, I confess it was to my relief."

"That 'senior physician' would be Ellesmere, I suppose."

She nodded.

Wyre frowned. "I assume this patient is still locked up at Wood's Close. We could request an interview. He might know something. About your fiancé's whereabouts, I mean. It's worth a try." There were no other leads, he didn't say.

"That was the strangest thing, Mr Wyre. There was no

formal committal. Whoever this man was, he was free to come and go as he pleased."

Wyre thought for a moment. "Much as I dislike Ellesmere, it sounds as if his intervention was justified."

"Robert was furious at having his patient taken from him." Miss Crawford brought her other palm down on the notebook's dark cover, trapping it like some large, black insect. "But the loss merely strengthened his resolve. He told me he already had enough to guarantee the attention of his peers. These are his notes, Mr Wyre." She held out the book. "They are his only consolation. He believes when the public sees what he was labouring at, they will understand why he set foot in this awful place, and his reputation will be repaired."

Wyre doubted that. He took the book from her, feeling a little pull before her fingers released. Limp, well-worn vellum covers, with a name, *R. Aspinall*, tooled in gilt. He opened it. The sight caused his breath to hiss between his teeth. That flowing hand – identical to the one that had recorded those wicked descriptions in the loose page that fluttered to his feet in Leighton's apartment. How the devil had Leighton come by a page of Aspinall's case notes? He felt a second chill flash along his limbs – the man Miss Crawford's fiancé had been treating was the misrule at the centre of the plot to murder the Duke of Cumberland. Aspinall's patient had been Mr Parlez-Vous.

Struggling to control his trembling fingers, he turned to the first entry. It was dated 27 November 1809. Even to a psychological amateur, Aspinall's staccato observations clearly plotted a mind utterly lost to reason. That such a creature might even now be dressing a Duke!

Mechanics of the release of seminal fluid a monomania. No improvement here!!

Nakedness a spur only when coupled with distress.
*

Exists on a continuum????
Tremendous potential to violence over time. Repeated dreams of slicing living flesh.
*

Massa confusa!!
Claims God is a hare or snake.
*

Proclaims diversity is a unity.
Believes Christ is a suspended spider.
*

Claims to have eaten human κόλυθροι.

Wyre could guess what lay beneath the Greek characters. The notes went on like this for pages and pages. Near the back, he found a jagged stub of margin. He was sure it would match up perfectly with Leighton's torn-out leaf. With staring eyes, he returned the volume to Miss Crawford, who clutched it to her breast as if it contained a set of wedding vows.

"The lunatic described here," he said, trying to control his breath. "Do you know his name?" It would be better to have Aspinall, but the mad-doctor's notebook might be enough to give the case what William called its lights.

"Robert wouldn't divulge it. He was forbidden."

That hope dashed, new, uncomfortable thoughts began to form in Wyre's head. Leighton must have known all along that Parlez-Vous had murdered Thomas in Crispin Street, known he'd been the one who'd taken a hammer to the fly. And he'd said nothing. Wyre thought back to that most calm, most collected voice in his ear. Would he recognize it again if he heard it at St James's? His life might depend on it. With Leighton gone, the only person

Wyre knew for certain could identify the assassin was Robert Aspinall, and he was a ghost. Well, there was always Ashcroft and Ellesmere, but he doubted they could be induced to give up their patient. Besides, he didn't trust either man to give a straight answer to anything. Even Ellesmere's horticultural practice seemed to be an allegory.

No, time was short and the Palace was the place. It was time to try the strength of his own wings. He'd do it for Leighton's sake, and for the Duke's, and – he was honest enough to admit – for his own. God's mills would grind, but there was no bread yet.

He followed Miss Crawford and the half-dressed landlady down again. If anything was clear, it was the importance of preserving a channel of communication with Miss Crawford. If the inquest failed to turn up a Parlez-Vous, her bendyman fiancé was the Duke's best chance. Some way would have to be found to combine both lines of investigation.

Theatre-goers, sensation-seekers, punks and their reeling swads formed a ceaseless tide along Vere Street's uneven pavements. Wyre was about to step into the hum and bustle, when Miss Crawford turned to press a coin into the landlady's dirty fingers. The woman's mouth formed a tragic, absurd O, her eyes pits. Wyre almost pitied the sordid collapse – until Miss Crawford leaned forward, and kissed her lightly on the cheek. Those fine, dark lips next to that sensuous maw!

A short walk brought them to Great Windmill Street, an out-at-elbows district of broken flagstones and transoms minus half their fanlights. Miss Crawford's lodgings lay above a bakery. At the bottom of her dark, cast-iron steps, tucked away at the side of the building, she drew a banknote from her skirts.

"Your fee, Mr Wyre."

A heavy dray, laden with barrels, thundered by.

He held up the note. Ten guineas, to be drawn on a Bath and Wells bank. His eyes met hers. "Shall we consider it a retainer instead? If, that is, you still wish me to take Robert's case."

She gripped both his hands, the gesture both tender and urgent. But no kiss on the cheek for him. They agreed the moment she received any news of Aspinall, she would write to Wyre at St James's, care of the old bird, Mr Read.

"If you're sure it won't impinge." Her voice was barely audible now.

The lawyer made his way back to Mrs Mason's apartment, those three elements – The White Swan, Wood's Close, St James's Palace – circling each other now in his imagination in a strange tableau where a white bird beat up through a beech copse against a bleak façade.

3.

JACKADANDIES

41. The Penetralium

Wyre woke in sodden sheets, his breath coming in hot gasps. He thought of St Lawrence on his gridiron, braising sweet and black. The day's slow burn had already begun ... Leighton! It sunk in all over again, the loss of what his friend used to call, jokingly, their double singleness. Groaning, he reached for his watch, a wedding gift from Rose. The dial showed an enamelled river scene with a picturesque bridge; if only he could dive into its suburban cool. Half past eight. He was due at the Palace in an hour. Throwing on his best legal-blue jacket, grabbing his leather bag, he dashed downstairs, wheeling out Leighton's dandy-charger from the foyer.

After teetery beginnings, blue bag slung over his back on its shoulder strap, Wyre got along tolerably well (the action *was* like skating). Wobbling to a halt at the bottom of St James's Street, he dismounted in front of an enormous crowd that had gathered there. It craned collectively for news, generating what, in the fashionable way of speaking, would be called a tumult of mighty harmonies, while above the mob waved a forest of placards, many of them advertising sectish sentiments. A balloonist floating with the whole city beneath his feet might see the fluid bedlam on the ground as a choreographed show, beautifully silent.

Wyre pushed his hobby horse through the unruly crowd, the Palace's twin octagonal turrets looming, their red-brick gothic filigrees somehow managing to be both grand and childish. A row of high shuttered windows gave the appearance of gun ports: he imagined them opening, cannon muzzles being nudged out to deliver a broadside onto the commoners below.

On the cobbles ahead, a brown straw figure dressed in crude approximation of a royal livery crackled into wayward sparks, and he heard the faithless valet Sellis denounced as a smut-ball, frenchified molly, Tyrant's henchman, extorter, cuckolded husband and escaped lunatic. A gamut of possibilities. In the middle of the throng, a hooded man sat hunched over two jangling wooden figurines, evidently meant to represent Sellis and the Duke of Cumberland. The valet's marionette, his hair an ominous slick, brandished a sabre in time to the other's fiddle.

The puppet gazed up balefully as Wyre drew level. "Remember wot you are. Eyes yer may 'av, but they see not. Ears yer may 'av, but they hear not. Speak yer may, but not a word more than is set down for yer."

Wyre pushed on, arriving at a makeshift cordon. The postings there regarded his cries of 'Courthouse' with rehearsed scepticism, eying his yellow running machine dubiously. Eventually, one of the swads lowered his firelock and waved a languid finger for him to pass.

Best had done his bit. He was in.

He trundled the running machine beneath a low arch. Suddenly, an insulating silence seemed to hang over everything. Liveried manservants moved about the grounds on flagstone paths like gorgeous high-stepping birds.

Someone was waving from a porched recess atop a narrow flight of steps . . . a nattily dressed man with oiled hair. Wyre went over.

"Mr Paulet," the man on the steps explained, as he reached the bottom of the steps, "valet to his Royal Highness the Duke of Cumberland. You're to come with me, sir. Mr Read's waiting." He smiled good-naturedly. "Some find the layout of St James's something befuddling." He pointed at the dandy-charger. "I'll find someone to take it to the stables."

Wyre followed Paulet along passages lined with tapestries; most of them rang the changes on hunting and allegorical scenes – hunters cornering a stag, peasants watching in a horseshoe as a boar was speared. It was the peasants' thinly stitched limbs, rather than the doomed animal itself, that evoked the fraying openness of the living body. In a couple of places, Wyre caught a whiff of caramelized wood. He remembered last year's lurid newsrag reports: sections of lead roof descending in liquid torrents, maids forced to flee in their petticoats.

"Almost there, sir," Paulet said over his shoulder, opening a yellow baize door to reveal a modest-sized ballroom. As the valet led Wyre across an expanse of sprung parquet, he crooked his left arm, exaggerating the bounce, playing the chaperone of some debutante or steely marchioness.

A blonde-haired, chignoned woman was arranging flowers along the window bank in a colourful transposition of the natural world. Shapely, dressed in a pale green dress, she worked confidently, none of the self-effacing mien of a servant. Her lips were rosy, astonishingly so, but the effect against her ice-white face was disturbing. Her blue eyes gleamed with an intensity he'd encountered only in felons convinced they were blameless. Two little girls, their hair up in yellow ringlets, played at her feet.

"This is Mrs Neale, sir," Paulet said, as they drew near. He stopped, and waved at the children. "She's awful good with blooms. She's been teaching her maid, Margaret, some of her tricks. Between them they'll soon brighten the place up."

Neale? This must be the wife of the Duke's man, the hero of the hour. *Up to his beaver hat in it*, Yardley had claimed. There was a blemish under the woman's right eye, which she'd evidently tried to conceal beneath a shimmer of paint. A birthmark or rash, perhaps a bruise.

"The flowers are for the King's birthday, Mr Paulet. We're doing what we can to raise the spirits of the house."

"It could do with a lift . . ." Paulet clucked his tongue, "everything that's happened." He gave the children another little wave. "This is Mr Wyre," he pantomimed with his lips. "He's helping Mr Read with his investy-gations."

Mrs Neale took her hands from the spikes and sprays of her window tray, wiping off nothing on her apron. She was what Rose's conduct books described as poised.

"The sooner things return to how they were, Mr Paulet. The Duke raised a cuckoo in Joseph Sellis."

"His Highness was duped like the rest of us."

They set off again. The matching baize door at the other end opened onto a short stretch of corridor, which in turn led to an antechamber and two adjacent three-quarter-sized doors. Paulet indicated the left one.

"Valet's Room, sir," he announced. He rapped sharply, cocked his head, rapped again.

Hands clasped behind his back, jacket heavy at the cuffs, leather blue-bag at his feet . . . the man standing at the empty hearth was Bow Street embodied, a man of the old stamp. So this was Leighton's 'old bird', Mr Read. He must have been on the cusp of the grand climacteric, but still looked vigorous. Powerfully built, too.

"No need for introductions," the Chief Magistrate began, eying Wyre with obvious suspicion. "The Secretary of State's office has been in touch. Friends don't come much higher." He smiled without warmth. "Best must have been itching to get one of his men in place. Have to say, I was expecting Cavendish."

Wyre swallowed the slight. "Is this where Sellis's body was found, sir?"

Read scowled. "Don't worry, we'll get to the carcass in a minute. This is where the on-duty man, Neale, slept that night."

The Valet's Room was narrow, with an unusual coffered wooden ceiling and fireplace almost comically too large for the space. Apart from a hanging portrait of a queer-looking figure in a hat, the walls were unadorned. The bed was wooden-framed and ascetic; an ugly nail stuck out from one of the bedposts, bent in the middle from being badly knocked in. Someone didn't know their job. There was a desk with a hinged, leather-lined writing flap, a bedside table and a tallow lamp. That was it. A functional room.

Gules of light from the single window caught in the net of fine floating dust.

Wyre's eyes were drawn back to the portrait. Something was off. The sitter was decked out in a woman's full crimped coiffure, but finished with a gentleman's broad-brimmed feathered hat. It was left to a pair of breasts – improbably high – to put the question beyond doubt.

Read was watching with a bemused expression. "Let's drop this nonsense. What's Best up to?"

Wyre decided to keep things formal. "The Courthouse has intelligence pointing to a second attempt on the Duke's life. Even assuming the papers are right about Sellis's guilt, there may be an accomplice who – "

"Even assuming?" Read's eyes had narrowed to slots. "The evidence is plain."

"Mr Best's in possession of a manservant's note informing on a drummer-boy. It's signed 'Mr Parlez-Vous'."

Read snorted. "Some molly footman who saw a chance to dispose of a rival."

"Or part of a wider plot . . . According to the papers, the Duke himself told Mr Neale he feared a second assassin was concealed in his chamber."

"Forget the claptrap you read in the rags. Sellis was working alone." He sighed irritably. "We'd all have preferred it if Sellis had been taken alive. A public execution draws a line under things. Instead – " he jerked his thumb savagely at the window " – we've got a mob at the gate, shrugging itself up into a frenzy. It's like the fucking Bastille all over again. Everyone from clerics and shoemakers to revolutionary Goldilocks ventilating opinions." He rounded on Wyre. "Just see you don't add to it."

"Sir, one of your own agents, Mr Leighton, confided to me shortly before he died – "

"Leighton?" Read scowled. "Yes, I've heard you two were acquainted. Sorry to be the one to break the news, but the man was cracked. Did you ever consider that?"

Wyre couldn't let that pass. "When I last saw him, he seemed perfectly reasonable."

Read's lips formed a cold smile. "Madness often wears the mask of sanity. Have you ever heard of anyone volunteering to work as a fly? What, he didn't tell you? That's right, your friend was a jampot."

Wyre pressed his lips together. Just minutes into their first meeting, and their bearing had already hardened into mutual unease. "Mr Leighton thought Sellis a cog in a larger wheel. Shouldn't we at least consider the possibility?"

"Giff-gaff!" Read exploded. "Sellis was working alone. The empiricals prove it. You can't hide the sun in a sieve." He glared at Wyre. "Who'd you rather believe, me or some sodomite fantasist?"

212

"He wasn't a – "

Read waved his hand as if Wyre's objection was patently specious. "Let's not do the Corsican's work for him."

Charged silence. He needed to get things back on an even keel, or his time at St James's would be fruitless.

"You mentioned empiricals, sir."

"That's right. The first being that Joseph Sellis was a foreign lover of arseholes. That's what the maids think, and they're usually right about such things." He glared again. "The real scandal here was appointing the dog-fox as a royal valet in the first place. That was on the negligent side of careless. Did you know his family was gifted an apartment on the upper floors? Think anyone else got that treatment? Cumberland himself stood godfather to Sellis's fourth bastard, christened Ernest Augustus."

"The Duke's own name," Wyre said, more to himself than to Read.

"Fine way to repay his Highness." Read sniffed.

"Why would a favoured man behave in that way?"

"Weren't you listening? His wife claims he was from Sardinia, but members of the royal household say he was whelped in Corsica, Boney's own turd of an island."

Read stepped from the hearth, presenting an unimpeded view of the absurdly over-proportioned marble fireplace. Behind the dog-iron was a back plate that depicted the Sussex Protestant martyrs chained together, half-relief. Talk about desiccated humour. If the fire was meant to be their portal into paradise, it had trapped them in hell. On the far right was an old man, hands clasped in prayer, his face angled to heaven, shedding silver tears that glistened in the soot.

"Has Sellis's wife been interviewed?"

"She's on the list. We have depositions from half a dozen servants who, incidentally, agree on all the particulars.

Neale's account, too. Naturally, I started with that." Read stretched his chin clear of his collars. "First man at the scene. Hero of the hour."

Hesitantly, Wyre said, "Does his version accord with the Duke's statement?"

Read's expression darkened. "The Duke's statement? Damn it, man, Cumberland's recovering from an insult to the brain. I haven't spoken to him. Not officially."

Wyre was unable to hide his surprise. "I'm sorry, sir. It's just from the newspaper reports, I assumed you had."

Read looked uncomfortable. "Blame the attending constables. Or somebody bribed a servant. Word gets around quickly in a place like this." He pulled at his cuffs. "The inquest jury convenes on Friday. Yes, I know it's tight, but if you don't like it, take it up with the Court of Royal Verge. Besides, there's more than enough time to collect the remaining affidavits, if you don't drag things out unnecessarily. Cumberland's included, before you ask. His Highness wants this business put to rest as much as we do." The whitest flight of spittle landed on the magistrate's sleeve. "Anyway, what's to decide? Sellis's carcass was found in his apartment on the other side of the palace, where he'd fled after taking his master's own sabre to him. Both doors to the cull's private room were secured from the inside. The bastard slit his own throat when he heard guards at the door." He wiped his forehead with a dark blue handkerchief. "We found his slippers in one of the closets at the back of his Highness's bedchamber. Holy blood, man, the traitorous fucker's name was sewn into them."

As tactfully as he could, Wyre said, "Actually, sir, I wanted to ask about the slippers."

"Christ! Come and see them for yourself," Read thundered. They're exactly where we found them."

Wyre went after the magistrate. The door adjacent to the one to the Valet's Room led into a narrow passageway, which ran diagonally for some yards.

"You're about to enter Cumberland's bedchamber," Read said over his shoulder, stopping. "Don't worry, the Duke moved his sleeping quarters after the assault. We have the run of the place."

The Duke's room was tastefully, and expensively, furnished: a gilt wardrobe inlaid with ivory birds, a glossy table with fluted legs, an enormous sofa with velvet cushions. A mahogany hand-organ stood in one corner. Light streamed in through a bank of high, latticed windows. The royal couch itself was set into a deep alcove, lined with handsome cabinet wood.

"If a bed could tell tales, eh?" Read said, with a hint of the tavern.

If he'd understood the spatial lay-out, the Valet's Room must lie directly behind it, sharing the wall. Wyre leaned across the bed to give the partition a stiff rap – a hollow report confirmed the wafer thinness.

"Jesus wept, those are his Highness's silk sheets. Come on, the closets are this way."

At the back of the royal bedchamber was an antechamber containing three closets. The magistrate opened the middle cubbyhole, revealing a space just large enough to conceal a man. On a shoulder-high shelf stood a round dark-lantern, and on the floor a pair of crimson Arab slippers, looking as if someone had just stepped out of them.

Read scowled. "This is where Sellis waited for the Duke to nod off."

"Are you certain the slippers are his?"

Read beetled his eyebrows. "Whose side are you on?"

"Doesn't it strike you as a strange thing to do, sir? Removing your slippers to kill a man."

What he wanted to say was that inferring a killer from a pair of slippers was tantamount to starting with a verdict then working backwards to find the supporting facts. That was a tyrant's jurisprudence.

Grunting, Read bent to retrieve one of the slippers. "See, those are his initials." He handed it to the lawyer.

The extravagant slippers were leather, not silk as *The Chronicle* claimed. The ornate monogram itself was based around two letters, *J.S.* Wyre had a sudden vision of Mrs Sellis stitching devotedly at initials destined to become the very abbreviation of treason.

"May I ask who found them?"

"Mr Neale," Read said briskly.

"Has Sellis's wife confirmed these are her husband's slippers?"

Read looked warily at the lawyer.

"Sorry, sir, but I'm not sure they'd convince a Courthouse jury."

Read glared at him for a moment, then the damn broke. "Listen here, I couldn't give a tinker's toss how you wheedled your way into this investigation, or whose yard you polished, but just so you're aware, Best isn't the only one who can pull strings."

Someone a-hemmed behind them, a stout man with pronounced wings of greying hair.

42. Depositions

"Mr Adams, Coroner at the Court of Royal Verge," the man spoke, as he offered a pudgy hand. Shaking it, Wyre imagined how the radical Thelwall must have felt on being arrested by Walsh, forced to yield to system.

Adams turned to Read. "The surgeons appear to have

finished fighting over who gets custody of Sellis's bones. I'd be grateful if we could discuss the remainder of the inquest schedule. His Majesty is obliged if the jury could convene half a day earlier."

A deep furrow formed above the bridge of Read's nose. He reached into his blue-bag, drawing out a sheaf of documents, which he pushed at Wyre. "Digest these," he said. "Mr Adams and I have a few things to discuss."

While Read stepped outside with the Coroner, Wyre took a seat at the Duke's shiny table. He leafed through the legal vellums till he found Neale's statement. So, what did the Duke's shining white knight have to say for himself?

Deposition of Cornelius Neale, Valet to his Royal Highness the Duke of Cumberland,

Who, being on his oath, says he attended his Royal Highness to bed last night at about twelve o'clock; and after his Royal Highness had passed the yellow room, which he always does when he goes to bed, the informant shut the door and is very sure he locked it, and afterwards remained in the Duke's room until his Royal Highness had got into bed. No other person was in the room. The informant then went to bed in the valet-in-waiting's room adjoining the Duke's bedroom.

While he was in bed, a little before twelve o'clock, the informant heard his Royal Highness call out "Neale! Neale! I am murdered!" On which he got out of bed and met the Duke of Cumberland at the door. His Royal Highness declared the murderer was still in his bedroom. The informant says he seized a poker, and ran towards the yellow room, seeing the door, which he had locked before going to bed, wide open. He immediately stood on a naked sword lying on the floor. He took up the sword and asked leave of his Royal Highness to pursue the assassin, but his Royal Highness desired that he should not. His Royal Highness then leaned on the informant's arm, and they went together to the porter's room. The porter was ordered by his Royal Highness not to allow any person to leave the house. They then returned to the Duke's bedchamber and, on going downstairs, met Mrs Neale, whom his Royal Highness desired to summon Mr Sellis.

His Royal Highness, faint from loss of blood, lay down on his bed. He would not allow any of his wounds to be examined until the arrival of his surgeon. Instead, he desired the informant to look for the assassin, to find where he could have been concealed prior to the attack. The informant opened the door at the foot of the bed leading to a small room that has three closets. In the second of these, the informant found a pair of leather slippers with the name Sellis written in each; also a dark lantern. At this time, Mr Jackson arrived and the informant assisted him in binding up the Duke's wounds.

CORNELIUS NEALE. Sworn before me, John Read.

Wyre skimmed back over the document to find the bit about Neale's wife. So Neale was claiming *she'd* been sent to rouse Sellis. In *The Chronicle*'s fugitive account, hadn't Neale himself been assigned that task? It was a small detail, but most details were. That's why they were details. He turned, sensing Read at his shoulder.

"It seems we're working to a tighter schedule now," the magistrate said gruffly. "But it doesn't change things. The crux of the matter – " he pointed at Neale's deposition " – is right there in front of you."

Wyre looked at him. "Sir, Neale deposes his wife was dispatched to Sellis's private room. In the newspapers – "

Read rode over him. "We go by the official interview, not some news rat's fantasy." He pulled again at his tight collars. "Right, if you want to see Sellis, you'd better get a move on. He's not getting any fresher."

Leaving the Duke's bedroom, Wyre followed Read through a bewildering succession of chambers, ante-chambers and connecting halls, which the magistrate negotiated with the sureness of a trained retainer. Wyre spotted Mr Paulet in one of the long corridors: he was perched on a high ladder, unhooking a casement. The valet waved down at them, earning a tut from Read.

Fifty paces further along, they passed a flight of stairs leading off, which ended abruptly with a marble-effect door that looked as if it had been dropped from above. A heavy-set man was standing to loose attention beside it, a blue hat slouched forward over his eyes. He winked at Wyre. Leighton's world again.

When they'd moved on, Read anticipated Wyre's question. "Leads up to the Duke of York's tower. Lives there with his family. We're not to disturb him." He lowered his voice. "The maids tell me Princess Amelia is at death's door. York's half-mad with anticipated grief."

A wide corridor brought them into what Wyre assumed was the far wing. They climbed up to the second floor, where Cumberland's "cosseted favourites" lived, "all grace-and-favour", as Read put it. "The others," he added, "kitchen maids and such like, share the dormitories below. Breathing in each other's farts all night." He laughed unpleasantly.

Wyre paused at a narrow, unlit corridor that intersected the main passageway from the left.

"One of those bloody dog-legs," said the magistrate. "It goes down to the maids' little dens. Keeps them out of sight till they're called. Loops round, apparently, but I've not been all the way."

Wyre poked his head into the gloomy tunnel, immediately

hearing that perfectly calm voice at his ear. *Have a care.* He stepped back, heart hammering.

Read watched with a quizzical expression that said it all.

The carpeted passage widened out into a saloon or antechamber, empty save for a mahogany table and two high-backed chairs. The lacquered door at the far end had been forced; ugly splinters of wood protruded around the hanging lock.

"Come on," Read muttered, giving the door a push, "let's get it over with."

Sellis's body was stretched out on a plain, narrowish bed, with what looked like a badly tied crimson cravat at his throat. Wyre's stomach jumped, but he kept its contents down.

Two men were locked in discussion at the single latticed window in Sellis's off-duty bedchamber. They both turned. Wyre stared in mute surprise, recognizing the spectacled surgeon who just hours earlier had pronounced on Leighton's remains. Did Mr Cline make a habit of attending suicides? Of course he did. Self-murderers automatically belonged to the hospitals. But weren't they jumping the gun? The inquest jury hadn't pronounced its verdict yet.

A thought occurred to him: those scoundrels who took Leighton's body, they'd delivered him straight to the anatomy room! Wyre hadn't thought to ask, his intellect dulled by grief. The idea of Mr Cline's fingers inside his friend . . .

Surgeon Cline approached, and introduced himself to the lawyer as if the pair hadn't already met. Wyre found himself giving his name awkwardly in turn.

Before he could say anything else, the other man spoke.

"Mr Jackson, Royal Surgeon at St James's Palace. Pleased tae make yer acquaintance, sairrr." He had a disagreeable visage, pocked cheeks surrounded by flaming locks, the model of a Scotsman. The air around him smelled of cinnamon and acrid eucalyptus. "If you'd care tae gie our traitor a final ance over," he said briskly, waving at the corpse, "we'll arrange tae have custody transferred tae Mr Cline."

Wyre nodded, and moved warily to the corpse. The gaping wound in Sellis's throat had two pronounced lips, lumps of something waxy discernible between them. He'd been prepared for a slit throat, but this was practically a decollation. A sheet of coagulated blood had formed over the valet's shirt; a pellicle of blue pearls shimmered dully on the surface. The picture was completed by a dark, gelatinous pool of blood and mucus, which had soaked into the pillow.

Sellis's face was strangely placid, as if he were only practising death, like a Tibetan. Wyre paused at the palms, which lay flat and clean, facing the ceiling. How could a man cut his throat without fouling his hands?

It was difficult to estimate the valet's height. Five and a half feet, at a best guess; certainly low-sized. Sodomy stunted physical as well as moral growth. As for his age, not above thirty. Dark hair, olive skin, regular features. Handsome, even now.

Sellis's jacket, trousers and gaiters hung smartly over the back of a chair at the foot of the bed.

To the rear of the off-duty bedroom was one of those washstands with the out-swept legs. Beside the enamel bowl, which was heavily soiled with blood, lay a pearl-handled razor, neatly folded up. The oval shaving mirror was splashed with dried drops of blood, each of the spatters given a gloomy twin by the silvered glass.

Read turned to Cline, and grinned unpleasantly. "What do you say to our freak of nature?"

The surgeon regarded him with evenly. "An interesting choice of words. *Lusus naturae* come in many guises." He adjusted the bright ribbon that held up his spectacles, undoing them on one side. "I once heard of an infant boy, in all other respects apparently normal, who at eighteen months began to vomit. About that time, his abdomen developed a large protrusion. The boy's mother sought advice, to no avail. Two years later he was brought to me. By that time, the poor fellow was little more than a skeleton. On examining him I was able to palpate a detached tumour. He died within six weeks." Cline retied the ribbon into a bow. "Postmortem inspection revealed a cystic cavity filled with fluid not dissimilar to green tea – and floating inside was a foetus." The surgeon pulled the pretty ends tight. "For the duration of his short life, the lad had been carrying his own brother."

Cline's hands were small, eerily beautiful. Girl's hands.

"Such monsters don't exist," Read said bluffly.

"Oh, they do, Mr Read. God is most considerate in this regard."

"Considerate?"

"Indeed. Such cases give men of my profession a perfect opportunity to expand their knowledge. I assure you, the poor boy excited as much attention among surgeons as Bonaparte's movements that season." He smiled at the gathering. "Postmortem, or I suppose in the boy's case, postpartum investigation is essential to the advancement of real learning. Who knows what dissection of Sellis will reveal?"

"I'd prefer to see him quartered as a dish for dogs." Read sniffed savagely. "Anyway, sooner the foreign bastard's off the premises, the better. But before you cart him away, perhaps we could hear Mr Jackson's opinion on the cause of death. For the benefit of our Courthouse representative," he added, glancing sourly at Wyre.

"Hardly an enigma, Mr Reid," the Royal Surgeon said, lifting a bushy red eyebrow, "even tae the untutored. The cause was a single, self-administered wound tae th' throat, five or a scuttle inches wide, inch-and-a-half deep. Both carotid arteries sliced clean through. It would hae bin impossible tae staunch such a wound."

"And the instrument of destruction?"

"Only a razor could hae produced such a clean cut." Jackson pulled his lips forward into an tight circle, as if about to whistle a tune.

"Such as that found at his bedside?" Read said in the courtroom style. He cast a glance over at the washstand.

Jackson nodded.

"You concur, Mr Cline?"

"Diagnostically speaking ..." Cline moved to Sellis's side, resting a hand on the dead man's shoulder as if comforting a sick patient. "My esteemed colleagues in Saxony would no doubt speak of an arterial miasm."

"Rogues and rupture-healers," Jackson muttered.

"Let us say, then," Cline continued with a private smile, "that the fellow died from a morbid derangement of the vital force. I think we can all agree on that."

Wyre coughed tactfully. "Is it feasible Sellis could have produced such a deep wound with his own hand?"

Jackson's lips dilated. "Depth is nae obstacle tae a verdict ay suicide, Mr Wyre. The cut was made exactly between the hyoid bone an' the larynx, a weak point in the integuments. The incision extends through the pharynx, almost touching th' spinal column itself, but wi' a firm hain an' determination ay purpose, it's possible tae achieve. I've seen larger wounds inflicted by th' hands of suicides."

"But the evenness of the cut – "

223

"It would be a rude stroke ay reason tae suppose the signature ay a biathanate injury in the throat tae be irregularity frae want ay steadiness in th' hand. In that final act, suicides ur aft the calmest ay folk. The wound's regularity provides nae presumptive evidence ay homicide."

"Well, there it is," Read said, adding, in a blither tone, "I spotted a hulking fellow this morning down at the stables. Big as two men." He winked at the surgeons. "Imagine him in a clinch with one of the sulky little maids you see scampering around here. What a race of Titans might be spawned. Assuming the brute didn't split her in two."

Cline brushed something from his sleeve. "It's often believed when a female is put out with a much larger male the breed is automatically improved. The truth with animals and humans alike is that the offspring is typically of an imperfect form." He caught Read's expression. "Oh, yes, Mr Read. When it was the fashion in London to drive large bay horses, farmers in Yorkshire put their mares to much larger stallions than usual. The mischief to the breed was considerable, producing a race of small-chested, long-legged, worthless creatures. Curiously enough, if the female is proportionally larger than the male, the offspring is generally improved."

"Either way," Read said with a snort, "Sellis was a runt."

"Just as well for the Duke he was," Cline replied, miming a scything motion that began its arc high and descended with surprising rapidity.

Read gave him an incredulous look.

Wyre crossed to the washstand. The razor's white handle was smeared with congealed blood. "Was the basin found in this state?"

"Exactly in that fashion," Read replied, frowning.

"The scoundrel was attempting to wash the Duke's blood from his hands when they arrived at his door." He looked distastefully at the bowl. "Royal blood, that is. Someone ought to clean it up."

"And the razor, was it found like this, folded beside the wash basin? I'm just wondering how Sellis could have closed the blade after administering such a wound to his own neck?"

Read's lips twitched. "As a matter of fact it was discovered lying open on the floor, a little way from the bed. One of my constables picked it up by mistake, closed it and set it on the wash table. Don't fret," he said, sullenly. "He's been reprimanded."

Cline's lips formed an amused smile.

Wyre crossed to the small door at the rear of Sellis's private bedchamber. From what he remembered, *The Chronicle* claimed the door was fastened from the inside. He turned the handle, which yielded, opening into a passageway immediately lost in shadows. Wyre peered into the gloom – was it part of the side alleys Read had referred to? The lawyer turned his attention to the locking mechanism, an intricate system of inter-connected rods and levers, then stepped out into the passageway, closing the door behind him. Through the door he heard Read's muffled tones; he could guess what the Chief Magistrate was saying. He tried the handle again – as he expected, it was immoveable. Wyre rapped to be let back in.

Read glared at him. "I assume there was a point to all that."

"The lock, sir. It engages whenever the door shuts." He opened the rear door and closed it again, holding his finger up at the precise point when the spring snapped to.

Read looked unimpressed.

"The back door to Sellis's room wasn't fastened from the inside that night, sir. Not on purpose, anyway, and certainly not to keep someone out. It would just have seemed that way to anyone unfamiliar with the mechanism. Even Sellis would have needed a key when he entered his room this way."

"What's the difference?" says Read. "We're wasting precious time."

"It means the door needn't be taken as a sign of guilt."

"Christ, Wyre," the magistrate said testily, "we don't need a treatise on locks. Come on, we're finished here."

Wyre bowed at the surgeons, and followed his superior out.

As they traversed the antechamber, Read growled, "Don't you ever show me up like that again."

Wyre said nothing, but looked straight ahead. On the stairs, his thoughts turned to the lad made monstrous by his brother.

43. Fairy Tales

He remembered always demanding the same story from his nurse, the one where the queen begs for a cloth to be pinned to her caul at the block. He liked the bit where the crowd jeered as the executioner raised his axe best. The way his nurse told it, the head went with a lovely sickening thump and a little roll, followed by a slice of blood.

A long pause. The royal skirts begin to heave and tremble.

"What tricks are these?" says the executioner, stepping back, stumbling due to the weight of the axe. Curiosity overcoming dread, he pokes about in the Queen's garters with his foot . . . and there under her petticoats is Geddon her pet terrier. The executioner takes another swing of his axe, dividing the animal in two.

"And that's what happens to people snared by popish superstition." His nurse always finished the story that way.

He was a man now. A soldiering duke, no less. But the thought of Geddon smuggled to the scaffold under the queen's folds still made him quicken. He remembered hiding his twitching yard under the blanket. His nurse finding it.

Like always these days, his thoughts turned to his marvellous boy, White, awaiting sentence in a Bow Street dungeon. Constable Rivett must have creamed himself. 'Grab of the year', the rags were calling it. Well, that Public Office quim-licker would soon be enjoying a grab of his own, courtesy of Long John Kitson. When the inquest was concluded. When things had settled down.

Then he could visit his poor White. Comfort him the best he could.

Quite out of the question now, though. As if it weren't bad enough having that filthy magistrate worming around the house, a little Courthouse shuck had turned up. He'd find out who was behind that, and then they'd be sorry, too.

Poor White. He pictured his little darling bathed in dusty shafts of sun, the boy's perfectly hung gems with their light covering of hair, the day's vein the thickness of a crow's quill. Or was it an artery?

Snatches of choral music drifted up from the Queen's Chapel. *Dominus illuminatio mea*. He cared nothing for religion, but he could live quite happily in its harmonies. Elegantly posed questions, followed by perfectly resolved answers. *Dominus ad adjuvandum*. White used to scoff at the soaring voices. Gelded lambs, he called them. What else could he expect from a drummer-boy?

He lay back, making a fist of it – pictured his love's elastic coat – the oiled tip (*he gasped*) – peeled lychees and jellies – White's face a nun's in the midst of her rapture.

44. Taking Turns

The depositions were being taken in a semicircular office that rose to a dazzling cupola – the glimpse of outside as unexpected as it was astonishing. Read showed Wyre to his seat then left, muttering about needing a piss.

A tall man in a liveried jacket identical to Paulet's knocked and entered. Identical, too, to the one that hung over the chair at the foot of Sellis's bed.

"My master begs to know if you or Mr Read require any refreshments before you begin," the valet said in respectful tones.

"Refreshments?"

The man dipped his head. "A cup of tea, sir. Or Italian ice, or French punch?"

Wyre shook his head. "Thank you, no. I can't speak for Mr Read."

"If you should change your mind, just send for me. It's Neale."

The man Yardley had warned him against. He looked more closely. The face was pleasing enough; none of the obnoxiousness of Wardle's description.

"I gather you were the man of the hour."

The valet kept his eyes professionally focused somewhere over the top of Wyre's shoulder.

"I did my duty, sir. No more than that."

"Yes, I read about it in the newspapers. You kept your nerve. While you're here, perhaps you could clarify something for me."

"If I can, sir. Everything seemed to happen at once. But then everything always does."

"They say Sellis must have lain in wait in the Duke's closet. Why, before bidding his Highness good night, didn't you –?"

"Why didn't I check the closet, sir?" Neale said, with a hint of injured self. "I didn't check under his Highness's bed for hobgoblins, either."

Sarcasm from a valet? "Perhaps you should have. Were all the doors leading to the Duke's bedchamber locked?"

Neale appeared to consider. "That between his Highness's bedroom and my own was shut, but not locked. But I'm a light sleeper. If anyone had come by that way I'd have heard them."

"There's no other entrance to the Duke's bedroom?"

"Only through the yellow door, which I locked." He paused. "Sellis was in the closet all along, sir. That's where we found his slippers."

Wyre ignored that bit. "After the Duke cried out, tell me what happened then?"

Neale was silent for a moment. "I heard my master shouting in agony, and ran to him. It must have been a little before three o'clock in the morning. He bade me look for the assassin."

"How could you see to look? I thought there was no light."

"But there was a little moon," the valet replied insouciantly. "I noticed the door to the yellow room was open, and ran to give chase. As I did so, I trod on the weapon Sellis had dropped there. I recognized it immediately as the Duke's regimental sabre."

"And then?"

"I asked his Highness for permission to pursue the

villain through the house, but he forbade it. He instructed me to call the other servants."

"Why didn't he allow you to go?"

"Shouldn't you ask him, sir?"

Wyre regarded him. "You called the servants."

"Yes. Then we set off for the porter, but his Highness came over faintish. Loss of blood, sir. We were forced to turn back. That's when we met my wife on the stairs. His Highness asked her to fetch Sellis."

"Why Sellis?"

"You'll have to ask his Highness, sir."

Wyre frowned. "What was your wife doing on the stairs at that time of night?"

"The commotion had woken her."

"All the way over in the householders' wing? That *is* where she's quartered, isn't it?"

"Oh, it's not that far, sir," said the valet. "Sound travels so readily through these corridors."

"Another light sleeper."

Neale merely looked.

"So you were quite happy for a woman to wander on her own through the house when, as far as anyone knew, the assassin was still at large?"

"The Duke was giddy."

"That doesn't quite answer my question."

"Perhaps I'm not entirely sure what it is you wish to know."

"You stayed with the Duke the whole time? You didn't feel the urge to go after your wife?"

"I remained with the Duke till the Prince arrived followed by the Duke's other brothers."

Silence as the big names circulated in the air.

"There was no mention of that in the papers."

"No, I do believe there wasn't."

Read's imposing figure appeared in the door. He was accompanied by a secretary; the man was primped out in powder-blue collars and cuffs.

"Mr Read . . ." the valet said, looking past Wyre, "his Highness asks whether you wish to take refreshments now."

Read shook his head brusquely, and took the middle seat at the table. Neale withdrew with a bow.

Little Boy Blue fussed with his writing implements, lining them up like surgical tools. From his blue bag, Wyre took out his own accoutrements: soft calf notebook (another of Rose's gifts) and a short pencil of the kind that offered little resistance to the knife.

The first informant of the day was a compact man with florid cheeks.

"Matthew Henry Graslin? Yager to his Royal Highness?"

The huntsman corrected the magistrate's pronunciation, earning himself a withering look.

"We're authorized to examine on oath all persons who may have been witness to the attempt on the Duke's life." Read turned. "This is Mr Wyre from the Courthouse." (A dutiful inclusion.) "Now, Graslin, I understand you accompanied the others to Sellis's bedroom that night?"

"Roight, sir. I arriv'd at Mr Sellis's door with Mrs Neale an' Benjamin Smith, th' Porter. Sellis's throat wor cut. Frightened us, the thought the murderer wor still in the house."

A bumkin's accent.

"Why did you think that?"

"Can't say." Graslin shrugged. "Suppose cos he weren' caught, nor seen runnin' away, neither. I went fer help . . . called on Ball an' Strickland. Richardson, too. Them's servants, sir. We waited in the Porter's Room."

231

"What did you tell Ball and the others?" asked Read.

"I told 'im Sellis wor dead." The yager adjusted his green jacket. "Mrs Neale said, from what she'd seen, the Duke wor set to join 'im. By then, there wor soldiers waiting in the hall. I sat wi' Mrs Neale in the Porter's room while Ball wen' upstairs wi' the sentinels. Them as 'ad been posted to guard Sellis's door."

"Sign and you may go."

Graslin took the pen from the secretary.

"One thing, Graslin," Wyre said quickly. "Where exactly was Sellis when you found him?"

The nib hovered in Graslin's fist above the vellum.

"Do you understand the question?"

"Lying on his bed, sir."

"Did anyone else enter Sellis's room before Ball arrived with the soldiers?"

The eyes flickered back and forth. "Not that I saw."

"Not that he saw, Wyre," Read said, tapping his finger on the vellum for the yager's signature.

When Graslin was gone, Read turned angrily. "What the fuck was that all about? Your role's to observe due process, not interrogate."

"With respect, sir, Mr Best – "

"Mr Best . . ." mimicked Read.

"Surely the issue of whether Sellis was left unattended is relevant?"

"In case someone desecrated his corpse?" Read snorted. "I don't suppose Sellis would have objected to that."

(The secretary sniggered.)

"Every minute that elapsed after the attack should be accounted for. A court would expect it."

Best peered at him. "Are you suggesting I don't know my job? It's to accumulate facts, not emboss opinion – and it's certainly not to help you lather up a public frenzy."

A furious still descended, broken by the appearance around the jamb of an aged schoolboy's head, bald apart from a few wisps of white hair that formed arches above the ears.

"Get in here, man," Read barked.

The witness confirmed his name as Benjamin Smith, Head Porter.

"Your part in this business?"

"His Highness and Mr Neale called on me, about two in the morning, sir, desiring I should lock all them doors leading out of the Palace."

"I assume you did as they asked?"

He nodded. "A little while later, Mrs Neale called on me. Tol' me his Highness 'ad instructed her to fetch Sellis, but the devil had bolted his room. I went with her, sir, called through the door, but there was no answer."

"And then?"

"Mrs Neale tol' us to put our shoulders to it, sir. We found him inside. I cried out he'd been murthered. The blood was still gushing. Afterwards, they told us he'd had at the Duke."

Wyre paused. "What did you make of Sellis's character?"

"Oh, he was obstinate, sir."

"How did Mr Neale get on with him?" Wyre sensed Read's exasperation building.

Smith appeared to weigh the question. "They weren't what I'd call friends. Quarrelled once over the Duke's wardrobe." (Read snorted at that.) "I heard Sellis say he couldn't live with the Duke, if Neale was kept on. Said he'd rather work as a messenger boy." The Porter's voice dropped a little. "Sellis was a stirrer, mind. He painted a disgusting picture of Neale. I told him a foreigner like 'im would never secure another position, if he'd just lost one."

Read sniffed. "Sign here."

When the cupola door had closed behind the Porter, Wyre turned to the Chief Magistrate.

"Earlier, sir, when Neale came in about his iced teas, he said he'd helped the Duke to the Porter's that night. They were forced to turn back."

"Well, what of it?"

"Doesn't it strike you as odd? Their first act after the assault, to seek out the Porter. Wouldn't you expect them to wake the surgeon, and tend to the Duke's injuries?"

Read gave him a contemptuous look. "Cumberland's a soldier. *You* might have run for bandages, but his first thought was to get the doors locked, and prevent the bastard who attacked him from getting away."

Wyre considered that. "What about Smith's first impression on discovering Sellis. He used the word 'murder'."

Read gave him a look of bewilderment. "Who cares what Smith said?" He jammed his magistrate's seal into the bleb of wax at the bottom of the Porter's affidavit. "Fuck's sake, man! He found the Corsican bastard in bloody sheets. Anyone who saw claret in that quantity would assume foul play."

"You don't think it odd, sending a defenceless woman halfway through an unlit house when everyone, including her husband, believes the assassin's at large? That bothers me, to tell the truth."

"Christ's nails, you're determined to see complexity where there is none."

The next round of interviews was more run-of-the-mill, and Wyre began to wonder if he was seeking an otherness that simply wasn't there. His attention drifted to the slashed crinoline dress Miss Crawford had worn to Wood's Close asylum.

A set of linked raps dispelled his reverie – a touch of the

sailor's holler-and-reply. Paulet appeared in the doorway. Seeing Wyre, he smiled.

Read waved the valet over. "Where were you on the night of the attack?" He reeled off the formula like a tired length of ship's hawser.

Wyre took in the genial valet more closely – fleshy face, stiff carriage; something military about the upraised chin.

"I was in the page's waiting-room, Mr Read, with Mrs Neale and two of the maids. Ann and Margaret, sir."

"What did you discuss there?"

"A case of a missing poker, sir. Margaret was carping on about it something rotten. Said it must have been taken from the valet's bedroom. Found it that morning while she was dollying the sheets. Behind the bed. She asked if I was responsible. I told her it must have fallen there." His eyes drifted to the side. "It wasn't ours, anyhow. Not originally. No, it belonged to the Duke. York, I mean, not Cumberland." He resumed his subaltern pose. "But I wouldn't attach any importance, sir. Things tend to walk in this house."

Read gave him a stern look. "If there's anything else you have to tell us, you'd better do it now. If it comes to light later . . ." He let the pause speak for itself.

Paulet shifted uneasily. "I imagine Mrs Neale already mentioned the pistol, as if that was my fault, too."

"Pistol?" Wyre experienced the sensation of being on a boat and feeling the precise moment when it reaches deep water, that sense of yawning bathymetry.

"The one that hung from the bedpost, sir. In a red bag. I can't speak to it, though, other than to say it had a short barrel. I told Mrs Neale I didn't care for it. They can pop off on their own, can't they?"

The penny dropped . . . That bent nail on the bedpost in the Valet's Room. That's what it was for! Any thoughts he'd found the game-changer quickly vanished. No weapon had been discharged that night. An unfired pistol changed nothing.

Read had evidently reached the same conclusion. "If it disturbed you so much, why didn't you just take the blasted thing down?"

The valet opened his mouth to speak, then appeared to think better of it. "It was an odd feeling," he said at last, "knowing it was there, hanging above me. I told Neale that, but he insisted he wouldn't sleep without it."

"Was it hanging there on the night of the attack?" Wyre was sick of seeing the world in slices.

Paulet's arms were at his side, back on the parade ground. "I believe it was, sir. Can't say for sure. It wasn't my turn."

"Your turn?"

"In the Valet's Room. It wasn't my turn that night."

Read flipped open his watch, then ended the interview with a long sigh like the release of pressure in a cylinder. Paulet signed his name with a little flourish and left, heels echoing under the cupola.

"None of the other informants mention anything about a pistol," Wyre began when the doors had shut behind the valet. "Yet they all remember the slippers. Why does no one think a pistol suspended above the valet's bed might be important?"

Read scowled. "You're determined to make a laughing post of this inquest."

"A court wouldn't look past the fire-piece, sir, and nor should we." Glancing down, Wyre realized he'd cupped his palms on the table as if protecting a hand of cards.

"Sellis used a sabre on Cumberland, not a pistol. Then he slit his throat. He didn't blow his brains out. The pistol's irrelevant!"

"It tells us something. We need to recall Neale." Wyre's own firmness surprised him.

"Don't be absurd. He's already given his deposition. Any more questions could be construed as persecution. He's a hero in the Duke's mind, and rightly so. I won't have you endanger this inquest."

A smouldering silence; then, to Wyre's astonishment, with a pained expression, Read sent his secretary out with instructions to return with Neale.

They waited, both mute, Read busying himself with signatures while Wyre pretended to read over his own notes.

The valet entered at a march, the secretary following a short distance behind, cheeks flushed.

"I've already sworn my affidavit," Neale protested. "I'm sure his Highness didn't – "

Read cut him off. "When were you going to tell us about the pistol? Mr Wyre here worked it out."

There was a pause. "Is that why I've been called?" The valet glared at the lawyer. "What an absurd fancy he has."

"We'll have none of that," Read said. "Just answer the bloody question. I won't have evidence hidden from me."

Neale was clearly as surprised as Wyre by the magistrate's tone. "I beg pardon, Mr Read. The business with Sellis is still raw. Some months ago, he attacked my character. It happened right in front of his Highness."

"Attacked?" Wyre said. "How?"

"Sellis called me a thief. Mr Read knows about it." Neale glanced at the Chief Magistrate." The accusations were managed by Captain Stephenson, and all were found to be untrue. From that day, Sellis harboured a hatred towards me. For that reason, and that reason alone, I took measures."

"What kind of gun is it?" Read asked.

"Nothing special. Something small and double-barrelled."

"Was it kept loaded?" Wyre put in.

The valet nodded.

"Did you ever imagine shooting Sellis with it?" Read added, finally showing something of the interrogating style.

"Only if he came at me in the night." Neale smiled faintly. "Given what's happened, I'd say I was right to take precautions." He stood there with an air of boyish petulance.

"Was it hanging up on the night of the attack?" Wyre asked. Bow Street and Courthouse were finally working in tandem.

"As a matter of fact, it wasn't. Mr Paulet had made his feelings on the matter known that morning. To tell truth, it had become something of a bugbear between us, so I locked it in the valets' escritoire. I'm surprised it wasn't mentioned. It's there now, or at least should be, if you'd care to look."

"We'll check that," Read said. He glanced across at the lawyer. "Does that clear the matter up for you?"

"You didn't like Sellis, did you?" Wyre said, gazing levelly at the valet. "There's no point denying it."

The valet shrugged. "Why would I?" He looked at Read. "May I go now? His Highness . . ."

Read gave a curt nod.

Two maids were next on Read's list, the first a well-spoken kitchen girl with pursy lips. Ann Ruddock, in service for three years.

"Give or take a month, sir." She qualified her statement as if indemnifying herself against a future charge of perjury.

Read began.

"Did you ever see Mr Sellis carry a dark lantern?"

She smoothed her tunic over her midriff. "I saw it in his hand once before, if you please. It must have been three weeks ago. Mr Sellis was coming down from his bedroom. We wished each other good night."

"Describe the lantern for us," Wyre said. To his surprise, this elicited no groan of impatience from the Chief Magistrate.

"It was a round one, sir. Round and dark."

"Where were you when his Royal Highness was attacked?"

"In bed, Mr Read."

"In bed alone?"

"Mary Saxby and I turned in early that night."

"And did you hear anything?"

"There was a noise in the passage. The clocks had struck eleven. We thought it must have been Margaret coming to bed."

"Margaret?" Wyre said.

"Mrs Neale's maid, sir."

Yes, Paulet had told him that. "And *was* it Margaret?"

"She come later, sir. She'd been reading in the scullery and heard something. She didn't like to be alone after that."

"What was she reading so late?"

"Her gospels, sir."

The Chief Magistrate let out a long sigh, and called Ruddock forward for her signature. Two scratchy marks. Despite her elocution, she was unlettered.

Ruddock's place was taken by Margaret Jones, a couple of years older with a soft, round face. A few unruly strands of coal-black hair had escaped from the scallops of her bonnet.

"Four months, sir. Still settling in."

Wyre caught the residue of Welsh inflection beneath more recently acquired city tones, but there was none of the carneying, wheedling way of that people.

"What are your duties, Margaret?"

"When I'm not helping Mrs Neale, sir, I d' make the butler's and housekeeper's bed. Mr Sellis's, too, that is, when he kips in the Valet's Room. I'm supposed to lay the fires, but it's been too warm since I arrived. Haven't made one yet, sir. There's a spare bed for the Adjutant of his Royal Highness's regiment, when he comes to stay, sir."

"Was the Adjutant here that night?" It appeared he'd earned the right to a few follow-up questions.

She tossed her pretty head.

Read took over; gruffer. "How often did you prepare Mr Sellis's bed this last week?"

"Twice, sir."

"Is that the usual number of times?"

"T' be honest, it was the first time I dun 'em."

"I thought you said it was your job," the magistrate said sharply.

"Mr Sellis never asked me to do it, sir. Not till this week."

"Never asked you?" Read bossed his chin.

"He likes – " an alarmed pause " – *liked* Ann Ruddock to make it, sir. The two were friends."

"Kept each other warm at night, eh?"

"Ann was a comfort to him, sir. After Tranter, I mean. Tha's all it was, sir."

"Who's Tranter?" Wyre said.

Margaret glanced across at Read. "Duke of York's footman, sir. A particular friend of Mr Sellis and Mr Neale."

Wyre scanned down the list of informants. No Tranter was listed. "Where is he now, Margaret?"

She looked alarmed again. "It 'appened a month after I arrived. Did 'imself in, Mr Tranter did. In the stables, sir. We y'eard the shot, me n' Ann Ruddock. Constables arrived to look into it." She looked at Read again.

"Biathanatos, Wyre," the magistrate said in a quiet voice.

Another suicide? They were stacking up.

"We y'eard the shot," the maid repeated. "Woke us both up. They found Mr Tranter in the morning, sir. On the cobbles, with his brains blown out."

Wyre fixed her with a stern look. "You say Tranter was Sellis's friend. Are the houses of Cumberland and York in the habit of fraternizing?"

She tossed her head again. "The schedules are different."

"Did Sellis have many friends? In either household? Take your time."

"He kept to 'imself, mostly, sir. Liked to spend his free hours with his family. Either tha', or he was down in the stables, polishing the Duke's carriage. Used t' talk like it were his."

"Were you shown the items recovered from the Duke's closet?"

Read drummed his fingers.

"I saw the lantern," she said carefully.

The magistrate broke in. "We already know that item belonged to Sellis. Now, listen here, Margaret. On the night Sellis attacked his master, did he ask you to make his bed in the Duke's chamber?"

The maid's bottom lip began to tremble.

"Keep going, Margaret," Wyre said. "You've done nothing wrong. We just want information."

"That's right, keep going, missy. Why was Sellis so keen for you to make his bed that night?"

"I was in the Housemaid's Room, sir, wi' Sarah and – "

241

she screwed up her face in concentration " – Jayne Tetherhead. Mr Sellis came in an' said I was t' prepare his bed in the Valet's Room. He told us the Duke would ride out to Windsor in th' morning."

"So you made up his bed," Read said. "What time was this?"

"It would have been about nine o'clock, sir. Mr Sellis left. He mentioned something about dressing his Royal Highness for drinks wi' some uniformed gentlemen. When I finished, I returned t' the householders' side to give Mr Salisbury's sitting-room a quick tidy – "

"Christ, Wyre, are you following this? It's a bloody maze. And who's Mr Salisbury?"

"Duke's steward, sir. Mr Sellis tol' me to get the sitting room ready for the morning, in case it were needed before I got up. When the Duke was finished with him, Mr Sellis come through on his way to his bedroom. I asked if the Duke still meant to go to Windsor. He jus' give me one of his black looks, and said he hoped my corners were better brushed than last time."

"Where the hell's the sitting-room?" Read demanded.

"It's what we d' call the room in front of Mr Sellis's bedroom, sir. His private, off-duty bedroom, I mean. Not the one the valets share. It's a through room."

"A through room. God Almighty, Wyre, wish I had one of those." Read sniffed savagely. "So you were in the sitting room, having this cosy little chat with *Mr* Sellis. Quite sure you weren't in his bedroom?"

Wyre pushed down the image; but Read's line was interesting. After all, Sellis would have needed someone to keep all those doors – at least five of them – unlocked along his escape route from the Duke's bedroom back to his off-duty chamber. Was Margaret the accomplice? A Welsh snake in the grass?

The heat had settled in the Cupola Office. Little pearls of sweat dripped into Wyre's eyes. He reached for Rose's handkerchief, dabbing at his neck and brow, before folding the silk cloth neatly again on the desk.

The maid looked appalled. "Mr Sellis wished me good night, sir. Tha's all. He looked unwell."

"I bet he did," Read said, his face dark. "He was probably thinking about what he'd planned for later. Quite sure you're not covering for anyone? Tell us now, and things will go easier for you."

The girl's eyes widened. "No, sir. Honest!"

"Did he lock his door after bidding you goodnight?" Wyre asked.

"If he did, I didn' hear nothing." A blush that began just above the girl's abundant breasts spread up her neck, arriving at her cheeks. What a big activity voice was. It took a lot of blood.

Read looked unimpressed. "Let me get this straight. Sellis asked you, for the first time ever, to make up his bed in the Valet's Room, next to the Duke's chamber – " (her head bobbed vigorously) " – but then slept in his *off*-duty apartment, all the way over on the other side of the Palace?" He exchanged a sceptical look with Wyre. "That's what you're saying?"

She nodded again, her eyes wide.

"What did you do when he went to bed?" Wyre struck a kindlier tone.

"Jus' finished up in Mr Salisbury's room, then I went t' bed myself."

"And you slept like a baby," said Read.

"I read till I fell asleep, sir. I was woken at eleven by someone shuffling aroun' out in the passage, the one that d' run along the back."

"The back?" Wyre asked.

243

"Between our rooms and the main corridor. I couldn' get off again, then. A little later, Mary come to bed. I asked her why she was wandering about in the passage so late."

"Wait a minute," Wyre said, frowning, "Ann Ruddock is adamant she and Mary lay in bed waiting for *you* to join them. They thought it was *you* wandering about."

Margaret looked confused. "I was in bed with Ann, sir."

"So who the devil was in the passage?" Read demanded

"Dunno, sir. Mary said it wern' her."

Read gave her a contemptuous look.

Margaret began again miserably. "It was someone shambling along in old slippers, tha's what Mary said. Couldn' see his face." She lifted her head. "I said to Ann it must be the devil come to – "

Read held up his hand. "Thank you, Margaret. We have all we need." He slid her deposition across the table for her signature.

"Do you enjoy working for Mrs Neale, Margaret?" Wyre said as the maid signed with a surprisingly neat hand.

Margaret looked up. "She's always kind, sir." She gave a little curtsey and left.

Read shook his head. "The devil, my arse. Preachers on every street corner, banging on about deliverance. These silly girls lap it up."

"You do realize the maids' stories don't tally?" Wyre began. "That noise in the passage – "

Read waved his hand dismissively. "Ann Ruddock has her Marys and Margarets mixed up, that's all." He ran a finger round the back of his collar. "Christ, this heat! Look, forget the little vixens and focus on the important thing. Some bugger was creeping about, and we both know who that was."

"But shouldn't we interview the Duke of York about his footman, this Tranter fellow?"

"For pity's sake," Read said wearily. "I already told you. York's not to be disturbed. The Palace is co-operating with the inquest solely on that understanding. Only his doctors may see him. Anyway, the Tranter incident was months ago. It has no bearing."

Wyre unfolded his silk handkerchief again. The cupola's glass was a lens for the relentless sun; they were slowly roasting alive. (Even the secretary looked as if he'd like to divest himself of his powder blue jacket.) Wyre looked down at his handkerchief, his eyes settling on the pretty letters Rose had embroidered in the corner. *C.W.* What combination of happenstance and fortune had ensured those initials weren't the ones stitched onto a pair of slippers found in a closet one night at the Palace?

"The Duke of York was here the night Cumberland was attacked, sir. He ought at least to swear an affidavit. For the record."

"For the record? What are you, one of those Jacobins? A dirty democrat?"

"For the record," Wyre repeated, knowing it was hopeless.

45. Horse Play

At midday, two dark-haired maids arrived with dishes of cold meat and vinegar, followed by Paulet with plates and cutlery.

Had any letters arrived for Wyre? The valet indicated the negative.

Read picked at his meal then got wearily to his feet. "We resume at one," he said, and left without further comment.

Wyre reached for his pocket watch. That left almost an hour for what Leighton would call familiarizing himself with the terrain. If he couldn't quiz York, he'd have a gander at his stables, where Tranter met his end.

The coaching outbuildings were situated at the western limits of the royal curtilage, a stone's throw from the high brick wall that looked down on Pall Mall's widened pavements. If the pistol shot that ventilated Tranter's skull really had woken Margaret all the way over in the servants' quarters, she was the epitome of a light sleeper.

A stableman of stupendous proportions was working in the courtyard, forking dung into a huge pyramid. Villagers in Dean forest would call him a galligantus. He was so tall, he appeared closer than he really was. It had to be the hulking fellow Read had joked about so earthily to the surgeons – unless there was a whole brood of giants roaming the city: a modern-day Goliath and his brothers. Angels, unrighteous women, strange flesh. Wasn't that the heady brew? What would the Southcottians make of this man, a very beast of the Apocalypse.

The colossus grinned toothily, waving a vast arm slowly back and forth. A simpleton, then. One of Wyre's nieces was slow. He waved back, then headed for the cobbles where the maid said Tranter had lain. Wyre put his head into the stables, and breathed in a warm peaty aroma. The stink traps were well tended. Three oily-skinned horses greeted his intrusion with skittish neighs, pushing at their bits. Fine animals, nothing loose or leggy about them.

Leighton's dandy-charger leaned against the wall. So Paulet had been good to his word. The contraption seemed oddly at home among its equestrian rivals. Wyre didn't doubt ostlers around the country would soon be getting used to these mechanical geldings.

He spun round at a scuffing sound. Had the freakish simpleton followed him in? Instead, a chinny lad in green fustian stood at his shoulder. Heart hammering, Wyre grabbed the yager's collar and bustled him up against the wall.

"What the devil do you mean by creeping up on me like that?"

"Beg pardon, sir!" the youth said in alarm. "I saw someone going in as shouldn't. Didn't realize it was you, Mr Wyre." His eyes darted wildly

"How do you know my name?"

The lad hesitated. "We was told to keep away from you, while the inquest's on . . ."

The boy's cheeks were two mounds of cherries, lips like a Cheapside gash. Wyre recognized the signs a mile off.

"*Who* told you? Spit it out!"

"Mr Graslin, sir." The boy stared at his feet.

So he was good with names. Wyre decided to try him with some others.

"Ever heard of a waiter called Thomas?" He tightened his grip. "What about Robert Aspinall? Don't tell me you've never heard of the Vere Street gang. Friends of yours, by any chance?" (The boy blanched.) "I'll bet you were thick with Mr Sellis. I understand he liked to hang around the stables. Just like you." Wyre thrust him against the wall again, eliciting a satisfyingly sharp yelp.

"I 'ardly knew 'im, sir. Saw 'im a couple of times when I was returning 'orses. Mr Sellis showed me his Highness's barouche."

Wyre followed the lad's eyes into the shadows. Parked at the rear of the stables, next to a preposterous high-perch phaeton, was a fine carriage, all elegant blazons and elaborate Corbeau panels. A dickey box jutted out above the cabin at the rear. Wyre thought of Crispin Street and Thomas's letter.

"What about when you were off duty? Ever meet Sellis

in town?" The boy's eyes drifted away; Wyre gave him another shove.

"He took me once t' see the mad folk, sir. We went to the park afterwards, then on to a tavern. Can't remember which one. He kept me in ale th' whole afternoon. It was no more than that."

"Did he ever act improperly towards you?"

An appalled silence.

"If you tell me," Wyre said quietly, "I give you my word you won't be asked at the inquest. With us, it's just two men talking. With Read, you'll be under oath."

The hunter's face twisted in an agony of uncertainty.

"Out with it!"

"It was in the jakes, sir," the boy said, his voice strangled, "in the tavern. We got up together to piss. I made a joke about his . . . about it being all shrivelled up. He said if I dared touch it, I'd see it grow heavy soon enough. He took my hand and placed it there. I removed it at once, sir. Sellis laughed, and said he knew someone who'd pay with more than ale for such things, if I cared to meet him."

"You were in The White Swan, weren't you?" Wyre gave the boy's collars a twist.

"No, sir, not there, on my oath!"

Wyre sensed the deep convective stirrings of information. "You were there." He smiled grimly. "And it wasn't the last time you accompanied Sellis to that turd pit." Wyre imagined Sellis's hand creeping over the hunter's breast, reaching down.

The boy's eyes began to swim. "Sir, I've been caught before. Mr Nares the magistrate said next time – "

"Make a clean breast of it to me, and I'll see none of this comes out."

"I can't – "

"Make a clean breast," Wyre repeated. "No one will

hear of your behaviour. If you refuse, Mr Nares will hang you."

The boy's lips acquired a bluish cast. "Up in the private rooms, sir," he said; short syncopated bursts, "that's where they . . . where they set out beds. For the use of men who had a mind to be married, sir. Sellis told me . . . said there was a country gentleman come to town, an' if I gave him a wedding night I'd be paid handsomely. I stayed till midnight, sir, but no gentleman came. I told one of the other men, an' he said he was no country gentleman, he was the city. By then it was too late to go home. Sellis said I should lie with him instead. Two other stinkers came to the room, each promising a shilling if I'd turn my back." He took a deep breath. "Sellis brought me to several husbands afterwards. There were others like me, but White was the worst."

"I know all about the drummer-boy. Tell me about Sellis."

The yager appeared not to hear. "White wanted to quit the army, an' had almost saved enough – his new patron paid ten times what the others did."

Wyre stopped at that. "Did you ever meet him, this patron? Could you identify him?"

"Not that night, sir. Later I did, though."

"Who was he? Was this the country gentleman? Give me his name. Whisper it." He turned his ear to the boy's lips. "Was it Parlez-Vous?"

The boy shrank away. "He always wore a satin mask, sir. It covered half his face. Anyway, he never spoke to the likes of me. He was only interested in White." The yager's eyes slid back up to Wyre's own. "Everyone was, sir, 'cept for Mr Sellis. He was the only one who couldn't stand White. He told me he'd seen his – you know, seen *it*, sir. Said it was dripping. I thought that was just sour grapes, on account of not being able to afford White, once his price started to go up."

French dishes . . . Parson Church's gibe in his room at Mrs Mason's suddenly rang in his ears. "Did you ever see any Frenchmen in the Swan?"

The effect was immediate. "Fuck me, no, sir!" The yager shook his head vigorously. "It wasn't like that."

Wyre leaned in close. "Listen to me – "

The yager relaxed against the wall, and raised a trembling hand towards Wyre's shoulder, the other coming to rest on his hip. The lawyer shunted him hard in the chest.

"None of that!" He swore savagely. "Don't tell Mr Graslin about our conversation, or anyone else, and you may still come out of this unscathed. God knows you deserve the end of a yardarm."

He left the flagrant misrule framed against the golden coach.

The Country Gentleman . . . another piece of code to place alongside Mr Parlez-Vous. Unless they were the same man. While he was turning the yager's information over, he succeeded in taking a false turn. His confused doublings cost him a good ten minutes; when, at length, he arrived in the Cupola Office, the magistrate made a show of tapping his index finger slowly on the tabletop.

Wyre decided to say nothing for the moment about his encounter. This infernal swelter! He fished out Rose's handkerchief, and pressed it to his damp forehead, folding the silk square back up afterwards, and placing it neatly beside his notebook.

Jackson was called up next. He gave Read a condescending look. "Ah troost this won't be unduly protracted. I hardly need remin' the inquest the Duke's recovery hangs in th' balance."

The Bow Street man regarded him sourly. "A brief inventory of his Highness's hurts will suffice."

"Very well. Ah can teel ye, then, th' skull was penetrated obliquely puckle inches above th' right ear, enaw fur th' pulsation ay th' arteries tae be clearly visible. Only a mercy prevented part ay th' Duke's skull frae bein' completely bludgeoned away. There were several wounds ay lesser consequence – oan th' left arm, an' oan th' back ay his reit thigh. His Highness's hands were also injured when he fended aff th' sabre." (Wyre watched the secretary's wrist fly.) "That nae major vessels were severed was nothing short ay a miracle. As it is, th' loss ay bluid will take several days tae make guid. In that time, th' Duke should see nobody.""

Read sniffed. "I fear it will be necessary to trouble his Highness one last time."

"Indeed? But yer constables hae already spoken tae him."

"On the night of the assault," Read said, firmly, "the Duke was unable to recount the episode with full clarity. Understandably enough. Since then, more details may have returned." He cleared his throat. "The request isn't made on trivial grounds, Mr Jackson. The Courthouse – " he glanced at Wyre " – believes a second assassin may have made the Palace a home. Certain things need to be ruled out, and only the Duke can do that."

So the blame was being laid at Wyre's feet.

Jackson was silent for a moment. "Then ah must insist you grant his Highness a further day's peace. Tae attempt an interview any earlier would be folly in th' extreme."

Read nodded his acquiescence.

Jackson signed his deposition, glancing coldly at Wyre.

Neale's wife entered next. She was a little younger than thirty, attractive in the city fashion. Her pale skin had acquired a little colour since the lawyer passed her in the corridor that morning. Her blonde hair was tied back now, and glistened in the light from the cupola. That curious stain beneath her right eye . . . had it darkened?

"Mrs Ann Neale? Wife of the valet Cornelius Neale?"

She nodded.

"I couldn't sleep that night," she began. "When my husband's on duty I find it difficult. I must have decided to go for a walk. I heard an awful commotion and went to investigate."

"On your own?"

"It was my duty. In the corridor I met his Royal Highness leaning on my husband. The blood was dreadful." Her fingers crept to the fringe of her dress.

"Carry on, Mrs Neale."

"I summoned the other servants," she said, lacing and unlacing her fingers, "Mr Jackson, too. Then, on the Duke's instructions, I went to rouse Joseph Sellis." Her voice vacillated between poles of cool self-certitude and something more vulnerable.

"You weren't frightened?" Wyre looked at her intently.

"His Highness wished it," she said simply. "I knocked for Mr Sellis. When no one answered, I tried the door, but it was bolted. By that time, the porter was with me, and also I think Mr Graslin. I asked them to break it down."

"Why did you do that?" Wyre said. "Mr Sellis wasn't under any suspicion at that point."

She was silent for a moment. "I heard a gurgling noise, like water in a man's throat. I suppose it must have frightened me. The porter managed to get the door open. What he saw made him cry out."

Read tilted forward. "What did *you* see, Mrs Neale?"

"I saw Mr Sellis lying in his bed with his throat slashed. I sent Smith to fetch help."

Wyre frowned at her. "Was Sellis wearing his shirt and jacket?"

Mrs Neale nodded. Small, precise movements.

"Do you swear, under oath, you found him that way?"

Read was watching her intently.

Another nod.

"And the razor?" the Chief Magistrate prompted. "Tell Mr Wyre where it was."

"It lay on the floor, a little distance away."

Read clearly wanted this wrapped up. It was time to get to the point. Fast. "Were you ever left alone with Sellis's body?"

The question seemed to take her aback. "For a short while, I suppose I must have been. But only while Smith and Graslin went for help."

"And how long was that?"

"Not so very long. Mr Smith returned, and took me down to the porter's room, where we waited for the soldiers."

"Did anyone else, beside Mr Smith and Mr Graslin, enter the bedroom while you waited with Sellis?" Again, he sensed Read's irritation building.

"No one at all." She blinked. Bright, blue eyes; short, dense, blonde lashes. She was what Rose would call a catch.

"Finally, Mrs Neale, are the doors leading from the ballroom into the yellow room usually kept locked?"

"Both of them, Mr Wyre. They're always locked at night. All the doors along that way are. I lock them myself, or Margaret, my maid, does."

"No key was found in Mr Sellis's private, off-duty bedroom. How, in your opinion, was he able to move there so quickly from the Duke's chamber – right across the Palace?"

"Her *opinion*, Wyre?"

Miss Neale returned the lawyer's gaze squarely. "It seems reasonable to assume someone must have unlocked them."

"But not you, Mrs Neale?"

"Not me."

Read cleared his throat. "How long have you known Sellis?"

"Since whenever it was he arrived here. Five years, I believe."

"What would you say of his character?"

Her lip curled. "He was an intractable man. He couldn't abide being contradicted, not even by the Duke. He would never acknowledge himself in the wrong."

"Did the Duke treat him well?"

"With undeserved kindness. He gave Mr Sellis's wife and family an apartment on the second floor, quite near to Mr Sellis's off-duty bedroom, with a generous allowance of coal and candles. The Queen once presented him with a gift of muslin. Princess Augusta stood godmother to his daughter, and the Duke himself was godfather to his youngest child. We all found it a little – " she checked herself.

"A little what?" Wyre asked.

"No one else received such attention. A few days before Mr Sellis's death, the Duke invited him to ride in his carriage rather than on the outside in the rain. Inside, with him," she repeated. "He told my husband, who told me."

"Do you know what they talked about in his carriage?"

A shaft of light pierced the cupola, bleaching her face to a crimson mouth and two blue points.

"How could she possibly know that?" Read objected. He laid his palms heavily on the table. "Tell me, Mrs Neale, how did Sellis and your husband get along?"

"Well enough, I suppose. They weren't what you'd call close-bosom friends. Mr Sellis was high-handed with all the servants, and my husband didn't like that. But they worked easily enough alongside each other."

"I understand your husband was in the habit of sleeping with a pistol hanging from the bedpost when he was on duty."

Two red spots appeared on Mrs Neale's cheeks. "I don't approve of such things."

"But you didn't forbid it," Wyre said.

"I made my objections clear." A primness had crept into her voice.

"Before you went to bed that night – " Read took over " – did you notice anything out of the ordinary?"

"Only that it was devilish hot."

"Would you say," Wyre began carefully, "your husband is close to the Duke?" He sensed Read straighten.

"My husband attends his Highness. He dresses him. That is his job."

"Do you resent the closeness?"

"*Wyre* – " growled Read. He laid a hand on Little Boy Blue's wrist, preventing him from recording.

Mrs Neale looked slowly at Wyre. "How *dare* you!"

"Thank you, Mrs Neale," Read said hurriedly. "That's all."

After she left, Wyre braced for the inevitable. It came.

"You aren't prosecuting in the fucking Old Bailey now. We *know* who the culprit is."

"We're missing something, sir. Somewhere in this house, information is being lost. I have an idea how we might – "

Read gave a snort of derision. "People are a lot less complicated than your ideas. The guilt is Sellis's, and his alone. I'll admit you had me wondering for a moment, but the matter's clear now. And Wyre – " he gave him a withering look " – you won't get anywhere in this house alluding to Greek vices."

The Chief Magistrate pushed himself to his feet, and announced an intermission.

Wyre went off to look for the water closet. Paulet was in the corridor arranging empty flower trays along the window sill.

"Getting them ready for Mrs Neale, sir," the valet said genially. "As a matter of fact, I just saw her leave. Your inquest, sir, I mean. She looked out of sorts."

Wyre was taken aback. He liked the man, but that was bold. "I'm afraid I'm not at liberty to discuss the inquest."

"Of course not, sir. My apologies." Paulet moved one of the trays six inches to the right. "I expect her information set the cat among the pigeons, though." He dipped his chin, at the same time lifting his eyebrows.

"Her information?"

"About Mrs Sellis's suspicions, sir." He hesitated. "Sorry, Mr Wyre, have I got ahead of myself again?" He ran a finger down the side of his cheek.

"Why the devil didn't you mention any of this to Mr Read?"

"He asked for *my* account, sir. I assumed Mrs Neale would have given hers."

"So what about these suspicions?"

"Quite unfounded. Mrs Sellis got it into her head that her husband was being . . . how shall I put it delicately? That he was being pursued by Mrs Neale's husband." Paulet lowered his voice. "To show how cracked she was on the matter, sir, she also claimed his Highness was pressing similar claims."

Wyre looked along the corridor to make sure they were alone. "His Highness?" He frowned. "You mean, the Duke of Cumberland?"

Paulet looked uncomfortable. "I assumed you'd have heard the Palace talk by now, sir. I suppose it was Mrs Sellis herself who started it." In a strange gesture, he tapped a finger on a closed eyelid. "It upset Mrs Neale. That's why I imagined she would have mentioned it."

Paulet had just explained Mrs Neale's anger in the Cupola Office . . .

"To be honest, sir, I felt sorry for Mrs Sellis. The torments she must have endured, knowing her husband was three times a week next to the Duke's private sleeping quarters. Enough to unballast any woman."

"Are you suggesting *Mrs* Sellis was the – " Wyre stopped short of saying it. But a female assassin would explain why none of the strokes told.

"Oh dear, I'm not suggesting anything, Mr Wyre. It's not my place to do that. In any case, whatever Mrs Sellis might have believed, she'd have put up with it, so long as she kept her coal and candles, and those nice big rooms for her children."

Wyre blinked. He was sick of gossip. Sick of the air of the place. He left Paulet with his window boxes.

Now, where the hell was the privy?

46. Eye Contact

His 'dark spells', his mother used to call them, begging him to abandon pleasure for the insipidity of existence. A bitch of the first water, always playing one brother off against the other. Hadn't he also turned out well? Why not remonstrate with Prinny and his band of dissolutes: Hellgate, Poodle, Skiffy and Tinman. The sobriquets said it all. (Far better than his own, though, he had to concede.) Why not upbraid Yorkie for his own peccadillos? God knows, there'd been enough of them – a whole string of unwashed actresses and bankers' wives.

He rubbed the pit of his eye. Why assume the same standard of reason and taste for all? Good works were accidents, of no more consequence than the size of a man's nose, or the colour of his hair. The so-called moral law was no rule of life for him. A Duke should live as he saw fit.

His thoughts returned to the man on the stairs, back in that devilish house of contradictions. Neatly turned out in his yellow braided waistcoat. His physician's waistcoat. Yellow waistcoat, black notebook. Oh, yes, Mr Parlez-Vous had told him all about the book.

No notes. Under any circumstances.

They'd been plain. No record of visits, no mention of the sponsor. Surely the reasons were obvious?

But the man on the stairs had chosen to ignore the edict.

He was a practical problem now. And practical problems called for practical solutions. As a matter of fact, he'd been assured, one was already decisively – incisively – in train. And it amused Yorkie to call him mad. Well, madmen were always prudent in their own affairs. Wasn't their Royal father the exemplum?

He plucked the sham eye from its little bowl on the dresser, and dropped it into his palm, experiencing the roundness.

The heat when the eyemaker had formed the glass shell into a golden ball, and breathed in vision with a blowpipe ... The blood vessels were added with red glass, the iris with a smart loop of the wrist. Finally, the candle of the eye was introduced with a drop of black. He remembered the first time the eyemaker dropped the fiery orb into his hungry cavity.

Leaning his face to the mirror, he pulled his upper eyelid out, and spooned the ball in. A perfect eye that fooled no one. Not the man on the stairs, that thief in the night, stealing up from the edges of his blind spot.

47. Gutta-Percha

Wyre returned from the privy to find Rose's handkerchief gone. His inquest notes were also missing.

Read was blunt. "The room was left unoccupied, Wyre. The servants here are like any others. The handkerchief's one thing, but you should know better than to leave interview notes lying in full view." The magistrate seemed distracted, rather than angry. "Anyway, what took you so long? We've had report of a mortality."

The switch to the language of officialdom arrived like a punch in the chest. "Whose?" Wyre didn't need to ask.

"Some apprentice yager," Read said gruffly. "Got kicked by a horse. It can happen if you get too close. Maybe he chose the wrong end." He looked carefully at the lawyer. "He wasn't down to be interviewed, before you get excited. It doesn't have a bearing."

"A horse, sir?"

"One of the pretty fillies they keep in the stables. Stoved his head in."

Wyre doubted it. More likely, Mr Parlez-Vous had stood on the other end of a club-hammer, a stable iron, perhaps, dispatching his victim just like he'd bludgeoned the Bow Street fly in the service tunnel. He decided to keep quiet. It was too late for the chinny lad – and perhaps it was better this way. Quicker than the noose. Yes, he'd probably done the boy a favour. Mr Nares's fingers would have closed.

A bright-eyed scullery maid was up next, followed by three young things of the type that could be called comely. Each deposition had a tutored feel, almost wholly devoid of the quirky details that gave the life to personal experience.

At half past four, Paulet appeared with a letter in his outstretched hand.

"Communiqué-for-Mr-Wyre-care-of-Mr-Read."

The valet raised an eyebrow, a strange, plucked thing. "I believe it's from a client of yours, sir," he said, looking at a spot somewhere behind the lawyer's shoulder. "If I've understood things."

Miss Crawford, it had to be. Wyre's heart caught on his ribs. Some good news about Aspinall might put this whole thing straight. But any hopes he entertained in that direction quickly evaporated: the letter described what seemed to him merely another runaround. A child had come up to Miss Crawford in the park, and pressed a note in her hand promising information. The implausible site of enlightenment was The Cranes, a well-known dockside palace of demirepdom. *Five o'clock that evening . . . could he meet her?* She suggested the Lakeman's cottage, St James's Park. It wasn't far – but Christ, it didn't leave him much time. Obviously, she was going, with or without him. He cursed. Miss Crawford was what wags in a gentleman's club might refer to lickerously as a 'stunner', to be enjoyed discreetly from the corners of flickering eyes. Cranes men – some of the women, too – on the other hand, would look at her in the same way a half-starved cur would eye a plate of meat.

He begged paper from the secretary and scribbled a quick reply, handing it to Paulet.

Squaring his absence with Read turned out to be easier than he anticipated: the magistrate was quite capable of dealing with a few pot-washers and daisy-trimmers.

"Go where you please. We resume at seven."

Wyre left as quickly as he could without sprinting through St James's echoing chambers.

The sky over the park was a sweeping blue scrow. Squadrons of soft-billed birds swooped into thick clouds of insects, which hung like living ornaments over the lake.

"May I see the note?" he asked.

She reached into the frilly covering over a pocket hole, producing a scrap of paper.

"*News from the dead.* Signed – no one." Wyre looked up. It didn't bode well.

"Do you think Robert is meant?"

"It might not be him," he replied, disingenuously. "I've heard of The Cranes. All lawyers have. It isn't . . . seemly."

She caught his sleeve; the intimacy caught him off-guard. "I'm aware of the risks, Mr Wyre."

The horses at the St James's hackney rank were in bad harness, beset by swarms of flies. The waterman waved them over to a two-nag chariot. The buck cabby wasn't cheap, though – one shilling per mile, sixpence extra for every half-mile on top. Daylight robbery. Wyre climbed in after Miss Crawford. A used copy of *The Gazette* lay on the seat.

They set off along lanes edged by dark brick buildings, crumbling barracks, dye-houses, fulling mills and old limestone villas. Landmarks began to appear at unexpected points on the horizon. The cabby, who was apparently in a hurry to be in two places at once, had obviously been inducted into a differently connected city to the one Wyre was accustomed.

261

Miss Crawford sat in silence. Wyre unfolded the abandoned newspaper – a report of a tiger terrorizing an Indian village caught his eye. Suddenly, he was aware of Miss Crawford leaning forward. Her hair, so thick it could have been an intricate wig, flexed and swayed with the motion of the carriage. Walnut oil . . . He took the scent deep into his lungs.

"*There*, Mr Wyre – " she said, pointing, a look of strange intensity on her face.

He followed her finger.

murdered in his bedroom. Thomas, Covent Garden waiter, 37 years, died from a single penetrating wound to his liver. His landlord discovered him lying in thick blood. Thomas has been three times convicted of detestable crimes, including two unnatural assaults on other men. It is supposed death occurred during one of these habitual encounters.

So the story had finally appeared, neatly framed by a familiar narrative . . . No mention of the private chemical factory, though. Why didn't that surprise him? But what was any of it to Miss Crawford?

"A nasty business," he said. "As a matter of fact," he said, feeling a swell of pride, "I was with the investigator who found him."

Her cheeks were ashen. "Robert complained of a waiter he met in Vere Street, the night of the arrests. A man who deceived him in the most repellent manner possible. *His* name was Thomas."

One of their carriage wheels found a disturbance in the road, throwing them sideways.

"It's possible," he began slowly, "that this Thomas fellow – " he lowered his voice, though it was impossible

262

the jarvis could hear them over the great noise of the wheels
" – had a hand in the business with Sellis, the assassin
everyone's talking about."

"What does your Mr Read say?"

"He's determined to see Sellis as an isolated event. You
might as well argue the earth is flat than question that
view."

Little by little the formal city was becoming a sprawling
port town of wood-and-brick pilings, muddy banks,
wharfs and warehouses. Shopping squares ceded to fenced
yards, to high brick walls, dark with sun.

They were moving parallel with the river now. Wyre
squinted through the dusty glass sliders at ketch-rigged
cargo boats straining at slimy mooring posts. There was
a smell of fish on the turn. The whole district was one
enormous wooden hull.

"When I was a little girl in Spanish Town," she began
suddenly, "I saw a strange bird crouching. Its call was
high and rousing. Some of the birds in the islands have
calls like *Sweet-John!–Sweet-John!* This one sang *Whip-
Tom-Peter! Whip-Tom-Peter!* – over and over. I ran
home to tell my father. He didn't believe me. It might
seem trivial now, but I saw it, Mr Wyre." The intensity
startled him. She looked away. "I saw many things in the
islands."

"I'll make sure the right questions are asked," he said,
simply.

"I've been reading a great deal about the assault on the
Duke of Cumberland. Do you think Sellis really cut his
own throat?"

Wyre looked out again at the barren quayside. The
smell was getting worse. "It's easier to tell you what I
don't think," he said. "That Sellis was capable of carrying
out a frenzied attack on the Duke, then making it all the

way back to his bedchamber – through five locked doors – unaided."

"Is the Duke still in danger? Is the King?"

Wyre made a wry face. "With any luck, Sellis's accomplice will turn out to be a servant. Some unthinking miss who had her head turned by Sellis. Bit of a flashy devil, our Joseph." He rubbed his eyes, suddenly weary. "The only thing dividing the Valet's Room from the Duke's sleeping quarters is a thin wall. Practically just paper, like a Chinese lantern. Sellis must have known that; he'd slept on the other side often enough. So why would such a slightly built man imagine he could slaughter a soldiering Duke, six feet in his stockings, without rousing the on-duty valet? It doesn't make sense. Not that such inconsequential details seem to bother anyone."

"Oh, wasn't Sellis on duty that evening? It's what the newspapers imply."

Sugar Island inflections, more noticeable now.

"As a matter of fact, the attending valet that night was a man called Neale. He and Sellis were at each other's throats. We have witnesses to corroborate that bit, at least."

"Women aren't the only ones who know how to deceive," she said. "I've seen men play-act almost as well." She looked away again, the ghost of a smile on her lips. When she turned back, her face had regained its bleakness. "Robert's alive, Mr Wyre." She clasped both hands to her midriff, a shocking gesture. "I feel it . . . here."

The chaise trembled to a halt at an unkempt verge, parking up above baked river banks. Wyre gazed down. Had Aspinall met his end here, covered in lime, buried in the river sand?

Seabirds floated above on hot currents, folding the air. Their shrill cries – flat, static, hypnotic – competed with the *rawk-rawk* of gulls clipping water. A pair of boots flashed in front of the window as the driver vaulted down from his box. Wyre climbed out with rather less agility, and waited for Miss Crawford, feeling like a prisoner who had just managed to excavate his way out of one prison cell, only to come up in another.

Miss Crawford stepped out. Her foot slipped off the highest tread. Wyre grabbed for her, taking the dark woman by the waist. No hips; light as a feather. Cabby watched with a grin. Wyre reluctantly tipped him sixpence to wait.

The Cranes was a squat, bare brick building at the end of a fenced-off patch of stony ground, a row of river hoists rising next to it. Wyre stared down at the murky body of water. If there were any salmon or skegger-trout swimming among the weeds, they never broke the surface.

Tavern harlots milled about the entrance, taunting Miss Crawford as if she were part of the competition.

"Cum to dip yer tail in the Thames?" one of the punks called.

Colouring, Wyre shepherded her inside. Remote, pallid faces suggested hashish, confirmed by drifting coils of pungent smoke. On one of the wooden benches, a trull – her back mercifully to them – was bouncing in the lap of some leathery tar; the motion sent ripples of shock up her bare midriff. With each rhythmic rise, a pair of pendulous stones appeared beneath her, as if they were part of her own body. Wyre was pulling Miss Crawford to him in an effort to shield her, when a heavy arm fell across his shoulders. He spun round in alarm.

"He who seeks out trouble never misses it – ain't that the saying, Mr Wyre?" (His accoster was a man of fifty, who wore a hat fashionable a decade ago. He had a paunch, and his eyes were the colour of quince.) "Oh, don't mind them – " he nodded at the clinching couple. "The Cranes's a right temple of jollity. Yer soon get used to it."

"How do you know my name?" Wyre demanded.

Quince Eyes said nothing as he piloted them to a table near the back of the tavern. "How to get the most out of life," he began, when they were seated, his head moving from side to side like an owl's as he squinted into the shadows. "That's the question yer oughta be asking yerself."

Three heavily tattooed men, all with sailors' salt-cracked faces, were cutting cards a few tables away. Two juvenile females, their rudimentary nipples visible above their low-cut blouses, sat between the men. They looked bored by the game.

Snatches of conversation drifted over.

"Got nabbed by a big bastard of a hound …" said one, close-cropped with strong, flat features, a spreading symbol tattooed on his neck. In place of a nose, he wore a gutta-percha imitation, coloured to resemble flesh.

"Bite yer, did yer dog?" asked a squint-eyed albino with fleecy hair.

"Aye," Gutta-Percha replied. "Legs, arms, arse. The vicious cunt wouldn't let go."

"What d'yer do?" said the third man, a sheen of sweat imparting an aquatic quality to his skin.

"Caught hold of its front legs, like you're supposed to. Held on, one in each fist. Can't let go once you start that, mind, or they'll tear your throat out. Then – " from the corner of his eye, Wyre watched him perform a violent pulling-apart action. "Split the bastard's heart."

"What de owner say?"

"Fuck the owner, I weren't hangin' round."

A barmaid arrived with three mugs of dark beer. She set them down roughly, slops of creamy froth wallowing over the sides. Quince Eyes raised his mug. His other hand jiggled at his side, causing his cuffs to flap.

A piece of stacked-up enigma slotted into place.

"Your name's Wardle," Wyre said in a low voice. "I could have you arrested for failing to appear at the Vere Street trial."

"But yer won't."

Wyre regarded him. The intelligence better be good. "Tell us where Robert Aspinall is."

The man tapped his nose. "Plenty of time fer that."

"Tell us now and Bow Street might overlook your earlier behaviour."

Wardle's odd eyes flicked across to Miss Crawford. "Fine piece of porcelain you got there. Put her in a bell jar, set her on the mantlepiece – watch her beat against the glass."

"How dare you – " Wyre began.

"Funny thing," the man went on, turning to Miss Crawford, "way I 'eard it, your Miss Molly was slated to hang – come what may, if yer catch my drift. An' now, Mr Wyre, dread agent of the State, travels all the way to a dockside shitpot for a parley, hoping for a scrap that might lead him to the rum dog."

Miss Crawford looked at him coldly. "Mr Wyre's agreed to help me. He's being paid for his trouble."

Wardle peered into the gloom again. "Don't matter now. The time of princes an' kings is comin' to an end."

"You talk like a revolutionary," Wyre said in disgust. Flickering movement at the neighbouring table.

"Believe what you like, Mr Wyre. It won't change nothing. A new unity's coming. As fer the Palace, now – touch with kid gloves, an' you'll hear nothing, move nothing. Rain down violent blows – well, yer might just hear things resound."

"Are you capable of talking only in riddles?" (Across the tables, Gutta-Percha was still shuffling cards but the females had vanished.) "A life may depend on what you know. Where's Robert Aspinall, and why didn't you appear at his trial?"

Wardle gave him an inscrutable smile. "Ever hear of Joanna Southcott?"

"Of course. Napoleon's brother." So the man was a disciple, one of those convinced the nation's present ills would usher in a bright new age – after, that was, the conflagration had destroyed all but the sealed 144,000 elect. It seemed Wardle and his sort weren't averse to adding to those ills, if it meant speeding the arrival of the valley of sweet waters.

Wardle gave him a pitying look. "The Spirit communicates with her directly." He closed his lids, an ecstatic expression building on his face. "Before I was acquainted wi' Joanna's writings, what little faith I had was built on sand."

"Wasn't she tried for blasphemy?" said Miss Crawford.

The eyes sprang open. "They claimed she was the devil's dupe, but he is hers."

"We're in no mood for a sermon," said Wyre. "Is Robert Aspinall alive?"

"*Please*, Mr Wardle," said Miss Crawford, her lashes wet. "I can tell you're not a bad man."

He grinned. "To what purpose did the Lord's disciples warn men t' flee the temptation of the devil?"

"Hell's tee – " Wyre bit back the oath. "I thought you'd seen the light, or whatever you call it. I suppose it was in one of Southcott's ranting seminaries."

"Oh, I've seen it. I've read that woman's shining words." Wardle switched to a sing-song intonation: "The seven stars are seven angels, and the seven candlesticks are

268

seven." He stopped abruptly. "You want to know what really happened at the Vere Street trial? I made a wicked bargain, that's what – " his eyes began to shine again " – but I couldn't keep it. Not when Joanna's own trial was prosecuted so unjustly."

"A bargain?"

"For immunity from the law. But they wanted it all, Mr Wyre. Prisoners in indecent postures, shirts turned up on their backs, men stooping so low I couldn't see their heads, bare arses everywhere." His breath rasped in his throat. "Tokens of seed, Mr Wyre." He turned to Miss Crawford and leered.

"Who suborned your evidence?" Wyre said, his jaw tightening. "Who paid you to lie?" If this was Brockton's work, God help him there would be a reckoning.

Wardle leaned back in his chair. "Wouldn't know his name." He took a draught from his mug. "Grey hair. Proud."

"Is that all you can say?" The man could be describing anybody. Even Read fit that description.

Wardle lifted his shoulders. "I'm not concerned with minions. I wish to bruise the head of Satan himself, to 'elp bring about Joanna's prophecies."

"And who would Satan be?" Wyre smiled. "I suppose that's not his real name, either."

"The man I mean's a devil by nature, and a devil by practice." He drained his mug.

"Does this man have my fiancé?" Reaching across the table, Miss Crawford touched Wardle's sleeve.

His look became sly. "Some people seem t' think yer can dance in a net an' nobody sees."

"Enough enigmas. You're talking about Mr Parlez-Vous, aren't you?"

If the name meant anything, Wardle made a good job of

concealing it. Wyre was about to push him, when the man leapt to his feet, eyes wide and staring.

"What?" he exclaimed. "You've led his monster right to me!"

Wyre followed his gaze into the shadows, but saw nothing. Wardle, however, staggered from their table like a man who'd seen his own ghost.

"After him . . ." Wyre pulled Miss Crawford to her feet. "He knows where Robert is."

He still had her by the hand when they debouched into the bleached scrubland outside The Cranes. When he saw the leather strop, it had already begun its transit. He jerked his head back, almost pulling off Leighton's trick. The intersection was glancing, but enough to send him to his knees. He swayed there for a moment before a shod foot flipped him over. Then an awful weight pressing down on his ribcage. The strop rose again, dividing for a glorious moment the sun itself. A dim awareness of sharp cries behind him; a guttapercha nose floating above; a sudden blaze.

When the day's fragments reassembled, a dark, handsome face was staring down. Dark lips repeated his name till it sounded like a charm in some pagan ceremony. He swiped feebly at the air.

"Mr Wyre! I thought they'd – " Miss Crawford was crouching over him. Rolling over onto all fours, he retched noisily like a cat that had eaten coriander seed.

"Feckin' mollies," a punk screeched inexplicably from the tavern entrance. "Oughta be ashamed of yerselves!"

"Least the liddle 'un put up a decent foight."

Wyre struggled to his feet. Miss Crawford's pretty dress was stained with clay dust. Groggy, he tried to make sense of the dirt, of the insults. "Did they hurt you?" Another wave of nausea arrived.

"Dem jus' duppies, bwai," she replied softly – or something like that, her voice jumping with odd inflections.

Wyre gasped, spitting something greenish. He looked blankly across at the trulls.

"I'm perfectly well, Mr Wyre," she said in her usual voice. "You were right. I should have listened. It was a mistake to come."

The jarvis was leaning against his coach, watching with apparent amusement.

They travelled back in silence. Wyre's head felt like somebody had rung triple bob majors in it. As they trundled onto the bridge out of Southwark, Miss Crawford's fingers brushed his hand, closed and tightened. He let them.

"That gang was expecting us," she said at last.

He nodded.

"They might have killed you, Mr Wyre, and it would have been my fault."

The truth of her words arrived like an icy blast.

She was silent again for a moment. "Mr Wardle spoke of the prophetess. What possible interest could that awful sect have in Robert?"

Wyre thought he could answer that. He'd heard William discourse on Southcott's deluded philosophies often enough. "Joanna foresaw the war with France, or so her followers claim. They see the Tyrant as Antichrist intent on crushing all religion – though as far as I can tell, it's just lots of guff about thrones of clouds. If Wardle's role at the trial was to send the Vere Street gang to the scaffold, his sect must have thought its members in league with the French." To be fair, Joanna's lot weren't the only ones who believed that.

Miss Crawford appeared to consider for a moment. "Poor Mr Wardle. I'm sure he was decent, underneath. Do you think those ruffians hurt him?"

271

Wyre stared beyond the window. He seemed to be witnessing the destruction of the world: a bricolage of barbarous burning, the clattering of lipless jaws, cities plunged in darkness. Mercifully, his fantasy gave way to more habitual scenes: of crowds milling before shop façades, a sea of bobbing hats. But it was a city of utter strangers, empty and suspect. He picked a man out at random – out buying a gift for his wife, or his Cheapside mistress? Or (it seemed equally likely) for some broad-shouldered regimentalist in the Scots guards? A convert to the prophetess, or an agent of France, plotting a tremendous explosion. As the sun struck the tip of St Paul's, Wyre had an abrupt idea of a great carriage thundering down the nave.

Miss Crawford took her hand back. "Mr Wardle said Robert was meant to hang." Those large eyes, searching Wyre's own. He looked away. "Was the trial fair?"

"Wardle was cracked."

They turned into Panton Street, where a food riot was in full swing. Bread or blood agitators had halted a wagon, and were seizing sacks of wheat and potatoes.

—— *hanged than starve!*

Wyre turned away in disgust. He imagined one of Mr Shoreditch's new reaping machines trundling towards the rioters on cast-iron wheels, whitethorn cogs a spinning blur, cutting a swathe through the protestors.

48. The Phoenix of Sodom

Only a few patches of red paint clung to the cobbles at the St James's Square rank on the Mall. The war was bankrupting the nation. Wyre offered Miss Crawford his arm down from the hackney. For the hundredth time, he wondered what could possibly induce a woman of her calibre to devote herself to a misfire like Aspinall.

Across the pavement, a spidery figure in a tight hat was hawking pamphlets.

"*Phoenix of Sodom!* Know your enemy! Tuppence apiece."

Wyre looked disbelievingly: the hawker was a Courthouse colleague, Holloway, a sucking barrister a couple of years older than himself. His vinegary performances in court were effective, but for some reason he'd never enjoyed Best's favour.

Seeing Wyre, Holloway's fervent expression turned to one of discomfort, then defiance. "It's what people are thinking . . ."

Wyre took a copy of the pamphlet from a tottering pile, and opened a page at random:

. . . mockeries of bridesmaids found wallowing on beds with wretches of the lowest description, scores of unnatural monsters giving justice the slip. The fashionable part of the coterie is thought to be deep in secrets.

Rabble-rousing guff. There was even a passage fulminating against Mr Best, who was accused of personally presiding over the release of mollies.

Wyre gazed at Holloway in astonishment. "Hiding behind anonymous won't help you." He tapped the pamphlet. "Best will know it's you."

"It's what people are thinking." The barrister glanced sourly at Miss Crawford. "Those bawds in britches won't be put off by a stand in the stocks. They're like eels – dry them out, they resurrect in the next shower."

Wyre shook his head. "You shouldn't have dragged Best into your fantasies."

"Fantasies, you say? There's a secret society at work, if only you knew. Yea, even in the halls of power . . ." He began striking his pamphlet against the back of his hand in time to the rhythm of his speech. "A hidden web – poke it in one place, and it shakes somewhere else." His eyes shrank to tiny furnaces. "It's time to put an end to their cannibal philosophy! Time to rinse them out!"

"You've gone too far," Wyre said simply, tossing the pamphlet at Holloway's feet.

The barrister's only riposte was his cat cry, "*Phoenix of Sodom! Phoe–nix o' Sodom!*"

At the end of the Mall, the crowd that had been there since the beginning of the inquest into Sellis's death flexed and tensed. Wyre turned to Miss Crawford, suggesting they meet the following day. Aspinall was the key – he was more convinced of that than ever. Besides, Read didn't value his contribution, so what difference did it make?

"There's an intermission scheduled for three o'clock," he said. "We can meet at the east gate to the park."

"I'm sorry you were hurt, Mr Wyre."

He nodded, even mustering a half-smile Leighton wouldn't have disowned, before leaving her, setting off back to the Palace.

An elderly man leant against the green palings opposite Marlborough House reading something, one leg lifted to form a raised triangle, right foot pressed against the crook of the left knee. The dexterity was at curious odds with the few carefully combed back wisps of hair that still clung to the man's head.

"A prophet of plagues and torrents, our Mr Holloway," the old man said, lifting a copy of *The Phoenix of Sodom* as Wyre drew alongside.

Wyre regarded him cautiously.

The elderly gentleman touched his forehead, the vestiges of a military salute, perhaps, discernible beneath the casual gesture. "Glad to see that knock on the head hasn't put you off."

Wyre stared in astonishment, but before he could demand an explanation the old man was away, slipping like mercury between pedestrians. The lawyer watched him go, abashed. Should he just accept his private business was a matter of transparency to the outside world?

A mackerel sky hung above the brick towers. The sentinels at the barricade lifted their ceremonial weapons, this time without issuing a challenge.

49. Waiting Room

The message had arrived early that morning, and simply informed her James would be handed over at midday. From the look on the gaoler's face when she arrived at the Courthouse, she assumed she'd been summoned to collect a corpse. At her own costs. Her husband certainly smelled like a cadaver, but he wasn't dead; though not entirely alive, either. She'd stared at the gash in his forehead, at the thick amber fluid pulsing at the bony brim, building up in little pushes till there was enough to drip over and run down the bridge of his nose.

During those first hours, James had switched between intervals of thundering defiance, when he boasted he'd put the State to flight, and periods of uncontrollable raving, when he accused her of having lain with his gaoler before his eyes. Then he'd sunk into a sullen torpor, cursing his fortune for having taken up with molly bitches.

The door to the operating room creaked open, and the

surgeon put his head into the waiting hall. He was tall and grey-haired, and kept his eye glasses fastened around his head with a brightly coloured ribbon. Sarah rose to her feet.

"All done, Mrs Cooke," he said, motioning for her to join him in his theatre.

A man with a severely deformed frame, waiting with the other patients, struggled to his feet, throwing an invisible hook towards the operating room: "Mr Cline! Mr Cline!"

Sarah stepped inside to find the surgeon leaning over a basin of water in the corner, laving a little blood from his hands. Her husband sat quietly on a bloodied wooden chair.

"No dirty fingers for a few days," the surgeon instructed. "Give it a chance to heal."

She peered down at the shiny coin sewn into the neatly trimmed bone. Was that tent stitch? It looked like French Knot.

"The sixpence is on me," the surgeon said with a smile, adjusting the ribbon around his ears. He looked down at her. "How will you be paying for the rest?"

Sarah helped her husband up – he stank of deadening brandy – and led him by the hand into the waiting hall, setting him down on one of the short wooden benches. The other patients dotted about the bare atrium stared at the gleaming disc in his skull, the skin puckered around its edges.

"You wait here, James," she said, in a reassuring voice. "I won't be long."

She returned to the consulting room, put her back against the wall, bustled up her skirts.

50. Countrymen

Wyre gazed at the intersecting corridors, each a dizzying turn inward. The smart figure of Paulet appeared.

"The one you want's back there – " The valet pointed, his finger oddly curved. "It's easily missed, Mr Wyre, easily missed."

"I'm not going to ask where you got that," Read said, pointing at the welt, and scowling. "And you're not going tell me."

The Duke's under-butler, Joseph Strickland, was impeccably attired in a dark uniform, his frame canting slightly to the left.

"Sellis was civil enough," he began in a professionally remote voice. "I believe I saw him in his Highness's dressing room on the night of the attack. I was a little surprised to meet him." Strickland's smooth face bore a tiny fishhook-shaped scar that hung like a question mark beneath his lips.

"Why's that?" Read said bluntly.

"It wasn't his turn, sir."

Wyre had heard that phrase once too often. "What time would you say this was?"

"Oh, some time around eleven. Sellis looked at me oddly. I believe he may have laughed in what the maids would call a ghastly manner."

"What was he doing in the dressing room, if it wasn't his turn?" Read flapped at his ear with two fingers.

"His Highness often calls us on a whim. I believe there was talk of a visit to Windsor."

Wyre cleared his throat. "Tell me, Mr Strickland, what does a valet do?"

"It's a caring role, sir. He assists his master in dressing and undressing, keeps his clothes in good order, sees the housemaid lights the fires and fills the ewer, prepares hot shaving-water, airs his master's dressing gown, warms his slippers, combs his hair."

"Anything else?" Wyre made a play of studying him.

Strickland's lips twitched. "Nothing I'd be aware of."

The under-butler's place was taken by the broad-faced housekeeper, Sarah Varley. She laid a declaratory hand on her ample bosom.

"The problem's all them foreign types." She wrinkled her nose. "Thousands of 'em in London, all h'aspiring to be servants. Barely speak the language. Assassins in waiting, sir. That's what they say."

"Oh?" Read frowned. "What else do they say?"

She gave him a crafty look. "That someone paid Sellis to murder his Royal Highness."

"And do they also say you helped him? Don't look so surprised," Read added when the woman paled visibly. "Mr Wyre seems to think someone must have deliberately forgotten to lock the doors between the Valet's Room and the householders' private quarters. I'm beginning to wonder if he's right. How else could Sellis have made his way back?"

"Weren't me, sir." She stared at the polished floor like a recalcitrant child. "Perhaps you should ask Mr Neale."

Read frowned. "Explain what you mean by that comment."

"Well," she began hesitantly, "you know what they say about Sellis and Neale."

"I don't, but you'll tell us."

Wyre remembered Paulet's nugget about Mrs Sellis's suspicions.

"That the pair were always sneaking about the Valet's Room, sir." She squirmed beneath the Chief Magistrate's gaze.

"Mrs Varley – " Read's tone had acquired a dangerous edge. "Mr Neale and Sellis shared the Valet's Room. Mr Paulet, too, for that matter. There was no sneaking. Forget your petty gossiping. You're to give an account of your own movements two nights ago."

"But Sellis's preedy-lections were well known to the householders," she protested, an air of stubbornness coming through. "It's a wonder he didn't try to lead his Royal Highness astray." The housekeeper scrunched up her nose again. "Swooning over drummer-boys when the Duke went riding, thinking things no right-minded person would ever think. Not that the Duke would do anything like that," she added quickly. "To be honest, I felt sorry for Mrs Sellis."

Wyre doubted that. The very suspicions that had driven Mrs Sellis to distraction had been grist to this house-keeper's mill. What a place. "Did you ever see something of this kind with your own eyes?" he asked.

"*I* didn't, sir, but the servants used to laugh about it. Sellis and Neale once came to blows over a boy in the Guards. That's common knowledge," she said, glancing at Read, her face set. "It's a sin, sir. I won't have my beliefs squeezed."

"And what if we were to raise these allegations with Neale? Or better still, with Mrs Neale?"

Her face sank. "She wouldn't like it, sir."

"That's enough slum talk," Read said, a warning in his voice. "Tell us about that night. What did you see? *Actually* see?"

"I was with Margaret Jones," Mrs Varley said, more subdued now. "The lights were out in the passageway.

Neither of us like the dark. We passed Mr Sellis going upstairs, and wished each other good night."

"How did you know it was Sellis?" Wyre said. "You just told us it was dark."

"He carried a dark lantern. Mr Sellis has one of those."

"Did you actually see his face?"

"*Well*, Mrs Varley?" Read prompted.

She gave a little curtsey. "No, sir, not his face."

Shaking his head, Read concluded the deposition. The housekeeper signed her name in spidery characters, each one detached and determinedly independent.

"That rum bitch deserves a ducking," Read said as the door closed behind her. "There's not an incorruptible bone in her body. What's the matter?" he said, frowning. "Lost in the intellectual world?"

Wyre bit his tongue. There were hidden depths in the witness statements, things more vitally interfused, which Read didn't seem prepared to grasp. Why did the Bow Street man always wish to drag him back to the surface and hold him there?

"We're being fed a story. It's been rehearsed, but everyone's getting it slightly wrong."

Read simply regarded him. "You mean well, Wyre, I'll concede that. But don't you think the Duke's been through enough? A patriot wouldn't prolong this nonsense. The depositions agree in ninety-five per cent of the details, and that's sufficient for me. The other five per cent can be put down to petty vindictiveness or plain muddle. This whole thing's a waste of everyone's time and effort." He pushed his chair back roughly, and got to his feet. "Join us tomorrow, if you must. The inquest will be over by lunch. And Wyre, we'll be taking Cumberland's testimony. The Duke won't welcome schoolboyish theories. He's a man who wishes to be looked at, not into."

Read strode from the Cupola Office, followed by his secretary. Wyre watched them go, waiting a little while before making his own way out. Something important was eluding them; he hadn't changed his mind about that. The deponents' stories were too concordant, not enough of those little variations and telling discrepancies Courthouse prosecutors were trained to spot and jemmy apart. What did they *really* know? There'd been an attack on the Duke; someone had been heard shuffling about in the servants' passage; Mrs Neale had been sent to fetch Jackson and Sellis; Neale himself had ... The edges of the narrative were already beginning to fray.

Wyre pulled up sharp. He'd missed the piazza door. Paulet's word: *befuddled*. Hell's teeth, he'd gone practically all the way to the Valet's Room. Back to where he began. Perhaps that was just as well. It wouldn't hurt to look again. This time without Read.

A dark red ribbon marked the room as off-limits. Wyre slipped beneath it and gave the door a little push. Inside, leaning at the mantlepiece, both hands flat against the tiles, was Neale. The valet turned.

51. Conversations

Wyre decided to brazen it out. If he shouldn't be here, neither should Neale. Read had made it too easy for this man. He pulled the door to.

"The Valet's Room is out of bounds during the inquest, Mr Neale."

"Then you'll have to explain it to his Highness," replied the valet coolly. "He asked me to change the sheeting."

As outflanking gambits went, it was a good one. Wyre

was determined to keep his composure. "I trust the Duke's wounds are healing. I'd been meaning to ask you about them."

Neale smirked. "I'd have said that was Mr Jackson's speciality."

"Why don't you give me the layman's version. That's what you are, isn't it? A layman."

For an electrifying instant, Wyre thought the valet was about to rush at him, but his fierce look vanished almost as quickly as it had appeared.

"I can tell you what I saw," he said with a shrug. "The back of the Duke's right hand was cut across. There were gashes on his left arm; one of them looked deep. There was something on the back of his right thigh. He was also cut on his head."

"You saw all this in the dark?"

"I'd lit a lamp by then."

"While we're at it, tell me about Sellis's corpse. I know you were in his room that night."

"It's no secret," came the reply. "I told Read that."

"*Alone* with the body, I mean. Do you deny it?"

Neale laughed. "What a strange question." He appeared to consider. "People were coming and going. It's possible. Why do you ask?"

"I think Sellis had a co-conspirator, a slinker who goes by the name of Mr Parlez-Vous."

"Can't say I ever met him." The valet's lips buckled into a sneer.

"Down at the stables today, by any chance?"

"Mucking out isn't part of my duties, Mr Wyre."

"You knew Sellis better than most. Tell me, why would he attempt to slay his master?"

"Are you asking for my opinion?" Neale said, scornfully. "I thought you were after facts." He looked away.

"Sellis despised the principles of royalty, just as he hated religion. Anything that was moral."

"And you? Did you share those views? I've heard you two saw eye-to-eye on quite a few things."

"Oh?"

"The maids chatter, Neale. They've said some rather interesting things about the nature of your – " he let the space develop " – association with Sellis."

"Don't be absurd." His cheeks reddened. "Haven't you worked it out yet, Mr Prosecutor? The attack was intended to lay the blame on me. Sellis knew I'd be sleeping in the next room. The schedules are no secret, they hang in Mrs Varley's office. That foreign bastard intended I should be discovered with the Duke's body. He dug a pit for me, but fell into it himself."

Wyre sensed a fracture. "The servants say the two of you were often together in the Valet's Room."

"I've never found myself in an improper situation with another man, if that's what you mean."

"No? I hear the pair of you had a fight. From what I can gather, it sounded more like a lovers' tiff."

The valet took a step forward. "Who told you that? Scullery maids? Filthy creatures." He put out his tongue. "I did once fight with Sellis. What of it? It was my fault, if you must know. I pulled a newspaper out of his hands. But it was nothing. We made up immediately."

"Squabbling over a newspaper? Must have been quite a story. Someone you know get nabbed in Vere Street?"

It was a dry bite, and Neale smiled at it. "I don't have to indulge your fantasies, Mr Wyre. The Chief Magistrate has taken my affidavit. I didn't kill Sellis. Saying I did won't make it so. For your information, I was taken to see the corpse, and I assure you it didn't bleed in my presence."

"One other thing, were you acquainted with a man

named Thomas?" The valet's face gave nothing. "Someone studded him in his room last week. Professional job. Parlez-Vous' signature. This afternoon, an apprentice yager found himself on the wrong end of a horseshoe. I'd lay odds on you knowing him, too. While we're at it, Robert Aspinall hasn't been seen out lately. Friend of yours? I'm starting to think you're a dangerous man to know. "

The valet shook his head slowly.

"Drop the pretence, Neale. The servants look at you and see a hero, but I know better. Now, you'd better tell me who Mr Parlez-Vous is." The valet looked amused. "Fine." Wyre affected a shrug. "You might as well know you're my prime candidate."

"You'll have to win your promotion another way," Neale said with contempt, pushing past Wyre. The heels of his polished shoes created little detonations along the corridor.

The sun struck low in the lattice windows, filling the hallways with tincturing light. Ahead, Wyre discerned the outline of Mrs Varley. She was dusting off plant leaves.

"Piazza?" he said as he drew level.

"Next set of double doors." Before he could go, she reached out to touch his sleeve. "I made a bad impression earlier, Mr Wyre. I don't like flummery any more than you. But . . ." She faltered.

Wyre frowned. "*But*, Mrs Varley?"

"I didn't like to say in front of Mr Read, though I shan't sleep if I don't tell." Her lip began to tremble; another stern look from the lawyer elicited a quick stream of words: "They say, sir, the Yorkers do, that someone found the Duke . . ."

"Found him?"

"With Mr Sellis's wife, sir. Beneath a petticoat coverlet."

Wyre stared mutely. He remembered what Read had said about the Duke standing godson to Sellis's fourth child. That decision to give the brat the Duke's name, Ernest Augustus . . .

"Who found them in that situation?"

"Mr Sellis himself, sir."

"I thought you said – "

"I don't know what the house is coming to, Mr Wyre. There's Margaret lashing out at Mrs Neale in Birdcage Walk, and Sellis attacking the Duke . . . It's all topsides under."

"Margaret did *what*?"

But the housekeeper was already scuttling away, ignoring his command to return, her gait something between a hop and a dip.

Margaret had struck at her mistress? That dark blush beneath Mrs Neale's eye – not a birthmark, then. He struggled to absorb it . . . Margaret Jones, in thrall to her gospels. As for Cumberland being discovered with *Mrs Sellis* . . . the whole thing was taking on the character of a closet drama or, rather, Greek revenge tragedy. Had the Duke really made use of *both* Sellises, driving each mad with envy? He'd heard of such things. If true, both husband and wife might have felt they had reason to play the assassin. He fleshed out each scenario in his imagination: first, Mrs Sellis gratifying Cumberland to pay her ganymede husband back for having done the same, then punishing the Duke in turn by slashing him in the night. Next, Sellis: discovering his wife unhooked in the arms of his royal employer . . . Wyre winced. What man wouldn't wish to slaughter his cuckolder? If anyone ever abused Rose in that manner!

The piazza door appeared. Wyre stepped out into

blenching sun. Making his way across the nestled squares, he spotted a tiny, thin figure looking down at him from the Palace's helmeted garrets and cocklofts.

Watching, being watched. It was a way of life here.

He stopped by the stables to collect Leighton's dandy-charger, and wheeled it up the gravel path to the low arch that led out onto St James's Road. The crowd had thinned a little. Wyre lifted his leg over the bright yellow perch, leaned forward so his chest was resting on the cushioned perch, and pushed off.

He got halfway to Mrs Mason's apartments when he threw his heels down hard, swung the machine round, and plotted a new course for Great Windmill Street.

"There's no news – " he said quickly, seeing Miss Crawford's expectant expression. "I thought we might visit an old client of mine. I promised I'd keep him abreast, and I'm always able to think more clearly after talking to him. Differently, at any rate. The experience is a bit like becoming aware of your own tongue. Nothing's the same for the rest of the day." How absurd he must sound.

Miss Crawford merely nodded, stepping out of her doorway as she was, bare-shouldered, no pelisse. He watched as she went past him, one tiny hand on the dark iron railings. Rose's shoulder blades were smooth and fluted, whereas hers looked like two harmonic arches of a harp, with muscles for strings.

"Yours, Mr Wyre?" She stared at the yellow hobby horse, which he'd padlocked to a downpipe.

"Yes. It's a long story."

They walked the mile to No. 17 South Molton Street in humid air, saying little. There seemed too much at stake. How like hog's grease missing from a carriage axle was the lack of smoothing pleasantries – sooner or later the wheel would burn.

William's door made a scraping sound as if something had got trapped beneath the bottom rail. A mountain of radiating flesh greeted them in the doorway. Wyre flinched inwardly – he should have mentioned this strange side to William's character. Miss Crawford, however, showed no signs of discomfort, as if a full view of rolling regions was entirely in the usual run of things.

"Huguenot blood," the printer whispered to Wyre, his eyes shining with pleasure, as he showed Miss Crawford through the cramped hall to the parlour.

The table was its usual muddle of colourful sketches and half-completed oils-and-tempera. Today, there were also some intriguing head-and-tail-piece designs evidently intended for a larger project. A meeting with William was always a meeting across forms.

Face angelic, devilish, the printer fetched a dark decanter of wine, three glasses pressed to his pale, grey-haired chest. Pouring brimmers, he demanded a précis of the last two days.

"The whole thing's a thick, wet darkness," Wyre said, after conveying the gist of events (swearing William to secrecy first). "It's impossible to see through. You could hold the Palace in the palm of your hand, peer through ten windows at once, and still see nothing."

"Learn to see by the ear, through the tongue," William said, insinuating his own tongue through his lips. It flickered there.

Miss Crawford twisted the stem of her glass between finger and thumb. "Do you really think the Duke was attacked out of jealousy?"

"A terrible overreaction, if so," William said, chin propped on his fists. "Desire isn't an enemy to be brought under control. It helps make us what we are. Sooner murder an infant in its cradle than nurse unacted desires."

Miss Crawford looked uncertain. "I'm sure Mrs Sellis views it differently."

"My dear, when the passions throw us into violent agitations, we feel a thousand different sensations. It first awakens the animal fibres, and later the spiritual."

Wyre prayed William wouldn't start on his pet topic, the acclivity – sexual climax as the surest route to the divine being. That wasn't why he'd brought Miss Crawford here. Mercifully, the printer's wife arrived with a plate of cold meats and the three of them fell to discussing the hooks and reveals of the Sellis affair.

"So you see," Wyre said, having followed all his avenues to dead ends for the tenth time, "it's as if an invisible veil has been thrown over everything. It shouldn't hide anything, but somehow it does. Sellis is discovered lying on his bed, practically decapitated, but the razor, thick with his blood, is found yards away on the carpet. How could he have inflicted such a wound on himself, then toss away the blade? It defeats logic."

William snorted. "I hope you haven't been using logic as your yardstick."

In a quiet voice, Miss Crawford said: "People convulse when they lose large quantities of blood." Both men looked at her. "I've seen animals do it," she went on. "Sellis might have flung the blade from him in his death throes."

Her words struck the lawyer in the same way a child's painting can surprise with a garden of perfect serenity or a shipwreck scene whose boiling sea it is possible to imagine slipping beneath forever.

"But then there's Neale," Wyre continued. "He's a

provoking little coxcomb . . . but murder? The trouble is, all explanations seem equally plausible. It's a paradox of choice. Perhaps I've taken too much in."

"The dervish rejects nothing that's offered him," William said unhelpfully, resting his chin in the V formed by thumb and forefinger.

Wyre felt suddenly, unbearably weary. "My friend Leighton died in vain. I haven't uncovered an atom of hard evidence, nothing that troubles the official approach. Sellis will go down as a madpash suicide."

"Sometimes it's necessary to look inward at the sun," William said kindly, pouring more jingling claret.

"I don't like bright lights."

"Sir, you take only a professional view of things. I take a spiritual one. Experience," he added, with a mischievous smile, "is always a voyage to the end of the possible. Push forward, encounter the story where it is."

"Leighton used to say something like that . . ."

"Did he, indeed? Sounds like he was a fine fellow." William jumped to his feet, returning from his wall cabinet with a wooden fossil-box. Lifting the lid, he took out a spiral talisman; dull and rough on the outside, it glistened wetly within. "I purchased it from a female collector on the south coast." He held the stone to the lamplight. "She believed it to be some ancient species of maggot, ossified into crystal." He passed it to Miss Crawford, who stared as if struck. "I look at it whenever I need to remind myself of the impressions small lives can leave on hard objects."

Wyre sat back; the wine was making him dizzy. A bloom risen on Miss Crawford's dark cheeks. She asked for directions to the water closet.

The printer watched her go, waited a moment, then held up a finger for silence. A little pause, followed by a protracted tinkling sound. William's eyes gleamed like the figures in one of his rapturous pictures.

"Sometimes," he whispered, "the yard must be slack and slender, and sometimes extended and swollen. That's why the Creator made it of two bodies, not bony as in a wolf or dog. If its substance were formed so, it would be continually as hard as a stick, and a great nuisance to us."

A reply was beyond Wyre. It was time to leave the printer to his truths.

On the porch, William hugged them together in a wide embrace. "In a place of roses, children, be a rose. In a place of thorns, a thorn."

They'd gone a few yards along the uneven pavements when the printer's placid manner underwent an abrupt transformation.

"A new mode of existence is coming," he roared after them. "First the corroding fire. The gates will be consumed, their bolts and hinges melted." Wyre pressed Miss Crawford's hand as they dissolved into the fierce, chartered streets, William's voice still audible over the hubbub.

All this, even this house, will fall to the wrecking ball . . .

Wyre pulled Miss Crawford into him. She didn't resist.

"He gets like this sometimes, but it was important to me you meet him."

All too soon, they arrived at the entrance to Great Windmill Street. Wyre bid Miss Crawford goodnight.

"Thank you, Mr Wyre. For a few hours, I was able to – "

He took her hand, and raised it to his lips. The slightest pull.

Wyre waited till she was indoors, then unlocked the dandy-charger. Below the steps, the baker was at work, glimpsed through his floury, subterranean windows.

Still feeling the effects of William's dark wine, if merely wine it had been, Wyre pushed off unsteadily. He'd be going to bed nursing . . . How did William put it?

52. Mr Gew

Mrs Mason had laid the early edition of *The Gazette* at the foot of his bed. Most of the front page was given over to a spectacular rout at some northern Peninsula port or other (fifty cannon confiscated, a sailor's head attached by a single nerve), but it was a small paragraph at the bottom that caught Wyre's attention:

Yesterday evening a man's mutilated body was discovered floating in the Thames at Southwark. The top and back of the head had been shattered. The flesh was still tight, suggesting he was not long in the water. Bow Street refuses to speculate on the man's identity.

Was that Wardle's shattered cranium? Hardly the shining apocalypse Southcott had promised him.

He pulled on his jacket. It was the last day of the inquest.

Wyre stabled the running machine, the royal horses shifting uneasily, as if glimpsing futurity in the form of padded perches and wooden wheels.

Paulet was waiting at the steps, but Wyre declined his offer of guidance to the Cupola Office. It was time to demonstrate some independence, if only to a valet.

The day's first informant was Mrs Sellis. She was attractive, despite shadowy rings beneath her eyes. Fair-haired, though darker than Mrs Neale. She stood, hands clasped demurely at her lap, a perfect Venus pudica. Did she accept her husband's guilt, or did she know better?

Read began. "Was your husband in good health?" For once the question invited depth.

"Joseph complained of giddiness." Her tone was flat and oddly incurious. She despised Read – he could see it in her eyes. "I advised him to lie in the fresh air." She smiled bitterly. "But you mean was he mad." Her fingers tightened on the folds of her skirts. "He was as sane as either of you."

Read ignored that. "Were you aware he'd spoken to other servants about his wish to leave the Duke's service?"

"He may have alluded to it. I reminded him of our many advantages here, and told him not to make me unhappy by mentioning it again." She turned her head to the side. "Anyway, that was more than two years ago."

"Did he owe any money?" Wyre asked, in an effort to shake the interview out of the formal scheme into which it was settling.

She paused before answering. "If he did, I never heard him talk of it."

"*May have alluded . . . If he did . . .*" Read parroted. "Tell us everything that happened that night." His voice was sharp as gunshot now. "You're to leave nothing out."

She began again, but her narrative retained an unspontaneous quality. As she started to dilate on the Duchess's amiability and great kindnesses to her family, Wyre interrupted her.

"Tell me, Mrs Sellis, did your husband have any cause to be angry with his Highness?"

"The Duke was always kind."

Thinking of her coal and candles again. "No cause for resentment. None whatsoever?"

She appeared to consider. "There was one thing, but it was trivial."

"Humour us," said Read.

"Joseph used to ride everywhere with his Highness. In the spring, the Duke had a box built on his carriage. On the outside. I believe it is called a dickey. My husband was ordered to ride there. Joseph said it shook him." Her eyes dropped. "Riding backwards always made him ill."

He took notice at that. The Crispin Street letter had alluded to a dickey box. To precisely this grudge, in fact. At last an informant had ventured something that could be verified externally.

Read merely snorted. "Hardly enough to warrant slashing a man in his sleep. A dickey box!" He pulled a face.

"How often did your husband take his shift in the Duke's chamber?" Wyre asked.

"Three times a week. Neale and Mr Paulet were responsible for the other days."

"Did your husband and Mr Neale see eye-to-eye?"

The phrase took him to *her* eyes. Cornflower blue, like Rose's.

"They never got along." Her mouth twisted; then, in a voice perfectly even, she said: "Mr Neale is a fly-blown quim."

Read reacted to the word as if slapped. "Keep it respectable," he blustered. "You're a woman, damn it, and before the King's representatives! Now, what was the cause of their animosity?"

She stood silent for a moment, then replied, "Mr Neale insisted on sleeping with a loaded pistol, which he hung up above the valet's bed in a little red bag."

"We know all about the pistol," said Read, his manner perfunctory.

Wyre glanced at the magistrate. Surely, they weren't going to let this go? "Would you say," he cut in, "it was considered acceptable for a loaded weapon to be kept near the Duke's person?"

She gave a little shrug. "I've no idea. Mr Neale put it there."

"Why do you think he did that?"

She gave Wyre a withering look. "I believe you know why. In case my husband ever tried to enter the room at night."

"Why didn't your husband simply take the pistol down?" A lazy bluebottle landed on Wyre's arm. Its weight shocked him.

Her expression hardened. "Mr Paulet didn't like it hanging there either, but Neale made it a principle. My husband was forced either to accept the slight or allow things to come to blows, and I expressly forbade that. Joseph would have lost his position, which was precisely what Neale intended."

"You must have noticed your husband wasn't sleeping with you that night," Read said. "According to the schedule, he wasn't on call. Didn't you wonder where he was? Or perhaps you already knew. Why don't you explain his sleeping arrangements for Mr Wyre."

She smiled thinly. "Whenever my husband was on duty, he slept in the Valet's Room. When he was on call, he slept in his private bedroom. Otherwise, he slept with me in the family apartment. The assault on the Duke of Cumberland took place on one of Joseph's days off. And you're quite right, Mr Read, normally, in those circumstances, my husband would have spent the night in my bed. However, that evening my youngest child was ill. Joseph agreed to move out so Frances, my maid, could sleep with me and help care for my daughter. It wasn't planned. We decided on it that evening."

"What time did he leave you?" Read asked bluffly.

"It couldn't have been earlier than nine o'clock. My daughter was cross because her papa promised he'd read to her that night." She stopped, her face suddenly destitute.

"No mention of a trip to Windsor?" said Wyre.

She gave him a look of puzzlement.

"Who draws up the schedule of duty?"

"That would be Neale."

"So let me get this straight," Wyre said. "There are three valets, one of whom – "

"There are four valets," Mrs Sellis interrupted. "If you count Mr Gew."

"Gew?" He frowned. It was the first time the name had come up.

"A thin man, with a lean, chitty face. He was indentured to the Duke of York, but was always to be found with Paulet and Neale. The three were thick as thieves. Mr Gew even stood in for them on occasion. Strictly speaking, that wasn't permitted."

Read was shaking his head. "Forget it, Wyre," he said quietly. "The man she means was at the Palace barely more than a few months, and he left a week ago, well before the attack. We know all about him. If you must know, I have officers out looking for him concerning another matter. Petty theft. Articles belonging to the First Lady of the Duchess of York's Chamber. Christ, these titles."

Wyre looked back at Mrs Sellis. He suddenly felt a pang of pity for this woman – vulnerable, adrift, prey to Mrs Varley's rumour-mongering, to Paulet's slip of the tongue (*Mrs Sellis's suspicions, sir . . .*). There was no love lost in this house. Still, the question had to be posed. This was a Royal inquest, after all.

"Had you any cause to be angry with the Duke?"

Read straightened.

"None whatsoever."

"We've heard enough," Read said, waving the valet's wife forward. "If you've nothing to add, you may sign your affidavit."

Putting her name to it, she turned on her heel, her steps to the door small, deliberate.

53. Gristle

It was all too easy to imagine a dispassionate observer casting him mentally in the role of torturer. But the fact remained he was trying to cure this patient. This unspeakable monster.

He'd heard of a sect of religious enthusiasts in St Petersburg who willingly practised emasculation on each other, equating the procedure with the purest form of knowledge. The ultimate stigmata of piety, or so they held, was the 'great seal', thus termed because removal of the penis, scrotum and testicles left a flat, disc-like scar. Devotees embarking on this path away from worldly corruption usually began with the 'lesser seal', where only the testicles were taken, allowing micturition to be accomplished with greater ease. Those electing for the great seal were obliged to squat to urinate, as women did.

He'd read, too, of tribes in the Caribbean isles that practised mambo rites on kidnapped boys, which involved similar excisions, though perhaps these were mere sea-dog tales. The procedure in those dark places, he explained to the man strapped down to the wooden gurney, patting one of his shaved legs, was simplicity itself. (His eyes went to the end of the patient's yard, where the veins were hard and clotted like knots along a length of string, a shibboleth of habitual onanism.) The operator, he continued, merely seized the parts to be removed with one hand, and struck them away with the other. A nail was inserted into the urethra, preventing strictures.

In England, such things were conducted with rather more finesse. The surgeon made his incision a little above the place where he proposed to divide the spermatic cord, continuing down at an angle of thirty degrees. The hard matter was detached from the adjoining fat and a finger hooked beneath, allowing a ligature to be tied around the exposed cord, and pulled firmly. The loose scrotum could be removed with elliptical incisions, the edges brought together and sutured tightly. Not a speck of disease was left behind. Not a trace of corruption.

The fingers of the strapped-down man tightened around the gurney-rail.

Inexperienced surgeons, the medical man went on, were enjoined to take the utmost care in distinguishing between putrefying diseases of the yard and mere inconveniences such as warty excrescences. He knew of several lamentable cases where men's yards had been needlessly removed.

He offered his patient some brandy for the pain; the man drank greedily. The doctor rested his palm on a hairless thigh, picturing two gleaming lumps of gristle on a tin plate, a spaghetti of ducts and capillaries still clinging to them.

Something for Parlez-Vous to enjoy later, when everyone else in the house was in bed.

54. Push, Balance

Read threw his palms on the table with a slapping sound. With an exasperated tone, he announced half an hour's hiatus. It was eleven o'clock, and the heat had risen intolerably.

In his sopping shirt, Wyre traipsed outside. The rose garden lay before him; hoping its predictable geometries might imprint themselves on his own desultory thoughts, he entered through an arch of dense blooms. A green marble bird-bath marked the middle. He watched a sparrow at its dustbath – turning at the sound of crunching gravel. Mr Adams, the Palace Coroner, stood there. He didn't seem surprised to see the lawyer.

"Drawn to roses, Mr Wyre? I like them pink and glistening. No chance of that in this infernal weather, but they say we're building to a proper downpour. When the rage allays, the rain begins, eh?" He smiled. "I trust our procedures have met with your approval." His hatted head was framed by dry-as-bone petals.

They walked together, the trimmed borders curiously scentless in the still air.

"Tell me, Mr Adams," Wyre said, "was the jury given an opportunity to examine Sellis's body before it was gifted to Mr Cline?"

"They were shown the corpse exactly as it was discovered in bed."

"Did Mr Jackson point out the insides of Sellis's hands were clean?"

Adams tipped his hat at three holy sisters huddled around a fine deep red specimen. "I'm sure he did, if it was salient."

"You're aware of the rumours?"

The Coroner pulled up. "That the Duke killed his valet, or ordered him to be killed? Those rumours? Or that the Duke's a buggeranto, a philanderer, a lady's man, an unfeeling monster who buggered Sellis's wife, buggered husband and wife together, both begging for it in one bed?" Adams made a bony spire out of two long index fingers. "I'm aware of them, and of a whole concerto of variations." He showed the tips of his teeth. "The war with France is at a cardinal point. I dare say, in the Courthouse's cosseted halls, you feel sufficiently far removed from the horrors our soldiers and sailors daily face with fortitude. Imagine, if you are able, how their morale suffers with each hour the Duke, a general in his Majesty's army, is exposed to such disgraceful insinuations." He placed his head at a courtier's angle. "But the inquest's verdict will silence them."

"Such a hasty investigation is unlikely to satisfy anyone."

"Cumberland is one of the six Dukes who rule England. He will be the next King of Hannover."

Wyre started as a volley of musket sounded across the gardens. Adams didn't flinch.

"There will always be fantasists prepared to argue black is white, but sometimes things are just as they seem. In such cases, it is foolhardy to suggest otherwise."

"Am I to interpret that as a threat?"

"Dear me, Mr Wyre – " the Coroner set off again at a leisurely pace " – our French friends must adore you. Sodomy in valets' chambers, conspiracies of scullery maids and stable lads, foreign assassins lurking behind the arras. In just two days, you threaten to do for the royal house what the massed armies of the Tyrant have been unable to achieve in ten years."

"You mistake my motives," Wyre said quickly, conscious of how emphatically he was losing the exchange. "What if a second attempt were made on the Duke's life, or on the King's? I shouldn't want *that* on my conscience."

Adams rolled his weathered eyes towards him. "Sir, have you just imagined the King's death?"

"Of course not," Wyre said quickly. "You're word-catching. I meant merely – "

"Shall we debate that 'merely'?"

They reached the rose garden's entrance arch, now an exit. Adams stopped, turning. "There's a fisherman in Worthing prepared to testify that you asked him for passage to France." He tilted his head as if listening for birdsong. "Forgive me, is he confusing you with someone else?"

Wyre opened his mouth to protest, but Adams cut him off. "The inquest jury will return a verdict of *fell de se*. Suicide, Mr Wyre. Let us leave it at that." He ducked under the arch.

"Who'll believe an inquest conducted behind closed doors?" Wyre called after him, impotently. "Wrapped up in just two days."

"Accept the world, Mr Wyre," the Coroner's voice floated back, "or withdraw from it. The royals go on. That is what they do. When the King dies, God saves the King."

Two sealed letters were waiting at his place on the gilt desk. Folded inside the larger was correspondence addressed to 'Captain Stephenson, Duke's secretary'. Wyre's breath hissed beneath his teeth – the signature was a communication from beyond the grave.

"Well?" said Read impatiently, "What is it?"

Wyre handed him the letter. Read reeled off the contents out loud.

Sir,–

I am extremely anxious to know Yr decision concerning the Evidence I have produced against Mr Neale. I beg leave you will relieve me from this disagreeable suspense. I do not wish to live in the same room with a man I have accused as a rogue. Mr Neale cheats his Royal Highness in everything he buys. On Toothpicks he gains 50 per cent, by charging 18-pence for that for which he pays only one

300

Shilling. On Soap he charges 2 shillings for that for which he pays only 18-pence. No oath or promise is binding with him. I can no longer live with this monster.
I am Sir Yr Obt. Servt,
J. Sellis

He tossed the letter back. "Stephenson looked into all this at the time. The charges were unfounded, a blatant attempt to blacken Neale's character. It changes nothing."

Wyre peered at the letter; the characters seemed to struggle to maintain their vertical slant. Perhaps an expert would conjecture an escapist attitude, or some deeply seated emotional susceptibility. Could cruelty be inferred from those blunt downstrokes?

The second letter was a short note from Mr Cline. What it pleased the surgeon to call 'curious marks' had been discovered on Sellis's body. Wyre was welcome to call at the Guy's Hospital dissecting room. Wyre slipped Cline's invitation into his jacket pocket. No need to show Read that.

Read shot him a quizzical look.

"It's a personal matter, sir."

The Chief Magistrate muttered something about keeping private and professional business separate.

At two o'clock, Read called a halt to proceedings. The afternoon's interviews had been cancelled – half a dozen householders on the list were in bed. "Puking their guts up".

"Poison?" Wyre said, thinking back to Neale's attempts to press 'refreshments' on them that morning.

Read snorted. "More a case of flyblown salmon the bloody idiots couldn't bear to throw away as the cook instructed. Serves them right. Don't worry, they'll appear tomorrow – even if they're shitting their rings out. But

301

it leaves us with a problem." He looked uncomfortable. "We can't bring the other interviews forward. Apparently that's impossible at such short notice. Staff duty rotas." He snapped his collars forward. "We'll need more time. I'm going to push back the jury's verdict meeting by a day. Adams won't like it, but fuck the arrogant bastard. You can tell Mr Best that, as proof of the inquest's independence. For now, we might as well take the bloody afternoon off. Our audience with the Duke is at five. Make sure you're back by then, or not at all."

Wyre left directly for Guy's. He made his way down to the stables to retrieve Leighton's yellow dandy-charger. Sitting astride the contraption, he made a wobbly circuit of the courtyard. He was definitely, if slowly, getting the hang of the technique. Push, balance; push, balance. There wasn't much more to it than that, really – though steering remained a haphazard affair. The tiller was simply too narrow. Perhaps he'd make a list of possible improvements to present Bow Street with when he returned the machine. In return for having kept it.

He skated out into St James's Road, feeling a marvellous release. The late, low sun had made a cracked gold sea of the cobbles. On he flared (in his imagination, at least), the city's public squares and civic parks dissolving into green archipelagos.

Push, balance; push, balance.

55. Old Friends

Sarah pushed her ledger book aside. She waited until the brewery agent's footsteps had faded before burying her head in her arm and weeping bitterly.

The pittance she'd managed to get for her lease on The White Swan barely covered James's prison fees. The premises remained hers till the end of the month, for all the good that would do her. Her license was revoked, her windows boarded up.

She'd had only one thing left to sell. In that respect, she was back where she started.

Pattering footsteps on the stairs made her lift her head. She quickly dried her eyes on her sleeves – her two little Chinese girls stood at the door, elbows touching.

"We leaving now," Liu said. "Thank you, thank you."

"But you don't have any luggage . . ."

"Everything gone." Liu pressed her dark lips together. "Charlies take it all." She pointed to her head. "Only experience left. That weightless. Carry everywhere." She bowed daintily. Her companion followed suit, dipping at the waist in that awkwardly graceful way of theirs. Arms linked, they continued down the stairs, long tunics flapping at their ankles.

Sarah made her own way down. James glowered at her from the ale counter. He'd grown thin since his injury, but in other respects precious little had changed. He waved her over, eager to discuss his latest wheeze. They'd call on old friends – the light danced in his one good eye – on the old, familiar faces. They'd start with Mr Shadworth. That old bum-tapper must be good for some ready cash. He'd been a dedicated Swan patron throughout its glory days, practically their first customer. Yes, a little reminder of that fact ought to be enough.

Sarah stared. Kindly old Mr Shadworth . . . It wasn't right. She thought on her feet. Surely there was nothing, she suggested, to be had from that quarter. Didn't James remember his threadbare shirt? They'd be risking the magistrate for nothing.

James shrugged. Parson, then. Old quim-lips had raked in more shillings from his Sunday plates than they took on a Saturday night. Aye, they'd pay Parson a visit. Thought he was all respectable now, did he? They'd see how he liked being squeezed from the other end.

56. View Halloo!

Taking Leighton's leather strap, Wyre locked his wooden gelding to Guy's wrought-iron gates. The hospital's long stone wings were overlooked by a high brick clock tower, whose enormous hands showed half past two. Plenty of time to see what Cline had for him, meet with Miss Crawford in St James's Park, and return to the Palace for the Duke's deposition.

A porter directed him down a shallow flight of granite steps to a festooned door.

Cline appeared in the foyer in an unwashed surgical frock coat. He adjusted the coloured ribbon holding on his wire-rimmed glasses, and gave Wyre his hand. "My letter found you. I had my doubts. I should imagine the inquest's at a delicate stage, and perhaps new information will not be welcome."

"I hardly think they'd dare melt a surgeon's wax."

Cline smiled. "I'm told in France every letter, irrespective of sender or destination, is re-routed through Paris. Whole armies of penmen painstakingly transcribe each sheet, whether seditious tract, billet-doux or laundry receipt. The facsimiles are stored in gigantic warehouses along the Seine. Vast reams of information."

"Why go to such lengths?" Wyre said dubiously.

"France is too populous to supervise its inhabitants in

unfolding time. This way the authorities can sift through at their leisure, and none of the guilt is lost."

Wyre cast another sceptical look in his direction. "Yours wasn't the only communiqué to find its way to my desk whole. You'd be surprised at how many outside parties have felt compuncted to help in the investigation."

Cline directed a sharp glance at him. "Which parties?"

"Millenarians, mollies, the Tyrant's mameluk for all I know. It's impossible to tell – and in each case, the lead proved worthless."

"You needn't worry about my allegiances, Mr Wyre. They are to Hippocrates alone." Cline followed the lawyer's eyes down to his filthy frock coat. "Blood and pus – it's worn as a badge of honour around here."

"I believe you have something to show me."

Cline bowed slightly. "This way, Mr Wyre." He started to walk, leading Wyre through the hospital's labyrinthine corridors, finally arriving at a flight of narrow stairs that led down to a set of double doors.

"This is our Dissecting Room. What goes on here is not all that unlike an inquest."

Nothing Wyre had seen in Crispin Street could prepare him for Cline's human abattoir. Wherever he looked was a hollowed-out, gouged, flayed or atomized travesty of the male or female form. Many of the corpses had something else in common apart from their incompleteness: a band of raw flesh around their necks where the rope had tightened.

"Nature laid bare," Cline said, his eyes on the lawyer, "can be disconcerting. But anatomy is the alphabet of physiology. Without its lessons who would risk cutting for stone?"

"It may surprise you," Wyre replied, fighting to keep his voice steady, "but I'm not one of those who need convincing of the necessity of such places."

Near the double doors, two medical students were preparing a young woman for dissection; the air around her was salty and ferric. Her black hair and tawny skin – mottled with syphilitic scars – confirmed her as a member of the middle tinge. One of Cline's students started shaving her dark pubis with quick, deft strokes.

"You spend a deal of time in hospitals," the surgeon went on, "you develop a sense of indifference. The breasts, and down here – " he indicated the woman's natural parts, now bare and alien, fringed with purple " – the cunt." He leaned in, his manner fraternal. "We can dispense with the Latin. She's beyond theory now."

An eruption of dry skin at the base of her bosom and sores on her tongue put the cause of death beyond doubt. Pox – she'd been dripping with it.

"May I see Sellis now?"

With a touch of the showman, Surgeon Cline pointed to the far end of the chamber where a linen sheet had assumed the contours of a body. "After you, Mr Wyre."

At the gurney, Cline pulled aside the sheet. The valet's familiar olive features appeared, his handsome jaw held shut by a bandage as if he'd been gagged. As if someone were afraid of what he might say, even now . . .

An aroma of figs; cedar, perhaps. Some sort of light embalming oil, prolonging the indignity.

"When my students have finished, his remains will be returned to the county. It's customary in England to bury suicides at a three-went way, though I believe the stake through the body is now at the discretion of the magistrate." The surgeon opened his hands as if releasing a bird. "And so our traitor passes from the educated fingers of science to the ham fists of superstition."

"A verdict hasn't been reached yet." Until the inquest jury had met and declared a judgment, Sellis wasn't technically a self-murderer. "It might be premature to treat his body in this way."

Cline placed his head at a wry angle, a look that conveyed everything.

Had the scalpels of Cline's novices gone to work on Leighton's torso, too? That beautiful body, razed to its parts.

"Far better *post*-mortem dissection," the surgeon said, "than the living variety. If Sellis had been arrested, Read would have had him taken apart in the public square. Not even the dignity of privacy in those final, most revealing of moments."

"Perhaps that's exactly what Sellis deserved."

Cline gave a little shrug. "Needlessly cruel, socially useless."

Wyre looked back down at the valet's naked body. The surgeon's letter had mentioned marks, but other than the gash at the throat there was nothing blatant.

"It was actually one of my assistants who noticed it," Cline said, waving over the two frock-coated students. Together, they heaved Sellis's cadaver onto its front, and Cline slipped a bolster under the hips. With a wedge-shaped piece of iron, he prised the valet's elevated buttocks apart. "See for yourself."

Forcing himself to peer inside, Wyre saw around the puckered waxy orifice thin lines that put him in mind of a perverse attempt at the kind of counter-hatching William used in his drawings.

Cline traced the marks in the air with his finger. "You see all manner of peculiarities in this region, natural flowerings and outgrowths of various kinds. These here, however, are the result of deliberate action – of an assault calculated not to incapacitate so much as humiliate."

"The wounds appear fresh," Wyre said, fighting a rising sense of horror.

"Say unhealed, rather. They were inflicted mere hours before this unfortunate man's demise."

"Does Mr Read know?"

"Not from me. Would you prefer it remain that way?"

Wyre paused. Nodded.

Cline regarded the lawyer. "Would you say you're making any headway?"

Wyre smiled mirthlessly. "It's a tornado of fragments."

"That, sir, is a perfect description of the human body."

Lawyer and surgeon walked back through the unrisen Lazaruses. Before they reached the double doors, Cline stopped at a skeletal female cadaver. Was Wyre's capacity to take in the death of the body being tested? The tall surgeon combed his fingers through the woman's brittle hair. A raised line of livid lacerations ran between her shoulder and elbow. Before Wyre's imagination, a sudden image arose of rattling drive chains and flat-toothed cogs.

"Needles," Cline said, softly. "I drew more than sixty from her flesh. I believe she used a prayer book as a hammer. Her injuries are self-inflicted, a phenomenon seen all too often in those who suffer from womb." He patted the bluish shoulder. "I've known girls thrust splinters of glass into the least welcoming of places. Some grind it between their teeth." Cline's face remained as neutral as ever.

"Mr Jackson's adamant the Duke's attacker struck a sabre blow to the skull using such brutality only a miracle prevented part of the head from being carried away, but he permits no-one to remove the dressing. Tell me, Mr Cline, in your opinion, could any man receive such a wound, yet retain sufficient command of his faculties to swear an affidavit just moments later?"

Another little shrug. "The human frame, so delicate in certain respects, is all but indestructible in others. A few years ago, a young French nobleman was wounded in a skirmish with his Majesty's infantry during which a portion of his scalp and skull was sliced off by a sword. A painful drawn-out death from infection seemed certain to be his lot. The attending surgeon, an exceptionally resourceful man, swiftly killed a dog and cut out a corresponding section of its skull. This he knitched into the nobleman's wound, achieving a perfect cure."

"Did he survive?"

"He did. Unwisely, he told his friends about this miraculous operation, which in time came to the attention of the Archbishop of Paris, who promptly put him under the ban of the church."

Wyre gave him an incredulous look. "What on earth for?"

"For having a fragment of a bestial body united with his own. A dog-man, or man-dog. The nobleman was banished from all assemblies of the faithful for as long as the piece of canine skull remained in his head.

"What did he do?"

"He had the offending part removed, and the sentence of excommunication was duly revoked. Then he died."

"And the surgeon?" Wyre felt sure he knew the answer.

"Still exceptional, still very much alive."

"You seem to have spent a lot of time in France, Mr Cline."

"When I was a young man, it was the fashion to see as much of Europe as possible. The Grand Tour. Geneva, Paris, the Alps. I even ascended once in a balloon. Thanks to the present campaigns, people these days must make do with Bath and the Welsh hills."

Cline set off again, only to pause for a second time at the female cadaver parked beside the mortuary doors.

"One medical clique insists the human body is no more

309

than a flesh-and-bone house for our thoughts, a mere mechanism for the traffic of philosophical ideas. Another faction, smaller though equally zealous, maintains our thoughts are simply the means by which bodies are steered towards each other for the purpose of sexual union. No higher end than that." He smiled with an impish air. "The entirety of our literature, political economy, engineering feats – all by-products of that single, overriding imperative."

"And what, pray, is your opinion, Mr Cline?"

"That philosophers make entertaining dinner guests." The surgeon pushed up his spectacles, making another deft adjustment to the multi-coloured ribbon. "I know of anatomists who swear the mouth is the first hole to form while we are still eggs in the womb. Their antagonists are just as convinced this particular honour should be accorded the anus. I've always thought the position one adopts on the issue says something profound about one's outlook on life."

"Is this the medical equivalent of gallows humour?"

"The face is just public display, Mr Wyre. You have to look deeper."

"Deeper?"

"The things of greatest importance are actuated down there – " Cline pointed to the bulging organs of a male corpse on the neighbouring gurney. "And there also – " he gestured down at the female's swollen hairless pudendum. "Some men never get over the fact that women possess such things."

He escorted Wyre out, and up, through the maze of interconnecting passages into the bright courtyard. The roasting air came as a relief. Cline raised his palm to the sun as if he would seize it and toss it in the Thames.

"What is it like," Wyre said as they made their way to

the hospital's wrought-iron gates, "operating on a living person? Cutting into someone."

"Oh, it's not very elegant. Just blood, muscle and fat. Greasy. Gut is glibbery. Bone is cleaner than gut." He glanced up, tracking some high birds. "In some of the larger amputations or internal procedures you literally wade in blood. It clots on you. Sometimes, you find yourself standing above the scene, looking at it through foreign eyes. It takes on the character of a slaughterhouse. But you hold fast, Mr Wyre – " he suddenly clenched both fists " – you hold fast to the fact that you're curating, not butchering, the flesh."

The clock tower showed ten past three. Miss Crawford would be on her way to St James's Park. Thanks to Leighton's wooden gelding, he'd easily make it in time – no need to put himself to the expense of a cab. Then back punctually for the interview with the Duke of Cumberland.

There was always the chance Aspinall had resurfaced and was willing to put the finger on Parlez-Vous . . . What an entrance Wyre could make.

Cline saw him to the pavement, offering for the second time that day a hand that had been to the darkest of places. He raised his eyebrows at Leighton's dandy-charger, but said nothing.

Slouching against a wall opposite the hospital was a figure in a natty blue hat, the identical twin of that worn by the man who'd stood to slovenly attention outside one of those endless Palace doors. Blue Hat seemed oddly solid among the spectral platoons of pedestrians. He raised a finger to his forehead. Leighton's world again – a universe of feints and deceits dreamed up in the rooms of the Office of Surveillance.

Guy's clock struck the next quarter as Wyre threw his leg over the running machine, and cast off, those thin, scratchy lines vivid in his mind's eye. Whatever Joseph Sellis had been while alive, it was easier to decide what he was in death.

He'd gone along tolerably well for ten minutes, and was looking about for the turning to take him up towards Blackfriars Bridge, when he became aware of something other than the usual foot traffic, something low and loping, still some way off, but closing. Heat, he decided, shimmering up curiously in the form of an enormous mastiff? He cast another swift glance over his shoulder, but the chimera had evaporated. He'd taken fright at hot air. He put it down to the delayed effects of the ten-day parenthesis in his life.

At that moment, he caught his toe on a raised corner, which sent him veering off the pavement, down into the path of laden dray-carts and flying hackneys. Pulling at the tiller, he corrected course, mounted the pavement again, and – face screwed up in concentration – worked on recovering his rhythm. Now, where the devil was the turning? He scanned in both directions along the brittle avenue – and felt the hairs on his nape prickle . . . Through the shifts of late-afternoon light, it was there again. The dog. Not heat, then; no play of mind. Was he the only one who'd noticed the shuck prowling?

Frowning deeply, he kicked off at a smarter lick. Christ, but where was he? Without his noticing, the clean and neat shops had gone, replaced by rough affairs with tiny windows, and the taverns were little more than out-and-out trugging houses. Everything was run-down and cheerless, made worse by the all-pervasive stench of horse dung and stale sweat rising around him in the blazing sun. Ahead, the hospital's loquacious clock proclaimed another quarter. *Ahead?* But he'd come from that direction. With growing alarm, Wyre flung another quick glance over his shoulder to discover the dog was keeping pace. Panic washing through him, he swerved into the next side street, wrestling with the dandy-charger's woefully inadequate tiller. Whenever he turned, it was to find the animal following.

The beast knew its game, carrying its head high, no raking along, nose close to the ground. Wyre was sprinting on his seat now, sweat pearling off his forehead, muscles in his calves tightening into excruciating knots, heart straining against his ribs – a blown fox!

How had the animal tracked him? It hit him: Rose's filched handkerchief . . . Yes, a dog could get a man's scent that way. Someone at the Palace had made their move. This was view halloo!

Wyre's heels slithered over the flagstones, his legs those of a clockwork maquette's, joints pivoting on cruel nails. Half-dressed trulls peered incuriously from niches in the walls like grotesque alabaster figures lining cathedral naves. In desperation, Wyre pointed the dandy-charger's unresponsive tiller at the next alleyway, only to find his escape route tapering appallingly towards a high brick wall.

He heard the dog padding in behind him, a savage sound brewing in its throat.

Wyre let the running machine fall, scrabbled out from under the perch and backed towards the wall, terror gripping his chest. The dog came forward crouching, matching him step for step, the final stage all instinct.

With a desperate glance, he sized up the wall. Impossibly high – but nothing to lose. Wyre sprang to his feet, and launched himself, somehow hooking the tips of his fingers over the top. Clawing for purchase, finding some, he ran ridiculously on the spot, waiting for the hideous compression that would snap bone, hauling himself up, each division of a second registering in a strange attention to the crosshatch patterns of the brickwork, the name *Paston* stamped deep in the middle of each block.

His trailing leg – a tearing sensation – then Wyre was tumbling –

57. Court-Plaister

– landing sprawling with a thump that knocked the air from his lungs. The danger wasn't over. He could hear the dog jumping repeatedly at the wall, its claws scratching near the top. Scrambling to his feet, he tottered out into a wide thoroughfare, half-blinded by pain in his leg, straight into the path of a four-wheeler.

" . . . of the way, brickshit!" yelled the driver, pulling at the reins. More by luck than design, Wyre's fingers found the corner rail as the vehicle slewed past. He swung himself up onto the footrest, wrenching open the carriage door with his free hand.

Empty! In! With a sob, he slid the glass slider to, just as the great shuck slammed into the side of the coach, enormous paws reaching half-way up the window.

Then it was gone between the wheels, the coach springs absorbing the yelp.

Wyre staggered from the coach at the east entrance to St James's Park, where Miss Crawford was waiting, engrossed in a small, auburn-leather book. Poems by her 'young lord', no doubt. She raised her head, and stared aghast at the shreds of his left trouser leg. Tucking her book into her skirts, she rushed over.

Leaning on her shoulder for support, he recounted the action with the dog. His shin felt open, cold; standing was an agony. After listening in silence, Miss Crawford insisted he come to Great Windmill Street, just a short walk away; she had dressings there, bought in preparation for Robert's pillorying.

Wyre protested weakly about the interview with the Duke, but allowed himself to be led away, his thoughts shifting from the raw sensation in his leg to that smooth volume lying perfectly flat against her thigh.

Great Windmill Street was numbered curiously. Her building, No. 17, was wedged between 23 and 37. He hobbled up the narrow side stairs, helped by the dark woman. In the void below, the baker's window was dusty with flour.

Miss Crawford's rooms lay across a bare landing. Dark patches on the walls and ceiling. A single window looked out onto a blind side alley. She watched as he took it in. "I used the last of my savings to settle Robert's prison expenses," she said simply. "It was either that, or see my fiancé moved to the debtors' prison." She guided him to the single chair. "We ought to cleanse that wound. Dogs are dirty creatures."

She turned her head away modestly as Wyre removed his breeches. Just as well – he wasn't one of those dandies who affected to wear undergarments; instead, he pulled his shirt tails down and around, covering his loins like a savage's cloth.

He waited while she inspected his wound. By some miracle, it seemed the animal's jaws, which had made such a good job of shredding his breeches, had only grazed the skin. The blood on his trousers, she announced, could all be explained by a badly skinned knee. He must have got that when he landed on the other side of the wall.

She disappeared for a bag of salt and basin of water. Wyre studied the grated skin, struggling to understand how such a light injury could produce so much claret. He felt a pang of sympathy for the Duke ... If his wounds weren't fictional – a big 'if', he felt – what agonies they must have caused him!

Miss Crawford returned with her accoutrements. "After Robert's arrest," she said, kneeling down, tipping the salt into the basin, "my father presented me with an ultimatum." The salt sliding into water made a hissing, cracking sound that reminded him of St Mary's. "Either I abandoned Robert, or my father's house." She dipped the sponge, offering it to the raw flesh. (Wyre flinched.) "As you can see, I elected for the latter." She wrung out the sponge; his blood clouded the water in little brown expansions. "For propriety's sake, Robert took a room in Primrose Hill. Our plan was to found a retreat for the psychically afflicted. A childish fantasy," she added, with downcast eyes. "I see that now."

Her breath on his wet skin was electrifying. Feeling his shirt tails twitch, Wyre willed his mind to empty. If she noticed the curious folds, she betrayed no sign. How could she not have seen?

"Memories fade," he said, swallowing hard. "The public will forget his disgrace."

"They won't be allowed to forget," she said, dabbing the graze dry. Producing a court-plaister, she dampened the adhesive backing with wetted fingers. "My father – " she lifted her head, her eyes meeting his " – taught me never to attempt a union of lips with a dog wound. Better to leave it gaping. That way it won't fester." She smoothed the plaister out, pressing hard at the edges. "All done, Mr Wyre."

A fishy smell rose from the sticky square of silk and cotton.

She pointed at the torn breeches, which lay discarded in

316

a ragged heap on the floor. "You can't return to the Palace in those. Robert's about your size."

She disappeared again. While he waited, his eyes moved over the bubbling wall-paper, the dark blooms of ceiling mould. She deserved better. Much better. He also thought idly about Leighton's running machine, lying in the blind alley. In all likelihood, some enterprising young street ruffians had found it and sold it on.

Miss Crawford appeared with a pair of brown-and-yellow checked trousers folded over her arm. "Robert won't mind."

Wyre rose stiffly. Turning aside, he pulled them on. They fit well enough; a touch baggy at the front.

58. The Patron of Lepers

Miss Crawford's Montego salt did the trick. After a cup of strong Jamaican coffee, Wyre felt well enough to walk back to the Palace. He'd be cutting things fine. Read wouldn't wait. Or the Duke wouldn't.

The city's clocks had already struck five before he passed under St James's echoing arch. Walking along the endlessly intersecting corridors, he longed for Paulet to appear to show him the most direct route. Wyre stopped at a glossy door that stood a little ajar. His name, whispered. His first name, shortened familiarly to one syllable . . .

Warily, heart racing, he placed his hand against the finger-plate; the door swung inwards on well-balanced hinges, revealing a long room of dark cut-outs. The gloom seemed to have been sieved through itself. Heavy drapes blocked the light from the windows. Slowly, areas of detail materialized. Someone was at a wide desk, slumped in a high-backed chair holding a handkerchief to his mouth.

317

Like the patron of lepers himself, freshly hauled from the tomb, the man had undergone an appalling transformation since Wyre had last seen him, his cheeks sunken and yellowish, the eyes cold, relentless lumps.

"Soz, Kit," the words came in rasps. "I couldn't see any other way."

Fists clenched, Wyre took a step forward. "I saw your body!" he said angrily. "Cline was there. The smell . . . Was that someone's idea of a joke?"

"It may have been a touch theatrical, I concede." Leighton spluttered, wiping his mouth. "In my game, you make style a means to an end. The stink came courtesy of some bits and pieces Cline brought from the morgue."

"But the stretcher bearers. You were rigid to the touch."

"Not actual stretcher bearers. Which isn't to say the rogues aren't used to conveying dead bodies about the city. As for rigid, that was down to one of Cline's preparations. Induced the cold rigour of death. Tasted like shit, but it was enough to fool Solomon." Leighton drew evidently painful breath. "I was out of it, Kit. Cline told me afterwards you'd turned up. You weren't meant to see all that. It wasn't for your benefit."

"Then for whose?"

"Bow Street's."

That explanation might do for a jilted taproom trull, but Wyre needed more. "How did you get past the Palace guards?"

"Oh," Leighton said vaguely, "plenty of ways through the pampas. There are a good deal more undocumented comings and goings here than you might think." He wiped his brow. *Was that one of Rose's handkerchiefs?* "You wanted to know where I kept disappearing these last months. Intelligencing – " He coughed again. "Right up the arse of the enigma. I had my sights trained on the

Palace long before that love letter to Sellis turned up in Crispin Street." He winced again as if something deep within had unknit. "The story began months ago with the death of a footman."

"Tranter . . ."

"Bravo." The Runner doffed an imaginary hat. "Ventilated his own skull one bright morning. At least the Palace said he did. Bow Street went along with that, logged it as suicide. Read himself was there to oversee the investigation. Asked for especially. You see a pattern building?" Leighton tugged at his collar. "But one by one, my noses on the street started whispering." His face was desolate. "They whispered, Kit – and it was always the same name."

"Mr Parlez-Vous. I found your torn-out page of notebook."

Leighton looked admiringly. "We'll make a Runner of you yet." He doubled over as a spasm of coughs wracked his body. "It was Parlez-Vous who brought me to the Palace. I got myself taken on as valet to the Duke of York. Wasn't as hard as you'd imagine, or as hard as it should be. I reinvented myself as Mr Gew."

That was good as far as it went, but it didn't explain everything. "You knew the whole time what Sellis was planning?"

"What *Sellis* was planning? Come on, Kit, you saw the poor sap's hands. They were clean. Not so much as a smear of blood."

"Read says he must have washed them."

"How could a man who'd just cut his own throat calmly rise and wash his hands?" The Runner's eyes slid to the side. "It wasn't long before Cumberland picked me out for special attention." His smile twisted, till it was perfectly grotesque. "Everything you've dared to imagine

319

about the Duke, multiply it by the worse felon you've ever prosecuted. Didn't bother him in the least that I was his brother's man. The evening of the attack, I accompanied Cumberland to the opera. Did you know he makes model soldiers? He casts them in lead himself. Lines of pretty men, all poised to charge."

"Was Sellis one of his pretty men?"

"Sellis, Tranter. I believe there were others."

"Others?"

"He's done this before, Kit. When he's finished with them, he slaughters them like tin men."

Wyre shook his head slowly. "I need proof. My career's at stake, Leighton. More than that. This is my last chance to get Rose back." He frowned again at the handkerchief Leighton was using to mop his brow.

"And you'll have it. We returned from the opera, and I turned in for the night. On the way to my chamber, I met Paulet in the corridors. He told me Neale had made a private arrangement with Sellis. Something to do with accompanying the Duke to Windsor first thing in the morning. Sellis had agreed to ride in Neale's place. The *quid pro quo* was for Neale to take Sellis's shift that evening in the Valet's Room. It wasn't unusual for the valets to come to such accommodations among themselves. I was tired from all that yodelling and soon nodded off. Next thing I knew, Neale was shaking my shoulder. He told me to get up. Cumberland was asking for me."

"Neale woke *you*?" Not so much as a syllable of this had appeared in Neale's deposition. Then again, there'd been no mention of a Mr Gew, either.

Leighton nodded. "I sprinted to the Duke's bedchamber, where I found his Highness standing calmly in the middle of the room. His shirt was bloody, but otherwise he was well. His regimental sword lay on the floor. Let me say that again, Kit. Cumberland was standing calmly in the middle of the room."

"People who've suffered terrible shocks can appear quite serene," Wyre said slowly. He wished for a modicum of that calm himself.

"Neale went off to fetch the Duke's surgeon."

"Mr Jackson ..." Wyre said, picturing the smug physician. "It was supposed to be Neale's wife who went on that little errand. According to her own deposition."

"Mrs Neale was in the Duke's chamber when I arrived, huddled in a corner, staring straight ahead as if she were about to be turned off the scaffold."

"She shouldn't be there," Wyre said, feeling he ought to understand, but not being able to. "Cumberland and Neale are supposed to have met her in the corridors."

Leighton kept his gaze on him. "She wasn't there for long. She was sent off to fetch Sellis. It was Mrs Neale who returned with the news of his death."

That much, at least, chimed with *The Chronicle*'s account. Mrs Neale, all alone in the winding ways, charged with raising the dead Sellis.

"Jackson arrived next, but on his own. Neale didn't slink back for another quarter of an hour."

"What was he doing all that time?" Wyre imagined the valet crouched over Sellis, dragging the pearl-handled blade in a deep straight line. Yardley had all but said it.

"I can guess. But it hardly matters what I think, Kit. I'm *persona non grata*." The Runner sucked a scraping breath into his lungs. "But *you* could make people believe." Leighton pressed a hand to his side, face contorting. "I was present throughout Jackson's examination," he went on through clenched teeth, "and saw nothing to match the account of the wounds in the papers. The cut to the Duke's hand was easily the worst of it."

"Jackson claimed the vessels of Cumberland's brain were exposed." Wyre stopped abruptly. Before he went any further, there was something he had to know. "According to Read, Gew fled the Palace a week before the attack, suspected of pilfering jewels belonging to some half-royal pintail." He hesitated. "Why did you really leave, Leighton? Why promote your own death?"

He had never seen his friend look so old. When Leighton began, his voice was raw, but strangely subdued. "I sneaked out of the Palace, the old bird's right on that. But I wasn't fleeing, Kit." A spark of the old fire returned. "My plan was to return first thing in the morning with a picket of officers, and make the snatch. Arrest the whole fucking nest. But it was already too late for that. Or rather, it was always too late." His breath came in rasps that Wyre felt in his own throat. "I made it home, but just before dawn someone paid me a visit. A nightmare man, known in the field as Shadworth. He's about a hundred years old, but you'd better pray you never meet him." Another coughing fit. "I can thank the girls who hang around there for my existence. They sleep on the stairs. One of them must have taken exception to being ignored. Called him a 'quean'. Set up a right racket." Leighton smiled thinly. "I watched him through the keyhole as he came along the landing. While he was picking the lock, I was leaving by the window. But no one tips Shadworth the pikes twice. The Palace had me by the jacobs. With Bow Street in their pocket, there was nowhere for me to hide. Short of something spectacular, I'd have been strolling the old Elysian by supper time." His breath juddered. "That's where Cline came in. He and I go back." He gave Wyre a lopsided smile, a hint of the old Leighton. "As you've probably gathered," he added ruefully, "I appear to have taken a drop too much of his nasty."

"That letter about the stolen soap and toothpicks . . ." The words sounded absurd. "You put it on the table. You've been there all along, guiding me towards Neale."

"To his paymaster. Don't lose sight of Cumberland. I believe you'll be interviewing him shortly."

Wyre looked at him in bewilderment. "Why didn't you tell me everything from the beginning? I could have been trusted."

"I wanted to, Kit. Under the bridge, I nearly did. You were asking the right questions." He paused. "The fly wasn't looking into Vere Street. Not directly."

"Into *what*, then?"

"He was investigating Tranter's death. He got close, too. Shadworth ended him. I knew it instantly. It had all that bastard's hallmarks."

"You could have trusted me," Wyre repeated.

"I reasoned if the bee didn't know about the flower, the bee wouldn't pay it a visit."

Wyre regarded him, his unease building again. Risen from the dead, or the flames? "That name. *Gew . . .*" His mouth was suddenly dry.

"Spelled with a *gee*, pronounced like the heathen." Leighton's eyes met Wyre's, and held them.

"Why that particular name?"

"Oh, I don't know. Must have been something about it."

Wyre tried to burrow beneath the single syllable. Something lay hidden there. A French etymon, a *Joux* perhaps? "Who are you working for?" He took a step backwards.

Leighton pushed himself stiffly to his feet, his eyes still not leaving Wyre. "You have to understand, a lot of it was done *impromptu*. Very little was worked out beforehand." He edged around the desk. "Cumberland's a murderer, alright, but I wanted you to discover it for yourself." His tone was suddenly plaintive. "They regard us as an inferior species, Kit. The Duke played us valets off against each other in a royal shirt dance." His expression was savage now. "The Palace is at war. Cunt-lovers against buggers. Can you be sure where you stand?"

"You're Mr Parlez-Vous," Wyre said in a quiet voice. "You're the Tyrant's agent. The second assassin."

A few loose-jointed steps, and Leighton was behind him, cradling his head. No time to cry out.

"The Vallon business ..." Wyre's voice was made strange by the angle. "My God, you murdered your own partner, you traitorous – "

The crook of Leighton's elbow tightened. Wyre choked, his eyes bulging. Two thick, black lines began to close from the sides. Then the pressure released.

"I could keep squeezing. But what would Rose think?"

"Rose?" Wyre gasped. "What's she got to do with this?"

Leighton let him fall. Then he was at the window, sweeping back the drapes. He stepped out onto the sill, dropped.

The lawyer stared stupidly for a moment, then scrabbled to his feet. By the time he'd staggered to the window, Leighton was already a tiny figure in the pear orchard. Wyre yelled his name, both of his names, into the trees until his shouts turned into impotent calls for the guards, who did not come.

59. House Calls

Cross Row. Both parts of the address were apt. Sarah watched with foreboding as James climbed the steps one up from Belcher & Son. Grinning at her over his shoulder, he banged on the door.

A neatly oiled head appeared around the jamb. "You . . ." Parson Church's face dropped.

"Aye. Fancy that."

The clergyman quickly recovered from the surprise. Sarah doubted it was the first time enemies had arrived knocking.

"I'm glad to see you recovered, James. I prayed for you. For Sarah, too." He bowed his head piously.

"Course yer did, Parson. An' it looks like yer prayers 'av been answered." Her husband spread his arms wide; a showman's pose, but the sixpence sewn into his skull made everything look ridiculous.

"I'd invite you in . . ."

Her husband wasn't easily put off. "That's kind of yer."

A prolonged pause. "But I'm afraid I have company." He sighed. "Look, James, the old days, the old arrangements . . . well, things are different now." The door started to close on him, but her husband was quicker, wedging his foot inside.

"Listen, you molly shit-stamper," he spat, no pretence at civility now. "I've seen you up to yer stones in a soldier. I've seen you marrying men to each other – administering the sacrament, reeling from gin – "

From somewhere within the house, a voice could be heard. Parson glanced nervously over his shoulder.

"I've lost everything 'cos of you and your kind," her husband went on. "Look at my head!" He made an absurd fingerpost, and aimed it at the stitched-in sixpence. "You made more than enough coin off my back. I ran all the risks. All I'm asking is for some gratitude. Ten pounds, that's not asking for impossibilities."

Parson stepped neatly aside as a death's head ring came hurtling from the blackness. It struck Cooke squarely under the eye, knocking him off the steps, sending him backwards into the baking road. He lay there, mumbling curses, limbs flopping weakly like a landed fish.

The man Sarah knew as Yardley came rushing out, leaping bare-chested from the doorstep. Taking a run-up, he drove a brutal shod foot into her husband's belly.

"Hee-haw, Cookey!" Yardley cried, stamping on the landlord's fingers, producing a strangled yelp. He crouched, raising his fist high.

Sarah flung herself at him, clawing and biting, gouging flesh from Yardley's cheeks. Elbowing her off, bellowing, he turned and delivered a punch that felled her.

She sat on the road, swaying, the world oddly away. Gradually, she became aware of Parson looking down at her, smiling that sweet smile of his. Sarah crawled groaning through the dust to her husband. His stitched-up hole had begun to weep again. She draped a protective arm over him.

They remained in that position when the Poultry Compter magistrate arrived to charge them both with extortion.

60. Spoiling the Strop

When Wyre finally arrived in the Cupola Office, the Chief Magistrate was tapping a devil's tattoo with his feet.

"Where the hell have you been?" He jerked his thumb at the window. "His nibs is already in the gardens. I told you I wasn't going to wait." He noticed Wyre's yellow check trousers. "Have the fashions altered again, or did you have an accident?" He scowled. "Come on! Santa Maria. This heat."

Wyre said nothing. Soon he'd be saying plenty.

Six feet tall, muscular frame, thick neck, full, fleshy lips, a gold garnet ring glinting from one long index finger. The

Duke of Cumberland was an exercise in sublimity, finished off in pretty white kid shoes. If there was a single deficiency, it was in the eyes, which were curiously uncoupled, the light more profound in the right than the left. He was clad in an olive tailcoat, his right, silk-sleeved arm out, supported by a sling. There was a palm-sized graze above the left temple, and from beneath a medical skull cap, a scratch ran down, terminating at the eyebrow.

Cumberland leaned forward on a metal-tipped cane; over his shoulder, a manservant held a yellow parasol, shading him. "When I let it be known," the Duke began, looking sternly at Wyre, "that I was willing for you to join Mr Read's investigation, it never occurred to me this courtesy would be taken as *carte blanche* to pick apart my servants' words. You've behaved like a naturalist dissecting live dogs." His lips twitched. "As for the unfounded insinuations you've seen fit to throw at Mr Neale, I can only say it is fortunate for you this gentleman is not quick-tempered."

"Sir . . ." Wyre left it at that.

The Duke set off through the grounds. "Am I to understand," he said, turning to the Chief Magistrate, "the jury now convenes tomorrow? I believe I left clear instructions. The business was to be concluded this evening."

Read attempted to bow as he walked, dipping absurdly. "By lunchtime tomorrow, sir, the inquest will be over. Its outcome will be incontestable. *Felo de se.*"

Two sulphurous butterflies tumbled above thick bushes of buckthorn. In the distance, chicken coops shone in slanting inflections of light.

"Words, Mr Read. Mere air-propelling sounds. You hear so many of them in this house." He pointed his cane, gripping it beneath its brass marotte, which was carved in the shape of a fool with long peaked hood and cleft chin. "What the great do, the lesser prattle about. They delight

327

in imagining what they cannot see into." His lips twitched again. "It can't be helped. I've made darkness my secret place. You see that tower over there?" He indicated with his stick. "My brother York has his study at the top. He's afraid of heights." His smile conveyed the irony. "I, on the other hand, adore precipitous places. They make me giddy, and I enjoy the sensation, so long as I know I'm safely placed. But I always make sure I am."

"Sir," Wyre began, "it may be rash to dismiss the possibility of continued threats to your well-being." (Read gave a little snort). "It seems likely Sellis was in communication with a club that met at a certain tavern in Vere Street."

The Duke pulled up. "Mr Read?"

The magistrate's face was dark. "Where are you getting this rubbish from, Wyre?" Turning to Cumberland, he said, "It's the first I've heard of it, sir."

Too late to stop now. "There's reason to believe the plot against you was concocted in The White Swan. In all likelihood, it involved sympathisers of the Tyrant. It would be prudent to work on the basis that a second assassin remains at large in the Palace."

Read shook his head pityingly.

They arrived at a walled orchard; a trowel and basket of bulbs lay next to the wicket gate.

"A second assassin, you say?" The idea seemed to amuse the Duke. He waited for his manservant to unlatch the gate. "I suppose, looking at this trowel – " he gave it a prod with his walking stick " – you'd infer a gardener?"

Read coughed tactfully. "Mr Wyre means well, but he's let his imagination run away with him. Now, if he could say *who* the Courthouse believes this assassin to be . . ."

The Duke trained his eyes on Wyre as if he were correcting the parabola of cannon shot. "The Chief Magistrate asked you for the name of this assassin."

The proverbial 'now or never'. "A French agent," Wyre answered slowly, "who goes under the alias of Mr Parlez-Vous." It felt as if he were being steadily annihilated. "The man found himself employment here, and styled himself Mr Gew. But I knew him as Leighton. He took us all in, I'm afraid. He fled the grounds just half an hour ago. If officers are sent to his known haunts . . ." The phrase sounded ridiculous on his lips.

"Parlez-Vous," said the Duke, "who is really Mr Gew, who is actually Leighton." The thinnest of smiles. "Three-in-one, like the divinity himself." He turned to Read. "But you disagree?" The Duke's questions had the finality of statements.

Read glowered at Wyre. "The man Mr Wyre's referring to was a Bow Street officer. But if the Courthouse had troubled to share their theory with me, I would have set them straight." A look of discomfort spread over the magistrate's face. "As a matter of fact, sir, I oversaw the man's placement at the Palace myself."

Cumberland frowned. "His *placement*?"

"It followed the death of a footman earlier this year, a troubled young fellow called Tranter. But Leighton let us all down. He used his position to knuckle jewels from a big house in Mayfair. I had men out looking for him. Then last week, his body was found in a dive near Cheapside. He'd swallowed arsenic. Took the easy way out, just like Sellis. Whoever Mr Wyre believes he saw running from the Palace, it certainly wasn't Leighton."

Wyre opened his mouth to protest, but the Duke waved his cowled stick dismissively.

"I leave such affairs to you, Mr Read. They do not interest me. Let us continue with my deposition. I'm tired, and wish to withdraw."

"Of course, sir."

"Very well. It began with a clicking noise. At first, I thought some bat had flown against me. They find a way in sometimes." Cumberland cast his eyes around the orchard as though expecting to see one of the twilight creatures flittering between the fruit trees. "In my dream, I received two blows on my head and, when I woke, two more. There was a low flame on my table, but I saw no one. I leaped from my bed and opened the nearest door. From the darkness, someone struck me on my right thigh. A sabre blow." The Duke glanced at Wyre. "I knew it to be such because I saw the weapon flash in a looking glass at the foot of my bed. I couldn't find my pull-bell. Later we conjectured the villain had severed it. I called out for Mr Neale, who was sleeping next door."

Cumberland's good hand went up, adjusting his black cap. (Wyre stared at it. If he yanked the silk to one side, would he find a bloody gash, or smooth, unbroken skin?) "Mr Neale came running. He observed the door to the yellow room had been flung open. Usually when I am in bed, it is locked." The Duke trapped a thrusting flower between stick and fingers, tearing it head from stem. "By the door lay a naked sword. I never heard the man who struck me utter a single word." He turned to Read. "The assassin must have fled through the yellow room and from there made his way to the other side of the house, to the householder apartments." The Duke walked a little way in silence.

"And then, sir?" The Chief Magistrate prompted delicately.

The Duke looked up. "And then, sir, I made my way downstairs with Mr Neale. I ordered him to make sure the doors were secured. In the corridor we met Mrs Neale, whom I instructed to fetch Mr Jackson. I also asked her to rouse Joseph Sellis." He paused. "At that

330

point, I came over totty-headed, and was forced to return to my bedroom. Mr Neale accompanied me there for safety. While I lay on the bed, that gentleman conducted a more thorough search of the room, during which he discovered the sabre's scabbard discarded in the closet, along with Mr Sellis's slippers and a dark lantern. I've seen Sellis with it before. Small and brown, with glass sides and tin sliders." His eyes met Read's, holding them. "Sellis was the man."

"Mr Neale remained with you the whole time, sir?"

"He did, and was a great comfort."

Wyre coughed respectfully. "May I ask, sir," he began carefully, "if you'd recently given Sellis any cause for anger?"

"*Cause?*" The Duke's cheeks flushed. "Cause to attack his master?" He looked away scornfully. "I am not one of those Lords who fling lumps of bread and cheese among the crowd for votes. I treat all men with the consideration they deserve. He had no cause."

Read jumped in. "I gather Mr Neale's wife went with the porter to fetch Sellis. Was that when they discovered him in his room with his throat slashed?"

That was putting words into the Duke's mouth.

"From heathen ear to heathen ear." The Duke's lips curled.

They reached a raised pond full of leaves, flies and frogs.

"By which time, sir," Read went on, "Mr Jackson arrived to tend your injuries. Is that correct?"

Wyre couldn't believe his ears. The Chief Magistrate was blatantly feeding his informant. "Perhaps we should give the Duke an opportunity to answer in his own words."

"It was quite as you say, Mr Read," the Duke spoke. "Mr Jackson arrived to tend my injuries."

"Are you quite certain you sent *Mrs* Neale to fetch the

surgeon?" Wyre said, still unable to square the idea of the slight blonde woman being dispatched alone through the dark passages. "Might it have been Mr Neale?"

With a thin smile, the Duke said, "Do you imagine I don't know them apart?" He raised his eyebrows. "And now you have the salient details."

Read thanked him for his time, dipping absurdly again. The secretary brought his pencil down on his notebook in an exaggerated full stop.

Slowly, Cumberland turned. "Oh, Mr Wyre." He lifted his injured arm from his sling, fumbling for something in his jacket. He cursed, more a sigh of exasperation. "I beg your pardon, gentlemen; my little finger was almost severed. Thomas?" His manservant reached a slender hand into the Duke's pocket, retrieving a pearl-handled razor. "Ah, there it is. A beauty, isn't it?"

The Duke passed it to Wyre. He turned it in his hand; the blade bore the stamp of its maker. The instrument seemed to collapse the space around it. "Was this Sellis's?"

"It was. I asked Mr Read for it, and he consented. It has a fine edge. Sellis didn't spoil the strop . . . Kept it wet, as he should, with drops of sweet oil. It serves as a memento of that night." He looked from Wyre to Read. "Gentlemen, I've changed my mind. I shall remain in the orchard a little while longer, until the air becomes too sticky. Good evening." He made a curious gesture with his hand, as if releasing a dove.

Read dipped again. Without another word, and not meeting Wyre's eyes, he left with his secretary. For a moment, Wyre was alone with Cumberland, who regarded him with an expression poised somewhere between distaste and amusement. He made an awkward bow of his own, and followed Read. The magistrate, however, took the path curving back to the Palace. Wyre's way lay in the opposite direction, towards the octagonal towers, to the city beyond.

At the piazza, he glanced back down to the orchard. The Duke was still visible, standing beneath his apple trees. A man had arrived to clear the leaves from the brazen surface of the pond.

4.

MARTYR'S TEARS

61. Balk Space

The morning's dry air was full of flies and floating seeds. Most shops had closed for the day, and a solemn silence hung over the city; people drifted along the pavements with bleached, immobile faces. All the newspapers carried identical accounts. Wyre peered into *The Gazette*.

29. August 1810. This day, at Windsor, about twelve o'clock, departed this life her Royal Highness the Princess Amelia, his Majesty's youngest daughter, succumbing to the disease that had baffled the art of medicine, to the great grief of all the royal family.

Ladies to wear black bombazeens; plain muslin or long lawn; crape hoods; shamoy shoes and crape fans. Undress: dark Norwich crape. Gentlemen to wear black cloth without buttons on the sleeves; cravats and weepers; crape hatbands; black swords and buckles. Undress: dark grey frocks.

Beneath the death notice was an advertisement extolling the medicinal virtues of stramonium, whose effects the Worshipful Society of Apothecaries described as a gorgeous clouding of the mind. Perhaps this was the sensation experienced now by the Princess as she floated beyond the breathing world. Wyre stopped at a narrow cross avenue intersecting St James's Street, and conned along the shop boards for a giant coffee pot marked *Habib's*. Cline had suggested meeting there, rather than at the Palace. He'd have his reasons.

337

The sky abruptly turned hazy. Wyre raised his eyes in astonishment as he was engulfed by tiny scraps of airborne paper like snow, or snow indeed. The flakes settled on his collar. Everywhere else remained summer. A sweet odour of wood smoke cleared up the mystery. In a shop yard nearby, two men of the borough were tending a bonfire.

The coffee house's window was filled with biggins, drip-pots and silver percolating machines, presenting a baffling involution of tubes and spouts to the street. A Persian proverb hung over the door. *One cup of coffee is worth forty years' friendship.*

Surgeon Cline was waiting for him inside, a freshly cut rosa mundi gracing his button-hole.

"All roses," he said, matter-of-factly, following Wyre's eyes, "were originally white until changed to red by a single drop of Venus's menstrual blood. Do you have a creed, Mr Wyre?" He pointed at the lawyer's copy of *The Gazette*. "An apposite enough question, perhaps, on such a morning." The surgeon scratched his nose with a slender finger. "Personally, I've always found the last shreds of superstition hardest to shake off. After you left Guy's yesterday, I treated a prostitute for syphilis. She told me she was an unfortunate girl and would happily leave that way of life. The hardening and thickening was very advanced."

At the counter, a thick-set Turkish émigré fixed a burlap bag of pulverized beans across the mouth of a juddering water urn, and opened a tiny tap to activate the grounds.

To the hiss of copious steam, Wyre asked, "What do you think the Princess died from?"

Surgeon Cline sniffed the air. "I think she succumbed to roses."

"Isn't everything these days supposed to be curable? Was there really no remedy?"

338

The elegant, spectacled man shrugged. "Not nitre and rhubarb. We can discount that now. Perhaps Peruvian bark."

Wyre's coffee arrived. Cline waved away the offer of sugar. "None of your blood-sweetened beverages, Habib. He'll take it as it is." He sipped from his own cup.

"Your letter found me," Wyre said, adding, "it was waiting in my lodgings, neatly folded on my writing table."

Cline didn't respond.

"I would have sought you out, in any case, this morning." He levelled his gaze at the surgeon. "I met Leighton, you know."

"Ah, Mr Leighton. And how was he? When I saw him last, his throat was bad." Not an atom of embarrassment.

"Well, he wasn't dead, for a start," Wyre answered, his eyes not leaving the surgeon's face. "Who is he really, Mr Cline?"

"I'm afraid you're asking the wrong person."

Wyre hesitated. "I've said nothing of your role to Mr Read."

Cline appeared to weigh this, at length saying, "You ask me who Leighton is. I can tell you he carries an old injury to his shoulder, which troubles him at night, especially when the weather is wet. He has a growth on his ankle, but it's been there since childhood, and doesn't worry me in the least. Beyond that – "

"Enough subterfuge!" Wyre struggled to keep his voice down. "I know you helped him stage his own d–" He bit his tongue. Heads were turning. "I suppose you helped him with the wound he supposedly received from Vallon. Another sham," he said bitterly.

Cline's face was expressionless. "I know nothing of that. As for those overripe stage props, he paid me five pounds." The surgeon took another sip of coffee, replacing his mug on

339

the table with precise movements. "Some years back, I was acquainted with a poet." He pushed his spectacles up his long nose, tightening the coloured ribbon as he spoke; red, blues and whites – the shades of the tricolour, it suddenly occurred to Wyre, though they were in the wrong order. "Inspiration used to strike at the oddest moments. I often saw him running into a shop to beg scraps of paper. He used to carry his verses home in cheese wrappings." The Guy's man leaned back. "Doctoring is a more methodical business, much more like an Ignatian meditation. In that respect, perhaps it's not all that different from being a lawyer." Amusement broadened into a smile. "Or a Bow Street Runner."

"The inquest into Sellis's death is almost over. Read looks certain to get his way. The verdict will be returned as suicide, and things will simply go on as before."

"Things always do. That is why they are things." Cline smoothed finger and thumb over his upper lip as if grooming an invisible moustache. "Skin, Mr Wyre, is the most interesting of materials. Nothing man-made I know matches it. Extremely elastic, very tough. You have to slice through the superficial layers, then go back again over your line to make your way in."

"Some people seem to think Sellis managed it in one go," Wyre commented wryly.

"If so, he would have made an excellent surgeon. Just think, in those final moments he was both surgeon and patient." Cline regarded Wyre. "A little over two years ago, a man was delivered to my anatomy room. His oesophagus – " Cline pinched his own Adam's apple " – had been cut as deeply as Sellis's. In itself, nothing unusual. I see a dozen such cases each year. But as I walked home yesterday with Mr Cooper, a colleague of mine, I happened to remember something said by the man who'd

340

brought in the corpse back then. He told me that when the fellow had been alive, he'd driven princes around the city."

"I don't suppose you have a name?"

The flicker of a smile. "He arrived in a hessian sack, and the man who donated him was the kind it is unwise to press for answers." Cline's eyes drifted past the display of coffee machines to the world outside. "Are you familiar, Mr Wyre, with the concept of 'lust murder'?"

Of course he wasn't.

"The sexual body calls forth desires in certain individuals the majority find repugnant. A while ago, a women in Faubourg Saint-Germain was imprisoned for removing the scrotums of her lovers while they slept. She used the skins to make purses. But the key to the pathology is repetition. Put simply, Mr Wyre, it doesn't stop. Unless, of course, the perpetrator is apprehended. But they rarely are."

"Are you suggesting *Sellis* was the victim of – "

"I'm suggesting precisely nothing. Drawing inferences must be your business."

The ensuing silence was the dynamic hush of a Quaker meeting. Wyre flipped open his watch . . . due in the Palace in half an hour. He got to his feet, reeling a little from Habib's coffee; he fished for a silver tuppence, which he placed on the table, bust up. The surgeon slid it back with a look that said it all.

Paulet was waiting at the piazza entrance. "Morning, sir," the valet said cheerfully. "Mr Read's already arrived, but I'd give him a few minutes, if I were you. He's got Mr Adams with him." In a stage whisper, he added: "They've changed the jury foreman at short notice. Mr Read's not happy."

Wyre gave him a curt nod. No small talk this time. He

set off. As he passed the trellised hunting scenes, punctuated by endless doors, an image rose of Mrs Neale and the Porter banging on that to Sellis's off-duty sleeping quarters. Had Mrs Neale's husband been on the other side, wielding a razor? And had the cool, blonde woman known? It hardly mattered. In mere hours, the inquest jury would proclaim Sellis's death biathanate. It would enter the record.

All the latticed windows along the east wing were lined with black cloth. Servants scuttled around, arms heaped with dark crepe wreathes in preparation for the Princess's funeral. Did the corridors come full circle? If he ran quickly enough, would he see the back of his own head?

He pulled up abruptly. It wouldn't do. It wasn't good enough. Putting out an arm, he stopped one of the passing servants, a fair-haired girl with limpid eyes. "Where can I find Mr Neale?"

Wyre followed the serving girl's instructions, finding himself in a windowless, oak-panelled side passage. He turned the last corridor, and almost collided with Margaret, running at full pelt in his direction, hems clutched in one hand, cheeks streaked with tears.

"What the devil, girl! Watch where you're bloody going."

The maid turned to him, eyes gleaming. Whatever she was about to say was lost in heaving sobs. She pushed past, and was gone. He'd heard Palace vixens were highly strung. Welsh, on top of that.

A percussive clack of billiard balls sounded along the passageway; Wyre followed the sound to a door that stood a little ajar. Through the crack, he saw the valet crouching over a table, lining up a shot with his mace. Taking Sellis's letter from his jacket pocket, where it had lain since the previous day, Wyre burst in, and slapped the letter down onto the green baize, the side of his arm sending an ivory ball spinning off into balk space.

The valet started, turning with blazing eyes.

Wyre spoke first. "You seem to have the run of the place."

Neale quickly mastered himself. "His Highness likes me to practise every day. It helps him raise his own game." The colour still high on his cheeks, he resumed his crouching position, cannoning a white into the reds, scattering them.

Wyre pointed to the envelope. "Aren't you curious to see who it's from?"

Neale snatched up the letter, giving it a cursory glance. "The accusations are false. Read could have told you that."

"You deposed under oath that you assisted Mr Jackson in binding the Duke's wounds."

"If I said it, then I must have."

"No." Wyre shook his head. "Jackson had finished tending to the Duke by the time you returned."

Neale's face betrayed no emotion. "And what, pray, was I about all that time?"

"You were helping a dead man into bed."

Neale shifted the mace from one hand to the other, as if considering whether to attack the lawyer with it. "Some dogs will bark at thunder, but you'll find we don't like yappers here."

Wyre ignored that. "Joseph Sellis folded up his clothes. He hung them neatly over his chair – even turning out the collars to keep off the dust. Only moments later, he's supposed to have slashed his own throat."

"Even if I'd set off with the intention of murdering Sellis," Neale said coolly, "his room was locked from the inside. They had to break it down. How am I supposed to have got inside?"

343

Wyre regarded him. "What was Sellis to you, Neale? An accomplice who'd lost his nerve? Someone you needed to dispose of before he had a chance to drop you in it?" He leaned in closer. "Or was he something else?"

"Don't be absurd." The valet made a show of lining up a new shot.

"There's no use trying to hide fire with straw."

His eye still on his ball, Neale replied, "Wouldn't your time be better spent looking for the man who owns the tinderbox?"

"And who would that be?"

Neale turned then, and gave him a withering look. "Nothing in the world could induce me to confess to a crime I didn't commit. Sellis was an Italian brothel-rascal who planned to murder and rob his master. Fortunately for everyone, he couldn't even finish off a sleeping man."

"That's a good story."

"Think what you like." Neale shrugged. "The jury will reach its own verdict." With a resounding crack, he sent the white ball careening off three cushions into a pocket.

Wyre pointed to the trembling net. "You've run a coup. And Neale . . ." he added, retrieving Sellis's letter from the cushions, "I mean to sink you."

Read was sitting hunched over a document. He looked up with spidery eyes as Wyre entered.

"Mr Best wasn't pleased to hear about your little piminy yesterday. Whatever passes for a talking to at the Courthouse, you can expect one when you return." He ran his index finger slowly along the gold-leaf border of the great rectangle of green leather on the desk. "Any *more* private investigations I should know about?"

Should he let the magistrate into his coffee with Cline? No, Leighton was a dead topic for Read.

The older man drove a broad fist into his cupped hand. "Come on, let's get this over with. The jury convenes at midday. I need to finish my report. Christ's fingers, I just want to be out of here."

The morning and early afternoon sessions took formulaic depositions from three housemaids, a prick-me-dainty of a footman, two scullery maids and a kitchen boy. Then it was the turn of those servants who'd fallen to the salmon. More of the same tutored, seamless narratives. When the signatures had been collected, Read arranged the vellum into a stack and passed it to his secretary. "See these are conveyed to the jury foreman. If he hasn't changed again." He turned to Wyre. "Write your report. I've accommodated you in every way. That should be reflected."

Wyre looked at him, startled. "What about the jury? I assumed I was to – "

"Go home, Wyre," the Chief Magistrate replied simply. "Watch a play. Or a hanging. They'll be dropping that White boy this evening. Half past seven, I believe. Most irregular. If you leave now, you'll still get a place near the front."

Wyre's protests were useless. The arrangement between Read and Best covered the duration of the depositions, and not a minute more. Read was playing it to the letter. Wyre was beaten.

62. In the House of a Bad Man

Wyre left the Cupola Office; it felt like he was falling through the corridors, rather than walking along them. He caught sight of his reflection between two antechamber mirrors, and sensed the ranks of himself closing in from both sides. He crossed a long, ornate Chinese carpet with a distinct impression of not gaining any ground. Wyre stopped at a water closet, and stepped in. Digging his yard out from under his shirt tails, he relieved himself into the ancient valve contraption, listening to the water drum on the cast-iron bowl. The whole time in St James's . . . he'd seen nothing, achieved nothing. He'd been sent from pillar to post by mollies, disciples, agents, valets, never even getting close to the penetralium itself. He and Read had done no more than draw their fingers across the surface of a great lagoon. As for plumbing its depths . . . For a start, Jackson had all but escaped the inquiry, though Wyre was as sure as he could be the Royal Surgeon had embellished Cumberland's wounds. As for Neale – Sellis's co-conspirator, or destroyer, or both, he'd done enough to swing. Even Mrs Varley knew more than she was letting on. A cudding housekeeper! On top of it all, he'd nothing to give Miss Crawford in return for her retainer. The chances of finding Aspinall alive were tiny, and diminishing with the hour.

Perhaps molly briefs *were* all he was good for. The flushing mechanism engaged at the third attempt. He felt too harried to occupy himself with the flowery ewer of water on the table nearby. Threading his way along the corridor, the sense of something, an unwanted part of himself – residue – was palpable. Read was right. It was time to go home.

"*Mr Wyre –* "

A woman's voice . . . To his left, a door opened inwards, revealing a vertical sliver of unbonneted head. Margaret Jones – Mrs Neale's maid, cracked on religion. Her features contorted, anguished, she waved him in, closing the door behind him with the flats of both hands as if she wished to shore it up against something unimaginable. Her dark hair was tricked up – something of the Roman about her. Her skin had that pallor the Italians called *morbidezza*. How had she known he'd pass this way?

"Are you quite well, Margaret?" he said in as casual a manner as he could muster, as if being beckoned by women into strange interiors was in the usual run of things.

She buried her face in her short, powerful maids' fingers, and wailed: "Mr Wyre!"

"If you have anything to say, you'd better say it now," he said, more sternly now. "The jury's about to convene." A caged linnet at the back of the parlour turned on its perch. "Out with it, child," he snapped. "It's your duty to report bad deeds to the authorities."

"They'll burn for it, sir!" she said in a strangled voice.

"Who will burn?" Wyre showed her the expression prosecutors reserved for cutpurses in the dock.

Her fingers dropped to her pinafore. "Mr Hill, our preacher, warned us about sins of the flesh. We stood out in th' rain to y'ear him speak of their dirtiness. *What will it avail, but vengeance?*" A strange light appeared in her eyes. "I saw the devil in the gravel pit."

Wyre sighed inwardly. Another dupe of the millennium. "You listened in the rain?"

"If you d' love the gospels like the Welsh do, you wouldn't mind a drop of wet."

"Who will burn?" he repeated.

"I dun' like to tell, sir. His wrath will strike th' whole municipality, turn all our hours t' ashes." She buried her face in her hands again.

Why such obsession with the city's spiritual profanation? Hadn't there'd been enough of that kind of talk? He decided to play along. "Destruction, Margaret? You mean like the cities of the plain? That's what you mean, isn't it? It's what the church says two men together will bring. You mean sodomy, don't you?"

Her lips parted at the word. "Mr Hill tol' us to spit on the ground an' wash our tongues. He tol' us to spit hard."

"Such creatures should be hauled into bright light," Wyre said, nodding, stepping into her rapture. "If all men were like that, it would be the end of life."

Tears made dirty tracks down her cheeks. "Mr Hill says tha's how the Welsh lost their lands. In torrents of vice."

"That's a bit hard on a whole nation, Margaret. But vice is indeed the royal road to hell. Tell me everything."

"Not here, Mr Wyre. There's too many maids about. They listen at doors."

She should know. Minor employees were an integral part of the never-sleeping ear, the never-blinking eye. Read had dismissed the Palace's scrubbers and potato peelers too easily.

They both had.

The maid brushed away loose strands of dark hair that had become stuck to her cheeks. "We'll go there, sir . . ."

He gave her an inquiring look.

"To the black pit itself."

Margaret's route to the Duke's bedchamber was direct and swift, cutting into the narrow service corridor – a dank passage with steep corners. In a matter of minutes, they were standing outside the twin three-quarter-sized doors, one sectioned off with a velvet ribbon; then they were moving in file along the diagonal aisle to the royal quarters. The sun was low now, practically level with the room's window. A mass of dark hung behind the glowing orb.

"What did you see, Margaret? Tell me. It needn't go further."

She smoothed her pinafore down over her midriff.

"I'd come back t' fetch th' dirty linen." She gestured at the closets to the rear of the Duke's chamber. "It were late, sir, almost eleven." Those ridiculous Welsh inflections, stronger now. "I y'eard voices." She went over to Cumberland's bed, half-perching on the edge, and pointed to the paper-thin partition. "They was coming from the Valet's Room."

"That wasn't the first time you'd heard things, was it, Margaret? You've sat on this bed before. Listening. Who told you to do it?" He looked at her hard. "Was it Mrs Sellis?" He pictured Margaret sitting on the Duke's silk sheets, jotting down the vile sounds she heard in that small, neat handwriting of hers.

"No, sir. It wern' Mrs Sellis." Her expression was sullen now. "Anyway, it were different this time. It sounded like someone were – " She bit her tongue. "It were different," she said simply, wiping her eyes. "After it stopped, I gathered up the linen an' left. I took the back way, sir, which passes the rear door to the Valet's Room. It was a little ajar." She looked up at him, then immediately cast her eyes down again. "Sometimes the latch dun' fall properly."

"You were spying, Margaret. What did you see?"

"Two men . . . at the foot of the valet's bed."

"One of them was your master."

"He wore a royal coat, sir. Scarlet and gold lace. Blue cuffs and collar."

The maid was describing the Duke's regimental jacket.

"What was he doing, Margaret?"

"Standing behind the other man."

"An Italian wedding . . ." Wyre's lips were dry. "Who was the other?"

She looked at her feet.

"*Who?*"

349

"Mr Sellis, sir." Margaret stifled a sob.

The degenerate swine. He regarded her, suddenly mistrustful. "Did Mr Neale instruct you to tell me this? You like him, don't you? I heard you had a set-to with his wife on Birdcage Walk."

"Lies, Mr Wyre," she said plaintively.

That soft, mendacious Welsh face. He fought an urge to slap it. If any of this was to convince a judge, he'd need details. The intimate variety. Was Margaret good for them?

"Did you see the Duke take out his yard?" A formula he'd posed countless times before.

Margaret eyes widened in alarm. At first he thought she'd make a dash for it, but instead she gave a short nod.

"You're quite certain of that?"

"Every woman knows, sir," she said in a trembling voice. "It were a fat, pale-headed thing."

"And did he place it inside Sellis?"

The sluices burst. "I've heard of a maid," she sobbed uncontrollably, "who had to stand in the pillory for reporting on her master. The judge said she couldn't have recognized what he'd done without taking part in the guilt herself."

Wyre recalled the case. "That's untrue, Margaret. Tell me what they did."

She used her pinafore to wipe away tears. "Wha' Mr Hill warn'd us against." Her face fell as if she'd fallen victim to a salvo. "Sir, I'm a good woman in the house of a bad man."

"Be precise, Margaret. I need to know *exactly* what they did. You said it was different this time. Different *how*?"

A palpable agony of indecision, then: "Mr Neale was there."

Wyre's heart caught on his ribs. "In the room?"

"He was watching 'em, sir. He held a pistol t' Mr Sellis's head. It were cocked, sir."

Wyre stared. "You're quite certain? If this is fiction, there will be consequences."

"I ran off, sir, an' met Mrs Neale in the corridor. She asked me where I'd been so late. She asked me if I'd seen Mr Neale."

"And you told her?"

"I told her I hadn't."

Wyre struggled to take it in. The maid had just placed all three men together that night. Two brutes, one man brutalized. Was the picture finally beginning to acquire what William would call its lights?

"You should have told me all this earlier. Now it may be too late."

"Will I be punished, sir?" says Margaret, twisting a blue locket ring around her finger; enamel, heart-shaped.

Wyre imagined a pair of strong arms thrusting her up against the wall, hands moving under her rose-coloured petticoat.

"Will I be punished, sir?" she repeated.

"There's no proof of what you say, Margaret. It's no more than hearsay."

Her eyes dropped, and moved slyly to the side. "The sheets from that night are still in the closet."

What? He looked at her carefully. "Show me."

He followed Margaret to the closets at the back of the Duke's bedchamber. In one of the cupboards was a pile of neatly folded linen. She pulled out a crumpled sheet from the bottom. How had it survived the washing rota? In one corner, the Duke's lion-and-unicorn was visible, picked out in coloured thread. His initials danced above. *E.A.* Margaret carried the linen to the bedchamber's window, and shook it out. Then she held it up to the light.

351

Transparent patches ... Wyre had seen such translucent stains untold times before – on linen sheets, jackets, shirt-tails, cuffs. There was no mistaking it.

Seed.

He left Margaret standing by the latticed windows without answering her question –

– and pulled up sharp in the hallway. What was the name Cline had given to such things? *Lust murder.* You damned idiot, Wyre. It had been staring him in the face from the moment he arrived.

Tearing aside the ribbon that placed the Valet's chamber out of bounds, he pushed open the tiny door. The bent nail at the top of the bedpost was a beckoning finger now. Business-like, he drew a line with his eyes from post to fireplace. The iron backplate was cast in alternate glints and shadows by the shafts of last sun. He through the burning martyrs – there was the old man, clasped hands raised to heaven. The light ricocheted off his tears.

Tears that shimmered through the soot.

He dropped to all fours like a supplicant. So Tranter had died shortly after Margaret arrived at the Palace. That made it, what, April? Already unseasonably warm; not much call for fires.

He touched a finger to the old man's tears, then pressed a fingernail into them. It left an impression. Lead. Soft, compacted fragments. Wyre swivelled round, calculating a line from bed to fire plate. The ricochet must have sent the bullet ... more or less ... *there*, to the right of the door where a patch of plaster took the light differently from the surrounding surface. Scrambling to his feet, he went over, heart hammering against his ribs. The plaster was rough, a clumsy repair. If he scraped away, would he find buried in the lathes the deformed remnants of the slug that ended Tranter before the footman's body was moved and dumped so unceremoniously outside the stables?

He fished around in his waistcoat pocket for the key to Mrs Mason's apartment. He could dig the bullet out with that, present the evidence to Read.

He stopped, and slipped Mrs Mason's smooth key back in his pocket, knowing he was too late. The verdict would already have been delivered. Even if his rough calculation had yielded the right spot to delve – and now he began to doubt – time had already rendered the bullet inadmissible. Any new evidence would have to wait for a re-trial, which would never happen. A bullet worth, literally, a King's ransom? There wasn't a strongbox in the country that could keep such evidence from walking. Even if he made it to the retrial alive, all he had was a theory, the airiest of citadels, easily dismissed along with all the other fantasies of conspiracy being rehearsed in taverns up and down the country.

Head bowed, he headed in the direction of the piazza exit, pausing at a door marked *KEY ROOM*. There was always the outside chance someone had handed in his notebook. It was a vestige of Rose he was unwilling to give up. His handkerchief, too; though he doubted he'd ever see *that* again.

Benjamin Smith's head appeared. The white hair and boyish complexion was a singularly unpleasant combination. "Nothing of that kind, Mr Wyre. No 'ankychief. No notebook, neither." Along the length of one wall, dozens of square-tooth keys hung from hooks. Smith followed the lawyer's eyes to a conspicuous gap. "Them along the top are for the state rooms," he said, pointing with an arthritic finger. "Them in the middle's the public rooms, west wing. An' them along the bottom . . ." He grinned. "Servants' dormies. That's where the maids cuddle up at night."

353

Wyre looked at him sharply. "You have keys to the private bedrooms?"

The Porter nodded.

"For Sellis's, too?"

Another nod. A smidgen of uncertainty had crept into Smith's face.

With a yawning sensation in his stomach, Wyre stared at the space beneath the hook. It was a tiny void, but it seemed to suck the whole room into it. "That was Sellis's key, wasn't it?"

"One of 'em, sir. He had two, did Mr Sellis. Two doors to his room, see. The spare for the one that opened into the rear passage went missing th' night of the assault."

"And you didn't think to mention this to anybody?"

"Mr Read spotted it," answered the old man defensively.

"Mr Read *knew*?"

"Wrote it down, sir. In his little notebook." The Porter looked away. "He 'adn't lost his, see."

Wyre shook his head. What did it matter now? What did any of it matter? He stepped out into the hallway, and set off again for the exit that would bring him onto the piazza, and away.

And stopped. Things had gone far enough. Even a moral victory was a victory of sorts.

At the foot of the stone stairs leading down from Smith's den of keys, Paulet was chatting with a girl on her knees next to a steaming bucket.

"The Seddon Room?" Wyre demanded, as the maid rose to let him pass. He looked dubiously at Paulet. "You always seem to be on hand."

The phrase triggered a smile. "These corridors, sir. They're something befuddling. It's the great long room downstairs, across the courtyard, you'll be wanting. The one they 'ardly never use."

63. Deluge

When it arrived, the rain was the kind that could beat fruit off trees. Pulling his jacket collars up around his ears, Wyre hurried across the courtyard's gravel paths, now slushy conduits. Palace gardeners moved through the flower beds with protective hessian sacks that abrupt gusts of wind threatened to tear from their fingers. He turned into a cloistered walkway, the quickest way, according to the ever-obliging Paulet, to the Seddon Room. The inquest jury would have arrived at their verdict. Perhaps everyone had already left.

He reached the low arch Paulet had described. It was decorated with snakes eating their tails. A stocky man stepped out of the shadows at the dripping entrance. He wore a burgundy long coat, his blue conical hat pulled down against the weather, eyes slits beneath the reinforced brim. Wyre made to go round him; the other mirrored his steps. He went left – the same; a dance in place. Wyre stood still, water cascading from his hair.

The man tipped back his hat. That misshapen nose, there was no mistaking it. Wyre stared through sheets of rain at the stocky waiter from The Sun.

"Ev'ning, Mr Wyre," the waiter called across. "At the centre of the storm again. Quite certain yer don't aspire to become th' storm itself?"

The eloquence was a slap across the cheeks.

"What are you doing here?"

"Just a bit of bollocks. Feeding the mystery."

It sank in. "You're one of Cumberland's men," Wyre shouted over the slaps of rain and noisy squalls. "You might as well know I intend to make the Duke answer for his deeds."

"Nah." The waiter gave him a look of disdain. "You've

355

got it all wrong. My master's York, and he'd probably applaud yer ambition." He tilted his face up to the hanging clouds. "But then there'd be the scandal to consider. Yorkie's baby brother in the dock?" He smiled, frowning at the same time. "I don't think so."

"I won't shrink from my duty."

The other gave him an appraising look. "You've got a strong belly, I'll give yer that. Tipped enough nasty in your soup to down a cow."

Had he heard right?

"Think of it as a parting gift from ol' Leager and Oakden. Good hearts, both of 'em, who didn't deserve t' dangle."

The mention of those two soiled names had only one meaning: he was staring at a lieutenant in Yardley's molly regiment – a corps within the Duke of York's own corps. In William's terms, the cup within the cup. Was this the penetralium itself? It was certainly payback. Retribution for failing to indict Neale, for failing to salvage Sellis's sullied reputation . . . and, it seemed, for having had the temerity to do his duty from the Prosecutor's bench. So he was to be ended under a pagan arch. He almost felt resigned to it.

"The dog – " he yelled over the gusts. "I suppose that was you, too."

"Nah, you've got Cumberland's people to thank there. Tend to get ahead of themselves, that lot." The man wiped water from his eyes. "We were all saying, us York men were, how well yer did to get away from the General. Years of experience, that mutt. You're a man of hidden resources."

"I'll call the guards."

That elicited a smirk. "'Arf of 'em are wiv us, Mr Wyre," he said, stepping towards Wyre. The waiter drove a fist into the lawyer's stomach that sent him spluttering to his knees. "That's from the Vere Street boys. Would have been worse, if I'd had my way, but Yardley thinks you'll have yer uses in the future."

"Best ... will ... uproot you," Wyre said between sucking breaths. "You and your kind ... are a disease. Human effluvia ..."

"And you, Mr Wyre," the lieutenant said, "are like a once-respectable woman reduced to the condition of a whore, begging every physician to inspect her stinking parts." He knelt; Wyre felt the man's wet lips at his ear. "When the old donkey blows his horn, it's time to cock yer hay an' corn. Ain't that what they say, Mr Wyre?"

He clutched at his assailant's sleeve, but the waiter flicked him off contemptuously. Whistling cheerfully, the man vanished into the cloistered walkway beyond the arch.

Somewhere, a solitary mistle thrush was trying in vain to sing the sun back.

Wyre flung the enormous door to the Seddon Room open on its hinges, and staggered in, his cheeks burning. The inquest chamber was set out like a courtroom, with a dock near the middle, but the benches were empty. He registered a set of double doors on the far wall – the jury must be inside, still deliberating. He wasn't too late! In the far corner, standing at one of the Seddon Room's tall windows, Read was conversing with the Duke. Adams and Jackson stood to the side. All four were looking at the lawyer.

"I won't be party to this," said Wyre over the booms of the storm, stumbling towards them, clutching his belly. "This inquest's a sham!"

"Hell's despair!" exclaimed Read. "Remember whose presence you're in." He took a menacing step forward.

Momentum swept Wyre along. "One of the maids saw

you with Sellis," Wyre said, looking past Read's shoulder to Cumberland, who was framed by flashing geometries of light.

"You're making a fool of yourself," Read growled.

"It's quite alright, Mr Read," said the Duke, his face displaying mild amusement. "Let him say his say. Adams ... Jackson. If you wouldn't mind."

With courtiers' bows, Coroner and Royal Surgeon stepped out into the corridor.

Read remained, his look black.

Wyre appealed to the magistrate. "Neale murdered Sellis, I'm sure of it." He was suddenly unsure. "But it was at the Duke's behest. Neale stole the key to Sellis's back door – it went missing from the Porter's room that night – and surprised Sellis while he was shaving. That's why the jacket and trousers were neatly folded over the chair. The sound of dropping water reported by Mrs Neale, the shuffling in the corridor that frightened the maids ... Not Sellis. Both down to Neale!"

"Mystery-mongering," the Duke said in a quiet but perfectly audible voice, his eyes tiny points. His black silk cap had made of him a demonic cardinal, or an antichrist. "You're worse than a pamphleteer."

"One of the maids saw you," Wyre said, voice rising, "in the Valet's Room, standing behind Sellis. You were – "

Read leaped forward and wrestled the lawyer to the floor, smothering his mouth with a broad hand. Wyre kicked and bucked, but the magistrate was the stronger man. In seconds, Wyre was pinned. He was aware of the Duke standing over them both, watching them struggle.

"Tell me, Mr Wyre," Cumberland said, looking down, "did your father beat you till the stick broke?"

"Why didn't you allow Sellis to leave, as he desired?"

Wyre said, choking against Read's hand. "All this could have been – " He cried out in pain as the magistrate's knee drove into his abdomen.

The Duke raised his cane. "Let him speak, Mr Read."

Wyre strained against Read's hold. "They hang men for what you do!"

"I could almost get used to your familiarity, Mr Wyre. But not your fables. I am guilty of precisely nothing. I exist in a state of grace."

"Ask him to remove his cap," Wyre said, trying to make eye contact with the Chief Magistrate. "You won't find anything more than a few light scratches." The girl with the needles – that's what Cline had been trying to tell him. "All self-inflicted . . ."

"An ingenious confection," Cumberland said. Then, in a sharper tone: "Get up, both of you. Enough!"

Read allowed the lawyer to rise, but kept his arms pinioned behind his back.

"You're wrong," the Duke said, pacing. "I wasn't in the valet's bedroom that night. You'd be more likely to find my brother there than me."

"Lies!" Wyre's cheeks burned. "You had Tranter killed, too. You blew his brains out in the valet's chamber. Leighton cracked your case."

The Duke stopped abruptly. "Can you prove this, or am I expected to set fire to my own beard?"

Wyre turned to Read. "The bullet hit the fire plate, sir," he said, with all the urgency he could muster. "It ricocheted back into the room. You'll find it buried beneath the plaster."

The Duke reached into his jacket pocket. *Shit!* Wyre strained against the magistrate's grip. Cumberland still had the razor.

"If your soul was on the outside," he yelled at the Duke,

359

struggling, frantic now, "it would be a black flapping thing. Someone will sit at your gate in judgement."

"There goes your imagination again." The amused expression reappeared on Cumberland's face. He opened his hand to reveal a silver pocket watch. He tapped the timepiece smartly, and glanced at the double doors. "The jury must be debating the finer points. While we're waiting for them to return, let's put Mr Wyre's theory to the test. The Valet's Room, gentleman." He extended his good arm. "Shall we?"

They followed the Duke, Wyre frog-marched by Read. The householders they met coming from the opposite direction kept their heads down, but Wyre felt their eyes on his back.

Rain sheeted against the Valet's Room's latticed windows, backed by dark shadows.

"Well, Wyre?" Read pushed him away. "This had better be good."

Rubbing his aching arms, Wyre went to the door jamb and ran his fingers over the plaster. It was perfectly smooth. Had it ever been anything other than that?

The Duke watched for a moment, pulling at his cuff. Finally, he said, "You were right in one respect, Mr Wyre. Right to surmise Sellis was an extortionist. But there was no impropriety. I have never thought of him in that way, and the very idea is repugnant to me." He glanced through the window at the dark clouds. "But you'll know better than most the mere accusation of a certain crime is sufficient to ruin a man. Physical injury – " he lifted his bandaged arm " – is bad, but injury to character far worse. Mr Sellis demanded a thousand pounds."

The lawyer said nothing; his ears filled with a strange roaring sound.

"Are you getting this, Wyre?" Read said. It seemed none of it was news to the Chief Magistrate.

"At first," Cumberland went on, "I contemplated paying off the villain." He shrugged, an odd gesture for a Duke. "However, on the night of his demise, Mr Sellis informed me the price of what he called his silence had doubled. Such a sum was impossible to procure discreetly, even for a royal scion. I explained this. Again he threatened me with newspapers." He smiled thinly. "I informed him I'd sleep on it, and give him his answer in the morning. Perhaps Sellis correctly guessed my intention to turn the case over to Bow Street. That night, he struck at me as I slept. The rest occurred exactly as I deposed." He took a deep breath. "So you see, Mr Wyre, I neither committed murder, nor caused it to be committed." He moved to the arched fireplace. "Shall we adjourn the flames, and forget this confusion of ways?"

Wyre stared from one to the other, weighing the Duke's story against Margaret's, against Leighton's. *A royal shirt dance?* It made some kind of sense: a molly scandal of such proportions would deliver a crushing blow to the nation's morale . . .

He breathed out. No . . . It was creaky as a newlyweds' bed. He shook his head. Slow, deliberate movements.

"I came to pursue the case," he began, "wherever it took me. It has led me to you."

The Duke stared at him for a moment. "Come, Mr Read," he said at last. "Mr Wyre knows what he's about. The jury will be wondering where we've got to." With his good hand, he pulled his lapels together. "By the way," he said, as if inquiring about a trifle, "who was the maid?"

Wyre pressed his lips together. His heart tightened to a clenched fist.

361

The Duke nodded. "I thought so." He left the Valet's Room, giving no sign at all of having registered the enormous figure that had appeared behind the frame, looming.

Read turned in the doorway. "You idiot, Wyre. I told you to go home."

64. After the Fire

In an old column from *The Gazette*, Wyre remembered reading about very large human ribs unearthed by Spanish peasants ploughing a field. The fragments were of such proportions, the ignorant joskins believed they'd discovered the relics of a wandering descendant of Rapha. Scholars from the university at Valencia dismissed the bones as whales' ruins.

"But whales are denizens of the sea," objected the villagers, who complained for years of a conspiracy.

An oddly dissociated corner of Wyre's brain weighed the respective arguments, bumpkins versus scholars, while a central core of self screamed at him to act – and quickly.

The colossal stablehand had been forced to crouch low to squeeze under the doorframe; once inside, however, he was surprisingly fast, advancing with arms spread wide like a playful uncle come to catch a child.

"A hide comes sooner or later to the tanner," he said, his voice incongruously reedy.

Backing away desperately, a tide of terror washing through him, Wyre screamed for Read. With a thud, his heels knocked against the skirting. Trapped.

The giant drew back a ham-like fist. The belly clout seemed to slow as it approached, its half-second transit splitting off into ever-more generous divisions. Wyre had time to speculate how Leighton would react in his place; whatever the man was, he'd throw punches wherever he found a target. He remembered him once trying to explain fear: *Let it make you clever.* He seemed to hear Leighton's voice at his ear now. *Dive and deceive! Fuck's sake, Kit, what are you waiting for?*

The lawyer hurled himself sideways just a fraction too late. The behemoth's knuckles scraped the edge of his ribcage, and sensation drained from one side of his torso. The deflected fist continued on its unstoppable trajectory, smashing through the lathes of the wall. Wyre had an absurd image of the hand sticking out on the Duke's side, debris dropping onto those silk sheets. He fell to his knees, groaning pitifully.

The colossus yanked out his hand, knuckles sticky with blood. Plaster exploded into the valet's bedchamber in a great puff. Squeezed now into the far right-hand corner of the room, preternaturally aware of the infinite segments into which the ninety-degree angle he was occupying could be parcelled, Wyre knew he had no chance of making the door.

The monster stooped, like a boy tickling for trout. He found one. The tentacle-like fingers closed over Wyre's ears, clamping, hauling him up, lifting him clean off his feet. Wyre hung there, kicking, staring helplessly into the enormous face –

– which suddenly creased into a thousand folds, all leading to the cavernous mouth, which let out a high bellow.

Then Wyre was falling, landing in a heap, clutching at his burning neck, waiting for the enormous boot to snap his spine. When he dared to open his eyes, he saw, absurdly, a wizened man, limbs arranged in a fighting

363

pose, facing the giant. The lithe old buffer who'd accosted him on the Mall! In spite of his years, the man moved with mercurial ease, sending a crunching fib into the giant's midriff. Goliath roared like a goaded bear. He swung his fists wildly, unable to land a punch. With strange speed his opponent slid under the great scything arm, uncoiling a counter-coup straight from the shoulder, catching the outlandish figure a clean blow on the sternum. For perhaps the first time in what Wyre imagined must be an atrocious career of violence, the giant took a step backwards, his face registering uncertainty.

From nowhere, a blade appeared in the old man's hand, which he jabbed up, aiming for somewhere deep. More by accident, it seemed, than design, a palm the size of a spade intersected with its deadly path, and was speared through. Wyre's rescuer attempted to retract his weapon, but it was pinned between bones. Howling, Goliath swiped with the back of his good hand, this time catching his opponent across the face, sweeping him away to the ground. The titan stared at his palm, contemplating a puzzle of steel and flesh from both sides, then wrenched out the blade, blood whipping. He tossed it aside; it skittered across the floor, coming to rest a few feet in front of Wyre, who inched stealthily towards it.

With another high bellow, Goliath stamped over to where the old man sat, dazed from the blow. To Wyre's horror, an enormous boot to the midriff sent the old man up in the air like a flipped coin. He came down hard, but somehow managed to struggle to his feet, the bone of one cheek paste. In a blur of movement, he whirled round a fist, striking the giant again on the chest, the height where any normal man's head would have been. What in any other situation would have been an ender, merely provoked a wild charge. The old man sidestepped neatly, sending his knuckles after the giant; they crunched into the small of his back, drawing another enraged squeal.

Wyre snatched the knife from the floor, waving it triumphantly. His saviour, distracted by the sudden movement, turned, and was caught by a cudgelling blindsider that dashed him to the ground. This time he did not get up.

The giant stepped over his foe, and raised his vast foot. The old man's eyes flickered . . . Sweeping a thin leg round in a last-ditch effort, he succeeded in clipping one of the mighty ankles. Losing balance, the giant windmilled with his long arms, but did not fall. Recovering, he bent at the knees like a spider, and gathered up his prey in an absurd paternal embrace before hurling it against the wall, dislodging the portrait of the woman in the broad-brimmed hat. The painting fell at Wyre's feet.

Blood drained from the old man's ears and nose; yet even now he made a feeble effort to raise his guard, some martial protocol, lodged deeply in the muscle.

The great foot came down, pressing onto the slender ribcage with a sound like that of a carriage wheel moving over gravel. Wyre groaned.

Goliath turned at the sound, and stepped towards the lawyer, an ogre a child might meet on some clammy, nightmarish bridge of the imagination. Light-headed, Wyre held up the portrait as a pointless shield, bracing for the blow that would cut all ties

It was Read who appeared around the cracked gilt frame, entering the Valet's Room at double pace, a Bow Street issue pistol held at full stretch. A fizzing spark, then a clock's tick of balanced nothing and an explosion almost too distant from the flash to be part of it. Finally, an appalling belch of smoke.

The giant's features contorted. "Mr Read?" he said mournfully, staring over his shoulder, clutching the saddle of his back. Then he dropped to one knee, emitting a drawn-out keening sound, like that of a baby.

Read dropped the pistol into his left hand, cocking it again with the thumb of his right.

"Still breathing, Wyre?" he said from the corner of his mouth. He spat a second slug into the muzzle.

Seeing Read's methodical work, the monstrous man scrabbled for the window, tipping his bulk head-first through the sash bars, his broad shoulders breaking them as though they were tinder wood.

Weapon reloaded, Read dashed to the window ledge, feet crunching on splinters of glass, pistol levelled over his left forearm. He crouched, rose, feinted left and right, looking for the shot. Wyre pictured the ornamental trees, which must be forming an occluding screen.

Cursing under his breath, the Chief Magistrate lowered his pistol. He turned, moving towards Wyre, the standard-issue 'dag' hanging at his side. The lawyer stared, eyes widening.

"Don't be ridiculous," Read muttered, and with his other strong hand helped him up.

"You came back."

"Let's leave it at that, Wyre."

Together they went over to the old man, lifting him carefully into a sitting position. Each shallow breath made a sound like a cracked piston.

"I'm afraid he got away, Shadworth," the magistrate said, dandling him like an infant. "I'll have officers sent after him. He won't be hard to track."

This was *Shadworth*?

The man's voice was wind through reeds. "No need. Liver shot . . . Can't be staunched."

Wyre knelt by the elderly man. "You saved me from Cumberland's monster."

"Not Cumberland's – " something pink bubbled at Shadworth's lips. "York's man." He took another rasping breath. "Like me."

A pause as Wyre attempted to bring it within the scope of his senses. "I don't understand." In truth, he didn't.

"Cumberland . . . was in . . . Vere Street that night."

The gasping was horrible. "I thought he spent the evening at the opera."

The thinnest of smiles. "Some of the men . . . liked to call it that." Shadworth's eyes begin to cloud over like two pools stirred up with sticks. "Cumberland misused a drummer-boy in The Swan . . ." He broke off in coughs the lawyer felt as explosions in his own chest. "York's had us tidying up . . . after his brother for years. He shuns scandal like a Covent Garden ague . . ." The ghost of a lewd smile. "But he hates Cumberland . . . suspects him of giving Princess Amelia something nasty." The crumpled face seemed almost empty of blood. "That sweet girl . . ." the tiniest spark returned to Shadworth's eyes. "She was destined to join us after the fires. It was foretold she would live at Joanna's right hand as her sister."

Wyre stared. Disciple talk!

Shadworth's breathing was now even more unprofitable. He gestured for Wyre to lean in and, in quick pants, said: "There's one man . . . can place Cumberland in Vere Street – " He stopped, found a little air. "Someone who . . . saw him disgrace himself."

"Aspinall," Wyre said quietly.

The dying man nodded, pronouncing as two hasping syllables an address Wyre had heard several times in the last few days. "You'll find him there . . . What's left of him." More coughing, more pink. When the convulsions finally ceased, Shadworth was looking through Wyre, looking backwards. "The splendid gloves . . ." The eyes sagged. Sealed.

Wyre turned to Read. "Did you hear that? We should go immediately to Wood's – "

"Fuck – "

65. Loose Threads

" – off. None of it can be proved." The Chief Magistrate glanced down at Shadworth's body. "Accept it."

"If you dispatched officers to the asylum this evening, fetched Aspinall . . ."

"Aspinall in court, testifying against an heir to the throne?" Read smiled. He cast his eyes about a room that looked as if it had been struck by one of the prophesied earthquakes. "Someone will be here soon to tidy up. You'd better be gone when they arrive."

"Shouldn't the inquest jury at least be informed?"

"I said you'd get nowhere alluding to Greek vices, Wyre. Long live the frigging King. Oh, and before you get any ideas about petitioning Best, if there was any justice in the world, that shitbird would be in the dock himself for aiding and abetting mollies. But don't worry, his time will come."

Wyre looked at him in bewilderment.

"He throws two or three lesser men to the dogs each year, and shields dozens." He looked at Wyre dubiously. "I assumed you were part of the scam."

Wyre looked numbly at the Chief Magistrate. Had Best sought him out – turning his and Rose's lives upside down in the process – not because of his prosecuting skill, but *lack* of it? "How much did you know about the Duke, sir. From the beginning, I mean?"

"Too much," Read answered, "and enough. England's at War. Now piss off."

Wyre made his way along the corridors, one side a dull ache, his neck and head feeling like another man's. Shadworth, at least, had still believed Cumberland could be stung. He'd spent his dying breath giving Wyre a shot at it. Pointless looking to Bow Street for help, though. Read had made that clear. Wyre had a stark choice: return to Wood's Close as a private citizen, or do nothing at all.

A maid startled him, arms laden with more of those damned wreathes, as she emerged from a panelled door hidden between tapestried hunting scenes. The whole Palace was wrong! Doors that looked like walls, walls made of paper. There was one thing, though, he was going to settle before he left. What did chess players call it? The natural move? He was about to make it. He stepped in front of the maid, barring her way.

"Where's Mr Neale?"

She looked at him with alarm. "In his private rooms, sir. If he's not on."

"*Not on*," Wyre mimicked. "This house is a disgrace."

He strode off in the direction of the householders' grace-and-favour apartments.

The valet was perched morosely in front of a large mirror, one slipper half-on. Neale spun as Wyre entered, and began to protest the intrusion. Without saying a word, the lawyer marched forward and planted a fist squarely on the man's chin, knocking him from his chair.

Neale stared up from the polished floor. "Are you mad?" He climbed warily to his feet, nursing his jaw.

Wyre braced for a counter attack, but Neale merely turned and took a seat at his desk. "Fine, you'll have your truth."

"I know it already," Wyre said. "You murdered Sellis on the Duke's orders. You stole a key to his room."

"That's not what happened." A quarto volume lay face-down on the desk. Neale turned the book over, resting his hand on the spread pages as if about to recite a few choice lines. "Since one version of events seems to be as good as another, you might as well hear mine." He let out a long sigh. "I had no key to Joseph's room. I never needed one."

"Joseph, now?" Wyre taunted. "What did you get up to in his room? Spot of thread the needle?"

Neale's eyes drifted to the window. "We were friends. Close friends. It would scarcely have been possible to be any closer. If you wish to hang me for that," he said, looking back at the lawyer, "you're welcome to try." Neale rubbed his jaw. "The knot would be a release." Wetting the pad of his third finger, he idly turned the pages. "Cumberland smoked us out. I suppose one of the maids traded a secret that hurt no one in return for some fleeting capital. He summoned us to the Valet's Room. I was prepared for dismissal, arrest even, but what took place there that evening was unthinkably worse." Little pearls of perspiration had collected along his upper lip, hanging there.

Wyre gave him a sceptical look.

"The Duke began by threatening to expose us to our wives." Neale's lips twitched. "I assure you, my wife would not have understood. He offered to lift his threat – but on one condition only." He paused. "Perhaps you can imagine what it was. Palace valets, the Duke told us, had always accommodated their masters in that way, when it was asked of them." His voice became impassioned. "I wish he would melt like wax!" He blinked back tears. "Poor Joseph bore the brunt. You were quite right, Mr Wyre, my angel did wish to leave the Duke's service. But he was a loving father, and in his own way a loyal husband.

It was more important to him than anything to provide for his family. A few weeks before his death, he told me he'd found some sympathetic friends. They promised to find him a new position in a big house in the city. I would follow, in due course."

"Vere Street friends?" Wyre said contemptuously. "The Tyrant's agents, more like."

It hardly matters. We were betrayed. I have my suspicions. That same night, Cumberland summoned us and claimed his *droit* in the most despicable manner."

A mental picture formed of the valet lying on his belly on Cline's gurney, that obscene cross-hatch. The pieces dropped into place like billiard balls in their pockets: the Duke with the valet, one thrusting, eyes rolling, the other barely able to breathe; the razor unclasped, those livid slice-marks, the blood welling up like tiny beads strung along the finest wire.

"Joseph bore it for my sake. Afterwards, the Duke went to join his generals, leaving me to comfort my darling. By the time I returned to the Valet's Room, Joseph was gone. I suppose he was already hiding in the closets. It didn't occur to me to look. If only I had . . ." He screwed his eyes shut. "I remained in the Valet's Room. What else could I do? It was still my turn." His expression was suddenly desolate and remote. "At about midnight, the Duke stumbled back. I heard the door to his chamber slam. The rest of the night's events occurred just as I deposed. The only thing I omitted to say was I immediately knew the assassin to be Joseph. You asked why I didn't fear for my wife's safety when the Duke sent her along the corridors. Now you have your answer." He wiped away more tears. No longer needing to wet his finger, he turned another page of poetry, then closed the book.

"What about Tranter?"

"The pistol was the Duke's, not mine." His lips formed a cruel smile. "He couldn't raise the flag without it. Whether the footman's death was an accident or happened by design, I couldn't say." He cast his eyes down. "I helped move the body to the stables. I am so very ashamed of that." He buried his head.

Wyre studied him. Could Neale be induced to testify? He doubted it. But there'd be time to deal with the valet later. Now the clock was ticking for Aspinall. He'd head for Great Windmill Street, and Miss Crawford. Just as soon as he'd stopped off in South Molton Street. There was something there he needed to fetch.

He left to the sound of the valet's sobs.

66. Ketland & Co.

"I'm afraid it's the only way," Wyre said, after he'd laid the day's events bare for the printer.

William regarded him sadly. "I wondered if one day you'd call for it. But as for it being the only way, Big Tom Aquinas teaches there's nothing in the intellect that wasn't first in our senses."

The meaning evaded him. Wyre held out his hand.

"Very well." William took a deep breath and held it. He crossed to the tall mahogany drinks cabinet. Opening a tiny drawer, he retrieved a key, which he joggled in the brass lock of a larger compartment. From this box, he took a second key, offering it in turn to the locking mechanism of a still more substantial drawer. Nestling inside that, Wyre knew, was the pistol.

William passed the firearm to the lawyer. Only then did he breathe out. "If you're certain."

The dull weight in Wyre's palm felt oddly familiar,

though he'd hardly handled the weapon since buying it, and only once let it off in a field. The kick had made his arm hurt. He stared down at the dark stock, its fine touch-hole, the ornate stamp of Ketland & Co. on the lock's plate. The gun was beautiful. Mr Egg the gunsmith had explained how this particular model not only boasted what was called a Damascus twist, but also an improved pan and gooseneck hammer with a double arch for expelling damp.

"I'd like to have the Duke standing before me now," Wyre said, holding out the gun with a display of impotent bravado. He made a clicking noise in his mouth. "Point blank."

William lifted his bushy eyebrows. "Not so long since, physicians thought flowers shaped like testicles could cure sexual diseases." He reached back into the drawer, pulling out a powder sack then a handful of slugs. They clacked together in the printer's palm like glass marbles. "Has it ever occurred to you," he continued, "that our opinions on love between men might be similarly circumscribed by the times, that in this regard we're merely dupes of the Spectre?" He stared so furiously, Wyre could almost believe he was looking into the future itself.

A man of complex genius – and wrong on many things.

They exchanged a handshake. Wyre was about to slip the pistol into its purple velvet shoulder-bag when William put his hand over the muzzle. The lawyer felt him through it.

"Look at us, Wyre, two men, with death in between!"

67. Poultry Compter

The stench was worse than a Southwark ditch, worse than a tanner's yard. It was the smell of unwashed privates. Dirty snatch and arse. She used to scold her girls about it.

The Poultry Compter – so called because they used to sell chickens along these streets – was where all those accused of unnatural crimes were thrown in with the city's vagrants, debtors and prophets. Whole lengths of the prison's crumbling walls were shored up with props.

Ten ounces of bread a day, six pounds of potatoes a week, the allowance revoked if they failed to keep themselves clean. They were made to wear tufted thrum caps, though some had to make do with the tops of old stockings. Beef for those who attended chapel.

Each offender paid six shillings for garnish to the steward, who was himself one of the felons, elected by his peers. That, or a bushel of coals for the fire. If a person was poor, a decrepit old man told her when they'd arrived, as he'd peered down her pinafore, they never pressed it.

Sarah feared the old ones most. They'd already had her last shilling, and swore they'd have more.

Since they'd been dumped here after the business with Parson, her husband had sat in a corner, refusing to sleep, running a finger ceaselessly around the puckered edges of his sixpence. Sarah knew what he was thinking. He was probably right: the others would scratch and bite for it.

Within the inner gate, twenty common debtors were spread across two wards called Kings and Princes. Sarah wondered where Queens was. The wardens were supposed to keep the males and females apart after five in the afternoon, returning the women to a place called the Mouse Hole. A deal must have been struck that evening. She looked round the cell, which was dimly lit by what little low sun had come out after the storm. She was the only one of her sex still in Kings.

The man snoring lightly beside her, accused of forging bills, was low-sized and slight of build. He hadn't bothered fighting for one of the hard oak pallets raised above the draughts, padded with straw ticking. A ragged shape appeared at his side, and tapped him on the shoulder; a gimlet eye was sufficient to persuade him to crawl to a position where the breeze from the window was strong enough to ruffle his hair. A skinny man curled up like a frightened child on her other side also moved off.

From the opposite wall, her husband grinned at her as he watched the whole dumb show unfold.

Mr Wadd, the Compter's surgeon, was a youngish man who rattled when he breathed. He seemed to listen attentively as Sarah described the pain. He asked for names, which she did not supply – it would only be taken out on her later, or on her husband. And who knew how long the gaol in the chicken lanes would be their home.

She listened with detached interest when he mentioned a warrant he'd happened to see that morning on the Governor's desk. A weaver from the North, bludgeoned to death with his own tools. What was her maiden name again?

68. Arms & Emblems

If anything, Miss Crawford's smooth, brown face was more handsome for being puffy with sleep. Her amber necklace ignited in a slow shaft of sun.

Without prelude, Wyre told her he knew where Robert was being held.

"I had a vision of the Judgement," she answered in a distant voice, as she led him upstairs to her apartment above the bakery. "It's been a long while since I thought about the scriptures."

At her table, Wyre reeled off the day's contents, finishing

with his bout against the colossus, Read's most timely of entrances, and Shadworth's dying revelation about Wood's Close asylum.

"I'm coming with you," she said at last.

Wyre cleared his throat. "I don't imagine Ellesmere will give your fiancé up easily – " When he saw the resolve, he stopped. "Very well. We should leave while it's still light."

"I almost forgot, Mr Wyre." She reached across the table for an envelope slotted between the silver wires of an expanding toast-rack. "This arrived earlier today. It was sent to this address, but curiously has your name on it."

Wyre examined the neat seams. The letter bore the arms and emblems of the Belgian Court. He snapped the onyx seal. The finely woven sheet contained two short sentences above a name in speech marks. 'Gew'.

He looked up at her. "It's from an acquaintance of mine, letting me know he's well. He sends his regards." Keep the muscle on the stretch, indeed. So Leighton was on the Continent. Was Rose with him? As Read put it, it was too much, and it was enough.

The distant cheer of a crowd could be heard through Miss Crawford's open window.

"They're hanging the youngest Vere Street culprits this evening," Wyre said. Cunt-lovers against buggers. The words occurred to him. He half wondered whether he might have spoken them aloud.

Miss Crawford nodded, lovely in a sudden shift of light.

"Not yet seventeen," she said. "I read that somewhere."

The lawyer's hand reached across the table to cup Miss Crawford's own. She let it lie there.

Another cheer. The legal terms ran through his head. *Indicted for an unnatural crime on the 17th day of August in the fiftieth year of the Reign of this Sovereign Lord George the Third. By the Grace of God.*

Wyre rose to his feet, and tightened the strap of his purple shoulder bag. "If you're sure you wish to come . . ."

Miss Crawford stretched, putting her head at a strange angle, almost like a man hanged.

69. The Cup within the Cup

With a painful somersault of mind, Wyre realized Rose would never return to him. He stole a glance at Miss Crawford's bare arm lying on the cracked leather seats of the hackney coach, imagining that meeting. Her simple dress of cobalt blue stretched across her thighs. The curve of her ribs was visible. God, she was fine. In the gnarls of late light that infiltrated the unwashed glass sliders, her tawny skin appeared somewhere on a spectrum between fresh mahogany and cloves. As alien as a vagrant bird. And he wanted her – even more than he desired to see Cumberland in the dock. He wanted her whole. Heart, lips and thighs. Everything. She wasn't to withhold the smallest atom.

The city whipped away on either side of the coach. Why did she cleave to a skipjack like Aspinall? Was this the deranged loyalty of wives of legend who threw themselves on their husbands' blazing funeral pyres.

After a stretch of jolting cobbles, the hackney finally found its rhythm on the baked dirt road leading north of the city.

They arrived at Wood's Close as the sun was practically level with the asylum's crenellated battlements. The topiary peacocks, still wet from the evening's downpour, cast elongated shadows over the sweeping drive, their neatly clipped beaks distorted into grotesque maws.

Professor Ashcroft must have seen the hackney pull up. He was waiting for them, framed by the stout, hammer-dressed jambs.

Wyre led Miss Crawford to the porch. In his best Courthouse voice, he said: "We demand to see Dr Ellesmere. Immediately." The purple bag under his jacket seemed to take on weight.

Ashcroft regarded him steadily.

"We've been given to understand your colleague was less than candid in respect of Mr Aspinall's whereabouts."

"Given to understand? And what if my colleague is unavailable?"

"Then we'll return with Bow Street officers." Wyre played his cards, hoping the asylum Director wouldn't call a sight.

Ashcroft smiled. "Since you're clearly intent on pursuing this folly, we'll see if Dr Ellesmere is willing to receive you. But I warn you, he's at work in the basements and won't welcome the intrusion."

They followed Ashcroft into the main corridor, taking an abrupt turn under an enormous stone lintel. The way led into a narrow communicating passage. Wyre drew Miss Crawford closer. Recessed doors began to appear at regular intervals. They reminded Wyre of dark catacombs. Rooms to lacerate, not heal the mind. They arrived at a narrow staircase, which descended in a tight spiral; the curving iron banister was clammy under Wyre's palm. Miss Crawford's skirts brushed against him from behind. Someone had carved a crude image of Christ crucified into one of the stairwell's quoins.

A subterranean corridor led off at the bottom, tapering to barely more than three feet in width. High windows – the word was clerestories, wasn't it? – with upward sloping sills provided glints of light in the shadows. Why hadn't Ashcroft brought a lantern? Wyre frowned – the asylum Director was now merely a hazy shape ahead, then even that silhouette vanished.

"Ashcroft?" Wyre called after him. No reply, just mockeries of his own voice reverberating between the stones. He turned to Miss Crawford, his sudden uncertainty of purpose evidently apparent.

"Robert's down here somewhere in this dreadful place," she urged. "We can't abandon him."

Wyre ran his hand over the bulge of the gun-bag beneath his jacket, and nodded.

The next bend carried them into a stretch of humid dark; it was as if the whole corridor had been flooded with black steam. Ahead, flickering tongues of orange seemed to dance like marsh fire. They continued onward to the source – the unworldly glow was lamplight sieving through the grate of a heavy door. From behind the metal grille came sounds that might have been hollow groans.

The lawyer's fingers closed round the iron handle, and pushed down.

The room was long with a low, barrel-vaulted ceiling. Wyre counted half a dozen wooden gurneys arranged around a copper-plated cabinet like fanned-out playing cards. Five of the gurneys were empty. Dr Ellesmere's tall figure was bent over the sixth, his back to them. He gave no sign of having registered their entrance.

On a copper cabinet behind the physician sat a large, fluid-filled jar. Beside it lay a glass-handled wand with two prongs, connected by a length of spiralling cord to a brass plunger that travelled through the jar's cork. Behind the cabinet was a low wooden door. God knew what it led to.

Slowly, the doctor turned. He was dressed in a hard leather apron, scalpel hanging loosely in his fingers.

379

Stepping aside, he gave an unoccluded view of the man on the gurney, who was strapped down securely. Miss Crawford gave a little gasp of horror. The man – not Aspinall, thank God – was naked, his yard flopped back on his belly, a landed salmon. Beneath it . . . Miss Crawford's hand had gone to her mouth. The bag between the man's thighs was slit open down the middle, like a seed-pod with its contents removed.

With a sense of scrabbling for a hold at the lip of a precipice, Wyre fumbled under his jacket, his slow, heavy fingers struggling to locate the bag's puckered opening. At last, he had the pistol stock in his hand. He yanked out the weapon, aiming it at Ellesmere, pulling the gooseneck hammer back with a jerky motion.

"Leave him be," he cried. "Are you insane?"

The physician stared for a moment, then opened his fingers, letting the scalpel fall. It made a tinkling sound on the herringbone brick. Wyre advanced as Ellesmere edged backwards, a bizarre two-step. The physician stopped beside the cabinet and wiped his hands on his apron, each finger leaving a little slick of blood.

"The procedure is every bit as painful as it looks," he began, his skin unctuous in the lamplight.

At the sound of the doctor's voice, the mutilated man began to stir from his stupor, straining at the chin strap. He succeeded in raising his head a little, neck dissolving in rolls of flesh as he tried to peer over his belly.

"First, you get your man as drunk as you can," Ellesmere continued, "and then you have to be fast. As you can see, I've yet to apply the sutures. You're prolonging this patient's discomfort."

Wyre held the pistol level, looking along the top of it, past the white earthy rind of the flint. Only a yard of sharp air between them.

"They say we feel pain only when we resist it, Mr Wyre. But the point is the speed."

"We haven't come to hear truth from a madman. Tell us where you're keeping Aspinall."

"Truth ... fables ..." Ellesmere made a curious shucking movement. "I could tell you many stories about Mr Aspinall, each true in its own way. I suppose you knew – " he turned to Miss Crawford – "that your fiancé was briefly a physician to the Palace, employed by the Prince of Air himself?"

"What are you talking about?" Wyre said, the gun's weight pulling at his tendons. "Where's Robert Aspinall? Be quick about it."

The man on the gurney let out a low moan.

Ellesmere's eyes were viperish, focusing on the tip of the barrel. "It's quite true. One of the Palace's favoured own was receiving treatment in this house – for troubling dreams, Mr Aspinall's favourite topic. Your betrothed," he said to Miss Crawford, "was a very Joseph. I can't say I shared his enthusiasm for the brain's fantasies. People will take for granted that distempered dreams always portend something of consequence. They have a name for it. *Oneirocriticism*, if you can credit that. Dream of bright stars, you're in physical health, but woe betide if the celestial bodies should appear murky." He gave a snort of derision. "You might as well write a treatise on ghosts, or join the ranks of piping poets and opium-eaters. I find a scalpel answers all modern questions."

Wyre waved the pistol again. "If you've harmed a hair on his head . . ."

"The Duke of Cumberland himself made the arrangements for treatment," the doctor continued blithely. "Of course, your betrothed – " he glanced back at Miss Crawford " – wasn't told of his patient's true identity. We were all under a strict embargo to refer to the individual only as Mr Parlez-Vous." He caught Wyre's look. "I see the name is not unknown to you."

"Parlez-Vous is *Cumberland?* He'll suffer for it!"

Ellesmere ignored him. "The Palace demanded utter discretion. Your fiancé's pioneering treatise, *An Inquiry into the Nature of Dreams: Thoughts on the Imagination in Repose* – " he reeled off the title " – was well known to the royals. The family keeps a close eye on medicinal innovations. As a matter of fact, this wasn't the first time the Palace looked to Wood's Close for tactful service."

Wyre let the muzzle speak, waggling it left and right.

"Of course," the doctor said, nodding. "Time is of the essence. Suffice it to say, Parlez-Vous' case turned out to be infinitely more whorled – " he fanned out his fingers " – than anyone could have predicted. Dr Aspinall did his best, but the good man was over-tasked. I decided to take matters into my own hands, to your fiancé's not inconsiderable chagrin, Miss Crawford," Ellesmere's voice hardened. "He sensed, rightly, that a case had fallen into his lap with all the hallmarks of a sensation. I believe he actually thought he'd be allowed to publish his findings." The physician shook his head slowly. "Dear me, always at cross purposes to the world, always pulling against the tide."

Miss Crawford took a step forward. "For heaven's sake, what have you done with Robert?" The man on the gurney groaned as though answering her.

"The very notion of making public insights touching on the affairs of our ruling family . . . Quaint is putting it mildly. I demanded he hand over his medical logs, and in his presence fed the papers to the fire. And there things might have lain, Miss Crawford." The doctor's face darkened. "It wasn't until in subsequent private conversations Parlez-Vous happened to mention to me a small black notebook in which it appeared your fiancé had been in the habit of, how shall we put it . . . jotting things down. There had been no such book among the ledgers I burned, and I instantly knew it to be the true repository of his thoughts."

Wyre pictured the leather volume he'd helped Miss Crawford salvage from the wreckage of Vere Street's disgusting tavern.

"Such a gross breach of trust could not be permitted to pass unchallenged." The muscles of Ellesmere's face tightened. "I confronted your betrothed, tried one last time to impress on him the seriousness of his situation, told him in terms impossible to misconstrue that the Palace would not stand for it. He confessed to the notebook, but swore – on his engagement to *you*, Miss Crawford – that his journal no longer existed, that you'd consigned it to the flames yourself. LIES!"

Wyre struggled to keep his voice steady. "Tell me where he is. I won't ask again."

The physician shot him a contemptuous look. "Poor Robert Aspinall, a lightning rod for the complications of this world. I doubt he would have recognized Cumberland. His Highness was always disguised when he went out for his evening entertainments. I made representations to that effect. But the Duke was unwilling to run any risks." Ellesmere wet his lips. "Your fiancé's adventures in Vere Street, on that night of all nights, sealed his fate. Perhaps it would have been better for him if he hadn't survived his pillorying." His face set. "On St James's orders, I invited him back to Wood's Close. My letter was to imply that restoration of his position here wasn't out of the question. The Duke's own men were waiting to take him into custody. As to where he is now, Miss Crawford, I'm afraid I wouldn't know."

She shook her head. Those jerky clockwork motions again. "What could a man like Cumberland possibly have to fear from Robert? They suffered in the same way. Robert tried to treat him."

"Treat Cumberland?" Ellesmere was plainly amused. "No, my dear. I said the Duke made the arrangements, but he was not the patient. To be sure, the Duke has his own peculiarities of mind, just like his father. Parlez-Vous' insanity, however, was of an entirely different order. Sodomites are simple, spiteful creatures, prey to petty conceits and dreary jealousies. Their lusts are basic. Arse or cock, seldom both. They rarely form lasting attachments, nor ascribe any value to them, living entirely inside the present moment." He pulled at his sleeve like a conjurer before a trick. "Parlez-Vous' psychopathy, if you'll permit me the term, went far beyond such clear-cut models. Cases that bring new diseases of brain to light are rarer than proverbial hens' teeth."

It dawned on Wyre. "You plan to pass Aspinall's work off as your own."

Ellesmere smiled inscrutably. "Parlez-Vous despised sodomites, was consumed to the very substance with that hatred. Apart from, that is," he added, "a Palace valet called Neale. I believe you know him, Mr Wyre. Yes, curiously enough, despite all evidence to the contrary, Parlez-Vous was adamant he could be redeemed. Only, pity anyone to whom Mr Neale took a shine." He paused. "There was a footman, a Mr Tranter . . . and that White creature, of course, whom Cumberland was in the habit of loaning to Mr Neale as a reward. Oh, the Duke enjoyed dispensing his gifts." The physician's lips dilated again. "From what I gather – " he patted his coat as if feeling for an imaginary pocket watch " – the drummer-boy will have felt Parlez-Vous' noose around his neck an hour or so ago."

Wyre tried to resist the spreading cloud of unreality. "Who murdered Joseph Sellis? Was that also Mr Parlez-Vous?"

"Who would you like it to be?"

"I'll have officers brought here. You'll tell them."

Ellesmere frowned. "Forgive the lack of courtroom decorum in my summing up," he said, taking a small step back, "but you must know it was only ever about a few puckered arseholes."

Miss Crawford gasped. Wyre levelled the pistol over his left forearm as he'd seen Read do in the Valet's Room, crouching slightly, spreading his weight. "Last chance, you devil! Where's Robert Aspinall?"

The doctor gave him a curious look. "When you get up after defecating, Mr Wyre, do you feel there's always more to come out?"

Ellesmere reached behind him, and snatched up the glass-handled rod – blue sparks flared at its prongs – thrusting the instrument straight at the lawyer's chest. The pain drove out language; Wyre became a single crooking muscle, the doctor's grotesque rictus hovering above him, filling his contracting vision. A blank crack, somehow related to Ellesmere dropping his shocking points, his head expanding in a great red slop, the glass jar coming shatteringly down, its clear contents hissing over the brick floor. Wyre heard the emptied pistol clatter at his side.

Then Miss Crawford was kneeling next to him, her hand beneath his jacket, sliding into the pouch, taking a lead ball, tipping the powder sack. Even in his quiverish state, he noted the proficiency. She held out the pistol, straining at the hammer with two thumbs, forcing it back with a final click. Looked up, past him, her face flickering with strange blue lights.

Wyre twisted his neck painfully, stared over the body of

the mad-doctor in the direction shown by the pistol's muzzle. That side door was open now. An oddly familiar, advancing shape. Mrs Neale's features had undergone a terrible transformation since he'd seen her last. She cradled a second throbbing jar beneath her arm, and with a high whooping noise rushed towards them, outstretched pole fizzing.

Miss Crawford rose, one strap of her dress falling to the side, her fingers tightening around the butt of the weapon. That line, from her bare shoulder to the rod.

There followed a flash that seemed to gather all the room's dancing lights to it and the valet's wife fell backwards as if attached to an unseen wire that someone had tugged violently. When the pall of smoke finally lifted, she was sprawled backwards over a gurney. Slowly, she slipped to the stone floor.

Again, Miss Crawford was crouching over Wyre, hauling him to his feet. His whole body numb. Squinting down, he discovered two round sear-marks in his blue legal jacket. Heart height.

Somehow the pair of them were crossing to the side door. They passed Mrs Neale, whose jaw moved feebly from side to side as if she were trying to finish an anecdote.

He was in another room now, watching Miss Crawford stand beside a body on a raised stretcher. She didn't appear to look at the sutured line, but Wyre knew she'd seen it; recognized it.

She bent over her fiancé, her face that of a pretty boy (was he the only one who hadn't seen it?), stroking Aspinall's forehead with gentle motions Wyre felt suddenly as fire in his chest. A curious expression, like the turn of a sonnet towards a resolution of some kind.

Robert Aspinall's eyes opened, stared at the lawyer. Not the slightest flicker of recognition. Then the head lolled to the side, its pained features creasing into a wide grin.

Mad as the winds.

Wyre watched him for a moment, then turned away.

All gone. Rose, Leighton . . . and now Miss Crawford. But he'd be damned if he was leaving without the truth, even if it meant trying to thresh facts from fables in Ellesmere's story. Didn't it always come down to that? Wasn't that what William tried to tell him all along? The cup within the cup. Let him have a stab, then.

Mr Parlez-Vous was Mrs Neale, on whose extraordinary medical case Aspinall's fugitive, then Ellesmere's filched, treatise depended. Even in his final moments, Ellesmere had sought to hide her from the world until he was ready.

White had felt her pinch. Tranter, too, in all likelihood. Neale swore it was the Duke's finger curled around the trigger. But Wyre only had his word for that.

Treatment at Wood's Close. That was how the Duke had made his peace with Bow Street. Cure rather than punishment. A novel idea. It was in the air. Mrs Neale was the perfect testing ground. But the asylum had merely been an echo chamber for her sickness. She'd been a pretty bird in a bell jar. Wyre pictured the torn-out page of Aspinall's notebook, mentally reading its obscenities. Had Ellesmere egged her on, nurturing her hatred of mollies, recording her excesses in his study of one mind made two, the double character? Those regular visits to the Retreat, each time returning to the Palace a little madder, her jealousy more murderous.

His thoughts returned to the Duke's bedchamber. There was little doubt Mrs Neale had wielded the sabre. It explained why the strokes hadn't told. All those nights of knowing her husband slept with just a paper wall between him and Cumberland. Or not between them. Hadn't Paulet said as much (though he'd meant Mrs Sellis)? Wyre could almost sympathize with her.

As for Joseph Sellis, he'd been sacrificed for no other reason than to explain the Duke's injuries. He'd been as expendable as a lowly swad in the Peninsula game.

Who'd slit Sellis's throat, and how had they got into his room? There was only one explanation now. The missing key was thieved from the Porter's office by Cumberland and Neale as they planned their cover. He'd always thought it strange they'd gone there first, rather than to Jackson the surgeon. Wyre swept the mental drapery aside, pictured the sequence as it must have occurred – the injured Duke leaning on Neale as they made their way through the corridors looking for Mrs Neale, the unbalanced plaything of both men (Wyre had no doubt of that) – finding her, bringing her to the Duke's sleeping quarters. Leighton had arrived then in the guise of Mr Gew to witness Neale tending to the cuts on his master's skull – his own wife's handiwork – seen Neale set off on his murderous commission. How could Neale refuse? It was either that or leave his wife to the Palace fixers. Perhaps he'd pleaded with Cumberland as she cowered in the corner.

But there was more to it. Cumberland wasn't sentimental: he'd have sacrificed all his tin men and women, if he felt he could. No, Mrs Neale had insured herself. Margaret Jones, her ear at the wall, her eye at the keyhole . . . The Welsh maid had documented Cumberland's comings and goings for her mistress: all those outings to Vere Street as the Country Gentleman, all those visits to the Valet's Room, all those rides with footmen in the royal barouche (the dickey-box, indeed!). She'd transcribed all she'd heard. It was all neatly recorded somewhere.

And Read knew. Knew, and decided to protect the Duke from scandal. To serve England the only way he could. The story of Sellis's suicide worked for all parties. Read had warned him he wouldn't get anywhere with insinuations about Greek vices, and he'd been right. Puckered arseholes. The lawyer shook his head. Dirty places, and they'd cost at least three men their lives.

But what about that *contretemps* on Birdcage Walk? Perhaps Margaret's head had been turned by Neale, the man she'd seen in so many intimate situations. Had she tried to save him with her gospel graces? Perhaps her mistress's sharp blue eyes intercepted a glance too warm, inferring from it an understanding. The foolish girl had been playing a dangerous game. Margaret running that time, cheeks streaked with tears, from the games room . . . True to his type, Neale had spurned her in the end. But her God was a vengeful God. Margaret's swift retribution had been to tell Wyre what she'd seen in the Valet's Room. She'd been telling the truth.

He fought an urge to retch. How could these people bear to breathe each other's air?

And Leighton . . . Had the Runner's Bow Street superior stood back as the Palace set Shadworth on him? More likely, Read had done his best to protect him with that unlikely story about stolen gems in Mayfair. At least, Wyre preferred to think so. At any rate, Leighton was safely harboured in the Belgian Court. There was nowhere in England he'd ever be safe again. But it didn't make him a turncoat, just a man whose struggle with life was more complex than he'd known, or could have imagined.

None of this explained Thomas's letter offering hope to Sellis. William's words again – the cup within the cup. But now Wyre knew better what Sellis had been. Many things. Tormented victim of the Duke's violent desires, Neale's lover, dutiful father of four (the youngest of whom was imprisoned within the prison of the Duke's own name). What else? French spy, assassin manqué? Whatever Sellis was, was now succumbing to time's ultimate victory over the light embalming fluid that Surgeon Cline had used to clothe the dead man's worse than nakedness for all those student eyes.

Only the slippers left now, and they were easy. Mrs Neale's part in the charade was to fetch a dead man. She waited till the Porter and the other joskin left Sellis's bedroom before grabbing the first items that came to hand, concealing them under her skirts. Then she'd placed them where they needed to be, in the Duke's closet.

Read had known. Known and hadn't liked it. But he was a patriot. He believed in the war with France. Though not enough to see Wyre suffer. He'd come back.

As for Miss Crawford, and her truth. Those river-harlot cat-cries rang in his ears. She would always remain with Aspinall, their pact sealed in the cruellest terms. But he also knew, in that same instant, that despite it all, despite what he was, what she was, if she were only to ask, he would give up everything.

It was a story of sorts. A pattern even. But as his thoughts rested on an image of a Cumberland still most safe, most sound, he realized his was one chronicle among many.

Wyre crossed to a door that led outside into a little sunken courtyard. Alone now, he climbed its steps, Miss Crawford's voice gradually enfolded in another's. He emerged into a world barely recognizable from the one he'd left. Memory returned with a company of swifts, screaming their parabola over the gardens. One broke off, fixed on its own, solitary trajectory, its shrillness seeming to bend the air. Wyre imagined the wooded lands round the city already turning in the little creature's ancient brain into the ribbed, then level, sands of its endless summer.

Author's Note

I began this novel in July 2010, two hundred years – pretty much to the day – after the raid on The White Swan tavern in Vere Street. The idea for the book emerged from discussions of the Swan mollies' persecution with students who had opted to take my Romantic Eroticism course at Aberystwyth University. Buoyed by their enthusiasm, I launched into the project, estimating a year's work, at most, lay ahead. In the four years it actually took to close Wyre's case, close-bosom friend and fellow Romanticist, Damian Walford Davies, read every word, many of them more than once. His advice, encouragement and infallible ear were a unfailing spur whenever the complexity of the story threatened to get the better of me. Damian is one of the few who understands Blake "to the lees", and I profited from his wisdom in that respect, too. I owe another substantial debt to Susan Stokes-Chapman, who also read the entire manuscript, and insisted the plot make sense.

Like all good Romantics, I subscribe to the doctrine of "being there" – of footstepping, absorbing, and when necessary inhaling. First-hand familiarity of conducting surgical procedures, however, lay beyond my experiential horizon. For insights into how bodies are put together, and come apart – particularly into the wet work of chirurgy – I'm grateful to my good friend Wolfgang Spaeth. I have also been helped by my doctoral students, nineteenth-century specialist Ian Middlebrook, and the novelist Eliza Granville, whose expertise in the areas of cab history and memory, respectively, has been invaluable. Further thanks are due to Jayne Archer for her advice on folk remedies; and to Elaine Treharne, for early exchanges on the mythical Donestre, whose grisly devotions provided me with an entrée into The White Swan's taproom, and on up into the attics. Finally, thank you to Robert Davidson and Moira Forsyth at Sandstone Press; to Planet Magazine (who published parts of Chapter 19 as a podcast); to my literary agent Dominique Baxter at David Higham Associates; and to Veronica Foetz-Camm for liking Mr Shadworth.

I acknowledge the Department of English and Creative Writing at Aberystwyth University for generously granting me study leave to complete the first draft of this novel.

Aberystwyth, 17 December 2014